# circumstantial EVIDENCE

# circumstantial EVIDENCE

A NOVEL

JAMES SCOTT BELL

Nashville, Tennessee

4263-59
0-8054-6359-3

Published by Broadman & Holman Publishers, Nashville, Tennessee

Dewey Decimal Classification: F
Subject Heading: LEGAL STORIES
Library of Congress Card Catalog Number: 97-3344



**Library of Congress Cataloging-in-Publication Data**

Bell, James Scott.
Circumstantial evidence / by James Scott Bell.
p. cm.
ISBN 0-8054-6359-3 (pbk.)
I. Title.
PS3552.E5158C5 1997
813′.54—dc21 97–3344
CIP

1 2 3 4 5 — 01 00 99 98 97

# PROLOGUE

SANDY JOSEPH never saw it coming.

He should have. That's what he thought, in the final second of his life. You don't grow up Jewish in Flatbush and fight your way to the top of the movie business without street smarts. You don't have agents for Melanie Griffith, Julia Roberts, and Sandra Bullock hounding you about your next project unless you know how to play the game.

But tonight the champagne and music—hip-hop, gangsta rap, and a little Whitney Houston—had dulled his senses, as premiere parties always did. Funny thing was, this wasn't his movie. He was here for a friend who was taking a chance.

Charles Winning, a fellow New Yorker, had produced this movie directed by a film school whiz he hoped would be the next Spike Lee. It was a mishmash called *Red Ride 'N the Hood,* an African-American take on some traditional fairy tales, with a decidedly dark and twisted spin. Sandy actually liked it, though his marketing sense told him it was doomed—a not-long-to-video, twenty-million-dollar clinker.

So best to enjoy the party and keep Charles sipping the bubbly. Maybe for a night they could forget box office receipts and the Tuesday morning *Variety* and just sit back and have fun—even if the jam was mostly black kids decked out in urban outlaw. Sandy could never get into rap, urban, hip-hop, or dance. He didn't even know how to tell the difference, which was unhip, so he kept the dark secret to himself. He wanted the Beatles back. He'd even take the Monkees.

Something about the evening bothered him. Sandy wasn't a bigot. He knew the sting of bigotry himself. Black gangs had been on his case when he was a kid. He'd done some time in juvey in Brooklyn for things that might have gotten him killed. Black against white. That never left you.

This theme was reflected in the movie. Racist white cops, KKK members, bigoted bosses—they all got their comeuppance in the movie. To be fair, black violence against brothers was given a shot, too. But when one of the bad white cops ended up doused with gasoline, his flaming body screaming through the ghetto, the audience cheered wildly and long. Sandy felt the small hairs dance on the back of his neck.

But he didn't tell this to Charles as they sat together on the upper floor, where only brass, stars, and their guests were allowed. Charles was despondent enough. Sandy kept trying to lighten the load, but it worked only intermittently. By 11:30, Charles was near tears. "I've had it," he wailed over the din. "I'm walking. I hate this business."

"Come on, man," Sandy said. "This is your night. Enjoy it."

"It's going down the toilet."

"I liked it, pal. The kid is talented."

"But no one will *see* it. Forget talent! I want eighty mil!"

He wasn't going to get eighty mil. He'd be lucky if he got eight. "Finish your drink," Sandy said as he pulled two Cuban cigars from his jacket. "One for you, one for me."

They walked out to the parking lot and lit up. "It's OK, man," Sandy said.

"I'm toast," said Charles.

"Not even," Sandy reassured him.

Charles shook his head and looked at his shoes.

They stood for a few minutes in silence, then Sandy said, "Look, go home and catch some major Zs, all right?"

"I can't even keep my cigar lit," Charles answered sadly, looking at the cold stogie in his hand.

Sandy took him by the shoulders, turned him around, and pushed him back toward the party. "You gotta fight hardest when it looks the worst," Sandy said. "Don't ever let 'em see you sweat, pal."

Charles shuffled toward the theater.

Sandy handed the valet his ticket. The night was cooling off. A crowd began to spill out of the club and mingle all over the noted Hollywood Walk of Fame. Sandy wondered which stars were being tromped on by the young urban set. For some reason he thought of Don Ameche. *I bet none of those kids would even know his name*, he mused. *Who's going to remember mine?*

Sandy hung his head, then reminded himself he'd soon be home, by the beach, tooting a little blow. The latest shipment, part of which he'd sampled last night, was pure snow heaven. Who said coke was passé in the new Hollywood?

The valet pulled up in Sandy's silver Bentley, the pride and joy of the kid from Flatbush. Every time he drove the car—no, you couldn't call it a *car;* it was a chariot, a king's conveyance—Sandy Joseph thought about how nice it would be to drive through his old New York haunts with it. Just cruise on down the streets and wave at all the guys who never made it.

Sandy took out a five and handed it to the valet. Then he happened to look at his eyes. He didn't recognize the kid. He was young, black, thin, like so many others who were at the scene. No reason for him to stand out. But there was something in the eyes that said the kid recognized *him*.

"Do I know you?" Sandy Joseph said.

The valet shrugged and shook his head.

"You ever work at any of the studios?"

The kid shook his head again, anxiously this time.

"What's up with you?" Sandy said.

The kid's face drew suddenly tight. "Nothin', man. What's up with you?"

It was a challenge. An in-your-face. Sandy felt old instincts rise up. If it had been a few years ago, he might have put a hand on the kid's chest and shoved him. But it was late, and the whole scene was making him jittery. Sandy Joseph shot the kid a look and got in the Bentley.

As he pulled out onto Vine and took a right, Sandy noticed his cigar had gone out. He was fumbling for his lighter when he heard a click.

"Don't turn around," a voice whispered.

Adrenaline rushed through his body, wiping out the pleasant champagne buzz. Immediately, he knew it was a carjacking. How could he have been so careless? This was Hollywood, not Westwood. He should have looked in the back seat of his car.

"Drive slow," the voice said. "Turn at the corner."

*All right,* Sandy thought. *Easy. Do it all. You can get another Bentley. Your insurance is paid up.* He took a right on Hollywood Boulevard, which was strangely empty and soundless. The flicker of a porn theater marquee caught his eye. It was the brightest thing on the street.

"Take the car," Sandy said. "No problem. I walk away."

"Pull over," the voice said.

"No problem." Sandy eased the car to the curb and said, "You want me to get out?"

"Don't move."

"You can have it. I won't say anything."

"Quiet, please."

*Please? The guy said "Please"?* That's when he knew. That's when he realized it was over. He turned his head to the side.

"Don't turn around!" the voice commanded.

"Come on, man, come on! I got money. A whole wad! And I'm walking. I'm walking, I swear!"

Silence.

"I'm straight with you, man!" Sandy blurted. "Do me a solid. I walk. I say nothing. Come on!"

*Crack,* like the snap of a whip.

Sharp, quick. A burning in the brain. And just before oblivion, Sandy Joseph thought, *I should have seen it coming* . . .

# CHAPTER ONE

"I'M GOING TO EAT YOU for lunch, honey, and I bet I get the worst case of heartburn, too."

Tracy Shepherd looked into the man's eyes. This wasn't the first time he'd pulled something like this. Last time she passed him in the court hallway, he'd looked her up and down with a leer and winked an unmistakable invitation at her.

"You pulling one of your famous psych-outs, Mr. Beymer?"

"I do what is in the best interest of my clients," said Jackson Beymer. He was in his late forties, with dark, shiny, moussed black hair, dangling gold bracelet, and a thousand-dollar, deep-blue Armani suit. His voice was resonant, smooth, confident. "So, give my guy the deal, and I'll get my lunch down at Langer's. What do you say, girl?"

"Don't call me *girl*, or I'll scream for my daddy." Tracy tried to make it sound half banter, half bravado. It came out like a warble. She was never very good at this sort of thing. She was twenty-seven years old, had been in the district attorney's office three years, and still couldn't mimic the "boys' talk."

"I'm no sexist," teased Beymer. "I like all you chicks in the office."

Tracy shut her eyes and shook her head slowly. She felt a wisp of her dark blond hair fall over one eye, and she pushed it behind her ear.

Beymer said, "Look, you're a busy deputy, on the move, on the way up. But you're too busy. Aren't we all? Don't you want to get rid of another file? Bim, bam, boom, and you're home early."

He was right, of course. As one of the trial deputies in Department

128, she had the discretion from her supervisor to do just what Beymer was asking—offer a plea to a lesser offense, with a sentence much softer than the charged offense would bring. Another case file would be cleared. The office wouldn't miss it. The court wouldn't miss it, either, what with the overcrowding problem the three-strikes law was causing. And it *would* go down as a conviction. There really wasn't any reason she shouldn't go with the deal.

Except one. Beymer's client had messed up a woman and a child, and it wasn't the first time. He'd held a burning cigarette to the cheek of his twenty-two-year-old girlfriend, the mother of his four-year-old daughter. The daughter was screaming and crying as she watched. He'd whacked the girl with the back of his hand, which had sent her into a wall and bloodied her nose. Then he'd threatened to kill them both.

"I don't think so," Tracy said.

"Come on," said Beymer. "This isn't one of your street scum. My guy is a man with a job and a place in the community."

Tracy knew what he was getting at. Without saying as much, he was emphasizing that this was a white, suburban "incident," not a drug-peddling, ghetto crime. It should be treated differently. This was no thug. This was westside, not eastside. This was "my guy," not some gangbanger.

"You see, Ms. Shepherd," Beymer said, tugging at his crisp, French cuffs, "if you don't offer me this deal, we go to trial. And we all know what happens when I go before a jury." He leaned in closer. "Lunch time."

Tracy stiffened, trying mightily not to let her expression broadcast the tightening in her stomach. She'd tried nearly fifty cases during her tenure at the D. A.'s office, but they'd been misdemeanors. Drunk driving. Petty theft. One- or two-day trials mostly. In and out. Rote.

This would be different. She'd just moved into the felony unit, and now she faced the prospect of going up against the legendary Jackson Beymer. This was the man who had gained an acquittal for the

"Chinatown Slasher," a busboy accused of dismembering seven streetwalkers over a two-year period. Police had been sure they'd had the goods on Wayne Morishita, including DNA and hair trace evidence. But two things they hadn't counted on: They hadn't counted on Wayne Morishita being the troubled scion of a wealthy family, and they hadn't counted on that family hiring Jackson Beymer.

In the trial, televised on Court TV, Beymer had turned the scientific experts into blithering idiots. Not so much because he knew the science as well as they did (which was true), but because he knew how to leave out the technical jargon and use words the jury could understand. "Vivid words," he had said later on the "Larry King Show." "You have to make it real for the jury."

So Morishita had walked, just like the last dozen clients Jackson Beymer had taken to trial.

*Give him the deal.* Tracy's inner voice told her to do it. Everyone would understand. *Don't take on Beymer.*

She was seated at the prosecutor's table, the one next to an empty jury box. Beymer was leaning lazily on the edge, between Tracy and his client, who was at the defense table. Tracy leaned over. She wanted to see his face.

Beymer's "guy," Howard Sollomon, turned toward Tracy. He was young, only twenty-five, and looked like he should be modeling clothes in *GQ*. But his eyes changed when he saw Tracy. His mouth started to curl slightly to one side. He was saying, in his soundless way, that he knew she'd let him cop a plea. He had hired the best. No little deputy was going to stand in the way. No little deputy would be that stupid.

Tracy leaned back in her chair. Beymer was fiddling with his bracelet as he held his daily calendar in his other hand. "So, when shall we set it?" he asked.

"The trial?"

"The plea."

"No deal," said Tracy. Her throat was bone-dry. She looked around for a pitcher of water.

"You're not as smart as I thought you were," Beymer said, slapping his calendar closed. "What is it with you? You want to be a judge? Run for D. A. or something?"

"Did it ever occur to you, Mr. Beymer, that I might actually be thinking about the justice of this case? Did it ever occur to you that the victims might play into this?"

"Oh, spare me your law school speeches," scoffed Beymer. "Listen to a little real-world wisdom. You listening? Those victims, as you call them, want their man back in the house. They are not going to offer the testimony you need to convict. This will be one of the easiest cases I've ever tried, and you, my sweet, are going to wind up a loser on the front page of the *L. A. Times*. Is that really what you want?"

The scenario was all too real. It *could* happen just that way. And her so-called career would be over before it started. She could end up pushing papers in Compton. That would be just like Siberia. No, more like hell.

Tracy tried not to let the twitches she felt around her eyes spread to the rest of her face. "You're a good lawyer, Mr. Beymer," Tracy said as evenly as she could. "But so am I."

"Do tell?" said Jackson Beymer with a smirk. "How many felonies have you taken to trial now? Is it one? Two?"

"I've had my share of trials."

"Oh, sure, 'meanors. Drunk driving mostly, am I right? And just how hard is it to win a deuce anymore? Guy blows a point-o-seven or more, and any jury in L. A. is going to want to string him to the nearest telephone pole."

Tracy said nothing.

"Real tough. Back when I was starting out I actually won those suckers. Still could. But all you got now are lazy P. D.'s, sitting on their brains, wondering how fast they can plead out. How many *real* trials have you had?"

"I guess I have to start somewhere."

Jackson Beymer leaned toward her. His face tightened like a clenched fist. His eyes narrowed. Lowering his voice so no one else could hear, he spat through clenched teeth, "Listen to me, rookie. You better learn to play the game. You better learn how to do some favors, you understand? You want to last around here, you better get a little wisdom up there in that pretty little dome. Am I coming through?"

Tracy noticed her right leg was trembling. She tried to focus on Jackson Beymer's face but couldn't bring herself to meet his gaze.

*Give him the deal.*

It would be so easy. Just a nod of the head, a few marks on the file. Over and done with. She put her hand on her right thigh and rubbed. And at that moment she remembered something her father used to tell her. She could hear his voice saying, "Character is much easier kept than recovered."

Tracy pushed her chair back and stood up. "You'll have to take your best shot," she said.

Exhaling with obvious displeasure, Beymer said, "So you won't heed my advice?"

Tracy shook her head.

"You know, rumor has it," Beymer said, "you're a good, pure, clean example of Christian womanhood. That true?"

"Excuse me, but that's not relevant to—"

"Don't get me wrong. I think we could use a few more godly prosecutors, you know what I'm saying?"

"No. I don't."

"Well let me spell it out. Maybe you think you've got God, or Jesus Christ, or Pat Boone on your side. But don't be fooled." He leaned toward her and whispered, "In the courtroom, I am God."

"This conference is over, counselor."

For a moment, Jackson Beymer stood there nodding his head

slightly. Then he turned his back and went to whisper something in his client's ear.

A moment later Sollomon blurted, "But you said she'd take it!" Beymer whispered something else and then Sollomon shot a glance at Tracy, his eyes aflame.

Tracy had no doubt that, if he had the opportunity, Sollomon would take great pleasure in doing to her what he'd done to his girlfriend and child.

Tracy stepped out of the elevator on the eighteenth floor of the Criminal Courts Building. MaryLou, the county safety police guard, who was security on the floor, nodded at her.

"Mornin', Ms. Shepherd," she said. "How's it goin' today?"

"Don't ask."

"You look like you been snakebit."

"I have."

Smiling, MaryLou nodded. "A defense lawyer, right?"

"You got it."

"Who was it this time?"

"MaryLou, I—"

"Come on, tell me, I love to know. Was it Weitzman?"

"No."

"Public defender?"

"Look—"

"Give me a hint?"

Tracy laughed. "You are a hoot, MaryLou."

"That's what my mama always said."

"All right, who is the highest paid criminal lawyer in Los Angeles?"

MaryLou looked at the ceiling for a moment. Then a light seemed to flick on in her head. "Not Jackson Beymer!"

"The very same."

"Oh, honey, you stay away from that one! I seen him on TV. He'd eat his own young!"

"You know, MaryLou, I'm not going to argue that one with you. Now I *have* to go to work." She turned left and walked down a small hallway to the security door.

MaryLou called after her, "If he pulls anything, you tell me. I'll give him something to remember!"

Tracy smiled and waved. She punched in the three-digit code on the door, then entered the prosecutor's world.

It was a spare, functional place. No fancy carpets or wall art or office plants like you'd see in a Century City law firm. The only spot here that looked like that was "mahogany row," where the Los Angeles district attorney himself had his office.

Tracy paused to check her phone messages. A young intern named Becky walked over to her. "Duke wants to see you," she said.

"Now?"

"Pronto, he said."

"You know why?"

Becky shook her head.

"Thanks," Tracy said, starting down the hallway.

Frank "Duke" Gallegos was the head deputy of her central trials unit, a career prosecutor in his mid-fifties. He'd been in on Tracy's interview for the office and had in fact pushed for her hiring. Tracy liked him not only for his experience and wisdom, but for his deep laugh, which helped keep things light around the office. The office was always in need of a little levity. It was the nature of the profession, like with surgeons who have to deal with death all the time.

And she was warmed by the notion that Duke liked her, too. It was more than a mentoring relationship. Duke was becoming something of a father figure to her. Nothing would replace Dad, of course, but he was in Florida, and she was clear across the map. Tracy had the sense that Duke wanted to look out for her, and that was nice.

But when Duke Gallegos wanted to see someone "pronto," it was certain that something big was up. Tracy tried to think of any major mistakes she might have made in the last twenty-four hours.

She gave a quick knock at Duke's open office door, and he motioned her in. The head deputy's corner office was a little larger than the other offices on the floor and looked out over the sprawl that was L. A.'s new urban landscape. Directly below stretched the tentacles of the civic center, spreading outward toward the ethnic enclave of Chinatown—with its red-, yellow-, and jade-colored pagodas—and the barrio of East L. A. Up to the north, nestled in the hills, the light fixtures of Dodger Stadium were visible on days when the smog wasn't too thick. And all around were the freeways, the never-ending tangle of asphalt and exhaust fumes that tied together the outer reaches of the City of Angels.

"Sit down, Trace," Duke said. "Coffee?"

"Had some."

Nodding, Duke poured himself a cup from the little maker he kept on his credenza. "I gotta give this stuff up," he said. Then, after a big swallow, he bellowed, "Nah!" and started to laugh. Tracy laughed with him. She couldn't help being wrapped up in his personality. Short and stocky, like an old-time piano mover, Duke Gallegos was every inch a fighter. He'd been in the trenches more than thirty years, which helped explain why his thinning white hair remained in a perpetual state of disorder. And, as always, his tie was loosened, and his sleeves were rolled halfway up his thick forearms.

"So you're not busy enough," Duke said.

Again, Tracy laughed. "Yeah, right."

"None of you deputies are. You'd think this is a summer camp."

"Not like the old days?"

Duke winked. "You got it right. The office here is the largest prosecuting agency in the world. We got over a thousand deputies pushing a quarter-million criminal cases every year. But I think we got more *real* work done when I was a young buck."

"Well, just think of the example I have to look up to."

"You're a quick one, you are. Matter of fact, that's why you're here." Duke sat down behind his desk and took up a worksheet. "You hear about the movie guy who was blasted last night?"

"I saw something in the paper."

"Yeah, nasty. Sandy Joseph. He was pretty big. Rich. All those guys are. Makes me want to sell my life story for the big screen. Who do you think should play me? Tom Cruise?"

Tracy smiled.

"Maybe Harrison Ford," Duke mused. "We'll see. Anyway, I got to thinking. I'd like you to work on this one, starting from the ground floor. LAPD's got a couple leads. I want you with 'em."

"Me?"

"Yeah, beautiful, you. I already spoke to Bob." Bob Campbell was her supervisor, the calendar deputy in Department 128. He was usually the one who handed out the trial assignments in that courtroom. For some reason, the pattern wasn't being followed here.

"But my plate is full," Tracy said.

"I'm taking care of that." Duke put his feet up on the desk and leaned back. "It's time you moved up. A murder case. You're ready."

"Whoa." Tracy didn't know whether to laugh or cry. "I just moved into felonies."

"You're a fast mover. Bob says you can do it."

"I'm . . . flattered. But a *murder* case? Now?"

Duke's phone rang. He picked up. "Gallegos."

He looked at Tracy and then handed her the phone. "For you."

Tracy blinked, then said into the phone, "Yes?"

"Mrs. Shepherd, it's Wilma Olivera."

"What is it?"

"Allison's not feeling well. She has a slight temperature."

Tracy closed her eyes and sighed. When she opened them she saw Duke looking at her with concern. She covered the mouthpiece and whispered, "My baby-sitter. Says my daughter isn't feeling well."

Duke nodded and spun around toward the window.

"She wants to talk to you."

"I can't—"

"Hold on."

A moment later Allison Marie Shepherd, five years old, said, "Mommy, I don't feel good." Her voice was slow and weak.

"I'm so sorry, honey . . ."

"When will you be home?"

"As soon as I can. Mrs. Olivera will take care of you until I get there."

"Mommy?"

"Yes, honey?"

"I want you to come home now."

Tracy gripped the phone so tight her hand showed white splotches. "Oh, sweetie, I'll try . . ."

"Mommy?"

"Yes?"

"Love you."

Letting out a long breath, Tracy said softly, "Love you, too, sweetie. I'll see you real soon."

"OK."

Tracy hung up the phone, and rubbed her temples in a circular motion. "Sorry, Chief."

Duke spun back around and held his hands out. "Hey, no problem. The single-mother thing. I know how it is. I'm a nineties kind of guy."

"I try not to let it get in the way of work."

"I know that. And that's another reason I'm tapping you for the Joseph thing. Don't be scared about it. Everybody's got to jump in sometime. It might as well be now."

"But there are others who could handle it, with more experience. Conroy. Ricciardulli."

"Sure they could handle it." Duke plopped his elbows on his desk. "That's not the point. The point is, I want you to get your feet wet."

"You sure this isn't wet cement?"

"Meaning?"

Tracy inhaled deeply. "This looks like it might be somewhat big, you know? A famous person shot in Tinseltown? Glamour, glitz, gossip. I don't know if I'm ready. Maybe I should second chair."

"You're ready, or I wouldn't have picked you. And remember, you go into trial here and you get to hand off all your other files. That's the fun part. You get to give your full attention to this one."

"It'll mean some late nights."

"Always does. But you've pulled those before."

Tracy glanced out Duke's window, catching sight of a distant 747 easing down toward LAX. "I don't know, Chief," she said finally. "Can I think about it?"

"No."

The response was clipped, stern. It caught Tracy off guard. Then suddenly, Duke laughed, deep and rolling, and seemed normal again. "In all honesty, Trace, I want you on this one, and I want you to give it your all. I'll do everything I can to make it as easy as I can. But I want you there. OK?"

It was a directive, not a request. "OK," she said.

"Good. You're gonna be sitting in this chair someday. Maybe I'll oil it for you."

It was his way of dismissing her. Duke never told anyone to leave. But she knew from the way he said things when the conversation was over. Tracy stood up and started for the door, then turned back. "About my files," she said.

"How's that?"

"I'd like to keep one of them, if I might."

"Which one?"

"Sollomon."

"Sollomon?"

"The guy who burned his girlfriend and bloodied his little kid."

"Let Bob handle it."

"I'd like to be involved."

"Who's defense counsel?"

"Beymer."

Duke looked up and scratched his cheek. "Jackson Beymer?"

"Yes."

Flicking a pencil across the desk, Duke Gallegos said, "That's all you need. Going head to head with Jackson Beymer the same time you're doing your first murder trial. Why do you want that?"

"I don't know. Something inside me. I really want that one."

"We'll see." Tracy started to say something, but Duke put up his hand. "We'll *see*. Now go give LAPD a call and get started."

Tracy could only nod. Just before closing the door behind her, Duke said, "Welcome to the big time, kid."

The big time. Wasn't that where all the prosecutors in the office wanted to be? And there she was. Boom. Just like that.

But the only thought that pounded inside her head as she walked down the hall was, *I'm not ready for this. I'm not ready.*

# CHAPTER TWO

THE HUGE, WHITE FACE of Parker Center jutted skyward like a sheer rock cliff, a forbidding fortress at the corner of Los Angeles Street and Temple.

Named for William H. Parker, the legendary chief of police during the fifties and sixties, it was the central operating headquarters of the Los Angeles Police Department—eight floors of law enforcement technology and manpower.

Tracy flashed her ID at the front desk and was issued a visitor's sticker, then took the elevator to the fifth floor. The rows of offices looked not unlike those at the Criminal Courts Building, except there seemed to be more sunlight here. The cops had it nice.

Near the end of the corridor, Tracy came to the small office of Detective Stan Willis. Willis was the lead on the Joseph matter. A no-nonsense guy. Tracy had met him a few times in passing. The rap was, he didn't smile. Ever. Today was no exception.

"Yeah, come in," he said brusquely when he saw Tracy standing in the doorway. She entered and took a seat across from his desk.

Willis picked up a pink score sheet and held it in his stubby fingers. Looking substantially older than his forty-five years, Stan Willis was what the other officers called a "pug." That was a guy who looked like his tenure on the force had accumulated in lines around the eyes and flab around the gut. Other officers took pride in keeping up a hunk-like image. Not Willis. He was the kind who didn't care what he looked like, only that you feared him.

Tweaking the sheet with his middle finger, Willis said, "We know who it is."

"Already?"

"He'll be picked up today."

"That's fast."

"Hey, the best time to solve a homicide is within twenty-four hours. After that people tend to start losing their memories."

"Why is that?"

"Ah, they get afraid of what might happen if they're a witness. Especially in a gang killing. How would you like to be the only one on your block to testify against that group of thugs down the street?"

Willis paused. Tracy only nodded. That was a major problem in gang cases. She'd always wondered what she'd do if she ever had a case where the witnesses were boys from the 'hood.

Willis said, "Our boy is a kid named Murray, O'Lean Murray. Gang-banger. Likes to be called Licorice."

Tracy pulled a notepad from her purse and flipped it open.

"They had a party for a new movie," Willis continued, "*Red Riding Hood* or something like that. Black movie. Sex, violence, lots of mad dogging on The Man." Willis huffed some air. "Anyway, it was gang-banger central there, apparently, except 'the suits' were white. They usually are. One of them was our friend Joseph."

Tracy said, "Yes, he was doing quite well for himself. I didn't realize he did *Terror*."

"Made a boatload of money. Hope he had a will." Willis grunted, picked up a paper clip, and continued, "Witnesses everywhere, though reliability's going to be a question. They weren't drinking Dr. Pepper at this thing."

"Crack?"

"Probably, though we found more evidence of ice."

"Crystal meth?"

"Party down, huh? But we know Murray left the party at least a half hour before Joseph and this other guy, Winning, went out to the parking lot. Pretty soon Winning goes back into the party, and our victim orders up his car. Here's where premeditation comes in. Murray was in the back seat."

Tracy scribbled a note. "The car wasn't locked?"

"Oh, it was locked; the valet swears. But they keep the keys on a rack, and there was so much going on, with people in 'Vettes and Jags honking and screaming 'cause they had to wait two minutes, that anybody with a mind to could have lifted a set of keys."

"Or had the valet unlock the car."

"Why would he do that?"

"Because he knew the perp."

Scowling, Willis said, "You've got quite an imagination."

"We should follow that up."

"No need. I've already interviewed the valet. He knows nothing."

"But—"

"Let us handle the police work, Ms. Shepherd." He said it with a strict, official air. Clearly, he didn't want any young D. A. trampling on his turf.

"But if you're talking premeditation," Tracy said, "how would he know Joseph's car?"

"You ever seen a key for a Bentley? The thing probably costs as much as a Toyota."

"And what about motive?"

"I was getting to that, counselor. Motive: robbery. Who drives a Bentley? Someone who's loaded, that's who."

"So he wasn't marking Joseph himself?"

"Not specifically. Just the guy with the Bentley. We got two wits who saw Murray—one who knew him—talking to a guy near where the valet said the Bentley was parked. Next time they looked, the guy was gone, but Murray's looking around. Murray comes back to the kiosk. We figure he put the keys back then. Then, get this, he heads *back* toward the Bentley. That's the last we hear of him. Joseph winds up iced, and no one sees Murray again that night."

Pushing aside a lock of hair, Tracy asked, "Physical evidence?"

"Ah, the pièce de résistance. One of those gangbanging wool hats, the kind O. J. wore. On the seat of the Bentley. And what do you think we found?"

"Hair."

"Right."

"You don't know it's his yet."

"Don't worry. It's his. And that's all you're gonna need."

"Don't start the congratulations yet."

"What's the matter? You seem a little, uh, timid."

Tracy bristled. "No, that's not it at all."

"Then what is it?" Willis snapped.

"We just have to make sure the ducks line up."

"Ducks? What are you talking about?"

"I'm the one that has to assess the evidence to see if we should file."

"You're not seriously thinking a no-file, are you?"

"I'm not thinking anything yet. I just got here."

"And I'm telling you what we've got." Willis leaned on his desk with two supporting fists. "That should be enough."

Tracy wanted to say that was never enough. Cops made mistakes, like anybody else. If they didn't, they'd be the prosecutors, judges, and juries all rolled into one. But she held back. No use starting off on the wrong foot.

"All I'm saying, Detective Willis, is that I'm new to all this. I don't want to make any mistakes."

Willis leaned back and unloosed his fists. Then he nodded. "Duke phoned me," he said. "Don't worry. You'll be all right."

Tracy stood up. "Just one more question."

"Yeah?"

"The killing took place in Hollywood."

"Yeah."

"So why is it being handled down here?"

Willis paused, looking Tracy in the eyes. "Decisions are made," he said. "We'll handle our end. You just handle yours."

"Whatever you say."

At that Willis almost smiled. But he didn't.

Tracy spent the rest of the day finishing up the files she would pass on and started one on the Murray case. But the one she found herself turning to most was the Sollomon matter. The memory of Sollomon's eyes, and the crassness of Jackson Beymer, lingered.

Why was she so interested in this one? After all this time in the office, she had developed that professional outlook all good prosecutors need—the ability to be dispassionate. Without that, sooner or later the endless stream of victims and shattered lives would take its toll. A prosecutor had to care, but it did no good for anyone if that caring created an emotional wreck. That had always been the toughest part of the job for Tracy, and she was just getting to the point where her professionalism was erecting that layer of objectivity she needed to do her job well.

*So what is it about this guy Sollomon?* she thought. *Why can't I shake it?*

Then it hit her. It was the child. The child was in danger.

Tracy glanced at the clock: 4:30. She decided to cut out, even though it was early. She wanted to get home to her kids. She needed to be with them. But the traffic, as usual, was no help. The freeway was stacked up like a parking lot, and the bottleneck out of downtown was a trickle. It would be a long commute to Sherman Oaks. She'd just have to ride it out.

Tracy flicked on the radio. KNX—"all news, all the time"—was carrying a traffic report. Stall in the right hand lane at Highland. More trouble. *Great.* Half listening, half pondering what to make for dinner, Tracy drove on automatic pilot until the radio anchor mentioned the name *Sandy Joseph.* Tracy snapped-to and turned up the volume.

". . . the African-American community has expressed concerns about a rush to judgment."

*Rush to judgment? Sounds like the O. J. Simpson murder trial. Who have they got on their side, Johnnie Cochran?*

Another voice took over, from a taped interview: "Justice is what they should be after. Not another win, not another conviction, not another notch on the belt. *Justice*."

*Great. This is all we need to keep the peace in L. A.*

The anchor said, "Calls to the district attorney's office were not returned."

Tracy stiffened. *No one told me there were calls about the Murray case. Why wasn't I notified?*

She flicked the radio off and drove in silence. It seemed like an eternity before she pulled into her quiet neighborhood south of Ventura Boulevard. Finally she stopped in the driveway of her rented house. She put her head on the steering wheel and took a few deep breaths. Slowly, she got out of her car, grabbed her briefcase and noticed Mrs. Olivera standing in the doorway. Her comforting smile was a great relief. Wilma Olivera was a gem: a Christian woman from the next block who loved kids and charged a reasonable fee.

"How's Allison?" Tracy asked.

"Resting in the living room."

"Thanks for taking care of her."

"Was no problem," Mrs. Olivera said. Tracy threw her briefcase on an entryway chair and walked into the living room, where Allison was lying on the sofa.

"How's my pumpkin?"

"Bryce took all my stuff and won't give it back!" said Allison.

A boy's voice from the next room shouted, "I did not!"

"Did too!" yelled Allison.

"That's how it's been," said Mrs. Olivera, with a tired grin. "I told them they would have to settle this with you tonight. I told them no getting away with this."

Tracy grinned weakly. *If only I could have been here when it started; if only I could be here all the time.*

As soon as Mrs. Olivera had gone, Tracy summoned Bryce to the living room. She sat heavily on the sofa, and the kids jumped up on either side of her. Allison, her angel, on the left; Bryce, her seven-year-old, looking and acting like his father in so many ways, on the right.

"I didn't take her stuff!" Bryce said.

"Did too," said Allison.

"Wait a minute," said Tracy.

"And I'm sick!" Allison had tears in her eyes.

"I just borrowed her Silly Putty for two seconds," Bryce pleaded. "Then I put it back."

"Did not!"

Tracy's head was pounding. "Stop!" Tracy yelled. She felt both kids draw back a little. "I'm sorry. Sorry. Mommy's had a rough day."

"You always have rough days," said Bryce.

"I know, Bryce. I do have hard days, a lot. You forgive me?"

"Sure," said Bryce.

"I forgive you, too," Allison said.

Tracy put out her arms and enfolded both her kids. "Oh, how I love you guys," she said. She paused a moment, savoring the physical touch. Finally, she said, "And you two love each other, right?"

"Uh-uh," said Allison.

"No way," Bryce said emphatically.

"Hold it," said Tracy. "Yes, you do. We're a family. That means we always love each other. Even when we're mad. OK?"

The children said nothing. Bryce shrugged his shoulders.

"You understand what I'm saying?" said Tracy.

"Uh-uh," said Allison.

"Well then, let's talk about it over dinner."

Tracy let the kids watch TV while she cooked up turkey burgers. By the time they sat down to eat, the crisis seemed to be over. Allison even said Bryce could play with anything she had if he'd ask her first.

And when bedtime rolled around, they were actually playing Go Fish together. Then Allison brought Tracy the book she wanted read to her this evening: Dr. Seuss's *McElligot's Pool.* With her two kids, fresh in their pajamas, up on the bed with her, Tracy started reading.

"'Young man,' laughed the farmer, 'you're sort of a fool! You'll never catch fish in McElligot's pool.'"

A few moments later she was aware of Bryce's voice. "Mommy . . . Mommy . . ."

She opened her eyes. It had happened again. She had fallen asleep reading to her children.

"I'm sorry," she said. "Mommy's so tired."

"You're always tired," said Bryce.

She couldn't deny it.

Tracy woke up at 2:30 A.M. Her sleep had been troubled, more than usual. Now she was wide awake. Moonlight streamed in through the window. It was a crisp, full-moon night—the kind Ben had always liked.

Slipping out of bed, Tracy went to the window. She looked out and saw the bright, silver ball bobbing above the mountains. Soon the tears came, and she couldn't stop them. She could only hear her voice, seemingly distant and removed from her own body, whispering, "Ben . . . Ben . . . Ben . . ."

It had been two years since Ben died. The intense pain of grief had been slowly replaced by the steady gnaw of emptiness. Some of her well-meaning friends had told her this was the healing of God at work. He was slowly guiding her by the hand out of the valley of shadows, back into his wonderful light.

She wanted to believe that, desperately, but she couldn't. It was God who took Ben away, wasn't it? Or allowed it to happen? How did all that work out, anyway? The preachers and theologians had fancy names for it, but it all added up to the same thing. God was in control, right? Then how come he didn't control the bullet that ripped through Ben's heart? The question didn't have an answer. She had been looking, but it wasn't there. She wanted to put God on the witness stand. She wanted to cross-examine him, make him answer under oath.

*It's 2:30 in the morning. That's why I'm thinking crazy thoughts!*

But she had to admit that wasn't it. She'd been having these thoughts, or thoughts similar, for two years. She'd never had such thoughts before. Then the killer brought down her husband. That's when it all changed.

Ben Shepherd had been on the police force for four years. That had been the fulfillment of his lifelong dream. He told Tracy that on their very first date, like he wanted her to know everything about him from the very start. And his dream had been to be one of those cops that made a difference in the community. The kind of cop that people waved to and said hello, the kind that cut people a break when they needed it, maybe made the difference in a kid's life.

Because Ben had grown up on the mean streets himself—he was raised in the southern section of San Diego, where Latino gangs ruled—he had that special empathy for street kids.

And then one had blown him away—without warning, provocation, or remorse.

Looking out at the dimly lit yard, soft moonbeams falling through the trees, Tracy thought for a moment that she should pray. But no words came, and just as suddenly the desire left her. She only said one thing, and that was his name.

"Ben."

# CHAPTER THREE

ON TUESDAY MORNING, eight court days after arraignment in Division 30, O'Lean Murray's case came up for preliminary hearing.

Tracy walked through the doors at exactly 8:45 and spotted Chad Turturro, a deputy public defender, sitting at the defense table, hunched over a stack of manila files. "Morning, counselor," she said, plopping her briefcase next to his mountain of case summaries.

Turturro jerked around like a paranoiac. He was a short, fast-talking New Yorker whose hairline was receding like the Pacific Ocean at dusk. "What are *you* doin' here?" he said.

"I came to talk about Murray."

"You're not doin' the prelim, Dickerson is."

"I'm the prime on this one."

"Lucky you."

"Chad, I've always wondered. Do you keep that Brooklyn accent for appearances, or is that how you really talk?"

Turturro snorted a laugh. "Don't mess with me, lady. I know people. Now what is it you wanted to jawbone about?"

"What are you doing on Murray?"

Turturro waded through the files on his desk and pulled one out. "Oh yeah. I gave it a quick once-over. Murder one. Looks like an L-WOP, am I right?"

"Life without parole? These are special circumstances, Chad. We may seek the death penalty."

"Come on, kid's got no record."

"It was a robbery."

"No record, Tracy."

"Never been caught before."

Turturro exhaled audibly. "How come you're down here, really?"

"I told you, I've got the trial track."

"Already? Aren't you a little, uh, green?"

"Maybe I'm just special."

Turturro snorted. "Let's deal 'em. How low you willing to go?"

"Now?"

"Cop to manslaughter, and you can go sit by the pool."

"Can't do it."

Grinning like the Cheshire cat in a cheap suit, Turturro said, "I always thought you could do anything you set your little mind to, counsel."

"Not on this one," Tracy said.

"Public pressure, eh? Too hot to cop?"

Tracy shook her head. "It's not like that, Chad."

"Sure. Tell me about it."

"It's not. This one can't be reduced. Public pressure doesn't have anything to do with it. The facts do."

"Whatever happened to Christian charity?" Turturro smirked. "You're a churchgoin' kind of gal."

Tracy smiled and said, "The Lord is righteous; he loves justice."

"I love it when you quote the Good Book," Turturro said. "How would you like to quote it at me over dinner?"

"Chad—"

"All right. Look, he's gonna be bound over, and then we're gonna hold your feet to the fire. Reciprocal discovery, Miranda—if it ain't there, I'm gonna paper you and keep you up late at night."

"I wouldn't expect anything less."

Janet Dickerson, the grade-one deputy D. A. from the Van Nuys office, appeared at the defense table. "Having fun?" she asked.

"Mind if I watch the prelim?" Tracy said.

Janet, a short twenty-five-year-old with a battleground of thick, red hair, shook her head. "Why not? It should be short."

"You wish," Turturro mocked.

Just then the door to the lockup opened, and O'Lean Murray was led in by a deputy sheriff. He was clad in orange coveralls with L. A. County Jail stenciled across the back. His hands and feet were shackled.

"Sit down next to him," the deputy said, motioning toward Turturro.

"My lawyer?" Murray spat.

"Now the fun begins," Turturro whispered to Tracy.

Tracy perused O'Lean Murray's face. He was thin, with taut, wiry arms. His eyes were dark and angry, but Tracy thought they held a soft confusion, too. He didn't yet have the hardness of features she'd observed in other gang members. No doubt that would be coming soon. He'd do hard time in the joint, and that would be that. Cons didn't get out of there without a hardness of heart or face as a permanent scar.

A moment later, Judge Richard Halberstrom took the bench as the bailiff ordered everyone to rise and announced court was in session. Halberstrom plopped his robed and rotund body in his chair. Stroking his gray beard, he checked his docket. "People versus O'Lean Murray," he said gruffly. "Are the people ready?"

Janet Dickerson stood up and said, "Janet Dickerson on behalf of the people, Your Honor. We're ready to proceed."

"Defense?" said the judge.

Turturro stood. "Ready, Your Honor."

Tracy watched Murray. Watched his eyes. Tracy saw some fear there. Good. That's what the criminal justice system is supposed to impart.

"All right," said Halberstrom. "We have a motion to suppress, do we?"

"Yes, Your Honor," said Chad Turturro.

"Let's get on with it then."

Halberstrom shuffled some papers on his bench. Suddenly O'Lean Murray shouted, "I didn't do nothin', Judge!"

Judge Halberstrom looked up and scowled. "Mr. Turturro, instruct your client to be quiet."

"Be quiet," Turturro said to Murray.

"I didn't do nothin', man! Nothin'!"

"That's enough," Halberstrom barked.

"I'm tellin' you, I didn't do nothin'!" Murray shot to his feet, pounding his fists on the counsel table.

"Young man, you'll be quiet, *now!*"

"No way, man! No way!"

Halberstrom turned to his bailiff. "Take this man back to lockup," he growled.

"No way!" screamed Murray. The bailiff and a deputy sheriff closed in on him. They gripped his arms and began to pull him toward the lockup door. Murray shook free. "I didn't do nothin'!"

Suddenly he whirled at Tracy and pointed his finger at her, screaming, "You know it! You know it!"

Tracy blinked. Why was he pointing at her? Had he confused her with Janet Dickerson? He didn't know she was the one who would be doing his trial, unless Turturro had told him.

The bailiff put an arm around Murray's neck as the other deputy sheriff pulled him through the door. Murray could be heard screaming all the way back to lockup.

Janet Dickerson turned to Tracy, and with a wry smile said, "You're one of the lucky ones all right. This case should make the evening news. If it goes to trial, you could end up on the front page of the *Times*."

"Just what I need," said Tracy.

Janet motioned to the center of the courtroom. "So what do you make of all that?"

"Protestations of innocence? We hear it all the time. Gangbangers are con artists. It's all part of the game."

Janet nodded slowly. "If he was acting, he ought to get an Oscar."

"We're lawyers, not film critics."

From the bench Halberstrom said, "That's enough fireworks for one morning, Mr. Turturro. Ms. Shepherd?"

"Yes, Your Honor?"

"You assigned to this case?"

"I'm afraid so."

Eyes twinkling above his bifocals, Halberstrom said, "You should have a lot of fun."

Mona Takata opened up her brown bag lunch and squealed, "Tell me all about it! This is great stuff!"

Tracy smiled. "Slow down."

"I don't know from slow! Tell me, tell me!"

They were sitting at a little table in the corner of the CCB cafeteria, near the window that looked out on the thick, gray walls fronting Broadway and Temple. "This is supposed to be our weekly fellowship lunch, remember?" Tracy said.

"So we're here. Fellowship. Now tell me all about it." Mona, a raven-haired Asian-American in her early twenties, spread her arms out like gull wings. "You're gonna be big! I'm talking the 'Today Show,' the 'Tonight Show,' 'Geraldo,' 'Larry King'—"

"Mona!"

"—'Entertainment Tonight,' dates with Brad Pitt—"

"Will you stop?"

"Why?"

"Because I don't want to be big," said Tracy. "I just want to be good."

"You are, girlfriend. Look, I've been an investigator for the office for what now, nine months? And all I've ever heard from people is that you've got what it takes." Mona took a big bite of a turkey sandwich.

"To be honest, I don't want this case."

Mona, cheeks now bulging with sandwich, made a muffled sound that might have indicated shock.

Tracy put up her hand. "Don't spit your food out. I'm just saying I don't know if I'm ready for something this big yet."

After a big swallow, Mona said, "Duke wouldn't do this if he didn't think you were ready."

"I don't know."

"Sure. You've got the talent. You've got the brains. You've got the looks. A jury will melt in your hands."

"I wish I was that confident," Tracy said, sighing. "But I don't know—"

"Don't know what?"

"I don't know about the time. I'm going to have to be committed to this, fully committed. I'm worried about the kids."

Reaching out to pat Tracy's hand, Mona said, "Hey, don't worry about them. They're great."

"But I'm not there for them like I should be. It's starting to tear me up."

"I know. You didn't ask for this."

Tracy looked down at the table. "You're right. I didn't."

Mona took Tracy's hand.

"I get lonely at night," Tracy continued. "I miss Ben's touch. I mean, I can't even tell you. And the kids constantly ask me about him. It hurts, Mona. Like a fist inside me just pumping away."

Mona nodded and kept listening.

"Am I supposed to be here, Mona? I can't figure out what God wants from me."

Mona smiled then and reached into her purse for her familiar, thin, well-worn Bible. "You remember that verse you once told me about?"

Tracy tried to remember. "No."

Mona flipped open the Bible and started riffling pages. "I have it underlined. It was the one you said made you want to become a D. A.

Here it is—Psalm 89:14—*'Righteousness and justice are the foundation of your throne; love and faithfulness go before you.'*"

"Yes, I remember now. But there are other places to seek justice."

"Not like here. Look, I'm just a rookie investigator. I haven't been around the block much, but it seems to me like you've got the position to do real justice all the time. For the victims, and for the occasional mess-up who you know deserves to be cut some slack."

"I don't know."

"What's wrong?"

Tracy took a breath, then said, "Will you just do something for me?"

"Anything."

"Just pray for me," Tracy said. "Hard."

"I have been, ever since the first day I found out that you were a sister. So I'm right here for you, babe. You and me. Can't think of a better team."

When Tracy got back to the eighteenth floor she snatched her mail and phone messages, went into her office, and closed the door. She gave Mrs. Olivera a call and started slicing open the mail as she cradled the phone on her shoulder.

"The kids are fine," Mrs. Olivera said. "They want to say hello, of course."

"Put them on," Tracy smiled.

"Hi, Mommy," said Allison. "Bryce is calling me names."

"Am not!" Tracy heard her son's voice in the background.

"OK, pumpkin, let me talk to him now."

Bryce got on the phone as Tracy opened another letter. "Allison won't play any games with me," Bryce reported.

"Just try to be nice, honey."

"I am, but she still won't play."

"All right, but don't call her any—"

"Mom? Mommy?"

Tracy was silent, breathless.

"Mommy?"

She could hear his voice, but it sounded like it was halfway across the world.

"Mommy, are you there?"

"Yes, Bryce, I'm here. I have to go now."

"But what about the games?"

"I have to go. Bye, honey." She hung up quickly, vaguely aware this was probably the first time she had ever cut one of her children off on the phone. But she would have to think of that later.

Looking down at the letter in her hands, a trifold piece of plain white bond, she read again the two words in red crayon across the center one third of the page:

*YOU'RE NEXT.*

# CHAPTER FOUR

HE CROUCHED and listened.

He smelled the air.

He felt the ground.

All of the elements were dancing for him: rhythm of earth and sky. Soon it would be time.

The other man would never know, until the final moment. That was always part of it. How close could he come without an enemy sensing him? How close before he knew? That is the way to draw strength, if the enemy is worthy.

And how to know he is worthy?

Feel.

Watch.

He heard the noise and sensed the enemy drawing closer. Had he been his great-grandfather, the enemy would have been riding a horse, and he would have prized that animal. There had been no greater honor for the Blackfeet than to take an enemy's horse. The horse had lifted them from nomads tied down to the rivers and freed them to become the great tribe of the Plains. Stealing horses from the enemy was heroic and worthy of song.

Today, the enemy would be driving a Jeep. No matter. It would be done just the same.

His fingers curved around the smooth handle of the hunting knife in his belt. And he became aware again—aware that inside he felt nothing. Not even the thrill of the hunt.

For a moment his muscles went limp. The sound of the Jeep grew louder. He suddenly thought of his grandmother, her weathered face, her soft voice.

*Why now?* he thought. *Why do I think of her now?*

She was saying something, but he couldn't hear. He didn't want to hear. Not now. Below, the Jeep passed on the dirt road.

All thought left him. He started moving according to the ancient ways. Leaping from the rock, he landed like a lion on the road, just behind the passing vehicle. He began to run. The Jeep kicked up dust, coughing like a sick animal.

He pounced. Softly, he landed in the back seat. With all the bumpiness of the road, the ranger didn't notice. Now was the time to take his coup. Like his fathers. They would ride to the enemy and touch him. Not killing yet. No. Touching while he was still alive. Coup.

The ranger wore a Smokey the Bear hat. This would serve fine as a "scalp." He would have everything—horse, scalp, coup. Everything except the heart of his enemy. He did not know the man's heart, but he sensed it was not worthy.

He pulled the knife from its sheath. In one motion he tore the hat from his enemy's head and grabbed a handful of hair, pulling the head back starkly, staring into the shocked eyes—eyes that knew the terrible moment had come.

The last thing they would ever know.

"It's nothing," Duke Gallegos said. "A crank letter. You should be used to this by now." Tracy sat in Gallegos's office with the cryptic message on her lap. "But you can tell crank letters because they go on and on," she said. "They want to tell you exactly what they think of you and the case and the way the world has ripped them off. This is a pure threat."

"Somebody's just having a little fun with you."

"Fun!"

"Mind games, Trace. Look, do you think if someone wanted to actually kill you they'd telegraph it with a note like this?"

"I don't know, Duke, this is L. A. Killers like publicity. They get book deals."

"It's a prank, Tracy. The question is, are you going to let it bother you?" Duke sat down in his chair, simultaneously taking a swig of coffee. "Trace, this wouldn't be a case of nerves, would it?"

"No, it wouldn't!"

Duke put his hand up. "Take it easy. Look, I know what it's like. Butterflies in the stomach, your first capital case. Don't worry so much. Remember what my grandpappy used to say—the secret is not getting rid of the butterflies; the secret is getting them to fly in formation." He laughed his infectious laugh, and Tracy felt better. Somehow, just knowing he was here and available was comforting.

"Let me tell you about my first murder trial," he continued. "I was about your age, too, I think. I was helping out the lead prosecutor, Manny Madura. So the day before jury selection, he gets sick, comes down with some tropical thing that makes him so goofy he thinks he's in Denmark all the time. So who gets to pick the jury?"

"Little old you," said Tracy.

"Little *young* me. And I'm so scared the first thing I do when the panel comes into court is spill a glass of water on myself. Yep, Duke Gallegos, the toughest kid west of the Pecos, has wet his pants. It wasn't pretty."

Tracy could feel her nerves settling down. "At least I can say that hasn't happened to me yet."

"Count your lucky stars. So I stand up to address the first twelve in the box, and I say, 'Good morning, ladies and gentlemen. My name is Frank Gallegos and I represent the paper of California.'"

"*Paper?*" Tracy said.

"Paper. Not the *People* of California. No. I'm standing there with a big water stain on my nice gray pants, telling the good men and women who will assess my case that I represent the *paper* of California.

Well, not only did they all laugh, but I look up and see the judge in stitches, too."

"That must have made you feel just great."

"And then the judge says—we're only five minutes into jury selection, mind you—the judge says, 'Mr. Gallegos, do you need a recess?' And the whole courtroom cracks up again."

"That's awful."

"Awful? If there had been a rat hole in the wall I would have greased my sides and tried to slip in."

"So what did you do?"

"I just kept remembering something else my grandpappy used to say: 'If life gives you lemons, pucker up.'"

"I thought it was 'make lemonade.'"

"My grandpappy never did like lemonade. So I puckered up. I did the best I could under the circumstances. And you know what? The jury jumped on my side."

"Why?"

"Because they felt so sorry for me, that's why. I think they sort of took me under their wing. *We've gotta help this guy,* they were thinking. Well, I won the case. Going away. Afterward, I polled the jury. They all said what a great job I did even though I looked like I might faint at any moment. Some compliment, eh?"

Duke got up, came around the desk, and put his hand on Tracy's shoulder. "So what I'm saying is this. There are more than enough things in this job to make you want to bury your head in quick-drying cement. But you don't. You go on because you've got the facts and the law on your side. And the jury will love you for it."

He flashed that fatherly smile at her, and Tracy knew then it would be all right. She'd get through it after all. "Thanks, Duke," she said.

"That's my girl," said Duke. "Now, on another matter, I have something to tell you."

"What is it?" Tracy said.

"I'm handing Sollomon off to Levine."

"Levine! But he's—"

"Yes?"

Tracy hesitated. "I don't want to speak out of turn, but he's not considered . . . I mean . . ."

"Not one of our stronger trial lawyers?"

Grateful, Tracy nodded. "And he's got Jackson Beymer on the other side."

"I considered all that."

"Besides, you know how I feel about that case."

Duke put his hands up in the air, defensively. "I know, I know. But your feelings aren't the final authority around here."

The tone seemed unduly harsh to Tracy. Why should it be? She hadn't done anything wrong. She had been yanked from a case she wanted. If anything, Duke should be trying to explain his reasons.

"Listen," Duke continued, "I know how you feel, I really do. But we have to make these decisions all the time. You know that. The case was thin. And Beymer can do things to a jury, as we all know. And frankly this office can't afford a big loss right now. We have to be very, very careful of what we take to trial."

"I don't like this stuff."

"What stuff?"

"All the political considerations."

"You don't have to like it. Besides, I'm the one who has to think about it all."

"Chief, will you please—" Tracy stopped as Duke put his hand up and looked out his office door.

"I think we have a visitor," he said. She followed as Duke entered the hallway. A small knot of men and women were gathered near the entrance. Tracy noticed a man in the middle who seemed to be doing the talking. "Who's that?"

Duke said, "That is the next governor of this state."

The man turned and gave Duke a million-dollar smile. Now Tracy recognized him from the newspapers and TV spots. Rob Cavanaugh.

Forty-year-old candidate for governor. Up-and-coming. Movie star good looks, according to the papers. A sure winner.

He headed directly for them. His reddish blond hair was without flaw, and he wore a dark blue suit and patterned burgundy tie like a second skin. He was on the tall side, but he moved with the grace of an athlete.

Cavanaugh stuck out his hand and gave Duke's a big shake. "How are you, you old buzzsaw?" he said sprightly. "Keeping the streets safe for democracy?"

"You should know," Duke said.

"That I should." Cavanaugh turned and looked at Tracy. She noticed his eyes. Deep green.

Duke said, "This is Tracy Shepherd, one of our bright, young deputies. Tracy, meet Rob Cavanaugh."

Cavanaugh extended his hand. "Well I wouldn't want to be on the other side of the courtroom from you."

Tracy shook his hand. His grip was firm, warm. And his smile—it seemed to throw light. Tracy felt the unmistakable rush of blood to her cheeks. "Nice to meet you," she managed.

The small group of reporters closed in around them. Cavanaugh still held her hand. "Is she judge material?" Cavanaugh said to Duke.

"Let her get her feet wet in 'felony,'" Duke answered. "She's on her first murder case. The Joseph matter."

Cavanaugh released his grip and said, "I've heard about that one." He turned to Tracy. "So you're going to bring home the justice, are you? Great. I just hope justice is swift."

"I'll do my best," Tracy said.

"I don't doubt it," said Cavanaugh. "Would you mind a picture?"

For a moment, Tracy thought he was going to hand her a photograph of himself. Instead, he extended his hand again, and, instinctively, she took it. She heard the click of several cameras. Cavanaugh leaned toward her ear and whispered, "The political thing. Photo op and all that. I hate it. But it's got to be done, they tell me." Then he leaned back and said, "And where is your little piece of office heaven, Deputy Shepherd?"

"Um, back that way."

"I hope she has a nice view," Cavanaugh said to Duke.

"As good as mine when I was starting out," Duke answered.

"Mind if I ask you a couple of questions, Miss Shepherd?"

"Mrs. Shepherd," Tracy said.

"Ah."

"All right."

Cavanaugh smiled again and motioned for Tracy to show him the way.

"My office?" Tracy said.

"If you don't mind."

She looked at Duke, who gave her an almost imperceptible nod. "Why not?" she said, turning.

"You boys and girls stay here," Cavanaugh said to the cluster of reporters. "Grill Mr. Gallegos for awhile."

Tracy led him to her office.

"I appreciate this," Rob Cavanaugh said. "I just wanted to get, one on one, a couple of insights from you. You're a working prosecutor. I aim to be the prosecutor's best friend."

They sat down, Tracy behind her metal desk.

"You know much about me?" Cavanaugh said.

"Only what I read in the papers."

"And what do they say?"

Tracy shrugged, "Leading candidate, conservative, tough on crime."

"Check."

"Strong on traditional values."

"Does any place need them more than California?"

"You've got a point."

Cavanaugh leaned forward. "I know politicians always say they've got to get tougher on criminals, but I really want to do something about it. I mean, determinate sentencing. Ten years should mean ten years, not seven, or six, or five. And I want to tighten up the three-strikes law. No more arbitrary discretion. What do you think?"

"What I think may surprise you," Tracy said.

"OK, surprise me."

"I think we actually need more discretion. I think discretion is part of the prosecutor's job."

"Interesting. I always thought the prosecutor's job was to convict people."

"You're wrong about that, Mr. Cavanaugh." Tracy noticed him sit back a little.

He smiled charmingly and said, "How am I wrong?"

"According to the canon of ethics, the prosecutor is charged with seeing that justice is done. Not convict, but do justice. Sometimes that means filing a case and trying it with every ounce you have. But other times it means not filing. It means exercising your discretion not to seek a conviction."

"But won't that discretion vary from person to person?"

"Sure, but unless you want robots doing this job, that will always be the case. The system will never be perfect, but that's why you train people. Then you let them do their job."

Cavanaugh nodded. He was listening, really listening. *Imagine that,* Tracy thought, *a politician who actually listens.*

"May I ask," said Cavanaugh, "what your husband does for a living while you toil here downtown?"

"My husband was killed two years ago," Tracy said quickly.

"Oh, I'm sorry. I didn't mean . . ."

"It's all right. He was a cop with LAPD. He made a routine traffic stop one night in the Wilshire district. His partner was running the plates when Ben approached the vehicle. Two shots. It happened fast . . ." Tracy's voice trailed off.

After a pause Cavanaugh said, "He must have been a very fine man."

"He was."

Cavanaugh stood and offered his hand once more. Tracy felt a gentle assurance in his grip. "Mrs. Shepherd, thank you for your time. I appreciate it."

"Thank *you*," said Tracy. Rob Cavanaugh turned and left her office.

For five minutes Tracy sat at her desk, absently shuffling papers around, seeing nothing on them. Finally she shook her head violently and said out loud, "Snap out of it!" She looked up. Cheryl Itkin, her office mate, was just walking in. "Snap out of what?" Cheryl asked.

Tracy put up her hand. "Don't even ask."

---

It was nearly four o'clock when she got the call. The woman on the other end of the line had a husky voice, which warbled with tension. "My name is Kendra Murray," she said. "My son is O'Lean."

Tracy sat up straight in her chair. "Yes?"

"You the prosecutor?"

"Yes I am." Tracy was cautious. She would have to tread lightly on a call like this. She would have to take notes and immediately notify Turturro of the conversation. She grabbed a pen and legal pad.

"My son, he didn't do this thing," Kendra Murray said. "He didn't."

"How do you know that, Mrs. Murray?"

"I just do. I know my son."

How many times had Tracy heard that one? A parent, usually the mother, usually single, calling up to vouch for a son she couldn't control. Tracy understood the parental aspect, of course. The desire to protect—but usually it was just a clumsy attempt at an alibi.

"There is strong evidence against him," Tracy said.

"But I'm telling you, he wouldn't do it."

"He was identified by a witness."

"Won't you just talk to him?"

"I can't talk to him. He's represented by counsel."

"Please."

Tracy looked at the ceiling. "Mrs. Murray, your son is represented by a lawyer who is doing everything he can—"

"Everything? A public defender? He's got a thousand cases I bet. You're the one with the power." Tracy nodded to herself. The woman was not clueless.

"You don't know me," the woman said, tears evident in her voice. "I know you don't. But I wish you could just look him in the eye. I wish you could look in my eyes, ma'am. I have taught O'Lean to be in the world but not of it. I've taught him not to lie. He wouldn't do this thing."

"Are you aware, Mrs. Murray, of your son's gang involvement?"

"My son ain't in no gang! See, his friends are, but he's never been. They respect him 'cause he's an athlete. He's no gangbanger, ma'am, no way. Please, can't you help me?"

"I'd like to, Mrs. Murray," Tracy said, feeling like the words were coming by rote, "but he's in the criminal justice system now."

"System! He's gonna get lost in there! You know it and I know it. He's just a number to you, but he's a son to me!"

There was a pause, then the woman added, "The Lord is my God and my witness, and before him I say my son did not do this thing . . ." Her voice trailed off.

Tracy closed her eyes and breathed deeply. "Mrs. Murray, as a mother you—"

"I know what you're thinkin'," she interrupted. "You're thinkin' I'm just a mother saying anything to help my son."

"And there's nothing wrong with that—"

"But I have the truth on my side, too. Doesn't the truth matter?"

"Of course it matters. The district attorney's office represents *all* the people. And that means we don't take thin cases to trial."

"So the case against my boy is thin, is that what you said?"

"Not exactly. I'm saying we will continue to look at the case and do what we think is right, according to the evidence."

There was a long pause on the other end of the line. Tracy sensed it was a silence of despair. "Mrs. Murray," Tracy said finally. "Let me talk to a few people. I can't guarantee anything, but I can assure you that, as a prosecutor, I want to find out what really happened. That's the only way I can take a case to trial. Does that help?"

"Thank you," said Mrs. Murray, sounding relieved. "That's all I ask. You've been very kind. God bless you."

"God bless you, too, ma'am." Tracy replaced the phone, absorbed in thought, and sat back in her chair. She folded her arms behind her head and closed her eyes.

The phone rang again.

"Tracy Shepherd?" The voice was a man's, low and whispered.

"Yes?"

"Do you know something?"

"Excuse me?"

"Do you know you're going to die?"

## CHAPTER FIVE

THE TWO MEN at the sixth tee looked out over the expanse of perfect green that lay before them. To the right were the million-dollar-and-up homes that guarded the winding fairways and undulating greens. To the left, the rolling hills of Thousand Oaks, one of the last vestiges of "old" southern California—gnarled oak trees amid arid bluffs, with blue skies and white, fluffy clouds above.

The pair were quite alone. This was no surprise. The Lakeview Oaks Country Club was one of the most exclusive in the world. Half a mil to get in. A king's ransom to stay each year. But such exclusivity meant privacy, which is just what the members wanted. And what the two men wanted, especially today.

The first man was thin and nervous, moving erratically under an ill-fitting, light yellow sweater and loose, cotton slacks. His severely balding head made people take him for fifty or more, even though he was only in his early forties. He paused to light a cigarette, his tenth since the round started.

The other man, still sitting in the cart, filled out his golf shirt perfectly. He was in his early thirties, though his relaxed attitude made him look even younger. He looked at the first man with vaguely concealed frustration. "You smoke too much," the younger man said.

"Nasty, I know," said the lean one.

"Undisciplined. A man should have control over what goes into his body. You agree?"

"Sure."

"I don't value lack of discipline, Lefferts," the younger man continued. "In fact, it makes me edgy. I can't afford to get edgy. It makes me do things I'd rather not do."

Lefferts felt a slight chill but said nothing.

The younger man said, "So what do you know about her?"

After a deep drag on his cigarette, Lefferts said, "She's well regarded, though something of a loner."

"Loner?"

"She doesn't have a lot of close friends, at least not in the office."

"Why not?"

"She's a Bible banger. She tends to hang out with this . . . wait a minute—" Lefferts walked to the back of the golf cart where a leather satchel was stashed. He unzipped it, reached in, and pulled out a file folder. He opened it and read something. The younger man did not move. He kept his gaze at the flagstick 438 yards away.

"Mona Takata," said Lefferts. "Another Jesus freak."

"Now that's almost funny," said the man in the golf cart. "One might think this thing was going to shape up into a battle of the gods."

"I'm not sure I understand, Mr. Kohlbert."

"You don't have the philosopher's imagination, do you?" said Kohlbert. "You don't see the implications of things. That's why I am where I am." Suddenly, he laughed, "I am WHO I am."

Now even more confused, Lefferts just smoked.

"Don't know your Bible, I see. Well, never mind. I'll come back into your little world. Tell me about this Shepherd's professional status."

"Well, like I say, she's considered a hard worker, a good lawyer. But totally inexperienced at this level."

Kohlbert said nothing.

"So it's just right, in my opinion," the lean man continued.

"Your opinion had better be well tuned."

"Right." He felt another chill. "I've got the situation in hand. I'll be closely monitoring everything. You'll get regular reports."

"I expect no less," Kohlbert said. "Now about the other matter—"

Lefferts said, "It has been taken care of."

"Payoff?"

"Not yet."

"When?"

"Tomorrow I fly out."

"See that you do. The Bear Paw is one contractor I don't want to annoy."

*For good reason,* thought Lefferts. Silence hung in the air like a high lob to a tight green. Lefferts was waiting for another inquiry from his boss. That's how he liked to do things. Out here on the golf course. Business and pleasure.

Finally, Kohlbert looked at Lefferts and said brusquely, "Well, are you going to tee off or what?"

---

Tracy and Mona stepped onto the Metro train underneath the Los Angeles Civic Center. They took seats by the opposite door. "I don't feel comfortable around the office right now," said Tracy. "Somebody is seriously messing with me."

"You think you're a target?"

"Yes, I'm a target."

"What does Duke think?"

Tracy sighed. "He thinks it's just some crackpot and it will all go away."

"He may be right."

"So what am I supposed to do, sit around until this guy comes after me, and then we'll finally figure out he was serious?"

Mona patted her friend's arm. "You don't really need this, do you?"

"I've thought about walking away more than once."

"Seriously?"

The train doors closed, and the Red Line was off toward the end of its route three miles away. Tracy looked straight across the car into the darkness of the tunnel. "Sometimes the only thing keeping me there is not knowing how I'd provide for the kids. If I had that settled, I'd probably walk."

"You could look around, maybe go into private practice."

"But unless I go into a firm, we're talking about a year or more to get going. It's brutal out there for private practitioners. And what would I do? Criminal law is all I know. I'd have to be a defense lawyer."

Mona laughed. "Well now, there are worse things."

"Oh yeah? Name one." Now it was Tracy's turn to share a laugh with her companion.

The train made a stop. A couple of people got off, a few more got on.

"I've got the answer for you," Mona said.

"What's that?"

"Marry some rich guy."

"Mona—"

"A Christian, of course. But one with a lot of bucks!" Mona giggled. Tracy shook her head. At least she was loosening up some. That was what Mona was good at.

"So outside of nabbing a rich Christian husband," Tracy said, "what do you suggest I do?"

"Tell you what. I'll do a little snooping around, see what I can put together."

"On your own time?"

"Why not? What else am I going to do? I'm not married to a rich guy, either."

The train made its last stop. The two friends emerged from the escalator to the street across from MacArthur Park. The usual afternoon activities were apparent—old men poking at the grass with their canes, women walking babies, Korean and Mexican shop owners minding street displays. And scattered around, a few professionals were on their way to authentic Mexican or Thai restaurants. Or the New York style deli, Langer's, where Tracy and Mona headed.

The moment they got in and were shown to a table, Tracy heard the voice. "Well, well, if it isn't the next Marcia Clark."

Tracy spun around and saw Jackson Beymer sitting in a booth by the window, notching a little salute her way. He was seated with a man she didn't recognize. He wasn't wearing a suit, like Beymer, but wore a polo shirt instead. Under it, his muscles were obvious. He had a buzz haircut and didn't look friendly.

Tracy nodded at Beymer then turned away, but he said, "I guess the saner minds in your office prevailed, eh?"

*He could only be referring to one thing,* Tracy thought—*the deal involving Howard Sollomon*. "Some might call it sane," she said.

"And what would you call it?"

"A miscarriage."

Beymer chuckled and turned to his companion. "You hear that, Cliff? The prosecutrix over there doesn't think justice was done."

Cliff looked at Tracy. Their eyes met for a second. Tracy felt like she was looking into a living mug shot. *Must be one of Beymer's clients, out for a celebratory lunch with his lawyer.* Maybe Beymer had cut a deal on this one, too.

"So I hear you're handling the Joseph murder," Beymer said.

Mona leaned over and whispered to Tracy, "You want me to fling a pickle at him?"

Tracy suppressed a smile. "I can't discuss the case with you, Mr. Beymer. You're not the attorney of record."

"Lucky for you," he said.

Tracy said to Mona, "Maybe we'd better move." Mona nodded.

"Going so soon?" Beymer said.

"We have some confidential matters to discuss," said Tracy.

"I won't tell," said Jackson Beymer. "Honest."

Tracy and Mona walked to the back of the restaurant. Tracy felt the eyes of the man named Cliff on her back.

"I don't like him," Mona said, looking at Beymer. "He's a slime."

"I'm not going to argue with you," said Tracy.

"It's not very Christian of me to say that, is it?" Mona's eyes twinkled mischievously.

Tracy said, "I'm not much of an authority on what's Christian these days."

"Hey, what is it, babe? You got the Mr. Ed."

"The what?"

"The long face. What's wrong?"

"Well, for starters, my life has been threatened a couple of times."

"I think that's just hot air."

"Yeah?"

"Sure."

"You're the voice of experience, I suppose."

Mona smiled. "I may be young, but I've got the juice up here." She tapped her forehead. "It's a gift from the Lord."

Tracy nodded.

"Hey," Mona said, "how about coming to church with me this Sunday? Come to my place."

"Over the hill?"

"Oh, yeah. Come pray with us crazy charismatics, hey? You'll be lifting your hands and getting anointed all over the place."

"I wonder."

"Come on."

"I'll think about it."

"Just want to stoke your spiritual fire a little. I know you've been struggling, but I've been praying. God's going to bring you through."

"I know that somewhere," Tracy said. "Somewhere in the back of my mind. But that's where it's staying, Mona."

"All we need to do is jostle it a little."

Tracy looked down at the table, wondering if that was even possible.

---

Tommy Bear Paw stood on the corner across the street from the small, white church with the statue in front of it. The Virgin Mary, unmoving, unsmiling, but looking at something. No, not necessarily *looking*. But *seeing*. Her eyes were cast downward, but she could see. That's what it was. She could see things he could not.

Bear Paw was dressed in a red flannel shirt, light-blue jeans, and black boots coated with dust. His dry, black hair was blown around by the hot, desert breeze. He did nothing to put it in its place. Instead, he watched the Virgin as if expecting her to move at any time, as if she might lift her head and look straight at him and say, "Come. I will show you what I see."

*What is it?* Tommy Bear Paw wanted to know. *Why do you keep it hidden?*

It was almost three o'clock in the afternoon. That was the time, he knew, when the thing called Mass would be over and people would start out of the church. Old, desert-dwelling women, and a few of their men, indulged their odd rituals.

Why did they come? What was it all for? To get to *see*. To catch a glimpse of what the Virgin saw. Catholics were a strange sort, but there was something in that strangeness that drew Tommy Bear Paw.

Patiently, he waited. He was used to waiting. It was part of his life now, the new life that started shortly after he got home from that other desert. He had learned to wait, and he was waiting now.

A few trucks from the highway passed him by, making the connection through the small town to the interstate, heading north toward Albuquerque or south toward El Paso. He thought again about being a trucker. There was something about it he liked. You were always on the move, so maybe you'd be able to find something just ahead. And, you'd be getting away from everything that lay behind.

The parishioners were starting out now, some heading for the little dirt lot to claim their dusty Fords and grimy Chevys, a few walking toward the center of town to catch the bus. It wouldn't be long now, and then he'd have his chance.

For a few minutes, he let his mind wander. Usually, he didn't allow this. It was bad for business. But with the hot sun and dull surroundings, he let his mind loose like a stallion in the arroyo.

As usual, it went back to that image, when he was a boy. It had been a hot day, like today, and he had been working the ranch with his grandfather. Backbreaking work, as always, but they had taken a break, and grandfather had put him on the back of a horse and had ridden with him to the house. Grandmother had prepared a pitcher of cold lemonade. All three of them had sat in the shade and drank. It was the best drink he had ever tasted. His grandmother's smiling face looked as bright as the sun.

He snapped his mind back to the present. Now, he thought, the priest would be alone. Now was his chance. He walked across the street.

The Virgin looked down from her pedestal. Bear Paw stared once more into her eyes. *What do you see?* Quickly, he opened the door, entered the chapel, and closed the door behind him.

It was dark and cool inside. Rows of wooden pews lined each side of the building. Off to the right was a bank of candles under a stained glass window. To the front, the altar with a brass rail in front of it, and above it the image of Jesus Christ hanging on a cross. That part he didn't get. What sort of religion left its founder hanging in the aspect of death? Why would anyone want to come to this place and see that?

There could only be one reason: They saw something he didn't see. His grandmother had seen it. She tried to tell him about it, but that was before the war. And she had died before the bad things happened.

Bear Paw noticed an old woman in one of the pews, on her knees. He almost left then. He had wanted to be all alone, but he was here now, and there was nothing to do but finish it. He had a sense of timing, and the time was now.

He walked forward to the altar. He waited. He knew the priest would be there. And he was.

A moment later the balding priest came back into the chapel, now out of his robes and in a more casual, yet austere, black shirt with Roman collar. He was carrying some items in his hands. One of them looked like a golden cup.

"Can I help you?" he said.

Bear Paw did not answer right away. Years of doing what he did had ingrained the habit of sizing up the person he was confronting.

"You new in town?" the priest said in a friendly manner. Bear Paw judged him to be in his early fifties.

"I want to talk to you," said Bear Paw.

"Yes, all right. Let me just put this stuff down." He went to a table at the back of the altar and laid the items down. "Shall we go into my office?"

"No," Bear Paw said.

The priest looked at him quizzically. "You want to sit down right here?" He motioned to the front pew.

"Where is the place we can talk freely?"

"Freely?"

"Where you can't repeat what you hear?"

"The confessional? You want me to hear your confession?"

"I want to talk."

Looking at his watch, the priest said, "Would you consider returning at 4:30, I have—"

"Now," said Tommy Bear Paw.

"Well, all right then. This way."

The priest led Bear Paw to the single, small confessional near the back of the church. He nodded toward the curtain of what looked like a voting booth. Tommy Bear Paw threw back the curtain, went in, and sat on the wooden seat. The separating screen pushed open, and Bear Paw heard the priest say something in Latin, then, "How long has it been since your last confession?"

"I'm not Catholic," said Bear Paw.

"Then why are you here?"

"I want to make sure you won't say anything."

"I'm bound by my vows not to repeat what is said inside here. But I'm confused. If this isn't your confession, what is it?"

"I don't know what it is. I just wanted to talk to you. You're a priest. You tell people what to believe. You give up your life for this. Why?"

"You want to know why I'm a priest?"

"Yes."

"Because I felt the call of God. That's why anyone goes into the priesthood."

"How do you know the call of God?"

"Well, you pray. You seek God. You learn how to listen for his voice. And then there's this unmistakable pulling you feel, that your life won't be complete unless you give it up fully to the service of God. When you feel like it is something you can't get away from, you surrender to it." Bear Paw said nothing. The priest asked, "Have you felt the call of God?"

"No."

"Do you pray?"

"No."

"Do you want to know God?"

"No."

After a short pause, the priest said, "Why would you not want to know God?"

Rubbing the smooth wood of the confessional with his hand, Bear Paw said, "Why should I?"

"Well, he's the Creator of the world. He is everything. And he loves us."

"So you say."

"Do you mind," the priest said, "telling me what it is you do?"

Bear Paw pondered this for a moment. "I kill people," he said.

"Excuse me?"

"I kill people and get paid for it."

A long silence was followed by the priest's voice, low and tentative. "Why do you do that?"

"Why not?"

"Because it's against the law of God." The priest was sounding incredulous. Bear Paw figured no one had ever come into his little booth and said something like this before.

"I don't see God," said Bear Paw. "Tell me where I can see him." It was thrown out as a challenge.

"You . . . have to believe."

"I want to see first."

"It says in God's Holy Word that they are blessed who believe without seeing."

"Then God's Holy Word is stupid."

"Son, let me try to help you see it another way. Let us spend some time together. But please, you must promise me, you won't kill again."

No, he would not make such a promise. It was over. He had wanted to be shown something, but it had not been shown. He quickly pushed away the curtain and made for the door of the church.

He heard the priest's voice call out, "Wait!" But he didn't pause. He bolted out the door into the sunlight and began to run. He ran and ran until he could no longer see the church, or even the small town at the crossroads.

## CHAPTER SIX

*TODAY IS GOING TO BE NORMAL*, Tracy thought. *Even if it kills me*. Then she quickly erased the thought from her mind.

She was sitting in church, trying to keep her focus on the praise choruses, the collective prayers, the sermon. It wasn't working. *Maybe I should try Mona's church sometime,* she thought. But she really knew that wasn't the problem.

She kept thinking about work, about threats, about O'Lean Murray. And then her kids, no doubt happily snacking in Sunday school, but who seemed to be getting further and further away from her.

Despite her feelings about God, she still came to church because of the kids. There was no other way to do it. They had to be given what she had been given, even if she no longer had it.

*Today is going to be normal* . . . She thought about the normalcy of her church back in Michigan, the one she had grown up in. Mom and Dad never allowed opting out of worship as an alternative. On Sunday, you went to church. That was one of the nonnegotiables in life. So she had grown up in the church, her faith comfortably in place, but never challenged—until her mom met the cancer that would not be healed.

That had put her faith into a kind of freeze; not melting, but not hot, either. And then came Ben's death. She was still reeling. Reeling so much that she had, on more than one occasion, considered dropping off the kids at Sunday school and going to the local Starbuck's to read the paper for two hours. But she resisted because of her parents. She knew if she did that, the final thread might be broken—to the past, and eventually to God. She wasn't ready to take that chance. The chilling part was, she had begun to wonder when she might be ready.

She tried again to put her mind on the sermon. She liked Larry Young, the senior minister. He eschewed flowery oratory and kept things simple. His goal was to bring the principles of the Bible down to the practical level. The problem was not him. The problem was plain *believing* anymore.

Today Pastor Young was talking about the spiritual disciplines: prayer, fasting, Bible study, and so on. Even though Tracy was in and out of the message, she did manage to hear Young say, "Discipline means being in the habit of doing those things you know you must do, even if you don't feel like it."

He chose a couple of examples: the student who would rather not study, the athlete who would rather not train. And then he spoke about the parent who would rather work than spend time with his children. Young used the masculine pronoun, but it stung Tracy just the same. Even though she would rather spend much more time with her kids, right now it wasn't possible. The guilt started creeping in.

As soon as worship was over, Tracy tried to mingle with friends and engage in innocuous chitchat. But she couldn't even do that very well. She was too preoccupied to be much of a social acquaintance to anyone. She gave up trying and gathered her kids up from Sunday school.

It was time for the second phase. The children were in pretty good spirits on the way to the L. A. Zoo. They chatted excitedly about going, which animals they wanted to see most and how much cotton candy they'd eat. Tracy started to relax a little. Maybe she could pull this off after all.

Traffic and parking were their usual snarls. It was pretty crowded inside the gates, too. But once they were inside, it was like another world. Bryce saw the flamingos and his face lit up. "The skinny birds!" he cried, grabbing his mother's hand and pulling her toward the pond.

"Not much meat on those legs, huh?" said Tracy.

"How come they stand on one leg?" Allison asked.

Tracy pondered a moment. "Because if they lifted it up, they'd fall down."

Allison frowned at first, then let loose a big smile. "You're joking with me, Mommy," she rebuked. Tracy leaned over and pinched Allison's cheeks, then kissed her on the nose.

"Let's go see the snakes," Bryce said.

"Yuck!" Allison said. "I hate snakes."

"We'll get to the snakes later," Tracy said judiciously. "Let's just walk and see what we see." She began to stroll, loving the warmth of their hands in hers and of the sun on her face.

It was while they were at the giraffe exhibit that Tracy first noticed the man. He was youngish, maybe twenty-five, and wore a tight-fitting black T-shirt and light-blue denim jeans. His eyes were covered by reflective sunglasses, and his blond hair was shoulder length. When Tracy first spotted him he was leaning casually against a pole in the shade, looking directly at her. She felt adrenaline rush through her body even as she casually looked away to avoid sending a signal that she'd noticed him.

*No way,* Tracy thought. *Not here. Got to be my imagination.*

She reached into her purse, pulled out a pair of sunglasses, and slipped them on. She gathered the children to her. "Come on kids," she said as she gave a quick look back toward where the man was standing. He was still looking at her, with a slight smile.

Tracy pulled her children in the opposite direction. "But I wanna watch some more," said Bryce.

"Let's go, please," Tracy insisted.

"But he's gonna eat some hay!"

"Now!"

With a grumble, Bryce joined his mother and sister heading down the walk. This time Tracy didn't turn around.

"Mommy," Allison said, "you're walking too fast."

Tracy slowed slightly. "Sorry, honey, but let's keep moving."

*Please, not now. Not with the kids.*

She kept walking down the path, even though Bryce wanted to stop at the elephants. "We'll come back to the elephants," Tracy said. "How about some ice cream?"

"Well, OK," Bryce said with muted enthusiasm. Tracy started for the little food court near the entrance. That would be far enough. Get with the crowd. If there was something to all this, the guy wouldn't do anything in the middle of a Sunday throng at the zoo.

Or would he?

Tracy got in line for ice cream and took a quick glance over her shoulder. All she saw was a bustling knot of indistinguishable faces. No guy in a black T-shirt. She became aware of Bryce requesting a sundae. "Hey Mommy, if this was Saturday, we could get a Saturday!" He squealed with laughter. Tracy put her arms around her kids and pulled them in close. "I have to tell you guys something."

"What, Mommy?" said Allison.

"I'm glad God gave you to me."

"We're glad, too," Allison said, squeezing Tracy hard. "Right Bryce?"

"Right!"

"And we're going to have a great time today," Tracy said.

"And forever," said Allison.

"And forever," Tracy repeated. She cast one more look behind her and didn't see the man. She started to relax. Ice creams in hand, the Shepherd family found a table and sat down to plan what to see next. There was the aviary yet to see, and the polar bears, and of course the—

"Nice looking kids."

Tracy spun quickly and saw the man in the black T-shirt standing almost at her elbow. A million thoughts spun through her mind. Scream for a security guard? Run? Talk to him? Kick him as hard as she could in a place that would do the most damage? Or would she just be making a fool out of herself?

"What do you want?" she said. She noticed her children staring at the man silently.

"Just making an observation," he said. His tone was self-consciously charming, almost mocking. "I notice things. I notice you are here with your children. They are yours, right?" He gave a little wave to them and smiled. Allison looked down at her ice cream, but Bryce smiled and waved back.

"Well, we have a long afternoon ahead of us," Tracy said in a conversation-ending way.

"I was just wondering," the man said, "if you wouldn't mind a little company."

"No thank you."

"Because I notice things, and I couldn't help noticing you didn't have a male companion with you, so . . ."

Tracy stood up and faced him directly. "Not interested," she said. She started to move. The man slid in front of her, smiling. "Look, why don't we stroll a little bit and think about it, huh? You don't know me, I don't know you, but we'll never know unless we give it a try."

"I said I'm not interested."

"That's what you *said*, but what do you mean? That's what I'm getting at."

Tracy pulled out her ID from her purse and flashed it at him. "I'm a deputy district attorney for the County of Los Angeles. If you don't leave right now, I'll have you detained. Do I make myself clear?"

The man stared at the ID and for the first time seemed flustered. His face slowly tightened into anger. He kept his stare hard on her as he backed away slowly, finally turning around and disappearing into the crowd.

Tracy sat down heavily at the table, putting her head in her hand.

"What did that man want?" Allison asked.

"Nothing good," said Tracy.

"Did he want to hurt you?" asked Bryce.

"Maybe."

"Then he's mean!"

Tracy patted her son's head.

"Mommy?" Allison said. "Are you ever going to get married again?"

"Why on earth are you asking that?"

"If we had a daddy, he would protect us."

"Mommy can protect us!" Bryce insisted.

Allison looked confused for a moment, then tears started forming in her eyes. Tracy quickly lifted her daughter onto her lap, enveloping her in her arms. "It's all right, honey. You didn't say anything wrong. It's all right. We'll let God decide if I'm supposed to get married again, OK?"

Allison nodded her head.

"That's better," said Tracy. "Now let's go have a look at the monkeys, huh?"

That pleased the kids. As they walked, Tracy tried to shake off the encounter. But she spent the rest of the afternoon looking over her shoulder.

Rob Cavanaugh loosened his tie and sat back in the hard, uncompromising hotel chair. He hated hotel chairs. They never reclined—made it hard to unwind after a full day on the campaign trail. First there was the Kmart in Sunnyvale, a parking lot rally that gathered an assemblage of enthusiastic locals while annoying a few who really wanted to shop.

But the speech went well. The mini-Brown Bear flags flapped ebulliently in the breeze. The good people of Sunnyvale were Californians first and Americans second. The bear flags were a hit.

Then it was on to a live radio interview at a Bay Area radio station. A few hostile calls came in (one caller insisted Rob Cavanaugh was the reincarnation of Adolf Hitler due to his stance on abortion), but Rob handled them with the skills he had built during his climb up the ladder of local politics.

The radio host was impressed. He said no one had done that well on his show since Ronald Reagan stopped in during the 1984 reelection campaign. Not a bad name to be associated with.

After the radio appearance, it was lunch in the limo as the candidate made a stop at a public school in Oakland. He fielded questions from the fifth graders, the news cameras whirring, and had the whole classroom laughing. A definite media home run.

In the late afternoon, he spoke to the San Mateo Police Department, and then it was dinner with party honchos at the Fairmont Hotel in San Francisco. It was that same hotel which, for all its fame, had the stiff chairs.

Now he had the time he needed to think about it. Rob Cavanaugh had been trying all day, but there was always an interruption. Should he or shouldn't he?

He popped open his briefcase and took out his leather planner. He flipped to the back where he'd written the number. He checked his watch: 8:30. Not too late, not too early.

He picked up the phone and dialed the number.

Tracy answered in the stillness of her bedroom. "Hello?"

"Tracy Shepherd?"

"Yes?"

"Rob Cavanaugh."

*What on earth would he be calling about?*

"Hello."

"I hope you don't mind my calling you at home?"

"No, no problem. What can I do for you?"

A slight pause, then, "Look, to be right up front with you, I'm not very good at this."

"At what?"

"Calling and asking for dates."

Tracy swallowed. "You're calling me for a date?"

"I am. I'm sitting up here in San Francisco, and I'll be down in L. A. next week. I wanted to know if I could take you out to dinner . . . or something."

"Oh . . ."

"If this is a bad time for you, just tell me and I'll—"

"No, it's fine. I mean, it's more than fine. I mean, yes."

*You stammering idiot!*

"Great!" Cavanaugh said. "How about Friday evening?"

"Friday sounds good. I'll clear my massive social calendar."

"Great. I'll come by and pick you up around six. Does that work?"

"Like a charm."

"Friday then."

"Friday."

"Um, one more thing."

"Yes?"

"Maybe you should tell me where you live?"

She did. After hanging up, she sat in the stillness for several minutes. Thoughts jumbled around in her mind like Ping-Pong balls in an air tunnel.

*Don't be such a stupid schoolgirl!* She got up and made herself some warm cocoa. She sipped it, watching the late news but hearing none of it. When she finally went to bed, it took her over two hours to fall asleep.

# CHAPTER SEVEN

CHAD TURTURRO'S MOUTH plopped open. "Excuse me?"

"I want to talk to your client," said Tracy.

"You've got to be kidding!" Turturro dropped his briefcase near his desk in the public defender's office.

"Why do I have to be kidding?"

"Because your average prosecutor doesn't make this request."

"I'm not your average prosecutor," Tracy said with a grin.

Turturro thudded into his chair and reached for a brown bag. "You're a charmer, you are," he said, reaching into the sack. He pulled out a plump, red apple and held it out. "Offer you one?"

"Is it poisoned?"

"Hey, never thought of that!"

"I am serious about talking to your client."

"He says he didn't do it."

"I know. I want to look him in the eye when he says it."

Turturro chomped a big bite of apple and chewed thoughtfully. "You have a hunch," he said, his mouth full. He quickly chewed some more and added, "You think there's something wrong here, don't you?"

"I don't have any firm notions," she replied.

"Whoa, now that's an ambiguous answer."

"Come on, Chad."

"No, wait a minute. There's a problem with the case."

Tracy looked up. "This isn't a closing argument. I just want to talk to him."

"Cutie," said Turturro, "you got a date. Let me get on the horn."

He picked up the phone and dialed someone at the sheriff's office. When he hung up he said, "Let's do it."

"Now?"

"Now."

They rode the elevator to the ninth floor. They proceeded through a security door, down a hallway to the lockup. A group of county jail inmates sat on benches, waiting for their moment in court.

Chad took Tracy into a small attorney conference room. It smelled of dust and sweat, unrelieved by ventilation.

"Like it here?" Turturro said with amusement.

"Homey," said Tracy.

"Don't make fun. This is where I spend my vacations." He offered her a chair, a county-issue metal folding job with ersatz padding. Turturro threw his briefcase on the spare table and sat down. "This is strictly off the record, am I right?" Turturro said.

"Yes," answered Tracy.

"Unless it benefits my client, in which case—"

"In which case," Tracy interrupted, "I will do what I think is right."

"It must be nice to hold all the cards."

"I'm not a gambler, Chad."

"Yeah. I know. And that's the only reason I'm doing this. If it was any other prosecutor, I wouldn't be here. But I trust you. Now why is that, Tracy? What is this power you have over men?"

Tracy waved her hand. "We'll talk about it sometime," she said.

"Hmm, a dinner invitation, no doubt?"

Tracy thought ahead to Friday and Rob Cavanaugh. "Slow down, counselor," she said. "Let's concentrate on your client."

"Can't blame a guy for trying," Turturro grunted, then riffled through his briefcase and brought out some papers. The door opened, and a deputy sheriff walked in with O'Lean Murray. No one said anything as the deputy unlocked Murray's cuffs. It was as if everyone knew their parts, and no one needed to offer any opening remarks.

The deputy nodded at Turturro and backed out of the room as Turturro stood up and guided Murray into the third chair. Murray looked confused and more than a little frightened. Tracy tried to read every nuance of his expression.

Turturro said, "O'Lean, this is the prosecutor in your case, Tracy Shepherd."

Murray looked at her with a mixture of fear and suspicion. "What's she doin' here?" he said.

"I'll tell you," said Turturro. "Don't worry."

"What's all this about?" Murray said, his words falling over themselves.

"Listen," said Turturro. "As long as I'm here, you've got nothing to worry about, OK? I won't let you say anything, or Ms. Shepherd ask anything, that I don't think is appropriate. She just wants to talk to you for a couple of minutes, OK?"

"Couple of minutes?" Murray spouted. "What for? I didn't do it, if that's what she wants to know. I'm bein' set up! I didn't kill anybody! You hear that? I didn't kill anybody!"

"Mr. Murray," said Tracy softly. "I just want to ask you some questions."

"I'm tellin' you forget it! You're tryin' to make me say somethin' that'll hurt me!"

Turturro said, "No, O'Lean. That's why I'm here."

"Try to relax, Mr. Murray," said Tracy.

"Relax! You're tellin' me to relax? You're just gonna try to nail me, send me up to Death Row. Why am I talkin' to you?"

"If you don't listen," said Tracy, "you'll never know."

Murray shot a glance at Turturro, who nodded at him. He turned back and glared at Tracy.

"I'm not going to ask you about the details of the night in question," said Tracy. "This isn't like cross-examination. But I do want to know what you were doing at that movie premiere."

"I went to see a movie!" Murray said. "That's all. My friend and me, we went to see this movie 'cause somebody gave us tickets. I went to have some fun, that's all. I didn't kill anybody!"

"You ever fire a gun?" Tracy said.

Murray looked at Chad Turturro. "I have to answer that?"

"No," said Turturro. "You say the word, and this is over."

The kid glanced back at Tracy. His look was hard, distrustful. Tracy suddenly wanted to assure him that she had his best interest at heart, but why should he believe her? Maybe this whole idea had been a mistake.

"How come you're here?" O'Lean Murray challenged.

"I'll tell you," said Tracy. "Because your mother called me. That's why I'm here."

There was a pause. Turturro said nothing, watching his client. Tracy waited for a response. Murray seemed momentarily paralyzed. If he was a typical street tough, she thought, this shouldn't have fazed him. But even more unexpected was what happened next.

O'Lean Murray erupted into tears. He put both hands on his face and sobbed uncontrollably.

Stunned, Tracy looked at Turturro. "Hey, man . . ." Turturro said, putting his hand on Murray's shoulder. Murray kept sobbing, "I didn't do it . . . I didn't do it." Chad Turturro patted his client on the back.

Tracy opened her mouth to say something, but didn't. For several moments the only sound in the room was O'Lean Murray crying into his hands. Then slowly, imperceptibly at first, but building into undeniability, Tracy got a feeling on the inside. It was disconcerting, but it was also strong.

O'Lean Murray was telling the truth.

If there was any place he hated more than Compton, Detective Stan Willis didn't know where it was. Compton represented everything bad about his beloved Los Angeles. Once a normal suburban development, it had degenerated into just another epicenter of gang activity, drugs, prostitution, and despair.

*What we need,* he found himself thinking as he drove toward the Compton Police Department, *is someone to take over this whole country and put everything right.* That someone would not just get tough on crime, but would root out all the potential criminals, *before* you had a bunch of waste to clean up. That someone would appoint judges who wouldn't be afraid to give back to the cops some of the power they'd lost in the sixties; and that someone would be saying the same things as Rob Cavanaugh, the next governor of the state.

Willis pulled into the parking lot and entered the building. Compared to his home base, this was small. But it was still large enough to hold one very important witness.

"Hey, Stan," the desk sergeant, Tim O'Rourke, said. "You slumming?"

"That's about the size of it," said Willis. "Taylor's holding a wit for me."

"Yeah, he's expecting you." O'Rourke buzzed Willis through. He walked around the corner and saw Dan Taylor at his desk.

"Glad you could make it," said Taylor.

"Glad my backside! You think you've got some earth-shattering news."

"And what if I do?"

"Show me."

"What? No thanks?"

"Not yet." Willis never liked Dan Taylor. He was a smug little man, always trying to hit a home run and get his name in the papers. Thought he knew more than anyone. So what was he doing stuck in Compton? Hitting singles and pop fouls. But he strutted around like an all-star.

Willis suspected Taylor had a special jealous streak reserved just for him. They were roughly the same age, but Willis was working out of downtown and got assigned the major cases. So anytime Taylor could turn up a piece of the pie that Willis, or anyone else, had missed, it was another chance to show somebody up.

But Willis was especially interested in this one. It had to do with the Joseph case. Taylor had called and said they'd arrested a kid on a crack rap who had offered to share some information about a murder case if they'd let him go. As with any such overture, the police officers only said it might look good down the road if he talked. Taylor joined the discussion and the kid did talk.

Now, it was Willis's turn to listen. Taylor led him to a small holding cell. The kid was inside.

Keeshon Baker was about twenty, with the unmistakable swagger of a gang member. More specifically, a gang member convinced he had some information that he could leverage against the system. He sat up on his cot when the two policemen entered.

"Hello, Keeshon," said Taylor. "This is Detective Stan Willis, LAPD. He's interested in hearing what you've got to say." Baker looked at Taylor with a typical attitude, challenging him. Willis had seen it a thousand times before.

"I hear you got some information," said Willis, leaning against the wall.

"Maybe," said Baker.

"You going to give it to me?"

"Depends."

"On what?"

"If you deal with me."

Willis looked at Taylor who shrugged his shoulders. To Keeshon Baker, Willis said, "Why should I deal with you?"

"'Cause I got stuff you need to know."

"Sure."

"What, you don't believe me?"

"I don't know you, except I know you're a gangbanger and you're about to do a lot of time."

Keeshon Baker shrugged. "I done time before."

"Listen, dirtbag," Taylor said, "you play games with us, and we'll leave your can in here and let the judge sort it out."

Putting up his hand, Willis said calmly, "Let me have a few minutes alone with our boy here."

"What, you want me to leave?" Taylor asked.

"Just a few minutes, Dan. It might make things easier."

"I think I should stay."

"A few minutes, Dan," said Stan Willis with a bit more force. Frowning, Taylor walked out the door, letting it slam behind him.

Willis smiled at Baker, who said, "You the good cop in this routine?"

"I can be," said Willis.

"I ain't sayin' nothin' until you give me something."

"What is it you want, Keeshon? A reduced charge?"

"We can start with that."

"Put yourself in my place," said Willis. "I'm totally in the dark about why I'm here. You say you have something hot, but I hear that all the time. Plus, you're a jailhouse snitch. That doesn't wash the way it used to. I need to hear a little more about what it is you think you have."

Keeshon Baker folded his arms. "I got something on that movie murder case. You know, the guy who got capped down in Hollywood?"

"Yeah, I know. That's my case. Were you there?"

"Maybe."

Willis shook his head, so Baker said, "Come on, man, give me somethin'."

"Tell you what," said Willis. "If you've got something worth knowing, I'll talk to Taylor and maybe even let you walk. If—and this is a big if—you testify."

"I got no problem with that."

"Then we've got no problems. What is it you wanted to tell me."

"Well," said Baker, "I was outside at the parking lot, and I saw a guy hiding."

Willis squinted his eyes, indicating skepticism. "Just happened to see him, huh?"

"Look, I was at the other end of the lot, man, doin' my natural thing. The bathrooms were all crowded inside, see? So I was out there, and I saw a guy crouching and moving between the cars."

"What did he look like?"

"He wasn't a brother, if that's what you mean."

"You could tell?"

"I could tell."

"And?"

"That's it. You guys are tryin' to nail a brother on this one, and maybe he didn't do it. Maybe this other guy did."

For the first time, Willis stood up from against the wall. He began to pace slowly, back and forth in the holding cell, only occasionally looking at Keeshon Baker. Then he stopped and reached into his pocket.

What he pulled out made Keeshon Baker's eyes widen. It was a white, plastic toothbrush, or it used to be. The bristles were gone. A razor blade was embedded in the handle.

"You know what this is?" Willis said.

"Yeah, I know what that is," Baker said. "A shank."

Willis nodded, then tossed the weapon on the cot next to Baker. "You ever seen this one before?"

Staring at it, Keeshon Baker said, "How should I know?"

"You been in the joint. I want to know if it's familiar to you."

"What are you talkin' about, man? I seen all kind of shanks."

"That one. You ever seen that one before?"

With a confused look, Baker shook his head.

"You haven't hefted it," said Willis. "Go on."

Keeshon Baker reached for the weapon and looked at it casually. He started to speak, but then he suddenly realized something. *Something very, very wrong.*

Stan Willis waited until the prisoner looked him in the eye. Then he fired a single bullet into Keeshon Baker's head.

# CHAPTER EIGHT

"WHO IS THIS JOKER?" said the little boy, staring out the window.

"Bryce Shepherd!" Tracy rebuked. "Where did you come up with that?"

The boy shrugged his shoulders. "You're going out on a date, right?"

"Yes, I told you that."

"Well, I've got to look this guy over."

Tracy couldn't help laughing. Her seven-year-old had always had a biting sense of humor. Sophisticated in a way, which made it all the more hilarious coming from such a young one. Still, every now and then, he crossed the line.

"You are not to be rude, Bryce. Talking like this about a guest is rude. Do you understand?"

Again, the boy shrugged. This time, he looked down at the floor as he did so.

"Bryce, are you all right? Is there something you're not telling me?"

He continued to look at the floor. Tracy reached down, picked him up, and held him. He clung to her like a little monkey as Tracy walked over to a chair and sat down with him. "Maybe you're a little nervous about Mommy going out with a man?" Tracy queried. "Maybe you'd rather I just stayed home with you?"

"Will you?" asked Bryce.

"What about our guest, who wants to take me to dinner?"

"He can eat here. We can make grilled cheese sandwiches."

"That's a lovely idea, Bryce. Maybe another time?"

Bryce put his head on his mother's chest. He felt soft and warm. They sat there like that for a couple of minutes, then Bryce said, "Don't get married unless you ask us, OK?"

"Oh, Bryce." Tracy squeezed him. "Of course not. I'm not thinking of getting married. But if I do, you and Allison will be the first to know. We'll all talk about it."

"And take a vote?"

"We'll *talk* about it. Now you just remember to do what Mrs. Olivera says and—"

A knock at the door stopped her. "Is that him?" said Bryce.

"Let's just see." As she went for the door, Bryce ran along behind her. They both welcomed Rob Cavanaugh. He was dressed casually sharp—tan shirt, slacks, and loafers. The word *impeccable* shot into Tracy's mind.

"This must be the place," Rob said.

"Come in," said Tracy.

Entering, Rob put his hand out. "This must be Bryce." Shyly, Bryce put out his small hand and shook Rob's.

"How did you know his name?" Tracy said, surprised.

For a moment, Rob Cavanaugh looked embarrassed. But he quickly recovered and said, "I think Duke fed me that information. We were talking, and the subject of you came up. I hope you don't mind my talking about you behind your back."

"Only if it was good stuff."

"Always."

Allison and Mrs. Olivera came in from the kitchen. "This is a dear friend, Wilma Olivera," Tracy said.

Rob shook Mrs. Olivera's hand. "*Mucho gusto.*"

"*Hablas español?*"

"*Poquíto.*"

"*Es bueno!*"

"*Ojalá que se mejore pronto.*"

Mrs. Olivera laughed delightedly.

"And what was that all about?" Tracy asked.

"Just using my basic dialogue sentences from high school," said Rob. "Who is this?"

"This is my daughter, Allison." Allison had her head behind Mrs. Olivera's thigh.

"Hello, Allison. My name's Rob."

The little girl peeked at him with one eye. Rob leaned over, hands on his knees. "Would you like to see me take off my thumb?"

Allison brought her head around fully and nodded. Rob put his left thumb out, then grabbed it with his right hand. When he pulled his right hand up, the left thumb was gone. Tracy smiled at the saucers that were her daughter's eyes. Rob slapped his right hand down on his left, and the thumb reappeared.

"How did you do that?" Allison squealed.

"Very well," said Rob.

"It's a trick!" Bryce said.

"He'll go far," Rob said to Tracy.

"All right, give Mommy a kiss." Tracy bent over. Allison wrapped her arms around her neck and kissed her cheek. Bryce didn't move. "Bryce?"

The boy said nothing. Tracy stepped to him and kissed him on top of the head.

On the way to his car, Rob said, "You have a couple of great kids there."

"I think so."

"I hope to get to know them a little better."

Rob opened the rear door of the black Cadillac, and Tracy got in. A large man sat behind the wheel. "This is Stu," said Rob. "One of my shadows." The man turned and nodded. Tracy recognized him from the first time she saw Rob at the D. A.'s office.

The late afternoon sun was still shining as the car took off. "You probably want to know where we're going," said Rob.

"Do you want to tell me?"

"No." Then he laughed. "It's a surprise. I love surprises."

They took the freeway to the Highland off-ramp. At the bottom of the hill the car turned right, heading up toward the parking lot of the Hollywood Bowl.

"No way," Tracy said.

"Way," said Rob Cavanaugh.

"I haven't been here in years."

"I hope you like jazz. Tonight it's Earl Klugh and somebody else, I forget who."

"I don't care who." She smiled at Rob. He put his hand on hers.

As Stu parked the car in the VIP section, Rob slipped into a floppy hat and sunglasses. "My disguise. I don't want to do any hand pressing tonight, present company excluded."

They made their way to the box seats, Stu following like a burly butler, carrying a large dinner basket.

"I've never sat in the boxes," Tracy said.

"It's the only way to fly."

Rob and Stu set up the table, complete with tablecloth, and spread out a sumptuous meal. Shrimp cocktail, fresh fruit salad, and a Mediterranean main course that would have pleased the eye of a Greek chef. With the meal set, Stu left them alone. Tracy melted into her soft, cloth-back chair. The warmth of the afternoon had given way to a pleasant coolness. Rob poured sparkling water into two glasses and handed one to Tracy.

"To a few hours of peace and quiet," Rob said.

"Amen."

They drank.

"Tell me how you got into law," Rob asked.

"I guess I felt it was a way to make a difference," Tracy said.

"But there are other ways to make a difference. Why law?"

"I don't know. You can't do much these days without a lawyer being involved."

"Not always a good thing."

"I agree. I'm just trying to do the best I can."

Rob smiled and said, "You mean you're an honest lawyer? They exist?"

Smiling in return, Tracy said, "I suppose I should be insulted."

"Nah. It's just that it was so cold the other day I saw a lawyer with his hands in his own pockets."

Tracy winced. "That joke was funny the first hundred times I heard it."

"Sorry." Rob leaned toward her with elbows on the table, head cradled in his hands. "Tell me how you became a lawyer instead of, say, a cowboy."

Tracy laughed. "Well, if you really want to know . . ."

When Tracy graduated from the University of Michigan she had acceptances from some of the top law schools in the country in hand. Somehow she had aced the Law School Admissions Test—she was more surprised than anyone because test taking had never been her strong suit—and so she had her pick. She could have headed East to Yale, but being an Ivy Leaguer held no allure for her. Besides, she wasn't a big fan of blizzards. She'd had enough of those growing up in Ann Arbor.

That left schools to the West, most notably Stanford, Boalt Hall, and UCLA. The lure of the southern California sun had its way, and Tracy was off to become a Bruin.

Her father was both proud and sad. Tracy was his only child, and his wife had died two summers before, succumbing to a cancer that was virulent and unrelenting. Tracy never told her father this, but her mom's death was really the start of a slow, festering anger with God. She didn't tell her father because it would have hurt him too much.

Hal Shepherd was what the people in town called "a good man." He was respected, even loved, in the community, starting with the home church but extending well beyond. He ran a hardware store on Main, and was known for extending "crazy credit" to people. "Just pay me next time you come in," he'd say if the customer was a little short. And every Sunday he sang in the church choir. He did that for thirty years. Church life was as much a part of him as nails, saws, and chicken wire.

So when Tracy got ready to leave Ann Arbor for the beaches of L. A., the first thing her father told her was, "Find a good church out there as soon as you can." That was one commitment Tracy tried to keep. She did find a local church, a small congregation that had the same feel as her church back home, but her attendance was spotty. She started visiting a "megachurch" in the area, one that catered to the younger set, and that's where she ended up.

She took to law school, finding out she really loved the stories the cases told. The search for justice, the "golden thread" of the law, was always of intense interest to her. And the class she enjoyed most of all, wonder of wonders, was criminal law. For some reason, the idea of assessing moral blame fascinated her. Here was where the law was crucial, more crucial for her than, say, probate. As her wills and trusts professor said, "This class is about greed and dead people."

Tracy wanted more out of her law career than that.

The summer after her first year, she answered an inquiry in the placement office for an internship with the L. A. County district attorney's office. It was for the Van Nuys branch, and she had gotten the job out of fifty applicants. Her duties were to assist as many of the deputies as she could—pulling jury instructions, researching motions, keeping track of files—but the best part of the job was that she got to sit in court and watch trial after trial.

It was exciting to be on the front lines, to watch the search for justice unfold in some minidrama in which victim and defendant would place their futures in the hands of twelve jurors. She got to see how a trial was conducted, what tactics worked and what didn't. And she got something more, something she hadn't thought about. She got to look into the eyes of the accused.

That was really where she became aware of her sense about people in trouble. It was all in the eyes. Windows to the soul. Some eyes were dead. The light was on inside, but nobody was home. These were the eyes of the career criminals, and there was almost nothing anyone could do to change that look of lostness. What was more disturbing than anything else were dead eyes in the young ones—dead before their time.

Then there were the "dazed and confused" defendants, wondering how they had fallen into the legal maelstrom. At least there was hope for these people. In some cases the legal system accomplished its loftiest, though least realized, mission—rehabilitation.

Finally, there were the eyes of the angry ones, the defiant. What was curious about these was that they spanned the spectrum. The "hard cores" could have them, but so could the white-collar drunk driver.

Tracy got to look at all of them. And the truth was, she was not at all sure she wanted to be looking at them for the rest of her legal career. Sure, this was all interesting stuff on a philosophical level, but did she really want to spend her days trying to put these people away? She didn't know, until the day she saw Johnny Richmond.

It was near the end of the summer, and she was helping Gene Bisnow try a case of assault. They were about to start picking a jury when a sentencing matter came up. A prisoner, hands shackled behind him, was led in from the holding area by a deputy sheriff and told to sit down until his lawyer, who happened to be late, showed up. The prisoner walked over near a chair, but did not sit. The deputy didn't seem to mind.

Bisnow was shuffling papers at the counsel table, and Tracy had nothing else to do but cast some glances at the shackled man. He had the look of the outlaw biker—long blond hair, a bushy hang-down mustache, and heavily muscled arms with faded blue tattoos. He was, Tracy guessed, in his thirties.

She instinctively looked at his eyes, wondering what type he was. What she saw there was something different, something she had not seen at all, ever, in a courtroom. It was the oddest thing, but his eyes had an overwhelming sense of peace about them.

Busying herself with a couple of file folders, Tracy looked casually every now and then toward the prisoner. He hardly moved. He seemed perfectly content, in fact. At one point he turned toward the far wall, glancing up at the clock. That's when Tracy saw it. In his chained hands, even though they were behind his back, the prisoner held a Bible.

Incredible! Was this one of those guys who actually found peace with God behind bars? So many claimed to, usually before their parole hearings, but this one had no reason to be lumbering around with the Scriptures in his mitts unless he was serious about it. Tracy found herself standing and walking over to the man.

"Excuse me," she said.

The biker turned and looked at her. His eyes were soft. He may even have smiled behind the large brush over his lip.

"I notice you're holding a Bible," she said.

"That's right."

"Means a lot to you?"

"Everything."

"Well," said Tracy, "I think that's great. I wish you luck."

"Thank you."

The next voice Tracy heard was Bisnow's, ordering her to "get over here." The prisoner nodded his head at Tracy just before she turned around. "Are you nuts?" said Bisnow. "You can't talk to a guy without his lawyer present."

"I didn't know that," Tracy said, her face suddenly flushed.

"Well you do now."

Later she heard his name announced to the court by his slightly rumpled and sweating attorney. Johnny Richmond. And he was being sent away for four years of hard time. Even so, his expression never changed, not once.

"And that's when I decided I wanted to be a prosecutor," Tracy said to Rob Cavanaugh. The stars were just starting to sparkle in the clear evening sky. "I thought what better way to have an effect on people's lives. To see that real justice is done somehow. I don't know, does that sound dumb?" She looked at Rob, who smiled as he placed his hand softly on hers. "Doesn't sound dumb at all."

"All right then, Mr. Politician. Tell me about your world. How did you get involved in the rough and tumble of politics?"

"Thought I could make a difference, too. I was a small businessman and didn't like all the hoops I had to jump through. Started making noise on the local level. Some people heard the noise and thought I'd make it as a politician."

"You seem to fit the profile."

"Except for one thing."

"What's that?"

"A family." He said it matter-of-factly, as if it were just something he was reporting.

"Well, why not?" Tracy tried to sound quiet and objective.

"I don't think someone should get married just to please the conventional wisdom. I've had some advisors who've suggested I take the plunge quickly, but I don't respond to pressure. When I get married, it'll be for the right reasons."

Rob leaned back in his chair. "I almost did get married, though. Few years ago. The woman I was engaged to called it off a week before the wedding."

"A *week?*"

"It would've been a mistake, I see that now. Last I heard, she had fallen off the deep end after marrying some other guy. Sad."

The two sat in silence for a few minutes, and then the concert started. It was wonderful. The soft jazz and cool evening were perfect. Tracy couldn't remember the last time she'd felt so relaxed and happy. She tried mightily not to let the whole thing become intoxicating, but she was only partially successful.

All went perfectly afterward, too. They stopped for a cappuccino at City Walk in Universal City, talked about everything from the Dodgers to the Dorothy Chandler Pavilion, then Stu drove them back to her house.

"Thanks for a great evening," Tracy said at the door.

"Thank *you*." He stepped close to her, took both of her hands in his. Then he leaned over and kissed her. Eyes closed, Tracy floated like a bird on a summer breeze.

"I'll call you again, if I may," Rob said.

"You may."

"Good night." He turned and walked back to his car, giving her a wave before sliding in. Tracy watched until the car drove out of sight.

"Have a good time?" Mrs. Olivera said when Tracy came in the house.

"Very good. Thank you."

"It was my pleasure, Mrs. Shepherd. He's a handsome one."

"You don't have to tell me."

"I think—"

"What is it?" Tracy said.

"I think it's a good thing, your going out."

"You do?"

"*Sí*. I don't know how to say this, but I think . . . Mr. Ben . . ."

"Ben would want me to?"

"*Sí*."

Tracy thought about that all the time she was getting ready for bed. Would Ben approve? Should I be thinking about this at all?

No clear answers came, but one thing was certain. She slept soundly that night for the first time in weeks.

"You what!"

Duke Gallegos jumped out of his chair and began pacing around his office. He looked to Tracy like a caged lion whose food had just been snatched away.

"All I'm saying is that O'Lean Murray doesn't look guilty," said Tracy quietly.

"*Look* guilty? What is this, a fashion show? I don't care what Murray *looks* like. I care about the facts!"

"That's all part of it, Chief. The case isn't as strong as Willis had me believe. Some things are off. And on top of all that, Murray, who's going to be telling his story to a jury, sounds pretty believable."

Grunting, Duke rubbed his face. "I don't believe you're saying this. You've got exactly zero experience doing felony trials, and all of a sudden you're a psychic? You know what twelve people are gonna think in the face of all the evidence against him?"

"I have to make judgments, don't I? That's part of the job."

"You need experience for judgment."

"But I'm closer to this case than you are. This is what I see."

"Tracy, don't you understand?" Duke sat heavily on the corner of his desk. "This is a big chance for you. It can make you. One case can do that. That's what happened when Bugliosi prosecuted Manson. He didn't have to try any cases after that. He could write books and mouth off whenever he wanted."

Tracy nodded.

"But a case can break you, too," Duke continued. "I don't want to see you become a Lea D'Agostino.

That name was familiar to Tracy, too. D'Agostino had been a rising star in the office, known as much for her jet black hair and ruby red lips as for her success in the courtroom. Then, in 1985, she was assigned to prosecute movie director John Landis and four others for manslaughter. While filming the movie *The Twilight Zone*, a combat helicopter used in a Vietnam war scene exploded, fell, and killed actor Vic Morrow and two child actors.

The trial generated a lot of publicity, of course, being related to the movie business. But some things went wrong during the trial, and the verdict ended up being an acquittal for all the defendants.

It was the end of high profile cases for D'Agostino. But the ripple effects were felt all the way to the top, to then-district attorney Ira Reiner's office. Losing big cases usually meant trouble for the sitting D. A. Los Angeles voters had a history of voting out incumbents who lost media-drenched cases. Reiner lost in the next election.

*Is Duke feeling pressure from the top on this case?* Tracy wondered. *Does he have to make it "go" because of all the publicity?*

That was no comfort. *She* was the one who'd have to try it, and if she lost, then a head would need to roll. Hers, probably. "Duke," said Tracy solemnly, "what am I supposed to do? I see what's in the file. I talked to Murray face to face. You want me to see something that's not there?"

"I want you to put every effort into this case, that's what I want. You know how far out on a limb I went picking you? You're green, you're new, and I said, 'She can do it.' I said, 'She's the one who will go in there and put all of her energy behind it because that's her job.' Now you come to me with some fantasy about this guy being innocent? It's crazy!"

"I didn't say he was innocent," Tracy protested.

"It sure sounded that way to me! Now I want you to listen, and good. There will be no more of this nonsense on the Murray case. You take what you've got, and you try that murdering gangbanger and get the max on him. Understand? I don't want to hear any more about your doubts about the case."

Tracy sighed deeply. She started to say something, but Duke interrupted. "Because if you do, I'm yanking you off of it. I see any more hesitation, you're gone. You understand?"

She understood all right. "Gone" would mean an assignment to low-level cases, maybe even out of the downtown office and into one of the outlying courts. That could mean a worse commute, less time for her kids, the netherworld of career prosecutors.

Duke said, "I trust this is the last talk like this we are going to have."

Saying nothing, Tracy stood and left Duke's office. Her head felt like it was in a vise. She wandered back to her office and sat heavily in her chair.

She stayed for several minutes, rubbing her eyes, trying to focus. She had plenty of work to do but couldn't get up the energy. So she turned to her stack of mail.

Not much, though one envelope caught her attention immediately. It was familiar. She opened it quickly and pulled out the letter. It had the same, childlike scrawl. This time the message was:

*ARE YOU ENJOYING YOUR LAST DAYS ON EARTH?*

# CHAPTER NINE

RANDALL LEFFERTS kept the engine running in his rented Camaro. He wanted the air conditioning on. If he had to wait, he'd do it in comfort. Whatever comfort he could muster with $100,000 cash burning a hole in the bag next to him.

He lit the next in a series of cigarettes and puffed nervously as he tried to find some music on the radio that wasn't country. Finally, he got a scratchy classical station that was playing something that sounded like Mozart.

The afternoon sunlight gave the town an orange hue. This was desert country. He couldn't wait to get back to California, where the ocean breeze could cool his sweating head. Most of all, though, he couldn't wait to get this Indian thing over with. Fast.

The only other time he'd seen the Indian face to face was when he'd made the initial contact, back when NyDex Systems made its big move. Sherman Kohlbert had dispatched him to meet this "contractor" that had been referred by one of Kohlbert's old acquaintances, Jimmy Balbona—the same Jimmy Balbona who was now no doubt the cornerstone of some community. They never found his body.

But before his untimely demise, Balbona had done Kohlbert the favor of finding a reliable hit man. The Indian was good, precisely because he wasn't one of the silky-suited wiseguys who always wanted to work their way to the top. He was a mysterious loner, and that's the way he kept it. He did his work and didn't ask questions.

At that first meeting, Lefferts felt a chill run through his body unlike anything he'd ever experienced before. There was a look of such darkness in the Indian's eyes, it was like staring into a bottomless pit. Stare into that long enough, and a guy could go nuts.

The Indian was over half an hour late. This was the designated spot. Lefferts had told him what time, and he had been very clear about it. He threw his cigarette down on the gravel and crushed it out. He heard the tinking sound again. What was it? Something wrong with the air conditioning maybe? Perfect. Lousy duty, lousy car.

He thought for a moment about telling Kohlbert he was through, but the thought left immediately. It wasn't by accident Kohlbert had picked him, supervised him, and developed him for this job. Kohlbert knew he liked money, lots of it—knew he had two kids and a wife accustomed to a certain style of living. All supplied because of a rapid rise in NyDex. And doing a few special services.

They involved criminal activity, of course, but that part didn't get to Lefferts. He was not conscience-stricken about it. Everybody was involved in stuff like this, from the government on down. It was all about getting away with it and getting as much as he could. And if a few people got iced in the process, so it goes. There was nothing to look forward to anyway. The world spins on, and everybody dies eventually. Then there's nothing. So get what you can while you can get it.

Keep it, too. Randall Lefferts knew that when he chose to be Kohlbert's guy, he gave control of his life to the man. If Lefferts ever tried to leave, if he was ever perceived as a threat, he knew he *would* be looking into the dark eyes of the Indian.

No use going to the police, or FBI, or anything like that. Somehow, Kohlbert would find him, his family, and his kids. No, Lefferts was in for the long ride, and this stupid waiting was part of it.

There was another *tink*, and then another right after it. It was getting to be a little like Chinese water torture. Lefferts angrily opened the door, got out, and put his ear near the idling car's engine.

*Tink*.

There it was, only this time it sounded definitely tinny, like something hitting the roof of the car.

*Tink.*

He looked up. The Indian was sitting casually on the roof of the building, looking down without expression, except perhaps one of mild disdain. What was he doing? Lefferts stared in silence, letting his frustration have full sway on his face. He watched as the Indian reached for something in his hand, then let it drop onto the rented automobile.

*Tink.*

Pebbles! The jerk was tossing pebbles at his car! Like some sort of idiot schoolboy playing a prank.

"What do you think you're doing?" Lefferts yelled.

The Indian said nothing, his legs dangling over the side as if he might leap at any moment. Lefferts looked around nervously. This was supposed to be a simple exchange, done in obscurity. But if they stood around like this any longer, someone was going to come along.

"Get down off of there and come here," Lefferts commanded.

The Indian didn't move.

Cursing, Lefferts shook his head and momentarily turned his back. What should he do now? This crazy native was playing games with his mind, and there wasn't much Lefferts could do about it. He spun back around and prepared to shout out an order, but then he stopped.

The Indian was gone.

Now what? Wait until he pops out from some crack in the wall, brandishing a knife? The Indian was crazy, and he was alone with him. A sudden chill ran through Lefferts. Suppose the Indian killed him and took off with the money? What was to stop him? The law? Lefferts felt suddenly alone, like a rabbit who realizes the dogs are all around him.

Anxious minutes strained by. No sign of anyone. Lefferts did the only thing that made any sense to him—he lit a cigarette. As he puffed, he leaned against the Camaro, trying to appear casual. He felt anything but.

A crunch of gravel on the other side of the car. The Indian was there, staring at him.

"For crying out loud!" Lefferts exploded. "What are you trying to do? Are you nuts?"

"Who is the one who is nuts?" said Tommy Bear Paw, impassively.

"Huh?"

"The one who is, or the one who hires him?"

*Oh man!* Lefferts thought. *Get me out of here*. "You want your money or don't you?"

"Do you have a wife and children?"

Lefferts trembled. The last thing he wanted was for the most ruthless, unfeeling individual he'd ever met to ask about his family life. With a touch of anger, Lefferts moved toward the car. Tommy Bear Paw jumped in his way.

"What are you doing?" Lefferts shouted.

"You didn't answer the question."

"I'm not here to answer questions. I'm here to give you a payoff."

"There's time enough for money. What about your family?"

"That's none of your business."

"I can find out, but it's better if you tell me."

Now a real, creeping fear filled Lefferts. Whatever game the Indian was playing, he didn't want any part of it. But there didn't seem to be a choice.

"Look," Lefferts reasoned, "I'm just a go-between. You made a contract. I'm here to give you what's owed to you. What does my family have to do with anything?"

Still impassive, Bear Paw said, "I want to know what kind of man hires someone like me."

"I'm not the one. Like I said, I just go between."

"What kind of man are you?"

"Come on, will you—"

"Answer the question."

"No."

Tommy Bear Paw casually reached behind his back. When his hand came back it had a knife with a six-inch blade in it. Instantly, Bear Paw had the point of the knife under Lefferts's chin.

"Oh no, please," Lefferts said. "No, no . . ."

"You'll answer my question now?"

"I got a wife. Yes. Two kids."

"How old?"

"One's sixteen. One's twelve."

"What kind are they?"

"What kind what?"

Bear Paw put slightly more pressure where the knife pushed up the soft flesh. "Boy or girl?"

"Both girls. Please . . ."

"Family man, are you?"

"What's your point?" Lefferts almost burst out laughing at the irony of his words. His point was at Lefferts's throat.

"Do they know you hire killers?"

"No, of course not."

"So you don't tell them? You keep secrets?"

"Everybody keeps secrets."

"No. Men of honor do not keep secrets."

*This is insane!* Lefferts thought. *A murderer holding me at knife point, talking about honor?*

Slowly, Bear Paw lowered the knife. Then he reached out and touched Randall Lefferts on the shoulder, pushing it slightly.

"What—" Lefferts sputtered in total confusion.

"Coup," said Tommy Bear Paw.

"Huh?"

Bear Paw shook his head. "Just give me the money."

Lefferts practically jumped inside the car where the small gym bag was. He brought it out and placed it in Bear Paw's hands. Lefferts said, "You want to count it?"

"No need. I know where to find you if it's . . . short."

Lefferts's chest tightened. His breath didn't come easily—not even when Tommy Bear Paw turned and walked away from him. A sense of impending disaster hung over him, and it didn't leave him the rest of the day.

Tracy knew South Central Los Angeles well. Beginning around the Memorial Coliseum and fanning out southward from there, the area's mean streets were the scene of innumerable crimes. Tracy had been there frequently, interviewing witnesses, taking a look at crime scenes. But every time she'd done that, she had been in the company of a law enforcement officer or an investigator. Never had she ventured into that territory alone—until now.

Driving down Figueroa Boulevard, she was oblivious to the welter of street life around her. Her mind was focused on the thing she was about to do, and on the events immediately prior.

She was increasingly apprehensive about the Murray case. More specifically, about how Duke Gallegos was approaching it. Why was he so intent on going forward? Just the political consequences? Or was there more to it than that? Why had he tapped her in the first place? He told her it was because she was ready. But was that really the reason? She never felt less ready in her life.

Could there be another, more subtle, reason for her getting assigned? Was it, in fact, so she wouldn't make waves?

That was the most troubling thought of all. It would make her little more than a puppet in the midst of a game that was being played out, a game for which she did not know the rules, or even the players. She tried to quiet these speculations, but they kept returning. The only way she knew to settle all this in her mind was to keep getting as much information on Murray as she could. Alone.

There was something bothering her about Stan Willis, too. Were he and Duke working together on this one? Willis seemed just as anxious to push the Murray case as Duke. If Willis found out what she was about to do, he would probably throw another of his famous fits.

If all that wasn't enough, those mystery notes threatening her life were beginning to take a major toll. She was feeling the stress in her shoulder and neck muscles like never before. Headaches were becoming more frequent and severe.

Who was this mystery man? Should she turn the letters over to the FBI and let them start handling it? But if this guy, whoever he was, was seriously warped—and there was every reason to believe he was—that might push him over the edge. Perhaps there was a chance he'd just go away.

Sure. Just like that prosecutor in Chicago who had his own secret tormentor—he tried to ignore the threats, too. Then one night they found him in bits and pieces in an alley behind the all-night Steak House down near the Loop. That was five years ago, and they were still looking for the murderer.

Tracy almost missed her turn. She pulled down the street with its huge palms lining both sides and quaint but aging houses. Once, this had been a fashionable neighborhood, in the years before white flight and urban blight. Now the windows all had bars on them, and the doors had heavy, metal screens. These were less homes than outposts.

Kendra Murray's house was the yellow one in the middle of the block. Tracy pulled up and parked at the curb. It was fairly quiet on the street this afternoon. A couple of kids were playing with a jump rope two houses down. A little farther, Tracy caught a glimpse of what looked like a teenage boy, leaning against a car, looking her way. The two kids stopped and stared as Tracy walked quickly up to Kendra Murray's door and knocked.

A moment later a woman's voice said, "Yes?"

"Mrs. Murray? It's Tracy Shepherd."

"Oh yes." The door unlatched and a stout but strong-looking woman opened the door and pushed open the black iron screen. "Come in, please."

The living room was small but neatly kept. A multicolored rug covered most of the dark, dull hardwood floor. Some pictures crowded around on top of a small portable television set on a wheeled traylike table.

"Can I offer you a glass of water?" Mrs. Murray said.

"Thank you."

The woman shuffled into the kitchen. Tracy took a closer look at the pictures on the TV. They were family pictures of a woman, who was obviously Kendra Murray, a tall, lanky man, and two kids—one boy, one girl. The boy, Tracy surmised, was O'Lean Murray. There was a certain resemblance. There were various poses, some group, some individual. In one picture, the girl wore a powder blue cap and gown. She was very pretty.

"The family history," Mrs. Murray said as she stepped into the room. She handed Tracy a tumbler of ice water. "A lot of years."

"Is that O'Lean?"

"O'Lean, yes, and my daughter Kaliesha."

"Where is she now?"

"She's dead," Kendra Murray said quietly. "She was with some friends at a fast-food place one night. A shooting broke out, and she was in the middle."

"I'm so sorry," said Tracy.

"She was eighteen. She was going to try to get into college . . ." Her voice trailed off.

Tracy could think of nothing to say. This type of experience was beyond her. Her house in the Valley was only about twenty miles away. It might as well have been twenty thousand.

She felt a wave of sympathy for Kendra Murray but immediately pulled back on it. She was here for professional reasons; she couldn't let her judgment be influenced by emotion. It was not going to be easy. At that moment, Tracy wished she'd never heard of O'Lean Murray. She wished she were back doing drunk driving cases.

"Marcus is my husband," Mrs. Murray said, nodding toward the photos. "He's doing time now, hard time. He couldn't get the monkey off his back."

"Heroin?"

Kendra Murray nodded. "He tried, he did try. But you can't do it by yourself. It's too strong. I kept telling O'Lean. I told him every time his daddy got taken in, 'That's what happens with drugs.' I tried to scare him. He never took drugs."

They sat down, Tracy in a stuffed chair with worn arms. A little of the insides peeked out through a small tear in the fabric. Tracy pulled out a yellow legal pad from her briefcase, a pen, and a file folder in which she had some papers relevant to the case. On the file tab she'd written "Murray, O'Lean" in felt-tip marker. She tossed the file on a small table and put the legal pad on her lap.

"Mrs. Murray, I want you to know something," Tracy began. "My job is to find the truth. That's why I'm here. I can't promise you anything. I can't tell you how all this is going to come out. But I can tell you that if you're up front with me, it will be better for all of us. O'Lean most of all."

"I always tell the truth," Mrs. Murray said. "I'm a God-fearing woman. I don't play with the truth."

"Then tell me, was O'Lean involved in any gang-related activity?"

"I told you before, no!" Mrs. Murray slapped her hand on the sofa pillow next to her.

"How can you be sure?"

"Because I know my own son."

"But you weren't with him at school, or after school, or evenings when he went out."

"He wouldn't hide it from me. We could always talk to each other. He's my only child now, and he knows I'd do anything for him."

"Maybe that's a reason for him to hide this from you. He doesn't want to hurt you."

A look of sadness came across Kendra Murray's face. Tracy felt terrible about it. She was asking tough questions, maybe even planting the seeds of doubt in a mother's heart. But if she was going to get to the bottom of things, she had to do it. If O'Lean Murray was guilty—and there was that strong possibility—then it would be better for everyone concerned if it was established with certainty.

"O'Lean's not like that," Mrs. Murray insisted. "He's never been like that. He's been angry, sure—angry about his father, angry about his sister. But he took that all out on the football field."

"Did he attend church with you?"

"Sometimes. Not always. But I keep after him about that. I tell him his only hope is in the Lord."

"That's true."

"Are you a believer?"

"Yes, I am."

"Well, praise God!" A wave of relief seemed to wash over Kendra Murray, and a huge smile appeared on her face. "This is an answer to prayer! To have a God-fearing prosecutor!"

Tracy chuckled. "Is that so strange?"

"To hear tell. Oh, thank the Lord you're on this case. I know you'll get O'Lean out of there—"

"Mrs. Murray—"

"I just know it by the Spirit."

Tracy put up her hand. "Mrs. Murray, I need to remind you, my job right now is to prosecute your son. I can't promise you anything."

"No need, no need. I just know God is at work."

*Well then let me know about it, Lord,* Tracy thought. *I'm ready right now.*

For the next hour, Tracy listened as Kendra Murray recounted everything she could about O'Lean, from his birth all the way up to the night he was arrested. Tracy kept up as best she could, taking notes. By the time the interview was over, she felt her hand was about to fall off.

Kendra Murray thanked Tracy profusely as she left and kept peppering her good-bye with "Praise God." As Tracy walked toward her car, she felt a great affection for Kendra Murray. For this woman to have her faith intact after all she had been through, well, that was a real testimony. But it wasn't going to make prosecuting her son any easier.

Tracy unlocked her car, only vaguely aware of what she was doing. Thoughts streamed through her head, even as she started the car and began cruising down the small street. When she was almost to the corner, she snapped out of her reverie enough to realize she'd left the O'Lean Murray file at Kendra Murray's house.

Exhaling a frustrated breath, Tracy slowed and started to make a U-turn but then, suddenly, hit the brakes. She had almost hit a teenager, a boy, standing right in front of her car. He didn't move. He stared directly at her.

Before she could react, Tracy felt her door being thrown open and a large, powerful hand grabbing her arm and yanking her out. Her knees hit asphalt, then she was jerked to her feet. Seven or eight males were suddenly all around her. The one with his hand on her arm put his face just inches away from hers.

"You in the wrong neighborhood," he said.

# CHAPTER TEN

THE TWO MEN sat in the back corner of the noodle restaurant in Little Tokyo. The booths had high, wooden partitions. Nothing fancy, but privacy was assured. This had been their meeting place for two years, where details were discussed.

Stan Willis took a long swig of beer and let out a satisfying sigh. "Ah, that's good. It's hotter than a dog in a sweater out there."

Poking with chopsticks at his pan-fried noodles, Duke Gallegos said nothing.

"What's the matter?" Willis asked.

"You've overstepped," said Duke.

"Nah."

"I can't believe you iced a witness."

"He came at me with a shank, for crying out loud."

"Right."

"What am I supposed to do, take one in the gut?"

"Don't take me for an idiot, Willis."

The policeman drained his beer and waved for a waiter. He ordered another Asahi, then looked back across the table. "Nobody's taking you for an idiot, Duke. We're all on the same side."

"It's going too far."

"Whoa, wait a minute. How come you suddenly think you can draw a line? You knew what it was all about. You knew who you were playing with."

Duke pushed his plate to the side with the back of his hand.

"Now there's nothing left but to see it through," said Willis. "All the way. Don't worry. There's plenty of light at the end of the tunnel."

The waiter arrived with the bottle of beer and a frosted glass. Willis poured the suds and smiled. "Good thing I'm off duty. Wouldn't want to break the rules, now, would I?"

Duke felt sweat starting to form on his forehead. Things had indeed gone too far, but there was no getting out of it now. Willis was right. He had gone into the thing with his eyes open. It had all been laid out to him, the chance to finally realize his dreams. He'd been stuck in the head deputy position long enough. There was not a chance he would move up any higher in the office. If it even looked close, politics would come into play. The district attorney would have no hesitation shipping him out of central trials. He'd done it before.

If it was all political, he could play the game, too; all he would have to do is turn his head a few times and move some people around.

"Now there's something else," Willis said. "About Shepherd. She's been asking too many questions."

"I want you to keep your hands off her," Duke said.

"Who said anything about hands *on* her? All I'm saying is you better yank her. She was a lousy choice to start with."

"She was perfect."

"Well she isn't now. Take her off the case."

"I can't do that."

"Of course you can. You're the head deputy, aren't you?"

"I'm not going to. It would hurt her career."

Pounding his glass on the table, Willis erupted, "Who cares about her career? You want to give this thing a chance to blow up just because of some low-grade deputy's career? What are you thinking?"

"I'm thinking this whole thing was a mistake."

Willis said, "That's one thing you'd better not think."

Silence hung between the two men. Willis reached into his pocket and pulled out a few bills, throwing them on the table. As he got up he said, "Lunch is on me." Duke Gallegos sat alone in the booth for a long time.

Tracy could not shake the feeling of terror. Even though what had happened was nothing short of a rescue, it was still not the place she wanted to be.

The man was heavily muscled. He wore an undershirt, baggy pants, Air Jordans, and an Oakland Raiders bandanna around his head. He looked in his mid-twenties, pretty old for a gangbanger on the streets. On his left bicep was a tattoo of a face, someone vaguely recognizable. It was hard to make out all the features because the tat was deep blue, and the arm deep black.

They were in a garage, filled with car parts and a half-together motorcycle. The smell of gas and oil were strong. A bench with a weight set-up was prominent in the center.

"You don't gotta be nervous," the man said.

"What are you going to do?"

"I ain't gonna do nothin'," he said with a spit of anger. "Why you think I'm gonna do somethin'? That just the way we are here in the ghet-to?"

"I'm sorry," Tracy said. "I just don't know what it is you want."

"First thing is, I saved your sorry butt."

"I know."

"I didn't come along, lady, you'd be in sad shape about now."

"They did what you wanted."

"I got the juice here. This is my 'hood. I hold it down."

Tracy began to feel just a little bit more at ease. If he was going to do something, like rape, he'd have made a move by now. Instead, he was talking with her like he wanted her to know who he was.

"What's your name?" Tracy asked.

"Be Rajah."

"You're a gangbanger."

"You scared?"

"Yes."

"Should be. But I got nothin' 'gainst you."

"Why am I here?"

"I know you came to see O'Lean's mom. Nothin' goes down around here I don't know about. There's some things you should know."

Tracy leaned back on a worktable.

"I know O'Lean since he was a kid," Rajah said. "He ain't no banger. I kept him out."

"You kept O'Lean from joining a gang?"

"That's what I said." Rajah moved around with a sort of nervous energy, his eyes flashing all around, never staying in one place too long. "I seen he was a smart kid and a good athlete. I seen he could go all the way, make it outta here."

Feeling a little bolder, Tracy said, "Why take such an interest in his welfare?"

"Maybe 'cause my little brother got shot." He stopped and looked hard at Tracy. It was almost like he was challenging her not to believe him. She had no reason to doubt his story. It was an all-too-frequent scenario in South Central.

"I took to him, that's all," Rajah continued. "Thought maybe I could help him get somewhere, 'cause I wasn't goin' nowhere. It's too late for me, but it ain't for him."

"OK," said Tracy, "let's say he's not in a gang. That still doesn't mean he couldn't have done this thing, on his own."

"No way!" Rajah exploded. "I'm tellin' you. I know him. I know his set. And I know somethin' else, too."

"What's that?"

Rajah said nothing for a moment. Tracy watched him lift a chain off the garage floor. "You're comin' with me."

The fear returned. She had no control over the situation. Yet there was a reason she was here. She was certain. *Now is the time to put faith back on the line,* she thought. If there was going to be protection from on high, she had to rest in that assurance. She hadn't needed to call upon that lately. It was time again.

"OK," she said. "Where?"

The next several minutes were surreal to her. Here she was, an L. A. County prosecutor driving her own car with a drug dealer and killer as a passenger. Tracy knew you didn't get to be where Rajah was in gang culture without capping enemies and trafficking in drugs. Now, they were tooling down the streets like car pool buddies.

Rajah picked up her cell phone and said, "Nice phone."

*Nice phone? He's making small talk?*

He played with it for a moment, then flicked it on. "Mind if I call my attorney?" Then he laughed. Some joke. Tracy began to feel even more unnerved.

"Your batteries are low, lady," Rajah said. Tracy knew he was probably into dealing drugs, and that meant he knew all about cell phones and beepers and other electronic gadgets.

"Turn here," Rajah commanded.

"Can you tell me where we're going?" Tracy asked.

"We're almost there. Don't you trust me?"

Tracy started to say something, but hesitated. Rajah laughed. "Don't worry, lady. You're safe with me."

They were driving down an alley now, with decrepit buildings and dumpsters and refuse all around. A couple of winos leaning against a wall gave the couple odd looks. Rajah gave them the red eye—gang lingo for a cold, hard stare—and they turned away.

"Pull up here," Rajah said, pointing to what looked like an abandoned apartment building. Since the '94 earthquake, hundreds of buildings like this lay unused and unrepaired. There was no insurance money to bring them up to code, and it was a better deal for owners just to walk away.

This one was fairly tall, five or six stories. It had a cheap chain-link fence around it, with so many holes and bent areas it looked more like a fishing net thrown haphazardly on the ground.

"This way," Rajah said, getting out of the car.

Tracy followed him.

They went through a back door that was partially off its hinges. Inside, it was dank, dark, and smelling of urine and smoke. Small beams of outdoor sunlight shot in through the slats of boarded-up windows. Rajah led Tracy to a stairwell, and they started up. "Just hang behind me," he said.

Up they went, five floors. Just before reaching the top, Rajah turned and put his hand out in a signal to be quiet. That was the point Tracy started thinking about guns. She didn't carry one, but she had no doubt Rajah kept one handy. And maybe whoever was on this fifth floor had one, too. Or several.

Slowly, Rajah opened the door and peered in. He paused for a moment, listening, looking. Then he yelled, "Yo, Mickey D!" He waited for an answer. There was none. "It's Rajah, man."

Silence.

"Don't mess with me!"

After another pause, a voice that seemed far away said, "Come up."

Rajah nodded toward Tracy and led her through the door. They walked down a small hallway, with abandoned apartments on either side. Out of a doorway a few yards in front of them a shaved head stuck out. It had a scared face attached to it.

"Wassup?" Rajah said as they reached the door.

"'Sup," said Mickey D. Tracy took him to be about nineteen or twenty. He was small, especially next to the heavily muscled gang leader. He wore a large undershirt that flopped all over him, accenting his skinny arms, and baggy pants that seemed about ready to fall down. On his feet were high-top designer basketball shoes, the kind some around here would actually kill you for.

"Who's that?" he said, backing up and looking even more frightened.

"Chill," Rajah said.

"She the man?".

"She look like a man? She's with me."

The apartment was in a state of massive disrepair. Cracks in the wall went from ceiling to floor and were wide enough to put a book in. What had once been a carpet was now a maze of torn and tangled remnants. One of the walls had been graffitied heavily with gang symbols. There was no furniture save for a mattress on the floor and an old-style, vinyl dining room chair.

"This here is Mickey D," Rajah said. Tracy nodded toward him, feeling absurd. The exchange of pleasantries in a place like this was odd indeed. "He likes to hang at McDonald's, see? That's why we call him Mickey D."

"Man, what you bringin' people here for?" said Mickey, shoving his hands in the pockets of his pants. It looked to Tracy almost like he was holding them up this way.

"You got nothin' to worry about," said Rajah.

"I do, man," the other one answered. "I gotta keep breathin'."

"You alive, man. You look that way to me."

"I didn't do you nothin'. What you want?"

"Yo, I only wanna talk."

"With her around?" Mickey nodded toward Tracy.

"Like I told you, chill *out*. She be the one on O'Lean's case."

Mickey D's eyes got large and round. He took a few fearful steps backward. "No, man, I can't do no talkin' to her."

"Oh, man . . ." The way Rajah said it carried a tone of implied threat. Tracy could see its effect. The pained expression on Mickey D's face told her everything she needed to know about what was going on inside him.

"I can't say nothin'," Mickey D squealed.

"I think you can." Rajah took a step toward Mickey D.

Quickly Tracy said, "Excuse me." Rajah stopped and looked at her. "Before we go any further," Tracy said, "maybe you better tell me just why you brought me here."

Setting his eyes back on Mickey D, Rajah said, "My man here is what they call a witness."

"Shut up, man!" Mickey D spurted.

"Yeah, witness to a crime."

Tracy said, "You mean the murder O'Lean is accused of?"

"No," said Rajah, "but right before."

"Shut up!" Mickey D's protest was pitiful. He swayed nervously, like a flagpole in a windstorm. Shoving his hands deeper into his pockets, Mickey D looked at the ground.

"How so?" Tracy asked Rajah.

Rajah replied, "See, he was a parking valet at the party for that movie, *Red Ride 'N the Hood*. Yeah, he was right there when the guy who got capped picked up his car."

Tracy watched as Mickey D's face went through several emotional contortions. He began walking back and forth, a caged animal looking for a way out. Rajah remained still, smiling slightly. "And," Rajah said, "he's got somethin' to say about the cops."

"No!" Mickey D cried.

"See?" Rajah said to Tracy. "Told you I had somethin' for you."

"No way!" Mickey D shook his head violently.

Tracy reached for her calm voice and said, "Listen, you can't withhold evidence. If you have something relevant to this case you'd better tell me about it."

"I ain't tellin' nobody nothin'!"

"What is it about the police?" asked Tracy.

This time, Mickey D just shook his head and turned his back.

"I could have you taken in," Tracy said. "I could question you down at Parker Center."

"Nobody's takin' me no place."

Not knowing what her next move should be, Tracy glanced at Rajah. He answered her with his own look, one that told her he was going to take over.

"Listen, side," Rajah said gently, walking over to Mickey D and placing a hand on his shoulder. "I think you better tell her."

In a small voice, barely audible to Tracy, Mickey D said, "I can't, man. They'll smoke me."

"That what you're afraid of?" Rajah said.

"Yeah, man."

"What I thought."

With a sudden, tigerlike move Rajah lifted the scrawny kid off the ground and shot out onto the balcony, knocking the screen door right off its track. Flailing arms and legs splayed out around Rajah's massive body. Then the arms and legs disappeared.

Tracy ran to the balcony, where she heard an anguished scream. Mickey D dangled five floors above the alley. Rajah held Mickey D's leg with one hand.

"Talk, man," Rajah said.

"Bring me up! Bring me up!" Mickey D wailed.

Tracy said, "Don't do this."

Rajah didn't make any move to pull the hapless kid to safety. "I'm losin' you, man," he said calmly. Before she could protest again, Tracy heard Mickey D say, "All right all right all right!"

"Tell her now!" Rajah commanded.

Looking up from his precarious position, Mickey D started spewing words. "The cop who talked to me told me to sign a statement . . . so I signed it . . . but it wasn't what I said . . . he made it up, said I had to sign it and then disappear or else he was comin' after me . . . I don't want no part of this anymore!"

Tracy tried to piece it together quickly. If what he was saying was true, then Willis, who had to be "the cop," was involved in a criminal effort to falsify evidence. *Was it a conspiracy? Who did it involve? Duke? Or does this go even higher?*

"Bring him up now," said Tracy. Rajah complied, pulling Mickey D by the legs back onto the balcony.

"I'm meat!" Mickey D cried out.

Tracy said, "Don't worry! I'm not going to say anything."

Mickey D looked at her with a small light of hope in his eyes. "What you mean?"

"Listen," said Tracy, "what you're telling me, if it's true, is a bombshell."

"If it's true!" screamed Mickey D. "I was gonna be dropped on my head, man!"

"I know, I know."

"That cop is a *bad* cop."

"Maybe. I have to do more digging. But I also have to keep in touch with you. If you do as I say, you won't have anything to worry about." She could tell from his look that he didn't believe her. Why should he? She was from another world, one where people like him were treated as cattle for the slaughterhouse of what was euphemistically known as the "justice system."

"I always know where to find him," Rajah said. Mickey D's expression told Tracy that was true.

# CHAPTER ELEVEN

NEVER HAD SHE FELT SO LONELY in the midst of the sprawling eighteenth floor. It was like being on an island almost, surrounded by a sea you knew was full of sharks. You just couldn't see them above the surface.

Tracy sat at her desk, almost paralyzed. What should she do now? Who could she go to? Trust?

Her phone rang. "Tracy Shepherd," she said.

"Rob Cavanaugh."

Her pulse quickened. "Hello."

"I'm flying into LAX a little later. What are the chances of having dinner?"

"Dinner?"

"Yeah, you know, as in eating? People do that sort of thing in the evening."

"I think that would be great," Tracy said.

"Fine. I'll be in around 5:30. Would it be possible to meet you in Westwood or something?"

"Sure."

"There's a place called Benny's."

"I know it."

"Six o'clock?"

"Six o'clock."

"I'm looking forward to it."

"Me, too."

It was right after hanging up that the idea came to her. Maybe Rob Cavanaugh could do something about this whole mess. He seemed to have an in with the office, and with the police department. It would be a major favor to ask of him, of course. But he sounded like someone who wouldn't mind doing a favor—for her.

She smiled at the phone.

---

It was just past five o'clock when Duke Gallegos called her into his office. He had his back turned toward the open door as he looked out of his window at the snarl of rush-hour traffic below. Tracy gave a little rap on the door as she entered.

Duke spun around. "Come on in, Trace," he said. "Have a seat." She tried to read his expression, which seemed darker than normal. Something was troubling him.

"How you doing?" he said, sounding more like a therapist than a head deputy.

"I'm OK," Tracy said cautiously.

"You sure?"

"Sure I'm sure."

"Because if you're not, I want to hear about it. I want my deputies feeling good. Don't need any burnout."

"Duke, you wanted me to do nothing but concentrate on the Murray case. That's what I've been doing."

"Maybe you're concentrating too hard."

"What's that supposed to mean?"

"Trace, look. I know I came down a little hard on you the other day. Maybe I was wrong to move you into something this big so soon . . ." He let his voice trail off, as if she should make the next contribution to the conversation.

"It's not that," said Tracy.

Duke's face suddenly changed to intense interest. "Then what is it?"

Now what should she say? Should she let him have it with both barrels? Or was it too soon? If she poured it all out now, maybe he'd think she *was* going off the deep end. Something told her to hold back. A little warning light in the back of her mind. Maybe it was something in Duke's expression. Troubled, concerned, but something more.

Scared? That was wild speculation. Still, she was convinced now more than ever that something more was happening all around her. But she couldn't say anything. Not yet.

"Duke," she said, "The case is not as strong as it should be."

"Don't worry," said Duke. "Willis will take care of that."

The mention of Willis's name made Tracy shudder a little. What a strange choice of words, too: *Take care of that*. What was that supposed to mean? That he'd plug the holes in the case with something besides real evidence? The mere thought of it brought cold nubs to Tracy's neck. Was that what Duke was telling her?

How could she even speculate on that? Duke was like a father to her. More, he was a moral barometer. When she'd had doubts about cases in the past, he'd always been there to guide and comfort her.

She chose her next words carefully. "Duke," she said. "I'm not entirely comfortable with Detective Willis on this thing."

Duke's eyes registered an odd expression. It was not surprise, which is what Tracy had expected. It was more like realization, as if he had been expecting her to say something like this all along. "Comfort," said Duke, "is not what this job is about." He said it almost like a warning.

"Duke," she said, "I want to see justice done in this case. That's what we're all about, isn't it?"

Duke didn't answer right away. That pause was even more chilling to Tracy than the thought that Willis might be a crooked cop. Finally, he said, "We all want justice, don't we?" But there was no conviction in his voice. It sounded more like an apology.

---

The image of Duke's face—drawn, haggard—stayed with Tracy all the way into Westwood. It was a haunted face, and it was haunting her. Only when she pulled into the Village did the picture leave her, only to be replaced by another.

*Ben*. Suddenly, he was there in her mind, and she knew exactly why. She was about to see Rob Cavanaugh again, the first man she had dated since Ben's death. Now, the memories of Ben started flooding in, almost as if her mind were telling her to feel guilty about her feelings for Rob.

What would Ben want? Surely he wouldn't want her to remain alone. He had told her that on a number of occasions. He was a cop, and they both lived with the thought that he could be killed someday in the line of duty. She hated to talk of it, but every now and then Ben insisted. He believed in facing the possibility head on.

*If anything ever happens to me*, he'd say, *I want you to feel like you can find someone else*. Why had he said that? Because he knew her. He knew how deep her love for him was, how much he was a part of her. How hard it would be to ever find anyone she felt that way about.

Now, there was a possibility. Rob Cavanaugh could never *replace* Ben—no one would ever do that—but he could step alongside him in her heart. But she was having a hard time with that. A terrible time.

She pulled into the public parking lot across the street from Benny's, the quaint seafood restaurant where she would meet Rob. She parked, turned off the ignition, and remained in her seat. She wanted to pray, but found she couldn't. Her mind was reeling. With a deep breath, she opened her car door and headed for the restaurant.

She saw Stu as soon as she walked through the front doors. He was hard to miss. "Mr. Cavanaugh is waiting for you," he said, turning. He nodded at the hostess as he led Tracy through the restaurant toward the back. Rob was sitting in a booth in the corner, his back to the people. He looked up as Tracy arrived and smiled. "You made it."

She sat across from him. Rob nodded at Stu, who promptly disappeared. "The things I have to go through to enjoy a simple meal with a wonderful companion." In the next few minutes, Rob managed to put her completely at ease. He seemed to sense she needed time to relax, and so kept up most of the conversation himself. He ordered them both shrimp cocktails as appetizers, and by the time they arrived, Tracy was almost feeling human again. Almost. There was still that gnawing sense of something not right inside her. It wasn't about Rob, though, or Ben. It was about the case.

"Rob," she said, "how well do you know Duke Gallegos?"

He hesitated for a moment. "Why do you ask?"

"Just wondering."

"I know him about as well as I know a lot of my political contacts. We've been together at a number of meetings, talked on the phone several times."

"I got the impression he was a pretty close friend of yours."

"You know us politicians. Everybody is our friend, except the guy we're running against." He seemed to look a little more deeply at Tracy, then said, "Seriously, though, I like Duke Gallegos. I think he's a good man."

"I do, too."

"Is anything wrong?"

*Yes,* she wanted to say, *something is terribly wrong. But I don't know what it is.*

"Tracy," he said, his voice soft, "I want you to feel like you can tell me anything. Anything at all. Because there's something I want to tell you."

Suddenly, the air in the restaurant seemed very cold. It had to be nerves. But Rob didn't speak. All of a sudden *he* appeared nervous, almost childlike. He looked down at his bread plate and tapped it lightly with a fork.

Even though only seconds went by, Tracy couldn't stand the suspense. "What is it?"

Rob looked up at her. "Tracy, would it be too much if I . . ."

He paused again. Tracy nodded her head, as if she were trying to pull the next sentence from his mouth.

". . . would it be too much if I had you think about something?"

"Yes, of course."

"Tracy, I know it's soon. We haven't known each other for long. But I'm a politician, and it's in my nature to take the long-term view, you know?"

Tracy nodded.

"What I'd like," said Rob, "is for you to just think about, maybe, somewhere down the road, that maybe this—" he motioned around him, as if to indicate not only the immediate setting but the two of them—"would lead you to consider . . . marriage."

Tracy's face flushed. Her head went light.

"Don't answer me now," Rob said. "I just want you to consider it. Maybe I shouldn't have said anything."

"No, no," she said quickly. "I'm glad you did."

"You are?"

"Yes."

Rob slid around the booth until his side touched hers. She felt electric, every nerve sensitive to touch and feel. When he put his lips on hers, all the sound around her—casual conversations, guitar music on the speakers, the chink of silverware on plates—melded into a single aural sensation, the sound of waves whooshing on a beach at night, a warm night, as warm as she felt now, wrapped up in his embrace.

"Ready to order?" It was the waiter's voice. Tracy opened her eyes to see a twenty-something slacker smirking at them with his pad in hand. Rob leaned his head back against the booth and looked the waiter in the eye. "My good man," Rob said. "Give us a few more minutes."

"Uh, sure." The waiter nodded and sauntered off. Rob leaned into Tracy again, pressing his lips passionately against hers, and the room started to spin, transporting her to a strange place, like in the old cartoons where the character runs off a cliff and doesn't realize he's in thin air—doesn't realize it until he looks down and says, "Uh-oh" and drops like a rock.

She was in that place now. She dared not look down.

The evening ended in a haze as Tracy tried desperately to get a clear picture of what was happening with Rob. But that picture was no clearer than the hazy mist hanging over the west side, a rolling evening fog from the Pacific Ocean a couple of miles away. It enveloped her car as she got on the freeway heading into the Sepulveda Pass. Only the taillights immediately in front of her were visible. She'd have to keep alert.

She flipped on the radio—91.5, classical—to keep her company. Driving home in the dark had never been one of her favorite things to do. The music helped and almost made her feel like she was in a nice, relaxing dream. Good. Relaxing was just what the doctor had ordered.

She noticed the tailgater about the time she got to Getty Center Drive. The headlights were on bright, a stupid thing to do in the fog, and they were much too close. Another crazy L. A. driver who thought the public roads were a personal playground.

But maybe it was worse. Maybe the guy was drunk. Tracy wanted no part of this. She signaled for a right-hand lane change. This was a dangerous move in the thick soup. Some other car could be barreling down at sixty miles an hour, and she wouldn't see it until it was practically upon her. But the crazy driver was much too close. She had to get over. Straining her neck, Tracy tried to see all angles. Finally she slipped into the slow lane. She quickly looked at her speedometer. She was doing fifty-five, but now she'd drop down a little and let the crazy driver pass her by.

Only he didn't pass. She looked to her left but didn't see any car go by. Suddenly she was jolted by the reflection of light in her rearview mirror. The guy had pulled in behind her. What was he doing? Was this some weird kick? Some driver ticked off because maybe she'd inadvertently cut him off somewhere back around Sunset? Or . . .

When the thought occurred to her, it came in hard. And it seemed to make sense. *This guy was following her.* And he had been ever since she got on the freeway. She made the connection: *the threatening letters. Could this be the one?* Or was she overreacting? Letting her imagination run away with her?

The headlights stayed behind, almost mocking her. She thought of that old Steven Spielberg movie, *Duel,* the one where Dennis Weaver gets chased by a mysterious, deadly truck. She'd always thought that something like that could very well happen to somebody, someday. Now, maybe it would be her.

*OK, think* . . .

She was about to descend into the Valley, where she could take an off-ramp and head for the police department. And do what? Drive in, honking her horn, as the tired desk sergeant read a magazine? If she stopped, that would be more than enough time for a maniac to take a shot at her and still get away. Maybe it would scare him off. But maybe it wouldn't.

She could make a call on her cell phone. Yes, that was it. Call in right now, and have a black-and-white pull up and apprehend the guy. Reaching to the right, she felt around for the phone. It wasn't there.

But it had to be. It always was. It was her habit to leave it within reach at all times. It wasn't there now. When was the last time she had used it?

She hadn't. The last one to have the phone was Rajah, when they were driving in South Central. He had picked it up and made small talk about it.

Had he given it back? A panic started to take hold of her and wouldn't let go.

As Rob Cavanaugh slid out of the car in front of the Beverly Wilshire Hotel, Terrence Hagan was waiting for him. The Cavanaugh for Governor campaign chief was a trim, muscular fifty, with steel-gray shards running through his dark brown hair and the intense eyes of an experienced politico. Rob thought the same thing he always thought when meeting with Hagan: *Ah, the Puppet Master.*

And why not? The man knew how to pull strings. How to get things done. How to *win*. He was one of those Vietnam vets for whom the war had not been a horror but an opportunity. As a marine, he'd seen his duty and he did it. Now everything he did was seemingly out of duty. That's why he was a winner. He didn't quit.

There was a certain price to be paid, of course. If you were a candidate under Hagan, you pretty much did what he said. That's what he was being paid for.

"Evening, Governor," Hagan said.

Rob smiled at the appellation. "Counting our chickens early, aren't we?"

"I don't contemplate losing," Hagan answered. "Ever."

"That's why you were hired. But I thought you weren't coming in until tomorrow."

"We need to talk."

A few minutes later they were in the lounge, Rob sipping a ginger ale and Hagan a Dewar's on the rocks. Light from the dim lamps barely illuminated Hagan's face. "So how was dinner?" Hagan asked.

Rob cocked his head. "You knew about that?"

Hagan smiled his Marine Corps smile, the one that seemed to say, *Of course I knew.* "Well, it's good to know I'm in such capable hands." Rob's voice betrayed a bit of annoyance. This was the part of the process he hated: no private life. People knew where he was and what he did. Hagan especially.

"That's what I'm here for," Hagan said, swirling the ice in his glass. It sounded like bones dancing. "And I'm here to see to it that nothing jeopardizes our task."

"And?"

"You like this girl?"

"Yes."

"How much?"

In his head, Rob heard himself saying, *What business is that of yours? You can run my campaign, and you can tell me what babies to kiss, but I'm not going to let you tell me who I can and can't have dinner with.* The voice faded into the back of his mind. Of course, he was going to let Hagan have his say. There was no other way. He was in too deep.

"I like her enough that I'm thinking of asking her to marry me."

Hagan looked away, like he was avoiding an unpleasant subject. "I'm all for marriage, you understand. I've done it three times myself. And it's especially good for a young, conservative candidate with the family values riff." He looked back at Rob. "But you didn't clear it with me first."

"Clear it? Why do I have to—"

"You have to understand," Hagan interrupted. "There are certain . . . considerations."

"We're talking about my personal life here."

"You have no personal life." Hagan looked straight at him, daring him to challenge that assessment. "You gave that up when you were given the present opportunity. *Given*, I might remind you."

*No need,* Rob thought, *you're the Puppet Master.*

"This gal is the deputy D. A. handling that Hollywood producer murder case," Hagan said.

"Unbelievable." Rob looked at him with a mixture of awe and amazement.

"Not really. It's my job to traffic in information."

"So what about that information?"

"There are considerations," Hagan repeated. "No need to go into them now. Let's just say it's messy."

"But I don't see why. What better prospect for me than a good, and good-looking, prosecutor?"

"Leave the analysis to me. I'm the one that has to throw all the frogs in the pond and get them to hop in line. All I'm telling you is, I think it would be a good idea for you to, well, look in another pond."

A pair of revelers suddenly screamed from the bar, jolting Rob. He glanced over quickly and saw a well-dressed man and woman falling all over themselves in laughter. He suddenly felt contempt—for a couple who seemed to think nobody else in the world cared what noise they made, and for a process that had saddled him with a man like Terrence Hagan. Turning back to Hagan, Rob said with muted sarcasm, "Is that an order?"

The Marine Corps smile returned to Hagan's face. "I like that," said Hagan.

"So is it?"

"Is it what?"

"An order."

"Let's just say it's a very strong suggestion." Hagan finished his drink.

"And if I refuse?" said Rob.

Lowering his glass, Terrence Hagan said, "Why don't we leave that bridge standing until we come to it?"

Rob looked at him and said nothing. In his mind he saw a picture of a bridge, and then he saw it blowing up.

The lights were closer now. *If they were any nearer,* Tracy thought, *they'd be inside my car.* Whoever it was, he was sending a message. Maybe that message was, *You're next* . . .

She had veered off the freeway at Balboa and driven by the park, hoping to find somewhere where there were people . . .

*What good will that do?*

. . . or police or *anything.* But no matter where she went she would have to stop. Eventually she would have to stop. And then he'd have his chance.

She sensed she was coming to an intersection. A new wave of panic washed over her. What about the red lights? She dared not speed through in this fog even though she had the idea that to do so might catch the interest of a friendly cop. Then she saw it: the red, foggy glow up ahead.

Headlights behind, right at her bumper. Only one thing she could do and that would be to hang a severe right-hand turn. *Don't slow down, hope for the best.* That's exactly what she did. The headlights stayed right with her.

Coming out of the turn, Tracy heard a thump. She looked down on the passenger-side floor and saw a dark object rolling around. Her phone. Rajah hadn't taken it! It had probably been between the seat and the door and just got dislodged.

Steering with one hand, Tracy reached down and felt for the cell phone. It was an absurd position, she caught herself thinking—a Mr. Toad's wild ride through the L. A. fog, a madman on her tail, and her stretching out so far she couldn't even see above the dashboard. But she found the phone.

Sitting up, she let out a huge sigh, and then flicked the phone to "ready." Just a quick 9-1-1 and this would soon be over.

No beep.

Nothing.

The battery.

*No way . . . no way!*

No power.

Tracy screamed in frustration.

*God, where are you?*

Bryce and Allison flashed into her thoughts. Another intersection, another right turn.

Where would it end?

---

Mona Takata never watched late-night TV, but tonight she made an exception. She couldn't sleep. She tried for an hour to coerce her body into the land of slumber, but to no avail. She felt like she'd had a couple of espressos. Strange.

At first she chalked it up to some normal stressor with her job, something that was cooking in her mind somewhere but which she could not identify. Maybe one of her latest interviews, though she couldn't think of one that was anything more than routine.

So she paced around and finally turned on the tube, hoping some mindless entertainment, or maybe an old movie, would lull her with alpha waves and let her sleep.

She settled on an old movie with a dapper leading man and his wisecracking wife, moving around high society with martinis in their hands. It was actually pretty cute, cute enough for Mona to grab the "TV Guide" to figure out what she was watching. It was something called *Shadow of the Thin Man*, with William Powell and Myrna Loy. She'd heard about that series but had never seen one. She made a mental note to check them out at Blockbuster.

Fifteen minutes into watching the movie, the inner restlessness returned. This time it was stronger, impossible to ignore. It was more than some distant disquiet, too. This turmoil had a point to it, almost like a message. Could it be one of those special burdens? Her good friend, a missionary to Africa who always got together with her when stateside, was a strong proponent of the "insomniac's prayer." Whenever she couldn't sleep, she told Mona, that was usually a sign that God wanted her to pray.

*So maybe this is it,* Mona thought. *I need to pray, but for what?* The answer came immediately—Tracy. Tracy needed her prayers. *Now.*

This wasn't very surprising. Mona was well aware of the pressure Tracy was under, and of those mind-bending threats, and of her struggle with her faith. Or maybe it was worse than Mona thought.

She didn't hesitate. William Powell and Myrna Loy faded into TV darkness. Mona got down on her knees.

---

She had made a mistake.

Tracy knew that the minute the road began to snake into the hills. Why had she chosen this route?

*Maybe the guy will finally give up,* Tracy thought, knowing that she was not going to give in to him, that she would keep driving until she found a police convention in a parking lot or something.

But he didn't give up. And now they were up in one of those residential canyons between the Valley and Hollywood, and she had no other choice but to keep going. Maybe, on the other side, where the lights were brighter and the crowds heavier, Tracy would find a way out of the nightmare. That's when she realized the car behind her was not going to give her that chance.

She became aware of the lights moving to her left, then forward, like he was going to pass her. But he didn't pass. He came alongside her rear wheel.

Tracy looked hard in her side-view mirror, wanting to at least get a look at the maniac. But she couldn't see anything because of the headlights, now fully in the other lane. If a car came the other way, the guy would be history.

Then she felt the first bump against her fender. The rear of her car jolted to the right, and she had to fight the steering wheel to keep from careening off the side of the road. This was it. The maniac had made his move. He intended to finish her off right here and now.

*Oh God help me!* was all she could think. Then another thought, *If you're still listening . . . if you're still there . . . Oh God, please. . . .*

Another bump, this one harder.

*Oh God . . .*

Her car was on some dirt now, skidding. The sight of her headlights against the fog reflected back at her like she was driving into a curtain, but this curtain did not part. Suddenly a huge impact on the right side thudded her head against the driver-side window. And then a feeling of weightlessness. . . .

She was falling—she and her car were falling—backwards, down, down, down into the mist.

## CHAPTER TWELVE

FOR THE FIRST TIME in a long time, Duke Gallegos closed the door to his office. He never did this, even when talking to people. He always imagined a sort of force field around his door, like the people in the office would get a jolt if they tried to pass by when they weren't supposed to. It worked well. Duke's corner office was private even with the door open. But not this morning. This time he sealed himself in.

Duke went through his normal routine, plugging in the little coffeemaker, putting in a couple of scoops of the gourmet beans he'd had ground at Trader Joe's, filling the machine with water. That done, he sat in his chair and spun around so he could see out the window. He had a panoramic view—the morning was relatively clear—but the whole thing was something of a blur. He wasn't focusing on anything.

*Is this how condemned men look out of their cells?* he wondered. Knowing they have no hope, they just sort of set their eyes out the window and leave them there? Was this the existence on Death Row where he, Duke, had sent more than a few in his career? How was he any better off than they? If he had the same feelings now, what difference did it make where he was?

He stayed, staring off into space, for twenty minutes. Finally, he gave himself a mental shake, poured a cup of fresh brew, and turned to his desk. He had several matters to take care of, for which he was thankful. His professional instincts would take over. He would lose himself in routine.

A few minutes later, after checking his calendar for the tenth time, Duke heard a knock on the door. It was Bob Campbell. He had that look on his face, the one the deputies get when some slam-dunk case has just been blown out of the water by a strange, unanticipated twist—a key witness recanting or a victim admitting it was all made up.

"What is it?" Duke said.

"Have you heard?"

"Heard what?"

"Tracy."

"What about Tracy?"

"She was in an accident."

Duke stood up. "What?"

Campbell nodded. "Yeah. Last night. Her car ran off the road in the fog up on Coldwater. She's in the hospital."

"Oh no," Duke muttered.

"Hard to believe, isn't it?" said Campbell.

Duke Gallegos did not answer.

The suite at the Century Plaza was the size of a football field, or it seemed so. Sherman Kohlbert hadn't set foot on the gridiron since high school, when he'd made varsity as a small linebacker. What he lacked in size he made up with tenacity and what his coach called "focused meanness." That was really the time that Sherman Kohlbert decided he could have anything he wanted in life, by whatever means.

He'd gone to USC on a football scholarship, but even before playing a down decided his future lay elsewhere. Why risk a life-limiting injury? He wasn't going to make the NFL, and he didn't want to. There was more money to be made up north, in Silicon Valley. College life was actually holding him back.

But the one year he spent at the university had not been a total washout. There he had discovered Nietzsche and a philosophy for a new age. Here was a man writing a century earlier about eternal truths for our time. Nietzsche turned the sodden Christian world on its head. What counts here is not goodness, but strength. Not humility, but pride. Not charity, but selfishness. Not justice, but power. The problem with the world was not nihilism, Sherman Kohlbert concluded. It was that it was not nihilistic enough.

He pulled out an Arturo Fuente from his traveling humidor, a beautiful mahogany job that had been a gift from a grateful politician, and lit up. He took a seat in a chair, propped up his feet, and flicked on the TV with the remote. He wondered if he could get the golf tournament. Watch Tiger Woods. He loved the kid's style. He'd locked in about sixty-million dollars in endorsement money the second he turned pro, at twenty years old. If all went accordingly, Sherman Kohlbert would lock up ten times that much in the next couple of years.

ESPN was carrying the tourney. Kohlbert leaned back and took a leisurely drag on the cigar. Everything was set up just right. The cop should be here any minute. Kohlbert guessed he would be right on time. He was. The desk called up to ask if Kohlbert was expecting a man named "John Robinson."

"Sure, send him on up," Kohlbert said. Nice touch there, having Willis use the name of the USC football coach. Intrigue didn't have to be all drudgery. It could actually be fun.

On TV, Davis Love III hit a nine-iron from 140 yards, landing it just inches from the pin. Kohlbert nodded his approval. Love was a good one, no doubt. Didn't have Tiger's style, of course, but he could play. As Love started up the fairway toward the green, there was a knock at the door.

"Come in," said Kohlbert. Stan Willis entered and closed the door behind him. He wore a floppy sun hat, the kind some senior golfers wear. On Willis it looked ridiculous.

"Nice disguise," Kohlbert said.

"What do you expect?" Willis said with an irritated tone. "I'm not into this secret agent jazz." Kohlbert nodded at the sofa. Willis sat, sinking into the soft cushions. Kohlbert, peering down at the cop, smiled. "You follow the tour?" he said.

Willis glanced at the TV, then back at Kohlbert. "No."

"Great game, golf. It takes talent, skill, and mental toughness, not to mention a good dose of strategy. You have to manage the course, see. Anticipate where the trouble is, figure out a way around it."

Pausing, Kohlbert took a puff on his cigar and regarded Willis through the smoke. The officer shrugged his shoulders, as if to say, *Real interesting, man, but you didn't call me up here to talk about a stupid game played with sticks, did you?*

Then Kohlbert said, "Golf is like life in a lot of ways, isn't it?" Again, Willis shrugged his shoulders.

"You have to know how to avoid the trouble spots. An idiot can't play good golf. An idiot just hacks around the fairways, leaving divots in the nice grass and cursing his bad fortune when the ball lands in the water. But the truth is, it's not luck. It's the fact that idiots can't play golf."

"Mr. Kohlbert," Willis said, "what does this have to do—" He stopped when Kohlbert raised his hand.

"I want you to agree with me first," Kohlbert said. "Agree with me that idiots can't play golf. You agree with that?"

"Sure," said Willis.

"Then take a look at that." Kohlbert nodded to the TV. Tiger Woods was about to tee off. "Now watch."

The boy wonder in the Nike hat took a practice swing, then stepped up to the ball. One look down the fairway, a little waggle, a small movement of the feet. Then he torqued his lithe body and unloosed a ferocious swing that sent the white pellet through the air like a rifle shot.

Silently, the two men in the luxury hotel suite watched as the TV cameras followed the ball to its resting place on the fairway, some 320 yards from the tee box.

"Awesome," said Kohlbert. "And smart, too. The kid knows how to manage his game."

"Yeah," Willis said without enthusiasm.

"Tiger Woods is no idiot. That's why he's successful. That's why he's got more money in the bank than you will ever dream of. That is because you are an idiot."

Sitting up stiffly, Stan Willis said, "What's that supposed to mean?"

"I think you know," said Kohlbert.

Willis tightened. *Like a dog in a corner*, thought Kohlbert. Willis said, "If it's about the D. A., then I don't see what you're all hepped up about."

"You don't?"

"No. I told you I'd take care of her, and I have."

"Yes. Like an idiot."

"Look, Mr. Kohlbert—" Once more, Kohlbert's upraised hand stopped Willis.

"Don't you wonder how I found out about this little . . . incident?"

"I assume Lefferts."

"You are again incorrect."

"Well then?"

Kohlbert leaned back in his chair and stuck the aromatic Fuente in his mouth, leaving it there. He spoke around it, "I saw it on the TV news, you idiot."

"I don't like being called that," said Willis, staring coolly at Sherman Kohlbert. Kohlbert did not move.

"I don't really care what you appreciate, officer," said Kohlbert. "Your jerkwater attempt at staging an accident hasn't done anything more than call attention to your incompetence. And now it happens to have been picked up by the news shows. That is the kind of publicity I would prefer not having. You follow?"

"I did my best."

"Your best wasn't good enough. That's your problem. Offing the kid in Compton was major stupid."

"He could have blown the whole thing open!"

"So instead we get an Internal Affairs investigation of your incompetence?"

"I'm in the clear."

"But your name is out there. You're becoming a liability." Kohlbert again turned his attention to the tube. Tiger Woods was in a fairway bunker. The two men watched silently as the phenom grabbed an iron, dug his feet into the sand, and sent a staggering shot all the way to the green.

"You see that?" Kohlbert said. "Awesome! That's a shot only a pro can make, and then only one in a hundred. An idiot tries to make that shot, he's gonna shank it so bad he'll end up worse than before. So the message is, leave those tough ones to the pros. I got someone in mind who'll do it right. A nonidiot, you see?"

Willis looked at the carpet. "Is that all?"

"No, that's not all." Kohlbert's tone suddenly took a plunge in temperature. He got out of his chair, put his cigar in an onyx ashtray, and strode to the wet bar. He reached inside the black leather satchel sitting on the bar and pulled something out. He walked back across the room and held the item up for Willis. It was the size of a Tic Tac.

"You see that?" said Kohlbert.

Willis nodded. Kohlbert continued, "That is a chip. But not just any chip. This is made from a new synthetic the boys in R and D have cooked up. They tell me this is the first of its kind, though others are on the same track. Hard to believe, but this little sucker is probably going to be worth billions. You follow?"

Willis nodded.

"But," said Kohlbert, "if the timing is not right, if the ducks don't fall into a row, this little thing will be worth *spit!*"

As Kohlbert said it, he threw the chip as hard as he could across the room. It disappeared into the plush, white carpet of the hotel suite.

"Now I have strategized this course," Kohlbert said, returning to his chair and recovering his smoldering cigar. "That's what I'm good at. So I call the shots. You don't make another, I mean you don't even sneeze out of the wrong nostril, unless I say so."

Willis, looking down, said nothing.

"Because if you do, I'll hold you accountable."

At that, Willis looked once more into the face of Sherman Kohlbert, president and CEO of NyDex Systems. "You can't mess with an L. A. cop."

Kohlbert slowly shook his head. "If you believe that, then you're more of an idiot than I thought." Silence, and a plume of cigar smoke, hung heavily in the room. Tiger Woods lined up a twenty-foot putt, stepped up to the ball, and rolled it into the cup.

"You leave the lawyer to me now," said Kohlbert. "It will have to be taken care of without error. You just concentrate on keeping the D. A.'s office out of the affairs of that dead Hollywood Jewboy. You got it? You understand your role here?"

Almost in a whisper, Stan Willis said, "Yes."

"Good, good," said Sherman Kohlbert. "And don't take it so hard. Remember what Nietzsche said: 'Life always gets harder toward the summit.' But think about it. We're almost at the top."

Tracy awoke with her head on fire. Her first thought was that she was encased in flames and gas and broken metal. But there were no flames, no smoke, no noise. Instead it was bright, cold, and she was on her back.

A hospital bed.

She was alive.

Groggy, she recalled she had been driving . . . driving . . . and headlights behind her. Yes, that was it. The maniac. But what had happened?

Must have had an accident . . . yes . . . the falling. She'd been in an accident. Accident? *No, it wasn't an accident.*

She wondered if she could move. She raised both her arms. Immediately pain shot through them. Fire again, all through her extremities.

She moved her legs. More pain. But she thought, *Thank God I'm not paralyzed.* Questions started flooding in.

What day was it?

What time?

Where was she?

Where were the kids?

*The kids!* She tried to speak, to call a nurse, but only a sound like an old siren came out. But it was enough. A blue-clad woman was at her bedside immediately.

"Are you in pain?" the nurse said.

"Yes," Tracy managed.

"Let me get the doctor."

"My kids."

"Excuse me?"

"I have to see my kids."

"Don't worry about that," said the nurse. Tracy saw she was an older woman, about the age Tracy's mother would have been had she been alive. There was something comforting in that. "We notified your housekeeper—"

"Mrs. Olivera?"

"That's right, Olivera. She's with your kids now."

"Thank God. Can I call?"

"Let's take it one step at a time."

"Please."

"She already knows."

"My kids . . ."

"As soon as you're able."

*And just when will that be?* she wondered. *How long am I going to be in this place?*

"You have some people waiting," the nurse said.

"Who?"

"A friend of yours, Mona, I think. And a man. They're in the waiting room."

"Send them in."

"I'd better get the doctor."

"Please."

The nurse left the room. A few moments later Mona and Duke entered.

"Gee whiz, kid," Mona said, "where'd you learn how to drive?"

"Mona—"

"We almost lost you."

Duke stepped closer. "How are you feeling, Trace?"

"Like I was pushed into a trash compactor. Listen—"

"You take it real easy," Duke said. His tone was reassuring, but his face troubled.

Mona, ever smiling, chimed in. "I think Duke is going to give you a few days off. Isn't that nice of him?"

"Wonderful." Tracy smiled slightly.

"I've got even better news than that," said Duke. "You can have as long as you want. The first order of business is getting you back on your feet, better than ever."

"And a new car," said Mona.

"Listen to me," Tracy said quickly. "It wasn't an accident."

Mona and Duke looked at each other, then at Tracy. Neither said a word. Tracy continued, "I was driving home, in the fog. Somebody followed me, then tried to run me off the road."

"No way," Mona said incredulously.

"Yes," said Tracy. Her head was pounding. She closed her eyes for a moment, tiny explosions of red and yellow dancing behind her lids, and when she opened them up again she noticed Duke had turned his back to her.

Mona said, "This is incredible, absolutely incredible. The police, do they know?"

"I haven't talked to anyone yet."

"You've got to make a report."

"I will."

"Duke?" Mona said, "what are we going to do about this?"

Without turning around Duke said, "We sit down with the police and . . . try to figure out who might be a suspect."

"Right," said Mona. She smiled at Tracy.

Tracy said, "Chief?"

Duke turned around.

"Hey, don't worry," said Tracy. "It's not like it's your fault or anything."

Duke said nothing.

They stayed a few minutes more, until the doctor came and advised them to let Tracy rest. Mona leaned over and gave Tracy a kiss on the cheek, whispering in her ear, "I was praying for you last night. God laid it on my heart." With a final wave, Mona left the room with Duke Gallegos.

Tracy closed her eyes and lay still for a long time.

## CHAPTER THIRTEEN

THE DREAM BEGAN, as always, with the sound. A distant pop, like a firecracker down the street, then hundreds of them.

Lights came next, lighting up the sky like the Fourth of July in a park in the middle of America. Pretty, if you didn't know it was deadly.

From there the dream took one of those weird turns. It veered into a dark tunnel, as if he were running through it. Only the tunnel was about to collapse. Its walls were made of something infirm . . . sand. The sand was threatening to fall and bury him.

Forever.

At the end of the tunnel was a hand. He reached for it, grabbed it, but it didn't pull him out. The sand was around his feet, then his knees and before he knew it his thighs. Getting heavy, oppressive.

"Pullllll!" he shouted. And the hand pulled harder, and he was saved.

The hand was Dev Traynor's. Good old Dev. The only decent guy in the outfit. The only one who'd talk to him.

And then the lights got brighter, the sound more intense, like being trapped in a giant popcorn machine. Dev was smiling.

In the next instant, Dev was on fire, screaming, burning, arms flailing. One arm was covered with flame, like some serpentine monster made of exploding gas, and he grabbed the arm, just like Dev had grabbed his, only when he pulled, the arm came off, tore right out of the shoulder, and Dev's scream was louder and more tormented than anything he'd ever heard . . .

Tommy Bear Paw woke up then. Always at that point, he woke up, sweating, fighting for a breath. And he realized again: the worst part was not the dream itself. Oh yes, the dream was a nightmare, the only one he ever had. But it was always the same.

No, the worst part was never knowing which night it would come. He would have several dreamless nights in a row, sometimes as many as a month's worth, since the Gulf War. But the dream always came back, in full intensity, at some point or other.

There would be no escaping it—forever—his torment. The price had to be paid. He rolled off the folding bed, the springs squeaking. He looked at the digital clock in the darkness. The red numbers said 2:43. He knew it would be 4:00 or 4:30 before he'd be able to catch a little more sleep. Sometimes the dream came again, right away.

*The price.*

He should have taken the hit. Dev had things to live for. That only showed the universe was made of dice. Sometimes it came up snake eyes. Always after the dream, Bear Paw thought somewhere in his mind that what he did for a "living"—the irony of the term was not lost on him—was somehow a payback to the universe. He didn't follow the process any further than that. He was no shrink. He was a killer.

The house—a shack, really—was out at the back end of the Ramirez place, in a quiet spot away from the access road. Bear Paw paid a paltry rent, kept to himself, and the Ramirezes seemed happy with the income. And they left him alone. They didn't know he had hundreds of thousands of dollars, cash, in the locked trunk under his bed. They never would have suspected anything like that.

That's how Bear Paw wanted it. He had no desire to live with people, in the city. People asked too many questions. Out here, he would be left alone, and the desert reminded him of home.

The money was of little consequence. It was only a point of pride, a measure of his worth. And he was worth a lot.

It was dealer's choice as to what to do now. He could look at the sky for awhile, or try to read a magazine. Raul Ramirez, for some reason, dropped his old *Field and Stream* mags on the shack porch when he was through with them. Bear Paw always took them in and put them in a pile by the stove, but he'd never read one, not once.

There was no TV, so he wouldn't be able to take advantage of a great American tradition, falling asleep in front of an infomercial. At least there was beer in the small refrigerator. Bear Paw grabbed a cold Corona and flicked off the top. Then he sat in a chair and flicked on the radio. Maybe one of those talk shows could lull him back to sleep. The first thing he got was some loud, obnoxious kook screaming at a caller for being a "moron." The apparent subject was alien abductions. Not exactly restful.

Turning the dial, Bear Paw passed a couple of music stations—hard rock, country—then landed on a male voice that was soft, yet adamant about something. At first he thought it was a commercial. But it became immediately obvious this was not a sales pitch. At least, not for some product.

"Human beings," the man said, "do not live forever. That is the focus of this book. The starting point. Death is inevitable. It comes to everybody. As the saying goes, we all owe God a death. He who pays today doesn't need to pay tomorrow." Death? Bear Paw became immediately fascinated. Death was a subject he knew something about.

"If that is true, and it is, the writer asks, 'What good are all the things that I can accumulate in this life? I've had everything in my hands. Riches, women, pleasure, successes—all of it. And you know what they are like? They are like a soap bubble when it pops. They leave only vapor. It is all meaningless."

*Strange stuff,* thought Tommy Bear Paw. Not normally what you hear on the talk shows these days. He leaned back with his beer, intensely interested.

"Meaningless lives. No point to them. Nada. Under the sun, everything is meaningless. Are you getting the picture? We'll fill it out when we return after this."

The program cut to a commercial, something about auto insurance. What was he listening to? Of all the programs he could get, what was this? Some preacher man, probably. Some God talk show. But this guy didn't sound like most preachers he was used to hearing. Usually it was all hellfire and damnation, or load up your wallets by saying the magic words. Stuff like that.

This guy was different. He seemed, well, normal. Maybe a little like a college professor or something, but not some Bible smacker. And what about what he was saying? *Right on*. Death really was the end of it all. So everything you get out of life is just going to add up to a big fat nothing in the end, right?

*Right. Right on, Preach. What else have you got to offer?*

"Welcome back. I'm Rabbi Joseph Levine, and this is the 'Jewish Hour.' We've been talking about the great Book of Ecclesiastes, the one book that should be on every self-help shelf in America, taking the place of all the rest."

*Ecclesiastes? What kind of weird name for a book is that?*

"Written thousands of years ago, its message is as potent for our day as it was when it was first put down by the Teacher. We've talked about the inability of our age to deal with death. It is an age in denial. Well, Ecclesiastes tells us we have to face the facts. We can't deny it anymore. At least, if we are to live."

*Who wants to go on living?*

"What is the answer to this meaninglessness, this pain of existence? The Teacher tells us: 'Fear God and keep his commandments, for this is the whole duty of man.' And then the Teacher ends the book with these words: 'For God will bring every deed into judgment, including every hidden thing, whether it is good or evil.'"

For a brief moment, Bear Paw felt a charge rush through his body, like when an icy wind suddenly hits the back of the neck and the flesh kicks into bumps. The words were preacher kind of words, but didn't the guy say he was a rabbi? That's Jewish, right? Weren't they mainly concerned with taking over Hollywood?

Another commercial came on, and Bear Paw found he was sitting rigidly in his chair, not sleepy at all. He wanted the rabbi to keep talking. At least he was interesting. But apparently the show was over. A news report came next. Tommy Bear Paw flicked the radio off. He sat for a long time, finishing one beer and opening another. Then next thing he knew it was light outside, and he was slumped in the chair, his neck aching.

The clock said 8:15. What a night. Nightmares and weird dreams, and voices on the radio. All of it was a groggy memory. Bear Paw went outside on the porch and took in a breath of morning air. He decided he'd go into town for a bite to eat, and shave when he got back.

Old man Ramirez yelled at him from the back of the ranch house, waving his arm. He started toward the shack. Bear Paw stood there in his boxers, waiting for him. They'd had this sort of communication before.

"Mornin', Tommy," said Ramirez.

"Yeah."

"You got another call from that fellow, Wheeler. Looks like you got more construction work comin' up, *verdad?*"

Tommy Bear Paw nodded. "Looks that way."

"*Bueno*. Good to have work. Always good to have work." Ramirez turned around and waved backward at Tommy as he headed back to the ranch house.

*So it will be breakfast and a phone call in town,* thought Tommy Bear Paw. Another job. When you're the best, they keep on calling. And always with that silly name, Orlando Wheeler—gunnery sergeant out at Fort Ord. Tommy didn't like him, and he didn't like Tommy, but he had a name you wouldn't soon forget. So what better name for the sign?

The sign that said, *We have somebody else for you to kill.*

"You don't look so good, Mom."

Tracy had to smile. *Out of the mouths of babes!* She knew she didn't look good. More like Boris Karloff in some Universal horror movie from the thirties. Stitches on her forehead, discoloration around her eyes, bruises like oil spots on both arms. Innocent little Bryce was just calling it like he saw it.

They were finally together again, in the living room at Mrs. Olivera's home. Tracy reclined in an old, comfortable chair, feet up, while the kids stood by cautiously, aware they shouldn't touch.

"Thanks, sweetie," said Tracy. "Mommy doesn't *feel* so good, either."

"Looks owie," said Allison, wide-eyed.

"I'll get better."

"We'll help you, Mom," said Bryce. "We can clean up the kitchen."

Mrs. Olivera came into the room with a tray of cookies and milk. With tiny squeals of delight, the kids took their portions and sat down on the carpet, cross-legged.

"You'll have some, too?" Mrs. Olivera asked Tracy.

"Oh yes. I've been dying for some cookies." When she heard herself say *dying,* her thoughts immediately darkened. Happy as she was to be with her children again, she had to face the fact that someone had actually tried to kill her—and didn't succeed. That would mean another attempt. But when? Where?

That was when she looked at her children and decided it was time to tell them. "Kids, listen. You're going to be staying here with Mrs. Olivera for awhile, OK?"

"All day?" Bryce asked.

"A little longer."

"Night, too?"

"For a lot of nights, maybe. OK?"

"How come?" Bryce asked. His face, for the first time, showed a small trace of fear, as if he understood now that this meant separation. Allison merely watched, looking puzzled.

"Well," said Tracy, "it has something to do with my work. There's a reason you'll be staying here right now instead of at our house."

"Are you staying here, too?"

"No."

Allison's eyes suddenly filled with tears, and she started breathing quickly. "I don't want you to go away!" she cried.

Tracy, though sore and slow, pushed down the recliner and knelt down next to her little girl, throwing her arms around her. "I'm not going away, honey. I'm going to be close by."

"I don't want you to go!" Tears streamed down the girl's face, sobs escaping into her mother's shoulders. At that moment, Tracy felt a wave of hatred—hatred for the one who was causing this.

Tracy put out an arm for Bryce. The boy fell into her embrace. A sharp pain shot through Tracy's chest, but she didn't care. She noticed Bryce had tears in his eyes, too, though he was trying to hold them back.

"Listen to me," Tracy said quietly. "This is only for a little while. I'll see you a lot. I just won't be staying here. Think of this as a kind of adventure. Think you can do that?"

Allison looked at her brother. Bryce thought a moment and said, "Is this a dangerous adventure?"

Tracy nodded. "A little."

"Like Indiana Jones?"

"Maybe not quite like that. But we can pretend like it is."

"How come?"

"You know how I work to punish criminals, right?"

"Yeah."

"Well, criminals don't like what I do."

"They're mean," piped Allison.

"Yes, they are," said Tracy, "and because they don't like what I do to them they may try to get to me."

Bryce frowned. "Is that what happened when your car crashed?"

"Yes. So, for right now, you stay with Mrs. Olivera until I decide what to do, OK?"

"Where will you go, Mommy?" asked Allison.

"Near. I just don't want us to be around our house right now, and you like being here."

Wilma Olivera, who had been standing by lending silent support, said, "We have fun, don't we?"

Both kids nodded. The hint of a smile came back on Bryce's face.

---

"So what do you think of the joint?" Mona said.

"Joint?" said Tracy.

"I can call it that because my brother owns the building. But you can't go wrong with an apartment in a place called Guava Manor."

"I've dreamed of a place like this."

"Come on, it's furnished, clean, freeway-close. Your kids are only fifteen minutes away."

"I'll take it."

"Big bro says you can stay here as long as you like," said Mona.

"How do you rate?"

"He owes me, big time. I've helped him evict more lowlifes than I care to remember. He needs me. He's such a pussycat."

Tracy put her suitcase on the floor and shook her head. "I feel like I'm in the witness protection program."

"And your new name will be . . . Honey Chiles. How's that?"

"You're crazy," Tracy laughed. The laugh died quickly.

Mona stepped toward her. "Don't worry, babe. This'll blow over. The cops will eventually catch the guy."

"I doubt it," Tracy said.

"Why?"

"I haven't been feeling too good about the cops lately, let's put it that way."

Mona headed for the kitchenette and retrieved a couple of glasses from a box on the counter. "I brought you a few dishes and things. How about we have a couple glasses of water to celebrate?"

"Wonderful."

As Mona filled the glasses from the tap, Tracy sat on the sofa and looked around her new home. At least it was freshly painted. The carpet wasn't new, but it wasn't ragged, either. And it was on the top floor, so people wouldn't be pounding around on top of the ceiling. It would do. It would have to.

Mona returned with the water. Tracy took a sip and winced. "Good old L. A. water," she said.

"Nothing but the best for you, kid." Mona sat on the sofa next to Tracy. "I have a little idea."

"Little? I can hardly wait to hear it."

"I want to do a little more sniffing around."

"I don't want you getting more heavily involved."

"Come on, what's wrong with it?"

"It's not under your official duties, Mona. If anybody were to find out, you'd probably get bounced. It's not your case. And you know how the police are about interference."

Dark eyes twinkling, Mona said, "I like life on the edge."

"You may fall off someday."

"I'm not worried. You think if the devil pushed Jesus off the temple, the angels wouldn't have caught him?"

"Mona, I'm serious."

"I'm serious, too! God's on our side! Who can be against us?"

Tracy looked at the cloudy water in her glass. "I wish I could believe that again."

Mona put her hand on Tracy's arm. "You just watch."

Tracy nodded but said nothing.

"Now," Mona continued, "what are you going to do next?"

"I'm still assigned to this murder case. I'm going to spill it all out to Duke. I'm going to tell him I don't trust Willis, I think he's doing a lousy job, and I think the whole thing is a sham. I don't think Duke knows anything for sure, but I'm going to tell him to try and find out. This is a miscarriage of justice just waiting to happen. I'm the only one standing in the way."

"Of the train."

"Right."

"Then you'll need to get your strength back. I'm going to run out to Ruby's and bring us back the thickest, fattiest, juiciest chili cheeseburgers on the face of the earth. How does that sound?"

"You want to know the truth, Mona?"

"Always."

"It sounds divine."

# CHAPTER FOURTEEN

WHEN TRACY WALKED INTO HER OFFICE the next morning—limping slightly but feeling much better—a symphony of colors was waiting for her on her desk. Flowers, balloons, and cards were strewn everywhere around the office. Even her office mate, Cheryl Itkin, had celebratory items displayed on her own desk.

"We wanted you to be overwhelmed," said Donna Pedones, who appeared at Tracy's door. Tracy whirled and saw not only her fellow deputy, but a whole slew of them crowding in the hallway.

"Wow," Tracy said. "Thanks, guys."

Another deputy, Hank Conroy, said, "We always suspected you were a flower child."

Without missing beat, Tracy said, "That's going back to *your* time Hank."

Everyone chuckled, then Cheryl Itkin squeezed through into the office. "So how are you, Trace, really?"

"A little like scrambled eggs, but starting to feel more like an omelet."

Hank said, "So how'd it happen? You get careless, have a little too much to drink, what?"

Cheryl spun on him. "Not now, Hank. Let her get her bearings, OK?" She started shooing the group with her arms. They backed away, with a few more words of welcome and encouragement. When they were all out, Cheryl closed the door.

Tracy said, "Was all this your idea?"

"We wanted you to know we're glad to have you back," Cheryl said.

"Thanks." Tracy hugged her, gingerly.

"If you need anything," Cheryl said, "or you want to talk about things, I'm here, OK?"

"Thanks. But I think what I want to do now is just get back to work. I have to catch up on the Murray case, see where things stand." For a moment, Cheryl said nothing, her face registering a mild state of surprise.

"What is it?" Tracy said.

"Didn't they tell you?"

"Who tell me what?"

"Oh, I'm sorry, Trace. I thought for sure you were notified."

"About what?"

"They've taken you off of Murray. Conroy has it now."

Tracy almost fell backward, like she'd been kicked in the head. Suddenly she burst past Cheryl. "I need to see Duke."

"I don't think he's—"

But Tracy was already in the hall. Anger and hurt welled inside her. Duke should have told her. She shouldn't have gotten the news secondhand. More, she shouldn't have been taken off the case at all. *I can still do the work. I need to do the work.*

When Tracy got to Duke's office she saw he was with Bob Campbell. They both looked up. Duke didn't look surprised. He seemed more resigned, as if he had expected her.

"Come in, Trace," Duke said, rising. "I wanted to come down for your little welcome back party, but Bob and I here—"

"Cheryl told me I'm off Murray," Tracy said.

Duke and Bob looked at each other. Bob said, "I was going to tell you this morning as soon as I could."

"We talked it over," said Duke, "and decided it was for the best."

Tracy ignored Duke's gesture for her to sit down. "Without consulting me?"

"Bob and I thought it best that the file not languish during your recovery."

"I'm recovered now."

"Maybe, but maybe not. We were doing this out of concern for your health, Tracy."

"Well I'm OK now. A little banged up, but nothing that should stop my career in its tracks. I won't let it, and I certainly won't let it interfere with the Murray case. Duke, I've poured my guts into this case."

Duke persisted. "I talked it over with Bob, and he agrees. Maybe you got a little too close on this one. Maybe we shouldn't have put you into this mess in the first place."

"Mess?"

"A murder case so soon."

"But you were the one who pushed me, Duke, remember? I was the one who tried to get out of it!"

"I know, I know. Maybe it was just bad decision making all around. In any event, the main thing is to keep our eyes on what's best. That's my job. And this is for the best, believe me."

"Bob," said Tracy, "would you mind leaving us alone for a minute?"

Bob Campbell shrugged as he looked at Duke. Duke nodded an OK at him. Just before leaving Bob put a hand on Tracy's shoulder and said, "Sorry, Tracy." It didn't sound 100 percent convincing.

"Tracy, let me explain," Duke said, sitting on the edge of his desk.

"You already have, Duke." Tracy realized she was standing firmly with her arms folded in front of her. It was what her father had called her "attitude of defiance" when she was a child.

"Not fully," Duke continued. "But first I want to know if you believe I'm on your side."

"My side?"

"Yes. That I have only your best interests at heart."

"Duke, I've always thought that, and I want to keep on thinking it. But you didn't even bother to talk to me. Why not?"

"You were hurt—"

"Not my mind. I was still capable of rendering an opinion. You visited me at the hospital what, three times?"

"Four. Once you were asleep."

"So why didn't you bring it up to me then?"

Duke looked at the ceiling. He paused like that for several moments, then said, "There are other reasons to take you off Murray. But I can't go into them now."

"Other reasons?"

"Yes."

"Don't leave me hanging, Duke. What are they?"

He looked her squarely in the eye. "Will you trust me on this?"

"Do the other reasons have to do with me?"

"No."

"With my professional abilities?"

Shaking his head, Duke said, "Nothing like that, believe me. I'm the head of an entire central trials unit. You know what that makes me? The ringmaster of a circus."

"And we're the clowns?"

"Maybe that wasn't an apt metaphor." Duke rubbed his eyes with the heels of his palms. "It's just that I have to take in all of the information that comes my way, evaluate it, and do what I think is best. Not just for the individual deputies, but for the office as well."

*There are other reasons to take you off Murray . . .*

"Duke, I'm still not following you." Tracy's arms were still folded.

"Then that's my fault."

"One question, if I may."

"Sure."

"Is it political?" Tracy expected Duke would shrug that question off, but instead his face changed suddenly. For a second, a look of something like terror flashed through his eyes. But then, with what must have been the experience of the seasoned trial lawyer, he resumed his normal expression.

"Why do you ask that?" he said.

"Because I know some of the pressures you can feel up here: the old office intrigue. Maybe that's what's going on."

Duke let out a sigh, sounding almost relieved. "So that's it. You think it's office politics, eh? Well, let me put it this way. You've got a keen sense of insight. That's what's going to make you one of the best trial lawyers out there. Now can we leave it at that?"

Tracy let her arms fall to her sides. She sat heavily in a chair and put her face in her hands. She felt tears trying to force their way out of her eyes. She held them back with her palms. Without looking up she said, "Duke, what am I going to do?"

"Tracy, what is it?"

"It's a nightmare, that's what it is. Duke, someone is trying to kill me. And that means my children are at risk, too. I don't know what to do. I can't go to the police. They have nothing to go on. And in the middle of all this, the only thing normal remaining in my life is my job—what I do, here in the office. But now that's ripped apart, too. You're taking me off a case that I care about. This is the second one in a row, too. Remember Sollomon?"

*Sollomon. The look he gave me in the courtroom . . .*

"I remember," Duke said. "That was so you could give all your attention to Murray."

"Which is now history, too. Duke, don't let my professional life get shredded up, too. I need something to anchor me."

Duke did not answer. Tracy was letting out more emotion in front of him than she ever had, but she didn't care. She was through holding back. "Duke, I need help. What am I going to do to protect my family?"

With a long breath, Duke stood and said, "I'll do what I can."

"Thanks. I guess that's all I can ask."

Embarrassed, Tracy stood and began to leave. Duke said, "Come to me anytime, Trace."

Tracy nodded, but without looking back she left the office. The walls of the hallway seemed particularly cold and close. More than anything, she wanted to be away from all of it—the office, the politics, the questions, even the people. There were only four people she wanted around her just now—her two children, Mona, and Rob Cavanaugh.

Where was Rob? And how much should she tell him?

As a trucker, Rand Johnson had a rule—never pick up hitchers unless they looked like they had an interesting story to tell. He knew he shouldn't help road strays at all; that would be the better course. You never knew if one of them was going to go nuts on you, pull a gun or a knife or something, and tell you your trucking days were over. Or maybe you'd get someone who'd talk about alien abductions all the way from Abilene to Albuquerque.

But Rand was a gambler of sorts, and he liked company. Seventy hours a week on the open road will do that to you. Having a companion to jaw with could take your mind off things, like the discs in your lower back screaming at you for all the sitting, or the leg cramps from working the rig, and the neck pains from having to keep an eye out for all the lousy drivers. Rand Johnson figured he'd risk the occasional oddball for the chance to have an interesting conversation. Otherwise, he was a prisoner in his own rig.

So when he saw the Indian at the on-ramp with his thumb out, just past the Denny's, Rand took a chance. He'd never picked up an Indian before. Maybe this one would have a story worth listening to. "Hop on up here, friend," Rand said. The Indian did, wordlessly. He slammed the door shut, hardly giving the driver so much as a nod. "Where you headed?"

"Los Angeles," the Indian said, in a quiet voice.

"Well, I'll get you most of the way, if you can stand it. The shocks on my baby ain't what they used to be." Rand Johnson let out a generous laugh, the kind that invites the other person to at least smile. But the Indian didn't smile, he looked straight ahead as Rand pulled his rig onto the highway.

Music sometimes did the trick. Rand flicked on his radio, already tuned to the coast-to-coast country station he favored. "You like music?" Rand asked.

The Indian shrugged.

"I like this station, has all the good songs. You get your classics, like Marty Robbins doin' 'Sometimes I'm Tempted,' or Grandpa Jones and 'T is for Texas.' Of course, you got your Garth Brookses and your Clint Blacks, or, if you want your music straight, your George Straights—" Rand paused and chuckled. "But you want to know the truth, I like the funny ones. Your Ray Stephenses, your Lewis Grizzards. You heard 'They Tore out My Heart and Stomped That Sucker Flat'? You heard that one?"

The Indian shook his head.

"How about 'No Toilet Paper in Russia'? Huh?"

No response.

"Well, you can have your Beethovens and your Mozarts. I mean, those fellas were good for their time. But two hundred years from now, when they look back to the great music of all time, they're not gonna look at guys in powdered wigs. No sir. They're gonna say it was ol' Waylon Jennings and Willie Nelson and Hank Williams who were the geniuses. Am I right, or am I right?"

The Indian looked out at the desert landscape rolling by.

"What about you?" Rand said. "Whatta you do, friend?"

After a short pause, Rand tried once more. "What is it you're lookin' for, pal?"

The Indian finally turned and looked at the truck driver. Rand noticed, even with a quick glance, that the Indian's eyes were deep and distant.

"You talk a lot," the Indian said.

"Well, I drive a lot, too, and most of it's with my yap shut. I pick up a few roadsters now and then and figure we can both pass the time with a little friendly conversation." Rand was getting a little hot now. "Is that too much to ask?"

"Why do you do this?" the Indian responded.

"What's that?"

"Why do you do what you do?"

"You mean drive a truck?" Rand said. "Because there's no other way I'm gonna make me fifty grand a year, maybe sixty if I'm lucky. Truckin's all I know. My daddy was a trucker, and I didn't go to no fancy school, so that's what I do."

"That's all?"

"What else is there?" Rand had never been pressed on his reasons for driving a truck before. He found this turn in the conversation a little strange. "I mean, you choose your work and you do it, right? I'm lucky I've got a means of income at all, considering the economy. I could be out lookin' for work instead of hauling freight and making a living."

"What is it you live for?"

Stranger still. But this Indian seemed perfectly serious. Well, if that's the way he wanted the conversation to go, that's the way it would head. "I don't know what you're gettin' at, pal," Rand said, "but if you want to know what I'm doin' this for, it's for me, my wife, and my daughter. I got a little girl. She's eight years old. I don't get to see her much, as you might guess. But I guess that's as good a reason as I've got. They're out in Sioux Falls, if you want to know."

The Indian said nothing, so Rand said, "What about you? I'll ask you the same thing. What's your reason?"

"I don't have any reasons," said the Indian.

"Come on now, everybody's got reasons. You got a family?"

"No."

"Friends?"

"No."

"Oh, come on, sure you got some friends."

The Indian was silent.

"You got a job?"

"Yes."

"Well, there you go. You got some income, some people you work with maybe. So you're just like all the rest of us, pretty much."

Then the Indian said something Rand would always remember. "I'm not like anyone," he said. It was really the way he said it that made an impression on Rand Johnson, sort of a hopelessness mixed with a sense of loss. It made Rand want to reach out and offer a hand, but he was at a loss for what to say. He was no psychiatrist, nor did he want to be.

There was something else in what was said that made Rand's neck hairs tingle. Something that signaled fear.

Rand Johnson got scared. Later, he would analyze the whole conversation, and conclude—along with some insights from his wife—that a man who had no friends and was in such isolation from the world was a dangerous man. His wife would ask him to please not pick up any more hitchhikers. Please, for her sake and the sake of their daughter, just don't do it.

And he didn't. After the strange Indian, whom he dropped off in Bakersfield, Rand Johnson never gave a ride to a hitcher again.

# CHAPTER FIFTEEN

MONA TAKATA decided her friend needed two things, in bunches. The first, of course, was prayer. Mona was going to hang Tracy's name on God's to-do list each and every day. That was a given.

But there was also something Mona could do herself. She was, after all, an investigator. True, she worked for the office of the district attorney, and as such she was given assignments. But she had a thing called spare time. Why not use it to hone her skills? It could only add to her effectiveness, she reasoned. Besides, Tracy needed this kind of help and, if last night was any indication, she couldn't trust anybody but Mona for it.

Tracy had called Mona late in the afternoon, telling her she had to talk. They picked a stretch of beach in Santa Monica, by the pier. That had been Mona's suggestion. She figured a little fresh sea air would help clear the mind.

Mona had been the first to arrive, pulling into the public parking lot two blocks away and walking to the leaning palm tree they both knew. The air was still warm, but the sea breeze made it bearable. Mona kept thinking of the song lyric, *Another perfect day. I love L. A.*

Tracy arrived a few minutes later. Mona could tell instantly something was wrong. Tracy explained the events of the day, beginning with being taken off the Murray case. It was apparent that Tracy had spent the rest of the day dealing with conflicting emotions, including various forms of anxiety.

From the way Tracy talked, Mona felt she was nearing a crisis point. Who could blame her, after what she'd been through? But it was what she said about Duke Gallegos that really threw Mona.

"There's something wrong there," Tracy said. "I think Duke is covering up something or protecting somebody."

Incredulous, Mona said, "You've got to be kidding! How do you know?"

"I don't," Tracy replied. "Not for sure. But something tells me that. And I'm scared, Mona. I'm out on a limb now, and it's being sawed off."

"Easy, girl."

"Who can I trust anymore? Who?"

"Now, here's the key question," Mona said. "Do you think there's a connection between the guy who ran you off the road and the Murray case?"

Tracy said, "I don't think so. I think the guy who wants to kill me is Howard Sollomon."

"Who's that?"

"A guy I was prosecuting. I got taken off his case to do Murray. He ended up walking under a plea bargain, one I was against."

"So you think that ticked him off enough to want to get you?"

"I think so."

"Based on?"

"Nothing, except the way he looked at me in court."

Mona sighed. "That's not much to go on. You could be totally off on this one."

Nodding, Tracy said, "I know that. But I have no other ideas. You see why it's so frustrating? And on top of all that I'm living like a fugitive. I worry each day somebody's going to take my kids, and I can't do anything about it but run away."

"Don't worry about it. Would you do one thing for me?"

"What's that?"

"Put it in God's hands."

Tracy tried to do just that. Mona held her hands and prayed. Tracy admitted it was tough, but she accepted the prayers.

Now, as she neared the studio, Mona thought, *It's my turn.*

The gate guard seemed impressed with Mona's badge. Official business. "Yes ma'am, and you can find the offices of Joseph Productions right over there."

The Joseph employees were still in mourning. Vonda, the receptionist and gofer, was red-eyed when Mona walked in and introduced herself. The twenty-something girl dabbed her nose with a Kleenex. "I still can't believe it," she said. "I just can't. I mean, he was just sitting here it seems like, talking about a hot new property . . ." She choked on her last words.

"Have you given a statement to the police?" Mona asked.

"Yes, sure."

"Was it an officer named Willis?"

"I think so. That sounds right."

"Were there any other officers with him?"

"No."

"Did he find anything significant?"

"I don't think so," Vonda said. "He seemed a little frustrated, too."

"Frustrated?"

"You know, like he expected there to be something. Oh, that reminds me . . ." She reached into her desk drawer and pulled out a gray, three-and-a-half-inch floppy diskette. "When he was here, he asked about correspondence files, but we don't have much. Sandy liked to use E-mail. I forgot about this, though." She handed the diskette to Mona. "Sandy had me starting an archive of memos, faxes, and E-mail and stuff. I just started on it. This is all I have. Would you give it to him?"

"Sure," said Mona.

The door flew open and a young, well-dressed man bounded in. He had dark, thick hair and eyes that seemed to dart everywhere. Energy waves seemed to emanate from him. "What's up?" he said to Vonda.

Vonda said, "This is . . . I'm sorry . . ."

"Mona Takata, district attorney's office."

The man stuck out a hand and sniffed. "Oh, hey, I'm Foster Gifford. I worked with Sandy. Exec-produced *Terror.* This is all such a gigantic bummer."

*Bummer?* Mona thought. *This is how New Hollywood execs refer to murder? With sixties slang?*

Gifford sniffed again. "Was Mr. Joseph into anything that could possibly have a gang connection?" Mona asked.

The executive stepped back and frowned heavily. His face got red, or had it been red all the time? "Gang connection?" he said indignantly. "What are you talking about?"

"I'm just asking," said Mona. "Was he working on a movie or anything about the inner city? Was he shmoozing and making deals at that premiere? Anything?"

"You got it wrong, lady. Sandy was just in the wrong place at the wrong time." He put his hands on his hips as if to challenge her.

"Well, you may be called as a witness," said Mona. She took out two business cards and handed them to Vonda and Gifford. "If anything occurs to you, let me know." The two employees looked at the cards, then at each other. Mona said, "And one more thing. This meeting we just had is confidential. Don't tell anybody about it."

"What about the police?" Vonda said.

"Even the police."

"That's entirely weird," Gifford said.

"Maybe," said Mona, "but sometimes life is that way. Tell you what. You just keep this to yourselves, and in a few months I'll bring you a story that will make you one great movie."

Gifford smiled and shook his head. "Another wannabe screenwriter, huh?"

"Hey, this is the land of opportunity, right?" And with that, Mona left.

It was now 2:30 in the afternoon. The air was sticky and hot. Mona didn't have anything on her immediate calendar, so she decided it was time to eat. Carney's was just over the hill on Ventura; she could order up a chili dog with lots of onions and a great, big Coke, and she could fire up her laptop and start some notes on the Murray case—angles of approach, people she might talk to.

And she could take a look at this disk.

Carney's was in that slow time between the lunch-hour office workers and the dinner-hour high schoolers. *Perfect,* Mona thought. Not enough crowd to be a hindrance. She could eat her cholesterol bomb in peace.

She took a booth in the back and set up her Compaq on the table. She flicked it on as the waitress came to take her order. It was a sign of the times, thought Mona, that the waitress didn't flinch about the laptop. Even out-of-work poets had them now, at least in L. A., and they liked to sip coffee into the wee hours as they suffered over their deathless verse.

Mona had no intentions of suffering. She just wanted to make some notes. She fetched the diskette out of the pocket of her purse and stuck it in the disk drive. Calling up a directory, she found only one file, marked "Corres.txt." She accessed it from her word processor.

Immediately she was mesmerized. Sandy Joseph loved to write. What he kept—through memos, notes, and letters—was something like a diary. A record of his life. It would have made fascinating reading if it were ever turned into a book, one of those tell-all Hollywood tomes that came out once a season. This had everything summer beach goers went for—rage, flights of fancy, ego gratification, jealousy, and indications of power. Sandy Joseph was nothing if not full of himself.

Perfect reading along with a chili dog. Mona ate it with a fork, so she could push "page down" with her left hand as she ate with the other. Especially fascinating were the items that Joseph had set apart with "* * *." These appeared to be almost stream-of-consciousness notes not meant for anyone but Sandy himself, true diary entries if you will. Things like—

"* * *Stallone is a jerk. He sat across from me and talked like Rocky Balboa, like he was heavyweight champ, and then said he wanted $25 million, pay or play—this from a guy whose last five movies have gone down the dumper. Hello? Anybody home?"

"* * *Party at Malibu and you-know-who walked in. He'd go broke if he had to pay taxes on what he thinks he's worth."

"* * *The one great rule in Hollywood: Nobody knows anything. That's what I have to deal with day in and day out."

Mona found herself caught up in these snippets. It was like getting right into the head of a leading Hollywood player, seeing what made him tick. She almost forgot this was a murder victim she was dealing with. It was just fascinating reading, and it only got more interesting. Sandy Joseph, she discovered, had a drug habit. Ice—smokable methamphetamine. And he was not shy about admitting it.

"* * *I'm managing to control the meth intake. Good for me. It's America. You should be able to do what you want."

That was unique. An in-your-face apologetic for drug use. Sandy Joseph was a very odd man. Why would he be so open about it, even in an electronic diary? As she read on, she came across the hint of an answer.

"* * *This one will blow Julia Phillips out of the water. If I ever decide to publish it, of course."

The reference was to a writer Mona remembered reading about. Phillips was a former movie producer and a coke addict. She was eventually drummed out of the Hollywood community and wrote a scathing book about the movie business. She had named names and repeated gossip, and she appropriately titled her book *You'll Never Eat Lunch in This Town Again*.

Was Sandy Joseph preparing a similar tell-all tale? Why not? There were easier ways to make a million bucks, but Mona couldn't think of any. Unless it was drug trafficking.

*Drug trafficking.*

The thought stuck in the back of her mind. Sandy Joseph looked to be a big-time user. Might he also be involved in sale and distribution? If so, maybe that would explain the gang connection. Joseph was killed by a gang-style hit because of something that went wrong with a major drug deal. Then it wouldn't be a case of robbery murder against O'Lean Murray. It would be something much larger than that.

Mona made a note to herself, then finished her hot dog. But a sense of unrest descended on her. Something wasn't right, though she couldn't quite put her finger on it. It was the same sort of feeling she'd had right before Tracy's accident.

She started praying right then and there.

---

Rob called just before she left the office. "Did I catch you at a bad time?"

"No, it's perfect," said Tracy. "I just wish you were here."

"I am. I'm down in San Diego, but I'll be in L. A. tonight. Any possibility?"

She looked at the ceiling and laughed. How had he known she needed to see him? She practically flew out of the office, and not even the freeway traffic could dampen her expectancy.

For three hours she played games and read books with her children at Mrs. Olivera's. When it was time for bed, she took the kids into the guest room where they slept, knelt with them, and held hands while they prayed. For the first time in a long time, Tracy felt God was listening.

Rob called from a cell phone around 10:30. Tracy gave him directions to Mrs. Olivera's, and ten minutes later he pulled up in a black

Cadillac. Alone. "Rented," he said as he opened the door for her. "Tonight, *I'm* the driver."

"So where shall we drive?" she asked.

"Around," he said. "We can just talk."

"Works for me," Tracy said as Rob pulled the car onto Ventura Boulevard heading west.

"So I was down there at the Old Town Mall," Rob said, "giving a respectable speech, my regular stumper, when someone who I'm sure was planted by the governor's team starts yelling. She's a woman, maybe in her late twenties, and she starts screaming at me, accusing me of being a hypocrite."

"Why?"

"Probably because she was paid to do it. But it came down to me holding myself up as a champion of family values, and I don't even have a family of my own."

"That's not relevant . . . hey, I sound like a lawyer!"

"At least you're on my side! But you know, the woman had a point. Where do I get off preaching family values? Tax cuts and child credits? Voucher plans and school reform? I don't have any of those concerns in my—quote, unquote—real life."

"You don't have to experience everything in order to reach policy decisions about it."

"Oh sure, but what we're talking about is the core of my campaign. That's the heart of the matter. I'm running on the foundations of God, family, and country. And for some reason this state is hearing me. Governor Tambor, it's true, has had trouble and a touch of scandal. So that's helped me in the polls. But as we get down toward crunch time, this could become a major theme of his attack ads."

"I don't think it'll play."

Rob reached over and took her hand. "Thanks. But there's something I'd like to ask you."

Quickly, Tracy said, "Would you mind if we pulled over for a minute?"

"Sure, what's wrong?"

"I just need to tell you something."

"Is it about the accident?"

Tracy looked at him. "It wasn't an accident."

Without further conversation, Rob pulled the car to the curb. Red light from a pizzeria sign filtered into the car as the faint sounds of Italian music, mixed with the stream of boulevard traffic, surrounded them. Rob turned toward her, drawing his right leg up on the seat. "What about this?"

"Someone ran me off the road."

Rob sat silently for a moment, running his index finger along the leather seat. Then he said, "Do you know who?"

"Not yet."

"This must be terrible for you."

"It is. I've had threatening communications and had to uproot my children. My boss has been acting strangely, and this case I've been on has been ripped away from me. And I don't know why. That's the worst part of all this. I just don't know why."

"Have you gone to the police?"

"There's nothing they can do, Rob. They can't put protection on me and my family, twenty-four hours a day. I'm just out there, exposed. I don't know when it could happen again."

Rob slid close to her and put his arm around her shoulder. Gently, he pulled her head to his chest. He stroked her hair, and for several minutes the only sounds she was aware of were her breathing and the unremitting blend of sounds from the street.

In his arms, she felt not so much a sense of peace but of strength. His strength. Her cheek rubbed against his soft cotton shirt, comforting her.

Finally, Rob whispered, "There's something I'd like to do."

"What's that?"

"I'd like to introduce you at my next campaign stop."

Tracy sat up and looked at him. "Me? What for?"

"As my fiancée."

Her breath left her. She inhaled deeply. "Rob, this is happening so fast."

"This is the nineties, isn't it?"

"We hardly know each other."

"I know enough. And it's just an engagement. We'll have plenty of time to make up the difference. Say yes."

"I . . ."

"Will you?"

"Rob, listen. Every part of me is crying out to say yes."

"That's a good sign."

"But the first thing I have to look out for is my kids. They'll need time to get to know you. I can't just announce this decision to them."

"They're great kids."

"Do you understand about that? It'll take time."

"I can give you that time."

"What do you mean?"

"You said yourself you're in a dangerous situation here, right? You have your kids staying with someone else, and you don't know what might happen next. You feel vulnerable."

"Yes."

"I have an answer. Take your kids and come up to my house at Lake Tahoe."

Tracy sat upright. With the streetlights behind him, Tracy could only make out Rob's silhouette. "I'm not sure I'm getting this. You have a house at Lake Tahoe?"

"I guess I should say *on* Lake Tahoe. And it's more of a villa than a house. It's the place I go to escape the rigors of public life. It's beautiful, Tracy, right there in the pine trees, with a view of the lake that will make you sing hosannas to creation."

Tracy put her hand up in front of her. "Wait a minute. You're proposing that I leave my job and go up to your house to live with you?"

"Not *with* me. Not yet at least. I'm out on the road. The house will be yours. I only have a housekeeper and groundskeeper up there. It will be your safe haven, until we can clear up this mess you're in. But when I come up we'll be able to spend time together. I'll be able to get to know your kids. And then, when the time is right, we'll get married. I love you, Tracy. I want you to be my wife."

For some odd reason, a clip from the movie *The Wizard of Oz* flashed through Tracy's mind. It made her laugh.

"What's funny?" Rob said.

"I just had a hilarious thought," Tracy said.

"What?"

*"Surrender, Dorothy."*

Rob slipped his hand behind Tracy's neck and pulled her to him. He kissed her, softly, and she melted into the kiss.

"Can I take that as a yes?" Rob asked.

"Can I think about it?"

"No."

"Then you can take it as a yes."

Rob started the car up again and pulled back onto the street. An odd mixture of peace, excitement, and uncertainty rushed through Tracy. The decision she had just made was huge. She was giving up her professional career, at least for the time being, and committing herself to a man she barely knew. Yet. But the decision had been made as much for her children as for herself. She didn't want this restlessness for them anymore.

She put her head back on the seat as Rob drove on. Closing her eyes, she voiced a silent prayer. *This is from you, isn't it, Lord?* There was no sense of an answer, so she prayed again. *Help my unbelief.*

At that moment Rob Cavanaugh took her hand again. As they drove further into the night, he said, "I'm going to make you a very happy woman."

# CHAPTER SIXTEEN

DUKE GALLEGOS looked at himself in the mirror for a long time. For several moments it seemed he did not know the face that was reflecting back at him. Who was this person? Where had he come from? How had he gotten into my body? What were those accusations written all over his face? It was strange, and frightening.

An old episode of "The Twilight Zone" came into his mind. It had been one of his favorite shows as a teenager, the one show he never missed. It had been years since he'd seen a rerun, but he remembered most of the episodes anyway. And the one he remembered now was the one about the small-time hood in the cheap hotel room, who looks in the mirror and thinks he sees himself, but, instead, it's another self trying to get out. He spends the whole episode going around and around with this other self, until finally they switch places.

*Is that what's going on? Is that another self I'm looking at? Which one is the right one? Which one deserves to "live"?*

As he continued to stare at his own reflection, Duke's mind flashed to another memory. This time it was his swearing-in as a deputy district attorney, at the ripe old age of twenty-three. His parents were sitting in the courtroom where the ceremony took place, beaming with pride. They'd scraped and sacrificed to put their boy through college, then law school, and now here he was, embarking on a great career.

That had been one wonderful day. They'd all gone out to eat after that—his parents, his sister Maggie and her husband, and a couple of neighbors from across the street. A big old Italian meal at his dad's favorite restaurant, Rocco's, where the food was authentic and the waiters all knew your name.

Then, after all the toasting and wine and food, after all the expressions of pride and good luck, there was one moment that stood out for Duke above all the rest. The other family members were chatting among themselves when his father turned to him and placed his strong, calloused hand on the back of his neck. "Son," he said simply, "I'm very proud to be your father. You've brought honor to the family."

*Honor to the family.*

Duke looked away from the mirror. He ran some water and splashed his face. "So how about it, big boy?" Duke said to himself. "What are you gonna do now?"

"Duke, are you all right?" His wife's voice. "You've been in the bathroom for twenty minutes." *Yeah, I'm all right, like a fly in a web all right.*

"I'm fine," Duke answered. "I'll be out in a minute." And with one last glance at himself, he thought, *Good going, big boy. You even get to lie to your wife. Honor to the family, huh?*

When he emerged from the bathroom, Evelyn was waiting with a fresh cup of coffee. "I figure you'll need this tonight," she said. "How late do you suppose you'll be?"

Duke took the cup. "Thanks, honey. You never know with these strategy sessions."

"The law is a jealous mistress, huh?"

"You knew that when you married me."

"I wouldn't have it any other way." She kissed her husband's cheek, then drew back. "Is something wrong?"

"Just normal stuff . . ."

"You sure?"

Duke marveled at how well his wife knew him. He looked into her eyes and almost burst out screaming. His head felt like it was in an industrial vice, with the gears slowly turning. "Don't worry, honey," he said. "Everything's going to be all right."

He took a long sip of the coffee, then handed the mug back to Evelyn. He leaned down and gave her a long, lingering kiss on the mouth.

"Wow," she said. "That was a good one."

"Don't wait up for me."

"You know I will."

The thought of his wife waiting for him to come home stayed with Duke, even through the rain. A storm had swept through the Los Angeles basin, and it was really coming down. The old wiper blades on his Honda Civic could hardly keep up. He could see no more than fifty feet ahead, the refracted lights of the other cars moving in kaleidoscopic fashion around him. Straight ahead was a dark void, an urban black hole.

He reached Sunset and turned toward the ocean. Soon he'd be there, but he thought for a moment of just driving on. Straight ahead, until there was no more road. Boom, into the Pacific. Then it would all be over.

Except it wouldn't be, not for the ones he'd leave behind.

Evelyn.

Tracy.

He had to make it right. He stayed with the twists and turns, all the way to the Palisades—some of the most expensive real estate in the world. Then he spotted the place on the cliff, a darker shadow than the dark of the storm, rising into the night sky.

He reached the huge gate he had seen on two previous occasions, rolled down the window, and pressed the security button.

"Yes?" said a statical voice.

"Gallegos."

The gate slowly rolled open. Duke advanced up the long drive, dim lights from the house poking through the murk. He sensed the gate closing behind him, like in some old horror movie.

*Locked in. Have a pleasant night.*

Lefferts stood on the front porch—a porch the size of most garages—holding an umbrella. Duke pulled his Civic up to the curb. He jumped out and ran up to the door.

"Wipe your feet," Lefferts said.

"And a good evening to you, too," said Duke, wiping his feet on a mat that said, "Casa de Kohlbert" on it. *How quaint,* thought Duke. *Just like real folks.* The mansion was done up Spanish style, all Coronado tile and adobe. Nothing had changed since Duke had been here the last time.

"This way," Lefferts said.

Duke followed the nervous man through the portico, out through some double doors and into the breezeway. The smell of the sea mixed with the wind and rain. Lefferts put up his umbrella. He didn't offer it to Duke. He only picked up his pace. Duke quickened his. The guest house windows surrendered somber light. Lefferts opened the door and said to Duke, "The feet." Duke stepped in and onto a large mat, wiping his feet once more.

"Ah, the district attorney has arrived," a voice said from the living room. The place was dimly lit with three shaded lamps. Duke recognized the voice of Sherman Kohlbert. Followed by Lefferts, Duke stepped to the center of the room. Kohlbert, in casual attire, relaxed in an easy chair next to the fireplace. A small fire crackled, flashing orange light on the side of Kohlbert's face. In his right hand, Kohlbert held a glass with ice and what looked to Duke like scotch.

"Sit down, Duke," said Kohlbert. "Randall, bring Mr. Gallegos a drink, will you?"

"Not for me," said Duke. To Kohlbert's left, sitting with his head slightly bowed, was Stan Willis. Next to Willis, on the sofa, was a man Gallegos did not recognize.

"Not even a soda?" Kohlbert said.

"Nothing."

"Want to keep the head clear, is that it?"

"Something like that."

"That's good. For the most part, that's very good. But this is a social occasion. You ought to loosen up a little bit."

From behind him Lefferts said, "Have a seat." It was more an order than a request. Duke sat down on a soft, Spanish design chair.

"Good," Kohlbert said. "Then we're all here. I thought it was time we had a little face-to-face, because things seem to have gotten a little, well, sloppy—and unpredictable. I don't like unpredictability. I like to know who's going to win, whether it's Mike Tyson or the New York Yankees or the next governor of the great state of California. And right now we need to tighten up some of the loose ends."

Kohlbert paused, taking a sip of his drink. No one spoke. Duke glanced at the man he didn't recognize. He was obviously fit, sharply dressed, and seemed to be one of those people with an attention to detail. His expression said he was attuned to everything going on in the room. For a brief instant, he made eye contact with Duke. *Eyes like little daggers*, Duke thought.

"Now," Kohlbert continued, "for starters, I'm sure we all know about the little incident concerning Tracy Shepherd."

Duke shot a glance immediately back at Kohlbert, who returned the stare. "Especially you, Duke."

"Yes," Duke said. "I know all about it."

"You sound a little ticked off."

"I am."

The others in the room looked at Duke, who said, "You went too far on that one, Kohlbert. What makes you think you can go around knocking off my people? We're on the side of the law, and the law tends to take a dim view about murdering its own."

Through the odd dance of the firelight Duke discerned a slight smile on Kohlbert's face. "Is that so?" Kohlbert said.

"Yeah, that's so," said Duke, sounding to himself like a kid on a playground standing up to the school bully. Only this wasn't any school. The bully owned the playground and everybody in it.

"Then it would come as a shock," Kohlbert said, "if the law didn't give a rip about this little incident."

"What are you talking about?"

"That the law itself might have been behind the attempt at taking Ms. Shepherd out of the picture."

What was he getting at? Duke didn't know, though he picked up a tone of playfulness in Kohlbert's voice. Suddenly the connection was made. Duke stood up and looked at Willis. "You scum!" Willis's head bobbed up. He pointed his finger directly at Duke. "Don't get in my face, Duke, I'm warning you."

"You're warning *me?*"

The man standing behind Willis snorted in disgust, then Kohlbert said, "All right, guys. The both of you knock it off. We're here for business. Sit down, Duke." Duke, his eyes still on Stan Willis, slowly lowered himself back into his chair.

"That's better," said Kohlbert. "I've already made my views known about this incident to Detective Willis. It was a rogue move, and those kinds of things I won't put up with. Not at this point in the story." Duke watched Willis look back at the floor.

"See," said Kohlbert, "we're very close—all of us—to realizing our goals. That should make all of you see how important this stage is; and at this point I'd like us all to hear from Terrence Hagan who has, I think, some good news."

The man Duke did not recognize stepped closer to the fireplace, next to Kohlbert's chair. "Gentlemen, the campaign is going better than any of us could have hoped. The latest polls show Rob Cavanaugh leading Governor Tambor by seven percentage points. That's *seven*."

"You can see we have the right man for the job," Kohlbert said.

"Who is he?" said Duke.

"I beg your pardon?"

Duke came right back. "Who is this guy? He wasn't around when this all got started."

"Oh, he was around," said Kohlbert. "It just wasn't in our interest for you to know about him then."

Hagan glared at Duke while continuing. "But we still have two months before the election, so we don't need any bumps along the way. Unfortunately, this stupid attempt on Shepherd's life could turn into a huge bump. We've got to smooth it out."

A cold sweat began to form on Duke's forehead. "What does he mean, smooth it out?"

Kohlbert said, "Tell him, Terrence."

"We've simply got to finish what was begun," said Hagan. He looked at Duke, daring to be challenged.

"Finish?" said Duke.

Kohlbert said, "Tommy."

From the dark shadows at the far end of the room Duke saw something shift. There was someone else present, who had been there all along. Now the figure moved, like a black ghost, into the firelight. It was a man dressed in a flannel shirt and blue jeans. Duke thought he could make out long, black hair in some sort of ponytail. The man stepped up next to Terrence Hagan.

"This is Tommy Bear Paw," said Sherman Kohlbert. "Someone I am very proud of. He's that rare breed of professional these days who is actually competent. Does his job, does it well. He was the one who took care of our movie producer friend. We'll call him the muscle because I like those old, Jimmy Cagney type of words."

Duke looked at the face of the Indian. Tiny orange flames flickered in the dark eyes, which stared back at Duke with a dead emptiness. So he was the one who iced Sandy Joseph. Duke had always wondered who it had been. Willis wouldn't tell him. Now he knew. Duke stood up. "No," he said. "I won't allow it."

For a moment the only sound in the room was the snapping of the fire. Hagan and Duke faced each other like two fighters in opposite corners of the ring.

"Sit down, Duke," said Sherman Kohlbert.

"I don't feel like sitting down."

"So what you're saying is you no longer want to follow my . . . advice?"

"Take it any way you want. I'm through with this. This is a joke."

"Then why am I not laughing?" said Kohlbert, setting his drink down and rising. He was not as tall as Duke, nor as strong, but Duke felt fear. When it came to raw power, the prosecutor knew he was no match for Sherman Kohlbert. He only wished now he had never met the man.

Kohlbert took two steps toward Duke, who felt surrounded. Lefferts behind him, Hagan on one side, Kohlbert on the other, and the Indian on the perimeter. Only Stan Willis was still sitting down. Kohlbert said, "There's no stopping things now, Duke. You should know that."

"I don't want anything to happen to her," Duke said. He noticed his voice wavering, and hated himself for it. "She's completely innocent."

"She was your pick, if you'll remember," Kohlbert said. "You said she wouldn't ask any questions, she'd just do her job, she'd follow the manual. But she didn't, and for that I hold you personally responsible. Besides, what's one less prosecutor in Los Angeles? She won't be missed."

"Listen to me," Duke said. "I can talk to her. I can give you my assurance she won't ask any more questions. I know her. She respects me. I can handle it."

"Too late," said Kohlbert.

"She won't do anything else, I promise you."

"Your promises are meaningless to me. I look at results."

"I want out," Duke said. "Now."

"That's not an option," Kohlbert said. "You are going to become the attorney general of this great state. You are going to get the respect you deserve. When you were passed over for the central director's job you told me it was political, and you were bitter, and you didn't know what to do about it. Well, I told you what you could do, and you threw in with me. It was the right move."

"You've got it all packaged up nicely, don't you? You're going to have a governor in your pocket."

"*And* an attorney general. See, it wouldn't be good for NyDex Systems to be made, well, uncomfortable in the years ahead. Not if we're going to make a run at Microsoft. That's where you come in, Duke. Cavanaugh will appoint you the day after he's sworn into office. That's what you always wanted, isn't it?"

Duke looked at the floor. "I want her left out of this."

Kohlbert sighed impatiently. "The decision's been made. I assume you'll follow along, as always."

Duke knew then he would have to follow. He had cast his lot with Kohlbert, knowing there might be some unpleasantness somewhere. But he'd never thought, in his wildest imaginings, that it would come to this. The cold-blooded killing of an innocent deputy district attorney, one who had never done an intentional wrong in her life, and he had put her in that position. But he would get her out. Somehow, he was going to get her out. Even if it meant giving himself up.

. . . *honor to the family* . . .

It would take deception, but by now he could handle that. He had been practicing it for some time.

"All right," Duke said. "But make it quick and painless."

The Indian looked at Duke, who thought he saw a shimmer of emotion on the hit man's face—something like disgust.

"Good," said Kohlbert. "That's a wise choice, Duke. And forget about the messy details, will you? That's my department. Now let's be clear on what's going to happen in the next two months . . ."

For the next hour, Duke was hardly aware of the time or what was said. He heard himself grunting answers, but didn't really know why. He thought, off and on, about suicide. But each time he rejected it. Tracy still needed his help.

When the meeting was finally over, Lefferts walked Duke back through the house to his car. The rain had subsided a little but was still coming down. This time, Duke didn't care if he got wet. He walked slowly through the rain.

Lefferts said nothing as Duke got in his car and drove back down the long driveway. The gate swung open, and Duke began his descent from the estate. It felt like he was descending into his own grave.

# CHAPTER SEVENTEEN

"SANDY JOSEPH was into drugs."

Tracy frowned. "How big?"

"Big," said Mona. They were huddled in the back of El Toro, a hole-in-the-wall Mexican restaurant Mona knew in the East Valley. If ever there was a place to get away from it all, this was it. "I'm thinking he could have been a major dealer."

"Sandy Joseph? Why?"

Leaning in, Mona said, "I'll tell you why. Did you know Sandy Joseph was about to be kicked off the movie lot?"

Tracy shook her head.

"Yeah. I did a little research. According to stories in *Variety* and the *Hollywood Reporter*, Sandy Joseph Productions was not going to have its deal renewed with the studio. That means he would have been out on the street looking for space and, more important, money to finance his pictures."

"So you think his murder may have been drug related?"

Mona took a tortilla chip and clipped off a corner with her teeth. "I didn't just ride in on a load of burritos," she said. "Yeah, it's a definite possibility."

"But I don't think O'Lean Murray is a gang member, let alone involved in drugs. It doesn't make sense."

"Unless O'Lean is being set up."

"Set up?"

"Yeah. It's not like they're going after the wrong guy. It's that somebody put the finger on the wrong guy *on purpose*."

Tracy shook her head. For some reason, that possibility had never crossed her mind. It was too much like some low-budget movie. But there it was, and it explained a lot of things. It also raised a terrible possibility.

"That means," Tracy said, "that Willis himself might be involved in this."

Mona raised her eyebrows.

Tracy felt like her face was suddenly white, as if all the blood had rushed to her rapidly beating heart. "Could Duke be involved in this, too?"

"It's just a theory," Mona said quickly.

"But it's a solid one. I just can't believe it. Why would Duke—" Tracy looked at the table and again shook her head.

"Let me say it again," said Mona. "It's just a theory."

"I'm getting out."

Mona stopped mid-chip. "What?"

"I'm leaving town."

"What are you talking about? Vacation? What?"

"No, Rob Cavanaugh has offered to put me up at his place at Lake Tahoe."

"Tahoe!"

"And I'll take the kids with me. I'll be able to get out of this whole mess."

Mona acted like she'd been hit in the chest. "Just like that?"

Sliding her fingers up and down her water glass, Tracy said, "Just like that. He's asked me to marry him, and I'm going to do it. This will be a chance to start all over, in a new place."

"But you hardly know the guy!"

"But everything points in the right direction. He's gentle, understanding, handsome—"

"Is he a Christian?"

"I think so."

"You think? Babe, that's the most important part. You can't get yoked to an unbeliever, no matter how good his resumé—or his bank account."

"I don't care about his bank account, Mona. What is this? The third degree?"

"Maybe," said Mona. "I just don't want you to make a mistake simply because you've got the heat on you."

"It's still a good move," said Tracy. "I've had it, and the most important thing is how it's affecting the kids. I've got to think about that more than anything else."

Mona laid another chip in the salsa. "We can beat this thing, Tracy."

"And we will. This is just another way to do it."

"So, when are you leaving?"

"Soon."

"Is this going to be our last meal together?"

Tracy put her hand on her friend's arm. "Only for a little while, until things clear up."

Mona nodded. "Then let's pig out."

---

The Santa Ana winds had just arrived, bringing a hot snap to the valley air for the first time in months. It felt good to Tommy Bear Paw. Like home, when he was a boy. The high desert often felt like this in the fall.

And with the winds came the brush fires. A heavy blaze was raging to the west, maybe in the luxury section of Calabasas, sending up a huge plume of brown smoke with an orange nimbus from the setting sun. He watched it for awhile from the open Jeep and thought of the signals of smoke his grandfather had showed him once, Manzanita branches and pine needles making the billows, and a woolen blanket controlling intervals. That had been a long time ago.

There was no activity at the restaurant across the street. He figured it would be another half hour or so. He looked back at the smoke, filling the sky like a blot of spattered ink. Or blood. The spattering was something he thought he had gotten used to. Blood never made a big impression on him. It had, in some odd way, been comforting. The warmth of it. The strength of it. Seeing it issue forth from the hunted was what made the hunt a victory. And he'd had many victories.

This last one, though, had troubled him. The elements had been the same, but the aftertaste was not. There had always been a sense of quiet after a kill. It never lasted very long, but it was strangely comforting—like something you expected. That's what was missing now. There was no quiet. Instead, there was a sense almost of rage. But rage at what?

He had felt, for the first time in a long time, like he wanted to scream. What was it? Why now?

In a way he was disgusted with himself. As he sat there, waiting and watching, he was being so . . . self-reflective—like all of the people he had grown up despising. The whites who lived in the cities, with their houses and BMWs, whose biggest problem in life was deciding what kind of espresso to order in the morning. These were the kind of people who sat around and wondered why their lives were so meaningless. They paid their head doctors a fortune in order to lie down and talk for an hour.

Now he was like them, looking for meaning.

Why now? Was it the people he worked for? He had grown accustomed to not asking questions. When people paid you, you did the job. You didn't ask the reason why. You didn't care what they looked like or believed in.

Only, this time he did seem to care. Somewhere inside himself, he was sickened by these people—these people who turned on themselves—and now they had dispatched him to kill this woman. Maybe that was it. He had never killed a woman before.

Never.

Warriors only killed other warriors; the women did not fight. His own woman had not been a fighter. That might have been what killed her. If she had only had more fight in her, she could have done something. When he'd gotten back from the Gulf, it was too late to find out what that might have been. Her brain was already eaten away, and the doctors said there was nothing they could do. She was in a coma and couldn't see him.

That was the beginning of the darkness.

Darkness was . . . quiet. He had lived in that quiet. Only now that quiet was being disturbed by thoughts.

*A woman is not a warrior. What were these men afraid of?*

Bear Paw shook his head, as if the shaking would get rid of the thoughts. This was no time to think. He would do the job. He would take the money, as he always did. He would not ask questions.

He would hunt.

Driving to Mrs. Olivera's, Tracy became more convinced that Tahoe was the right thing to do. She was a rack of nerves on the streets. Every set of headlights that came up behind her reminded her of what had happened. Like people after an earthquake who get anxious with each aftershock, Tracy would feel her skin tingle every time she saw a car in her rearview mirror.

*It is the right time to leave,* she thought. The tickets were in her purse, hand delivered by a courier from Rob's local campaign office. Tomorrow night. She and the kids would have all day to pack their essentials. Mrs. Olivera would keep track of the house until everything could be moved. Little details like that could wait.

Some big details, though, would take some creative handling. Like O'Lean Murray. He was innocent, she was quite sure, but what could she do? There had to be something, and she would think of it. This wasn't over.

And another detail kept hammering in her head: Duke. She could not believe that Duke Gallegos could have anything to do with Mona's theory . . . if it turned out to be correct. How could he?

She slowed to a stop at the light. Instinctively, she checked her mirror. Four or five cars were behind her. That's when she made her decision.

Taking a left instead of a right, she got on the freeway and headed toward Pasadena.

Tommy Bear Paw eased onto the freeway and wondered where she was going. This was not the way to her house, according to the information he'd been given. This had the look of instinct. The hunted had the instinct to survive. He sensed it. It was almost as if he could feel her insides churning with the life force.

Again, he felt odd. He hadn't sensed this before in those he hunted, and one more thing he felt—a very small, but very real sense of respect. He followed her for several miles, and then it struck him where she was going. Now that was a twist. It would be fascinating to watch. How would she react when she found out?

There was no hurry now. The job could be done at any time. He wanted to see where this trail would lead.

Tracy had been here only twice before, the last time for an office party in January—sort of a kick-off-the-New-Year-right party at the boss's house. It wasn't hard to find, though. There were only major cross streets to remember.

The house was a Victorian restoration, a nice place in a well-manicured neighborhood. Duke said he'd been there almost ten years. A bargain, he said, and he loved spending weekends messing around with it.

The street was lighted with the old-fashioned lampposts, part of what made this a quaint place to live. Some of Pasadena was in a time warp. A movie about the fifties could be shot here. It gave off a sense of peace and quiet. That was good. If she was going to give it one more try with Duke, she'd rely on that calm.

As Tracy pulled up to the curb across the street, she saw the police cars in the driveway and the yellow tape across the front door of the house. A small group of neighbors, some standing in robes and slippers, peppered the front lawns along the street.

She jumped out and ran to the open front door, not noticing the uniformed officer on the porch who stepped in her way and scared her to death.

"Hold on," he said. "You can't go in there."

Tracy tried to regain composure. "I'm Tracy Shepherd, D. A.'s office. What's going on?"

"You have some ID?"

"My purse, in my car."

"I'm sorry, but you'll have to—"

A voice broke in. "Tracy! Oh my God, Tracy!"

It was Evelyn Gallegos. Her eyes were red-rimmed and moist. She looked like she had been awake for forty hours straight, operating only on raw nerves and memory. Evelyn put her arms out and Tracy came to her, stopping at the artificial tape barrier. "It's Duke," Evelyn whispered, tears beginning to stream down her face. "Killed . . ."

"No . . ."

"Right here!" With a wail, Evelyn Gallegos collapsed across the police tape and into Tracy's arms.

---

In the night darkness, with the house and police the center of attention, no one would see him. This would be an easy one. He already knew the layout, of course, and with eyes still sharp, he watched the commotion, the police, the spectators, and the two women in the doorway.

Behind him a dog barked. He looked and saw it was a setter, one who was making it plain he did not like his domain intruded upon. Tommy Bear Paw spoke to him, low and soothing. *One animal to another,* he thought.

The dog stopped barking.

Tracy spent the next two hours at the Gallegos home. She answered questions for the investigator, someone from the Pasadena local, and called Mrs. Olivera's. She spoke to each of the kids, too, and neither one was happy about not seeing their mother before bedtime. She promised them both an exciting adventure. They would be going on a trip, on a plane. That made them happy.

Evelyn turned down a sedative and refused to leave the room where her husband's body had been found. As Tracy listened to her and the cops, bits and pieces of the story began to fall into place.

Duke had apparently come home midafternoon. He was in an agitated state, but not anything out of the ordinary. He did this sometimes on Fridays, knocking off early. He'd get away, come home, have lunch, maybe catch a nap. At times like this, Evelyn's habit was not to question him too much—twenty-three years of marriage had taught her that never worked—but to make him a nice lunch and tune in CNN for him. It was funny, she would remark later, how the bad news never seemed to make his moods worse.

This particular afternoon he didn't want CNN. For some reason he wanted to be alone in the study and have a beer. There was no beer on hand, but Evelyn said she'd be happy to stop off at Lucky's on her way back from the Chamber and bring some back.

Evelyn worked at the Pasadena Chamber of Commerce as a volunteer, helping to answer the mail. She liked to keep some of the crazy letters and bring them back to the house for Duke to read. It cheered him up, and she loved it when he laughed.

She stayed at the Chamber until 4:30, and then drove to Lucky's Market. The lines were long. By the time Evelyn got out with Duke's beer and a couple of plastic bags with sundry items she'd nabbed along the way, it was going on six o'clock.

She drove back and entered the house through the garage door. She didn't call out to Duke to come give her a hand with the groceries this time. She wanted to surprise him by bringing him a cold one. She had put a glass mug in the freezer before she left, and now pulled it out, all white and frosty. She popped the top off a bottled Budweiser and carefully poured it into the glass.

Holding the mug handle so none of the frost would be disturbed, Evelyn Gallegos walked softly toward the study. The door was open. She went right in. What she saw paralyzed her. Her hands went limp. The glass of beer fell and shattered on the floor.

Her husband was slumped in his chair, almost as if he had fallen asleep, his head thrown back. But this was not sleep. An ugly accumulation of blood covered his entire chest, as if some one had thrown a bucket of red paint on him.

Things were a blur from that point on. She managed to call 9-1-1, and the police arrived shortly thereafter. Her house became a crime scene, secured and gawked at, while inside she became a prisoner of the nightmare.

---

Tracy kept trying to make the jumble of events cohere into some logical shape. Duke murdered, but why? The police were treating it as a robbery since several items of value—Duke's own wallet, some antique watches, and an ivory statuette—were missing. But this scenario wasn't without problems. Nothing in the bedroom, where Evelyn kept her jewelry, was disturbed.

It could have been that the robber was surprised to find someone home. The house may have been cased, and Duke's being home in the afternoon wasn't anticipated.

Yet too many things were swirling around in close proximity—Joseph's drug dealings, the gang connection, and Willis's behavior. Was there some larger web she wasn't seeing?

Was there some connection between the attempt on her own life and Duke's murder? Or was all this just circumstantial, weak links in a perfectly innocent chain? No. This was all too close for coincidence. But who did that implicate? Willis? Or someone else, working with him?

Her next thought was the FBI. *Turn the whole thing over to the feds.* Get up to Lake Tahoe and marry Rob Cavanaugh and start life all over again.

That sounded very, very good.

# CHAPTER EIGHTEEN

AS SHE SAT IN HER CAR, watching the small office complex across Ventura Boulevard, Mona Takata felt like Kinsey Millhone, the detective character in Sue Grafton's series of novels. This was real, live, private investigator-type work, the kind of stuff Mona really wanted to do. There was more freedom here, and you were as good as your wits. Mona liked matching wits with people.

Now she was waiting to see where that slime bucket Howard Sollomon would go next. She didn't know what she was going to do when she found out, but part of the P. I. game was thinking on the run. She had a vague notion she'd confront him with the evidence and just watch his expression. Expressions were not evidence in a court of law. But out on the street, when you're sizing up a suspect, they could be very useful indeed. Mona always thought she was pretty good at judging books by their cover—especially when she jammed surprising information in the book's face.

She also realized this P.I. work was a lot of sitting. She'd been here since 10:15, and now it was past noon. Soon Sollomon would hit the street looking for lunch. There were several possibilities—a KFC, a local deli, a hot dog stand called Big Frank's, Abner's Sub Shop, and Denny's—all within easy walking distance. If he decided to get ambitious, he could find half a dozen more places east or west. Wherever he landed she'd land with him.

Mona flicked on the car radio and listened to the news. They were into the sports report—the Dodgers were heading for the playoffs—so the news about Duke's murder was probably past. She'd heard about it late last night, when another investigator from the office called her. Shock was not the word to describe how she felt. It was fear, too. Fear that something bad was reaching out from the darkness of whatever shadow Duke was in, reaching out for her friend Tracy.

This made it doubly important to find out what Sollomon knew. If he was the guy with the threats, there could be a connection. Her background check revealed that he worked in an escrow office, was still living with his girlfriend and daughter, and that he had more than a bit of a drinking problem. He'd never taken any treatment for it.

He'd gotten off the previous charge with two years' probation. He walked right out of the courtroom without doing any time. Tracy kept mentioning this case. It really bothered her, but that was life in the big city.

So Sollomon was a pipe bomb ready to explode at any time. Mona was ready for that possibility, with a nice little can of pepper spray that fit in the palm of her hand.

Sports moved on to traffic and weather. They were just getting around to the weekend forecast when Howard Sollomon exited the glass double doors of the office building and started walking east on Ventura. Grabbing her purse, a file folder, and her pepper spray, Mona Takata zipped out of her car, dropped a quarter into the meter, and followed Sollomon from the other side of the street.

He wasn't hard to keep up with. He didn't walk so much as stroll. It was one of those gaits a macho dude takes on, the I-own-the-street kind of swagger usually associated with skinhead teenagers or gangbangers. Sollomon looked almost funny—a clean-cut guy close to thirty years old who was walking like some prize peacock looking for premium birdseed.

At the cross street, Mona and Howard both waited for the light to change, then crossed at the same pace. Howard Sollomon turned into the little sub shop. Mona waited for the light to change again, then crossed the boulevard and walked straight into the restaurant.

It was pretty full. All the tables—maybe six in all—were taken, with several more patrons eating at the counter. Three people stood in the ordering line. A large, older guy in a white apron was whipping up submarine sandwiches as fast as his sausage-like fingers would allow.

Sollomon was eyeing the menu above the counter. Mona watched carefully, trying to decide if she should approach him now, with the element of surprise, or let him order his food and sort of ease into it. A moment later, the decision was made for her.

Howard Sollomon turned and looked Mona straight in the eye. Mona stared back, making no attempt to look innocent. What was the point? He had "made" her. She walked right up to him, more nervous than she thought she'd be, and said, "Is your name Howard Sollomon?" The man showed no sign of surprise or shock. His eyes were dark and almost dead. The word that came to Mona's mind at once was *lost*.

"Who are you?"

"Mona Takata, investigator."

"Who hired you?"

"I'd like to ask you a question—"

"You gonna serve papers on me?"

Mona opened up the file folder in her hand and pulled out the note with the crude, crayon message, *You're next,* written on it. "We have reason to believe that you sent this note to a deputy district attorney, Mr. Sollomon." She watched his expression.

Sollomon looked at the note—for about five seconds. Then he looked back into Mona's eyes. His expression did not change, and that's when she knew. *He was the one.* Someone confronted with such an accusation would at least look surprised, or outraged, or *something.* Howard Sollomon was none of these. He was as cool as the proverbial cucumber.

Without a hint of emotion, Howard Sollomon said, "I don't know what you're talking about."

Keeping the note in front of him, Mona said, "Then you deny writing this?"

"Yeah," Sollomon said coldly. "Now what?"

"Now we turn it over to the proper authorities," said Mona, slapping the note back in the folder. "You had your chance."

*Had your chance? Oh boy, that's good.*

Mona turned around and started to walk out when a hand grabbed her shoulder, a strong hand, and whirled her around. Now Sollomon's expression was different. It had the look, the one his girlfriend and daughter must have seen the night he messed them up. "You think you can pull this on me?" he snarled.

*Stay cool, girl.* "I'm not pulling anything. I have a job to do."

"Who do you work for?"

"That's confidential."

"Don't pull my chain, lady. I get real upset when that happens."

Mona fingered the pepper spray in her right hand, rolling the cylinder around and around. "What are you going to do? Hit me with a pastrami and cheese right here in front of everybody?" As Howard Sollomon looked quickly around at the crowd, Mona wondered how she ever came up with *that* one.

"Maybe we should go somewhere and talk," he said.

Bingo! He had taken the bait. Now sink the hook in deeper. "I don't think so. The authorities will be in touch."

"Hey, maybe we can work out a deal."

"I don't think so."

"Listen to me." He kept his voice low. "You're not going to get anywhere with that"—he made a dismissive gesture toward the folder—"but I might be able to help you."

"Help *me?*"

"Yeah, sure."

"How can you possibly?"

"I can give you somebody."

This was the talk of the typical snitch. In return for a "deal" they would talk, finger other people, bigger people. In a conspiracy case, or a drug-trafficking scheme, it came in very handy for prosecutors. But there was a downside. A lot of times the snitches just made the stuff up, hoping to con their way out of whatever trouble they were in. Howard Sollomon looked the part of the con man. Hadn't he conned his wife into dropping the charges?

"Who?" asked Mona.

"Oh no, not until we work something out."

"I'm sorry, Mr. Sollomon. You'll have to do better than that."

"No, missy," said Sollomon, his dark eyes not giving anything away. "*You'll* have to do better than that."

Mona stiffened. "I'll be in touch."

"I know you will," said Sollomon.

As Mona walked out, she felt the stare of Howard Sollomon slicing her up into cold cuts. She had what she came for. She was sure Sollomon was the one who made the threats to Tracy. He had all but admitted it by offering this "deal." Could she prove it? No. But Sollomon didn't know that, not yet at least. Her bluff had some legs.

But was there really someone else in all this? Who was it that he could "give" her? Or was it all just bluster by a man used to getting his way?

*Stay tuned boys and girls,* Mona thought on her way back to her car. *Stay tuned.*

---

Randall Lefferts thought, *I'll kill him. Someday, I will kill him.*

He stood stupidly in the middle of the motel room, a Motel 6 right by the freeway in San Fernando. The sound of trucks rumbling down toward Orange County, or up toward central California, provided a constant staccato of mechanized noise, and it was giving Lefferts a headache.

The stupid Indian was leaning against the door, eyeing him like *he* was the one who had some explaining to do. Lefferts no longer felt afraid of this weird aberration of humanity. Kohlbert had made it clear, in no uncertain terms, who was in charge of everything. If anyone ever became a loose cannon, if a certain hired hit man, say, suddenly decided to take out a certain right-hand man, that certain hit man would become dog meat soon enough.

That was certain. And the certainty gave Lefferts a new sense of freedom to manifest his loathing of this cigar-store freak. It didn't occur to him that the wish to someday actually kill the Indian rendered Lefferts something of an oddity himself. In his mind, this would be justifiable homicide. Now, to add insult to injury, this crazy breed was standing there telling him the job wasn't done, and he didn't really care what Lefferts thought.

"You better care, pal," Lefferts spat. "We're the ones who hired you. Kohlbert expects that those he hires will do what they are paid to do."

"The time wasn't right," said Tommy Bear Paw, with laconic indifference.

"You don't have anything to say about the time. Just do it."

"I will."

"Yeah, when? Next summer?"

The Indian did not answer. He stared.

"I came here to deliver the fee," Lefferts said. "I wasted a day getting this all set up, and you come up with excuses. Don't think this won't be remembered." His threat sounded strangely hollow. The Indian just didn't seem to care.

"Well?" Lefferts said.

"Well what?"

"When are you going to finish the job?"

"That's up to me."

"Make it soon. Or you'll be hearing from us, not in a nice way."

For a moment, Tommy Bear Paw looked Lefferts up and down, then reached behind himself and opened the door. He slipped out backward, never taking his eyes off Lefferts, and closed the door.

With a sigh of relief and some disgust, Randall Lefferts sat down on the queen-size bed. In his imagination, he came up with all sorts of improbable ways for the Indian to die, enjoying the fantasies and then wondering, only briefly, how he had become such a man as this.

# CHAPTER NINETEEN

IT WAS ONLY SUPPOSED TO BE a small service, a quiet memorial on a Friday afternoon. But the chapel was jammed, and there were twice as many people outside who had come to pay their respects. Police, prosecutors, defense lawyers, judges—they had all come to say goodbye to a respected member of the district attorney's office.

Tracy, sitting with Evelyn Gallegos, couldn't help feeling that Duke would be a little embarrassed by all the fuss. There was a portrait in the front of the chapel of Duke in a suit, smiling, looking out like a happy grandfather on all of his kin.

But there was another, more disturbing emotion inside Tracy. It had to do with doubts. Doubts about Duke, about what he may have been involved in. Something foul, though who knew what. She wanted to be convinced it was all just speculation. Maybe he really was murdered at his house on a sunny afternoon in a surprise attack by a frightened burglar.

Maybe . . .

Looking around the room, Tracy recognized many faces, without necessarily knowing their names. People she rode in elevators with, or passed in the hallways, or saw in the snack bar of the Criminal Courts Building. There was also one guy she wasn't happy to see. Detective Stan Willis sat in the back row, staring straight ahead. In an eerie sort of way it was as if he was detached from the proceedings, in a world of his own. Something was going on in that world. But what was it? Perhaps she'd never know.

It was a good memorial, with a few short speeches from friends and colleagues. Judge John Kirkendall wrapped it all up with the fitting epitaph that "Duke Gallegos was the kind of lawyer you'd want for anything. You knew he'd do his job, and see it through to the end."

Tracy felt good about sitting by Evelyn, being able to comfort her during the service. Several times her body quavered with sobs. It was all so familiar. Two years ago it had been Tracy sobbing, in a memorial to her slain husband, and the wife of a fellow officer had comforted *her*.

When the service ended, Tracy walked Evelyn down the aisle. As she did she caught sight of Willis again. This time he was looking at her, with a look she could not decipher. Never mind that, she said to herself, she would soon be gone and leave the whole mess behind her.

Outside the chapel the sun was breaking through the late afternoon clouds. *It might rain later,* Tracy thought. She always liked the rain because it washed away the smog. For a short time afterward, the dirt was out of the sky.

Evelyn Gallegos was greeted by some friends, and Tracy slipped back. She wanted to be there if Evelyn needed her, but assumed family and loved ones would begin their healing task. She felt a hand on her shoulder.

"Talk?" Walt Lindross said.

"Sure," Tracy said. Lindross, the district attorney, was a tall, rugged man who dressed sharply and spoke with an elegance that exposed his upper crust, Ivy League background. At fifty-five he had proven himself as a top prosecutor over the years and was well respected by his peers. That didn't stop the usual politicking that is endemic to the office, of course. In a couple of years he'd be up for reelection; already a couple of deputies were positioning themselves for a run at the big chair. Tracy doubted they would get anywhere, unless some sort of scandal involving a high-profile case hit. That was not out of the question. If the O'Lean Murray case became a powder keg, someone with political ambitions might be able to light a match.

Walt took her arm and walked her a little way past the chapel. "I understand," he said, "you're taking a leave of absence."

"That's right," said Tracy.

"It's certainly understandable. How long do you think it might be?"

"Truthfully? It might be permanent. I'm moving up north."

"That's a shame. I hate to lose good deputies. I've had my eye on you for awhile."

Tracy could hardly believe it. It always seemed like there was a big, block-wall barrier between the day-to-day deputies in the courtrooms and the big wigs of "mahogany row." Why would the district attorney have an eye on her? She was several rungs down, and usually all the information flowed upward through the different levels.

"Don't be too surprised," Lindross continued. "I'm not as far removed as I might seem. I've always been a courtroom lawyer, and I like to keep up on what my people are doing. I've had good reports on you, not just from Duke, but Bob Campbell and everyone else who's worked with you. You have what it takes to become a long-term asset to the office."

"Thanks, Mr. Lindross."

"Please call me Walt."

"I think I have to work up to that."

Lindross chuckled. "So be it—one of the hazards of sitting at the big desk. Anyway, that's how I feel about you. That's why I hate to see you go."

They were standing by a bougainvillea that spread itself upward on the side of the chapel. It covered the entire wall like a cloak. "It's not easy for me to leave," said Tracy.

"You sure you want to?"

"I'm sure I have to. I'm getting married."

"Well that's . . . wonderful. Really. You're not going to give up the law, though, are you?"

"It depends. There are still a lot of questions I don't have the answers to."

Putting a hand on her shoulder, Lindross said, "Please keep open the possibility that you may come back. Will you do that?"

"Sure."

Lindross nodded and then leaned back toward the direction they came from. Tracy opened her mouth and a little sound came out, as if she was going to stay something. Lindross hesitated. "Yes?"

Tracy wanted to tell him about O'Lean Murray, to voice all her doubts about the case, even to tell him that Duke's death might somehow be involved in all this. But she had been honest before, with the man she trusted most, Duke himself. Look where that got him. And she had almost been killed by a crazy driver, another piece of this puzzle. She hesitated to drop all this, in trust, on a man she barely knew.

On the other hand, she would soon be out of there. In good conscience, could she keep all her doubts to herself?

In the instant it took to run all these thoughts together, Tracy looked over Lindross's shoulder and saw a pair of eyes. They belonged to Stan Willis, and they were trained on her. He was perhaps fifty yards away, but the laser beam of his look was without question directed her way. Now was not the time, or place. "Nothing," Tracy said. "Thank you for the kind words."

"I meant every one of them." He walked her back toward the parking lot. She felt Willis watching them. As she got in her car, where she should have felt safe, Tracy instead felt a sense of foreboding—and *déjà vu*. She looked in her rearview mirror and saw Stan Willis still looking at her. A creepy, irrational fear gripped her as she started the engine.

---

Something big was going down. Willis knew it the second he saw Tracy talking to Lindross. What was she doing, spilling her guts?

What else?

That was one side, closing in. Then there was the other side, Kohlbert and his band of merry men. Who knew what they were planning? Too many mouths were out there, his included. Yes, they had paid him well, and there was more to come. But who knew whether or not they'd decide he was a liability?

No, they needed him. They needed Stan Willis, a cop on the inside.

Or did they? The confused thoughts pounded away at him as he sat in his one-room apartment. He'd taken the place in Silver Lake after Sherry left him. She'd taken the kids, and he didn't fight it, so what was the point of having a bigger place? After selling the house to settle the divorce, this place was just fine. Pretty quiet, too, considering. A guy could be left alone.

No one would know that he was fiddling with a couple of the street weapons he'd picked up along the way. No one would be pounding on his door, demanding entrance (as he had done to others so many times in the past). And no one would be looking into his window with high-powered binoculars—though he kept the curtains closed as a precaution.

On the table in front of him was the pick of the litter, a Glock-17 handgun. He liked the Glock, the Austrian-made beauty that the FBI and mass murderers alike favored. It was the gun Bruce Willis used in *Die Hard 2,* a movie Stan Willis saw four times. It held seventeen rounds of 9-mm bullets, automatically reloading the chamber after each shot. A guy with experience could empty the clip in ten or twelve seconds.

He'd taken it off a gangbanger in a shakedown in Culver City. That was always a good place to go off-duty if you were into this sort of thing. He'd bloodied the kid's face pretty good that night.

Willis rubbed the barrel of the Glock with a rag, wondering how long it might take him to empty the thing in a room of four or five. He wondered if that Indian would be quick, and made a mental note to take him out first—if it ever came to that.

He didn't like the way Kohlbert looked at him lately, or treated him. Guy thought he was Patton or something. Yeah, he could pay to be whoever he wanted. He could spread the marmalade about how he was going to take an underpaid, run-of-the-mill homicide cop and make him a special bodyguard and right-hand man—if he could follow directions.

Willis picked up another handgun, a Raven Arms .25-caliber, better known on the street as a "Saturday Night Special." It was small, easy to hide, light. It reminded Willis of the old-time Derringer the gamblers used to hide in their sleeves. That kind of weapon was a good backup in case you lost your primary. This one had come from the evidence locker. Lifting it had been too easy. Willis sometimes marveled that those guys kept anything at all in storage.

A half hour, then an hour went by, and Willis still patiently lifted, loaded, unloaded, loaded again, and polished the handguns. *Like a soldier getting ready for battle*, he thought. *Your weapon is your best friend. Treat it right.*

Yes, something big was going down. He didn't know if it would be him, or Kohlbert, or Tracy Shepherd, or who. But Duke was dead, and Stan Willis resolved that, if nothing else, he wouldn't be next.

## CHAPTER TWENTY

WHEN THE PLANE was finally airborne—when the smog haze below actually gave way to a glimpse of the Pacific Ocean—Tracy could hardly believe it.

Up to that point she had been busy enough getting everything together. The packing, the kids' things, the incessant questions about where they were going and why, the shuttle to the airport, snarls of traffic and ticket lines—all this had kept her mind occupied.

Now she and her two children were steadily climbing to thirty thousand feet and heading toward a new life. It was then that the decision became real to her. Closed off, in the air, leaving it all behind.

Bryce was glued to the window, straining to see the shrinking landscape and ocean below. Allison, in the middle seat, said, "I wanna see."

Tracy patted her daughter's hand. "When the seatbelt light goes off you can have a turn."

"I like flying," she said.

"It's fun, isn't it?"

"Like Disneyland."

"Yes."

"Can we go to Disneyland again?"

"Someday, sure."

"Do they have Disneyland in Lake Tahoe?"

"No."

"What *do* they have?"

What indeed? Tracy didn't know, either, except for the casinos, which interested her not at all. What would they be doing there? What would the kids do all day? What schools would they attend? What about all the details of setting up life in a foreign environment? She hadn't had time to sort any of that out.

"I'm sure," Tracy said, "they have lots of things." But she wasn't sure.

"Mommy?" said Allison.

"Yes?"

"How long will we stay?"

"I don't know. Maybe a long time."

"Can Mrs. Olivera come and stay with us?"

"I don't think she can, honey."

Bryce turned around. "Do we get free peanuts on this plane?"

They got the peanuts, and soft drinks, too, and the flight touched down a mere fifty minutes later. A car was waiting. The driver, a friendly man named Jackson, complete in chauffeur's uniform, stood at the gate with a hand-lettered sign that read *Shepherd*.

"Welcome to the North country," he said. "How y'all doin'?"

Bryce and Allison both said, "Fine."

"Good. Fine's a nice way to be."

Jackson helped them claim their baggage, then showed them to the limousine. Tracy smiled broadly as she got in. This might get to be a habit for a political wife.

*Wife*. How strange to be thinking it, but that was the reality, the reason she was here. She was going to marry Rob Cavanaugh.

*And live in this enormous . . . compound?* As the limo drove up through the gate, with pine trees lining the driveway and the sun streaking through in angelic rays, Tracy thought she was going to wake up and find out it was all a dream.

"You like it so far?" Jackson said from the driver's seat.

"Yeah!" Bryce and Allison wailed.

"Wait till you get a gander at the lake," said Jackson. "You're gonna love that. Oh yes."

The house was like an old English manor—stonework and wood columns, flower garden and cobbled walkway. The kids were ecstatic, bursting out of the limo, giggling, with Allison saying, "Cool! Can we keep it?"

Jackson laughed as he retrieved the bags from the trunk. "You want to keep this old house?"

"Yeah!" Bryce and Allison said together.

"And the lake, too?"

"Yeah!"

"How 'bout all the trees?"

The children looked around at the mighty pines jutting majestically into a pure, blue sky. "Can we?" Bryce said.

"Have to talk to God about the trees," said Jackson. "The rest is up to Mr. Cavanaugh."

Entering the mansion was like walking into another world. Tracy had been in plenty of big homes, of course, but not set in Wonderland. This was like some lodge you would pay hundreds of dollars a night to stay in: immaculate hardwood floors, country-style interior, a staircase to the second level. Tracy found herself wondering how Rob Cavanaugh could afford this place. Family money, maybe? Good investments? There was so much more to know about the man she would soon marry.

A middle-aged woman in a crisp business suit stepped into the foyer. "Hello," she said, "I'm Ellie Debussy, Mr. Cavanaugh's secretary." She extended a hand to Tracy. "Nice to have you."

"Thank you," Tracy said.

"And these are the children I've been hearing about." Ellie bent over to have a look at them. She smiled. The kids, shyly, each held Tracy's hands.

"This is Bryce, and this is Allison," said Tracy.

Ellie nodded at both and said, "Would you like to see the lake?" That ended the shyness. "Yes-oh-yes-oh-yes . . ." Allison fairly shrieked.

"Then let's go." Turning to Jackson, she said, "You know which rooms."

"Yes ma'am," the chauffeur said.

Ellie led them through the dining room and out the sliding doors, which led to an expansive stone patio. As soon as Tracy stepped out from the house, she was greeted with one of the most beautiful sights she had ever seen. Lake Tahoe spread out before her like a postcard come to life. Bryce and Allison were already running to the ornate balustrade, shouting, "Look! Look!"

"This is beautiful," Tracy said.

"A little piece of heaven," said Ellie.

"Some office you have."

"The job does have perks."

Bryce was the first to spot the stairway that led down toward the lakefront, where a dock and small boat jutted out into the water. "Can we go down there, Mom? Can we?"

Tracy hesitated and looked at Ellie, who said, "It's all right. We can keep an eye on them from up here."

Nodding, Tracy said, "Just don't get your shoes wet." The two children scuttled toward the lake.

"I can hardly believe this," said Tracy. "Just a few hours ago I was down in L. A. with a completely different life. Now I'm up here feeling like I'm in some movie about extremely wealthy people."

Ellie laughed. "I know exactly what you mean. I was working in downtown San Francisco only a few months ago. When I got hired by Mr. Cavanaugh, I had no idea I was going to end up working at his house on the lake. I couldn't have designed a better atmosphere, now could I?"

"How did you hook up with Rob . . . Mr. Cavanaugh?"

"Just a series of somebody knew somebody, who knew somebody else. I guess I got recommended along the way, but I didn't argue. I wanted to get out of the city, so I jumped at the chance. I guess you jumped, too."

Part of Tracy wanted to protest at that, but couldn't. She *had* jumped at the chance. As if sensing Tracy's sudden embarrassment Ellie said, "Come on, let's get you settled."

Tracy took in a deep breath of fresh air. "Let's," she said.

The kids were in their bathing suits, finally. Bryce had protested strongly, wanting to get his regular clothes all wet and sandy. Allison had broached the subject of testing the waters au naturel. But civility reigned, and Tracy allowed the kids to play and dig onshore while she stretched out on the chaise lounge, taking in the afternoon sky.

*Am I really here?* she thought. *Is everything going to be all better now?*

That's what her dad used to say when she was little and something bad had happened. She remembered one incident in particular, when Paulie Parrish, the bratty kid two houses down, had pushed her off her bike. She got a nasty scrape on her right knee, cried, and ran home to her daddy, who was working in the yard. He carried her into the house and put on the Bactine—somehow, he made it not sting—and a great big Band-Aid, then rocked her gently, saying, "Everything is going to be all right now." And it was. She didn't know what he said to Paulie Parrish's parents, but the brat never bothered her again. Daddy had made everything better.

Now he wasn't there, but in his place was a man named Rob Cavanaugh. Tracy felt a surge of feminist guilt, but just as quickly dismissed it. She'd never been a feminist, but she had been around plenty of them in law school and beyond. Tracy had always believed that a woman could work just as hard as a man and ought to be compensated on an equal basis, but she had clung to the politically incorrect position that men and women were actually different. So, although she would have found some way to deal with her situation, if a man like Rob Cavanaugh happened along with the power to make things happen, she was not going to refuse his help—or his love.

Bryce giggled at something down on the beach. Allison cried out, "Don't!"

*Yes,* thought Tracy, *life is going to go on just the same.*

*God,* she prayed silently, *thank you for taking care of us. I know I've been distant from you. I want that to end. I see your hand moving. You've brought us here, and you've brought this man into my life. I want to be yours again, completely. Help me to do it.*

And then, suddenly, she thought of someone else. He just shot into her thoughts, a picture of him, his face clear, his expression even clearer. It was the face of fear.

She was thinking of O'Lean Murray.

---

As the twelve jurors took their seats in the box, Kendra Murray's heart fell inside her like an iron ball. Somehow she had hoped their faces would reflect what she knew—that this was all a sham, a hoax, a travesty. She had prayed that these twelve citizens would know the minute they walked in that her son was innocent and the police were lying. But the faces didn't reflect anything like that, and she was powerless to say anything. Worst of all, though, Tracy Shepherd was not there. Why had God allowed that to happen?

The new D. A., a guy named Conroy, wouldn't even speak to her. Not a word. Not a returned phone call. Everything had to be done through her son's lawyer, but Chad Turturro was an overworked public defender. Nice enough, she guessed, but how much attention could he give her son's case? He always seemed to have a bunch of file folders with him. His mind seemed to wander sometimes.

The judge, a stern-looking older man with thinning white hair, said "Good morning" to the jury. The twelve, in unison, answered back. Then he told them that they were about to hear opening statements by the attorneys and that the prosecution would open first.

Kendra Murray looked at the back of her son's head, which was slightly bowed. She wanted him to turn and look at her, so she could smile at him. But he didn't turn around.

The prosecutor was now on his feet, standing before the jury. He was wearing a dark blue suit with a burgundy tie; he looked confident. "Good morning, ladies and gentlemen," he said. "On the night of September 23, one of this city's leading citizens, movie producer Sandy Joseph, was brutally, and in cold blood, murdered while in his car. We will prove to you, by the evidence presented, that the defendant, O'Lean Murray, committed that murder."

*Lord, oh Lord,* Kendra Murray prayed, with her eyes closed. *Let justice be done!*

It was night when he arrived, though the neon explosions from the casinos along the lakeshore created an artificial sense of day. Tommy Bear Paw didn't know why he decided to stop here. He had not gambled since the penny ante poker games in the army. He had never felt drawn to it. Gambling was for people who believed in hope. They hoped for the big score and so kept throwing their money away. Strange deal. Yet here he was, walking into the first casino, aware that he was looking for something. What? A connection, maybe. A reason to be doing something.

Not a connection with the people, though. He hardly noticed the rabble around him—the middle-aged women playing the slots, cigarettes hanging out of their mouths as they fed dollar after dollar into the machines; the high rollers at the craps tables, tossing down thousand-dollar chips as if they were bottle caps; the boozed-up out-of-towners who sat playing blackjack like so many robots, ordering more drinks from the scantily clad cocktail waitresses. None of this was of interest to him.

He only knew he had some sort of persistent twisting inside of him, an odd and unfamiliar feeling. He had thought about it all the way up Highway 50, ever since pulling out of Sacramento. Getting closer to his destination and his prey, he found himself thinking about her more than he had thought about anyone before.

It wasn't just that she was a woman, though that figured into it. It was more. She was dangerous. Dangerous to the men who had hired him. That was fascinating to him. Here was a woman with enough power that they wanted her dead.

He remembered a story his grandfather once told him. It was about an Indian scout hired by the provisional army in a Montana outpost. His name was Walking Deer, and it was said he could speak to the wind and the wind would answer him. It would tell him anything he wanted to know. His awesome powers of apprehension were utilized by the army in tracking down renegades, both white and Indian, with incredible success. But his success also became his curse. The captain in charge didn't trust him, always thinking there was some plan going on behind his eyes, that he would one day betray them all.

So the captain ordered a small group of his men to keep a constant eye on Walking Deer and to report to him anything they deemed suspicious. "All of these soldiers, afraid of one Indian," his grandfather had said. "It is fear that the white man has more than anything. That is why he is never at peace."

So it was fear that gripped the captain, a man named Connor, so powerfully that one night he could stand it no more. He woke up from a bad dream, took along his staff sergeant, and went out to the shack by the livery where Walking Deer slept. There they tied him up and hanged him, in the cowardly darkness of night. The next day, they told the other soldiers that Walking Deer had tried to kill them as they were watering horses.

That was not the end of the story. The spirit of Walking Deer remained, haunting Captain Connor to the point where a military board of inquiry found him guilty of murder, but insane. He spent the last years of his life in an asylum in Baltimore.

The connection here was obvious. This woman, Tracy Shepherd, filled men with fear. That was what gave her power. Was it that power that made him hesitate to kill her in the first place? Maybe he wanted to see more what that power could do and how it would affect those men.

Now, standing in a gambling hall, Tommy again wondered why he was here. He pulled out a crisp one-hundred-dollar bill, part of his installment plan, and sat down at a blackjack table. He tossed the bill to the dealer who counted out chips for him, and for the next two hours Tommy Bear Paw played cards, feeling neither empty nor filled.

Occasionally, during a break in the action when the dealer would shuffle, he would think of Tracy Shepherd, wondering where and how he would choose to kill her.

## CHAPTER TWENTY-ONE

TRACY AWOKE from the most refreshing sleep she'd had in months. Her bed was soft and warm, and she felt like cocooning for another hour. Soft light filtered in through the window. *Just another day in paradise,* she thought.

Her children were still asleep on the floor. They had wanted to sleep in the same room with Mom, not yet ready to be alone in their new abode. Allison gently snored, while Bryce was hiding completely inside his bag.

Tracy smiled. *At least we're all together,* she thought. And today Rob would be coming.

An hour later, showered and refreshed, Tracy and her kids came downstairs and met the daytime staff—a cook, a maid, and a groundskeeper, in addition to Ellie. They had prepared a sumptuous breakfast of eggs, sausages, pancakes, and freshly squeezed orange juice. "Better than IHOP!" Allison had squealed.

*Indeed,* thought Tracy.

They were almost finished when Rob arrived. He strode in wearing a flannel shirt and jeans, looking not like a political candidate but a cowboy in bunkhouse casuals. Tracy liked the look. It was comfortable, and comforting. She greeted him with a hug. Then she looked behind her and noticed Bryce and Allison smiling up at him.

"How you doing?" he said to the children.

Bryce said, "Fine," and his little sister echoed him.

"What do you think of this place?"

"It's way cool!" Bryce erupted. Allison said, "Yeah!"

Rob looked at Tracy. "And what do *you* think?"

"What can I say?" said Tracy. "Way cool!" She stepped into his arms again and melted there.

"What do you say we take a run around the lake in my boat?"

The kids cheered like it was an invitation to Disneyland. After changing into swimsuits, they all clambered aboard Rob's boat and started skimming across the shimmering body of water nestled in the magnificent Sierra Nevada.

"This is what I like most of all," said Rob, seated casually at the helm with Tracy beside him. The children, heads poking out of life preservers like fluffed-up ducks, sat in the back watching the wake. "The chance to be free of everything. I don't even bring my phone along when I'm in this boat."

"Nice," said Tracy, loving the wind in her face.

"I have an idea."

"A politician with an idea? That's novel."

"You'll like this one."

"Let's hear it."

"Here it is. When we get back to the house, let's find ourselves a wedding chapel and go get married."

"Today?"

"Why not?"

"I . . . wow."

"You like the idea?"

Tracy smiled. "I love the idea but . . ."

"But what?"

Looking to the stern at her giggling children, Tracy said, "I want the kids to have just a little more time to get used to the idea."

Rob put his arm around her. "I understand, but let's not wait too long."

"Where's your next campaign stop?"

"We have a swing through Orange County coming up next. Hagan tells me it's the key."

"Hagan?"

"My manager. Tells me what to do. I dare not disobey." He said the last in mock ominous tones.

"You haven't told me about him before."

"He's just . . . part of my political life."

"I want to share that part of your life, too."

Rob pulled her closer to him. "And you will."

"I look forward to helping you, Rob. In politics and everything else."

For a moment, Rob looked off at the horizon, his expression distant. Then he turned to her again. "I'll be off this afternoon. Won't be back until tomorrow. Will you stay?"

"You know I will," said Tracy.

"Good. What's the old song say? This is the start of something big."

For the first time in a long time, as long as she could remember, Tracy felt a perfect peace.

*This is crazy!*

As Mona Takata sat on the iron bench, she felt herself crossing the line. It was bad enough, her little charade in the deli with Sollomon. It was worse meeting with him here. If this ever got out, she was going to be cooked, or at least heated up quite bit.

Whose idea was this, anyway? Right, hers. She was the one who said they should meet, of all places, at the cemetery—quiet, sure, but with a sense of drama behind it. Meeting among the dead meant no one to disturb them.

Maybe the guy wouldn't even show up. Maybe he'd had time enough to figure out she was mostly bluster and wouldn't bite. Maybe he was playing his own con. He said he had someone for her, but that could be a complete ruse. She was sure he was the one behind the threats to Tracy. She just wanted to be sure he'd stop it.

If he was going to show, he was late. Mona tapped the bench with her fingers. She had one other stop to make. Trevor Peck, the brother of an old high school friend, was doing a little computer analysis for her on the disk she had picked up at Joseph Productions. It should be ready by now.

Fifteen more minutes went by. Mona thought about leaving, actually a little relieved. Sollomon gave her the creeps, and maybe she'd done enough to get him to lay off the juvenile attempts to scare Tracy. But before she could move, she saw him walking up the path. He lumbered, she noticed—sort of like Lon Chaney Jr. Maybe his face grew hair with the full moon.

"Thought I wouldn't show, didn't you?" he said when he reached her.

"What have you got for me?"

"Cut right to it, eh? OK. You got one chance."

"Forget the threats, Mr. Sollomon. You don't know what you're dealing with here."

With the faint trace of a sneer, Sollomon said, "Maybe I don't, and maybe I do. Maybe I don't believe you can do much of anything to me. You can't prove anything. You can't make me say anything."

"So why are you here?"

Now the sneer turned into a smile, but it was one of those smiles that made you nervous. "Insurance. I'm big on insurance."

"All right. I'm listening."

Only then did Sollomon sit down on the bench beside Mona. She felt herself squeeze in the opposite direction.

"First off," Sollomon said, "you give me a written waiver, with complete immunity."

"I can't do that."

"Then we don't talk."

"I'm not authorized."

"See ya." He stood up.

Mona recognized this little game of chicken. The first to blink loses. "Good-bye, Mr. Sollomon."

When he hesitated, Mona knew she wasn't the one with feathers.

"What assurances can you give me?" he said, looking a little nervous.

"Only personal assurances," Mona said, "but I'm a very trustworthy person."

"You know I have friends."

A clumsy attempt at intimidation. But even clumsy people were dangerous. "So do I," Mona said. "Now tell me what you've got."

Sollomon looked around, as if he thought someone might be listening. It was more than a little absurd to Mona, considering where they were.

Sitting again, Sollomon said, "Look, I didn't write that note. But I know who did."

"How do you know?"

"I just do, that's all."

"Who?"

"I need assurances."

"I already told you . . ."

"Look, I can't get into any more trouble." For the first time Sollomon looked more pathetic than dangerous. Mona felt the urge to say something like, *You should have thought about that before you hit your girlfriend and child*. But she held up and just listened.

"I'm trying to keep a new job at this title company. If they find out anything's going down with me, I'm out of there. Even if it's just a rumor or something. So I don't want my name in this, anywhere. I'm telling you I didn't do it, but I know the guy who did. How do I know? Because he works for my lawyer."

*And that would be Jackson Beymer*, Mona knew. "Are you talking about somebody in his office?"

"No, a guy who does odd jobs for him. Sometimes questions people."

"You mean an investigator?"

"Not exactly. He seems more like a bodyguard than anything else."

"What's his name?"

"I only know his first name: Cliff."

"And why do you think he's the one that sent the note?"

"I heard them talking one day, in the courthouse hallway, when I had to make an appearance. They were laughing about something and I asked them what was so funny. Beymer says, 'You know that D. A. who wanted to take you to trial?' And I say, 'Yeah,' and he says, 'I think she's gonna have to take a stress leave.' And then he looks over at Cliff, and they both start laughing again, like there's a private joke between them."

Mona waited for him to continue, but he didn't. He just looked at her. "That's it?" she said.

"What more do you want?"

"A little hard evidence would do nicely," said Mona, frustrated. "This means nothing."

"Oh, come on. It was obvious they were up to something with her, and Beymer does this all the time."

"Does what?"

"Plays mind games with other lawyers." Sollomon swiveled around on the bench and faced Mona directly. "He used to brag about it to me. He used to tell me why he's the best lawyer in America. Because he knows how to win the mental game. He told me 90 percent of winning a trial is to keep your opponent mentally . . . what did he call it? . . . disharmonized, or something like that."

"I don't doubt that," Mona said, "but that still doesn't give us anything about this note or the phone call."

"There was a phone call, too?"

*If this guy's lying,* Mona thought, *then he's doing a pretty good job of it.*

"Yes, there was a phone call."

"Male voice?"

"Male voice."

"There you go."

Sighing, Mona said, "That's not much to go on, I'm afraid."

Sollomon looked dangerous again, like a trapped animal. "You gave me assurances."

"Let me put it this way. I don't have any reason to doubt your story, yet. But I also don't have any reason to discount you, either. What you've given me today is just a little bit better than nothing, but not by much."

Sollomon stiffened.

"But I'll follow this up," Mona continued. "I'll do what I can to substantiate your story. But if I ever find out you haven't been straight with me, I won't take it well."

For a split second, Mona was scared. She wondered if she had overplayed her hand, if Sollomon would suddenly reach into his pocket, pull out a gun, and offer her permanent residency in the little memorial park that surrounded them. Suddenly she realized she'd left the pepper spray in her car.

Sollomon looked at her, his eyes intense like some latter-day Bela Lugosi. Then he said, simply, "Fair enough."

"Good-bye, Mr. Sollomon."

For a moment he paused, then stood quickly and walked away.

*An unsavory guy,* Mona kept thinking as she drove down Santa Monica Boulevard. But she was now convinced he wasn't the one. His story about Jackson Beymer and his bodyguard was bizarre enough to ring true. From what she'd heard about the "legendary" defense lawyer, he would stop at nothing to win. He was that driven. *And smart, too.* If he did indeed direct, or at the very least condone, the threats toward Tracy, he wouldn't leave himself wide open. There was probably no way to connect him. But if there was, she'd find it.

Mona pulled up to the apartment building off Melrose and parked. The neighborhood was nice, and she couldn't help wondering how a teenager, barely out of high school, could afford to be out on his own. It was a high-tech world, and if you were young, computer literate, had an ounce of ambition and a few contacts, you could make a fair chunk of change by freelancing for people. Setting up networks, analyzing problems, even helping old ladies surf the Net.

Todd Lloyd was just such a one. He greeted her at the door dressed in a Smashing Pumpkins T-shirt and blue jeans that looked like they'd last been washed sometime during Reagan's second term. He wore thick glasses, and his hair was long and stringy.

"I'm Mona."

"Chris said you'd be coming." He opened the door wide, and Mona entered a small computer wonderland. There were three stations in various parts of the apartment, the screens alive at each. Cables crisscrossed the carpet like a load of spilled spaghetti, while large-unit CPUs stood like sentries beside each location. Stacks of computer magazines covered the kitchen bar, and piles of technical manuals turned the floor into a maze. Scattered about in random fashion were two Domino's Pizza boxes, an empty Ben & Jerry's ice cream carton, several crumpled Jack-in-the-Box bags, and a cat.

Todd Lloyd, Mona determined, was a vision of the future. Soon a person would be able to stay indoors, have all meals delivered, and communicate with anyone in the world at the touch of a button.

"Watch out for the cables," Todd said, closing the door.

"Why don't you tape them out of the way or something?"

"It's no big. I just move 'em. Besides, Woz likes to play with them."

"Woz?"

"My cat. See?"

Mona glanced once more at the furry gray feline that was walking around, seemingly checking her out. "Nice to meet you, Woz," said Mona. "So did anything come up?"

"Maybe." There was an odd twinkle in Todd's eye, the sort one gets when holding a secret he knows you want.

"Todd," Mona said with some consternation. "Chris said you would give it to me straight."

"I just like to have a little fun. It's amazing how stupid people are."

Mona raised her eyebrows. Todd quickly added, "I'm not talking about you. I'm talking about the stupid people who think they can hit delete and nobody'll ever know what they had there."

He circled around the stack of computer magazines, opened the refrigerator, and pulled out a bottle of Coke Classic. Without offering one to Mona, he twisted off the cap and continued, "Yeah, especially people who haven't bothered to update their systems, like this guy whats-'is-name."

"Sandy Joseph."

"Whatever. So they delete their files but don't realize they're not really gone."

Mona shook her head. "Delete doesn't mean delete?"

The twinkle was there again. "Not in this world, Mr. Spock. In this world you have what is called the file allocation table that tells the operating system where a file is physically located. When you delete a file, that doesn't erase the data in the file. It only tells the operating system the space is now available for data. If you enter new data and it utilizes that space, then your data is overwritten. But until then it's still there, just not accessible until you goose it. That's where I come in."

Mona blinked.

"I just pick my way clean into the file allocation table, find the . . . well, trade secrets."

"So, what are you telling me? You found some files that had been deleted?"

"That's exactly what I'm telling you, Spock. And I'll tell you something more. I think this guy was scared when he zinged 'em."

"What makes you say that?"

"Because the files were all undisturbed. That tells me it was the last thing he did to this disk. Now why does a guy do that?"

Mona pondered that. "Why didn't he just destroy the disk itself?"

"Because there was other stuff on it he wanted. Stupid. Why don't people know how to use this technology?"

"What was on those deleted files?"

"You really want to know?"

"Don't mess around, Todd."

"Some beefy stuff."

"Show me."

Todd stepped over to a printer, pulled off a sheaf of papers and handed them to Mona. "This should keep you busy for awhile."

She quickly glanced at them, wondering exactly what she was holding. Todd handed her the disk. "Thanks," said Mona. "Good job."

"I know. That'll be a hundred bucks."

Mona almost dropped the papers. "A hundred bucks? Chris said you'd do this as a favor."

Rolling his eyes and shaking his head, Todd lamented, "I wish she would quit doing that! She's done that ever since we were kids, and just because she's older, she thought she could get me to fix everything her friends brought over, and then forget about me!"

"I'm sorry—"

"We sold lemonade one day. I squeezed all the lemons, *all* of them, and she took in all the money. When it was over, all she gave me was a quarter. A quarter! She said she was teaching me how to be a good employee."

Mona reached into her purse and pulled out a twenty. "Here, how's this?"

Todd took the money. "I guess it's OK."

"Just promise me you won't use it to buy pizza."

"Don't worry," Todd said with a smile. "Tonight is fried chicken night."

With a smile of her own—she was starting to like this kid—Mona left the apartment with the papers under her arm. She didn't even wait to get back to her place to begin reading them. She started right there in her car.

What she saw mesmerized her. She was holding the full confession of one Sandy Joseph, a major trafficker in drugs, practically bragging how he financed his movies and his lifestyle with profits from the cocaine trade. She was no expert in the structure of the narcotics trade, but she did know that those "at the top" are usually very powerful, very savvy business people. Not only that, they are well insulated from the bottom of their distribution pyramid. In that respect, drug trafficking was like any other successful business. Sandy Joseph, by his own account, was a success.

As she pored over the copies, Mona wondered why a man like Joseph would even risk putting these things down in written form. What had he to gain? *What if someone just happened to find them*, as she had? Then she remembered something she'd heard in a narcotics seminar a few years ago. The thrill of the drug trade is not simply in the making of money; it's in the getting away with it. Like gambling, it's no fun unless you can lose. Walking that thin line of danger is part of the rush. Maybe that's what Sandy Joseph was doing—feeling the rush. But then Mona read something that suggested a different theory.

Joseph was not just buying influence in the movie community. He was making political connections as well. Not all of them were above board; the notes suggested laundered cash to political operatives. Again, Joseph had insulated himself through several levels. Apparently, however, something had gone wrong with one of the contribution trails. Joseph intimated in one notation that he may have made an enemy, and as a consequence, his operation, indeed maybe his very life, might be in jeopardy.

So Sandy Joseph, seeing this proverbial writing on the wall, may have been readying a document to take other people down with him. Mona came to a list of names not connected to any other notes, but it was obviously, in some way, tied up with Joseph's nonentertainment productions. Mona read through the list, not recognizing any of the names.

Except one. It was the last name on the list, and it took her breath away.

# CHAPTER TWENTY-TWO

WITH A TWINGE of guilty pleasure, Tracy laughed as she and her children muddied themselves with abandon by the water. This was the most fun she'd had in years. When was the last time she had been completely in the company, and at the beck and call, of her kids? She couldn't remember.

The pure elation she felt with her children was coupled with the anticipation of Rob's return. He would be coming this afternoon, and he had promised to take them all out to a sumptuous meal at one of Lake Tahoe's best restaurants. She hadn't argued with that.

Bryce, poking the ground with a stick, paused and looked up at his mother. "Are you and Rob going to get married?"

"Yes," Tracy said.

Bryce went back to poking the ground. He didn't look happy.

"What's the matter, honey?"

No answer from the boy. Tracy reached out and stroked his hair back off his forehead. "Bryce?"

Without looking up Bryce said, "I don't want you to."

"Why not? I thought you liked it here. I thought you liked Rob."

"That was when you weren't going to marry him."

Tracy noticed Allison watching them silently. "Did anything happen to bring this on?"

Bryce just shrugged his shoulders. That troubled Tracy. She was sure he was feeling something that he wouldn't, or perhaps couldn't, articulate.

It was just fear of the unknown, probably. When it came to making a major change like this, kids were sure to feel some discomfort.

"Suppose we all just think about it, huh?" said Tracy. "Give it a little more time. Will you do that for me?"

Bryce still would not look up from the dirt. "I'm scared of him."

That was a jolt from nowhere. Scared of him? This had to be a child's irrational fear. Rob was one of the nicest, most caring men she'd ever met. How could anyone be scared of a man like that?

She wondered for a moment if Bryce somehow sensed something she didn't. But she quickly discarded that idea. No way. Rob had never been with Bryce alone.

"Honey, there's nothing to be scared about." Tracy tried to make her tone light. "Rob is a nice man."

"He's like Mr. Hanburg," Bryce said.

"Yecch," Allison added.

Art Hanburg had been one of their neighbors in Sherman Oaks. He lived down the street, alone, in a nice house. From all appearances he was a normal, decent individual, even though Tracy only knew him to wave at him as he watered his lawn. He liked to give out candy to the kids in the neighborhood. That made him pretty popular.

The only thing he didn't like, some of the older residents said, was noise. He was known to call the police on occasion to take care of a teen party that got a little too rowdy, or come running out of his house yelling at cars that were burning rubber down the street. But his worst loathing was for barking dogs. It was well known he had a running feud with his back-fence neighbor, who kept his Lab outside at night. The Lab barked incessantly. One night it stopped barking. It had been poisoned. Art Hanburg was questioned but never charged with a crime.

So it was disturbing to Tracy that this was the image Bryce brought to mind when thinking of Rob. Only time would make it right, and Rob would be here soon.

---

Tommy Bear Paw watched Tracy Shepherd with her children. They were on the lakefront digging in the sand and dirt. She was just like another child, but there was something more. She seemed to be connected to them in a way he had never known with anyone.

He sat against the knotty pine tree on the side of the hill, watching through binoculars. This was all so familiar to him. Scoping out his prey, getting to know their every move, was always part of his m.o. But there was something more here this time. He was actually interested in how this woman lived her life. He just wasn't sure why.

His thoughts turned briefly to the job. He obviously couldn't do it here, too many people around. It had been a mistake to allow her to come here. But he could deal with that.

He wondered how much of the story Cavanaugh knew. He didn't ask, didn't need to know. But it was curious to him. He'd never been involved with a conspiracy before. He'd done jobs for individuals. The whole nature of conspiracy was new to him, and he found himself comparing the relative strengths of each side. This bothered him.

He went back to work. He'd have to get her when she was away from the house. His instructions were to make it look like a robbery of some kind. No problem.

The problem was in his being bothered. He tried to shake the feeling, but couldn't.

Ellie came out onto the back patio and called to Tracy that she had a phone call. Brushing sand off herself as best she could, Tracy ran up the stairs and took the cordless phone from Ellie, who turned and went back in.

"Hello?"

"Tracy, it's me."

"Mona?"

"Yes."

"How are you, girl?"

"Just peachy, look—" She sounded tense. Even the short pause had anxiety in it. "I'd like you to give me a call in a few minutes."

"What—"

"From a pay phone. Don't you have some shopping you can do?"

"Sure, but what's this all about?"

"Go look for souvenirs or something, but call me." Then Mona hung up.

Tracy stood motionless for a moment, then hung up the phone. She found Ellie inside. "I need to run into town," she said.

"What is it?" Ellie asked.

"Just want to run a little errand for a friend."

"I can have Jackson run a car up for you."

"Is there a car I might borrow?"

"Is something wrong?"

"Not at all."

"Because if there was, you know Rob would want me to know about it." Ellie looked at Tracy squarely, as if trying to assure her it was all right to tell her anything.

Tracy smiled. "I just want to get out for a bit and pick something up for a friend."

"Well how about if I run you in?" Ellie said, and before Tracy could say anything else Ellie was crossing the room for her purse. "I could use the break myself. Why not bring the kids?"

"Yes, fine."

As Tracy readied the children to go—Bryce complaining that he'd rather stay and play on the beach—her sense of anxiety grew. It was irrational, she knew, until she had all the facts. That was her lawyer side talking, but she sensed something. Until she could talk to Mona, all sorts of imaginings were drumming around inside her. And she had another sense—vague but nonetheless present—that Ellie was coming along to watch her.

The drive into town was routine, with Ellie glibly talking about the sights and tourist attractions along the way. It seemed normal enough.

Tracy said she wanted to find a shop that sold tourist trinkets, and promised her kids they could each pick something out. That news was met with happy anticipation.

Ellie drove to a small shopping center, fairly packed this morning with the usual visitor traffic. "Don't you just love it?" said Ellie as they drove around until they found a space. "Urban blight comes to paradise."

Tracy gave a quick scan to the surrounding shops and restaurants. Ellie said, "I know just the place for you." With a child clutching each hand, Tracy followed Ellie to the boardwalk encircling the center. Ellie motioned them forward, right past a candy store that elicited squeals from Allison.

"Go there, go there!" Allison intoned.

"Maybe on the way back," said Tracy, pulling her daughter along. Already a sort of plan was forming in Tracy's mind.

The little shop with the trinkets was a few doors down, just past Salon Dominique. Outside were displays of postcards, T-shirts, and key chains. Inside, Tracy could see rows of hats and shelves with all sorts of those overpriced items tourist traps make their living on.

"Is this what you had in mind?" asked Ellie.

"Perfect," said Tracy.

"Let's go." Inside the kids began oohing and ahhing at the walls of knickknacks. For some reason, Allison attached herself to the key chains and started poring over them. Bryce wanted to try on a few hats.

Close to the cashier counter Tracy found a row of multicolored, Velcro-sealed swatches of nylon shaped into a form resembling a wallet. On each was a print in white ink of the lake with the mountains behind it. Above the mountains, in bold script, were the words "Lake Tahoe." The wallets were marked five dollars.

*Five dollars! No wonder some people have mansions on the lake.*

Tracy chose a lime green model, then stepped to the cashier. Immediately Ellie was at her elbow. "That was fast," she said.

"Right," said Tracy. "It's not the biggest decision I ever had to make."

"Sure."

"Would you do me a favor?"

Without expression, Ellie said, "Of course."

Tracy pulled out a ten-dollar bill—her last, she noted—and handed it to Ellie. "Have the kids pick out something small, and then would you mind taking them to the candy store? Have them get a little sackful each."

"What are you going to do?"

"I'm just going to make a quick call down south, see if everything is smooth without me."

"Why shouldn't it be?" For a moment, this sounded like an accusation, but Ellie quickly added, "I mean, I'm sure everything is fine."

"Just want to be sure. I'll be right back." Tracy turned and started out, half expecting Ellie to jump in front of her and question her further. But she didn't. This whole thing was getting to be too much.

Tracy thought she had seen a pay phone farther down the boardwalk. Indeed, there was a phone, and right now a young kid with long hair and a ring in his nose was using it.

*Great.*

Tracy stood close, so he'd know she was waiting. But he didn't appear to notice. He kept his face close to the unit, yelling something about a party that had already occurred, and was "the bomb."

Tracy scanned the place for another phone, but didn't see one. She glanced back over her shoulder, back toward the tourist shop, expecting to see Ellie there. She wasn't.

The kid was laughing now about something or other. Wasn't his time running out?

Tracy tapped her foot on the boardwalk, looked at her watch, and sighed.

"Complete gnarl!" the kid erupted into the phone.

*Get off, will you?*

No sign of Ellie at the tourist shop.

The kid hung up suddenly. Tracy took a step toward the phone, but the kid didn't move. He started fishing around in his pocket for more change.

"Excuse me," Tracy said. The kid looked at her like she was an alien intruder into his totally cohesive universe. "Would you mind if I made a quick call?"

"I'm callin' somebody," the kid said.

"I know, but this is urgent."

"Hey, we all got problems." He pulled out a handful of change and started pushing coins around with his finger.

"Listen, I'll pay for your call."

"Huh?"

"I'll buy your phone call for you. Just give me a couple of minutes."

The longhair looked at her skeptically. Then he shrugged his shoulders and said, "Sure."

Tracy handed him a quarter. "Thanks," she said.

"I'm rich," said the longhair sarcastically. Then he stepped aside.

Tracy grabbed the phone and dialed the operator. She got the recorded message giving her a menu of choices.

*Why do these recordings talk so slow!*

"Yes," Tracy said when the voice asked her if she would like to place a collect call. She looked back at the shop. No Ellie.

"Tracy," she said when asked for her name. Then a seemingly interminable wait while the connection was made.

Finally she heard Mona say, "What took you?"

"I'm here," said Tracy. "What's this all about? I just spent five bucks on a cheap wallet."

"I didn't want to talk over the phone at the house. I thought someone might be listening."

"I figured that. But this looks a little obvious too, doesn't it?"

"Listen to me. Get out of that house."

"What?"

"I'll explain it all when I see you again. But there is something very odd going on, and it starts with Sandy Joseph."

"Talk to me."

"We both know his involvement in the drug trade."

"Yes."

"But did you also know he was funneling money into politics?"

"No, I didn't."

"Yes. Several places, apparently. But there is one place that you need to know about."

Tracy said nothing.

"Rob, Tracy. He was giving major money to Rob's campaign."

Blood rushed out of Tracy's head. She grabbed onto the phone base to keep from falling.

"Trace, you there?"

"I'm here. How do you know this?"

"I uncovered some deleted files on a disk of his. Tracy, this guy was paranoid. He was prepping a big document implicating a whole bunch of people, then had second thoughts and wiped the stuff out. Only it didn't wipe. And one of the names he had listed is Rob Cavanaugh."

The world seemed to be withdrawing in fast motion around Tracy.

"Joseph was funneling money to Rob's campaign. I just don't know exactly how, but Joseph ends up dead. Maybe there's a connection, maybe there isn't. But there's something else."

"What?"

"Ever heard of a company called NyDex Systems?"

"Software or something, isn't it?"

"Big time. Joseph made some unflattering comments about a guy named Kohlbert."

"Who's that?"

"I did some checking on the Net. He's the guy who started NyDex, and from what I read he's pretty cutthroat."

Shaking her head, Tracy said, "What does this have to do with Rob?"

"I don't know. Maybe nothing. Maybe it was just another one of Joseph's connections, or maybe this guy Kohlbert is more ambitious than we know."

"Meaning?"

"Meaning taking a strong interest in Rob's future."

Tracy caught her breath and closed her eyes.

"Tracy," Mona said, "I want you to get out of there."

"Yes . . ."

"I'm sorry," Mona said. "Tracy?"

"Yeah?"

"Pray, will you? I will, too."

"Sure." But something in Tracy told her she would need some answers first. She'd need to know how much Rob knew about any of this.

"Can you get out?" Mona asked.

Tracy looked down the boardwalk and that's when she saw Ellie. She had Bryce and Allison at her sides and was heading toward the phone. "I've got to go!"

"Tracy, what's wrong?"

Tracy hung up quickly and turned around.

"Everything all right?" Ellie asked.

"Just fine," said Tracy.

"We got candy!" Allison announced, holding up a small plastic bag stuffed with multicolored sweets.

"That's wonderful," Tracy said, forcing a smile. "Let's go home, OK?"

"Did you get through to your party down south?" Ellie said, not moving.

"Yes, I did."

"A good conversation, was it?"

"Fine," Tracy said, noticing now her jaw was clenched. For a moment she met Ellie's gaze, which was cool and steady.

"Then we might as well be on our way," said Ellie finally. "After you."

*She knows something.*

Bear Paw had watched from the road, using binoculars to watch her every move. The way she had walked out of the shop, how she had snatched up the phone, how her body sagged at certain news—the body language was clear.

He found himself thinking, *Don't show it so much.* He realized then that he was watching her in a larger context. Sitting outside of the battle between this one, lone woman and the cabal who hired him, he saw the latest moves as part of the contest. How far could she go before the end? How much could she learn? What would be their reaction when they found out she knew?

They would scream for him to do his work, of course.

But for the time being, he watched.

# CHAPTER TWENTY-THREE

ELLIE DEBUSSY was going over some paperwork in the dining area. Tracy approached her from the stairs. "Something I can do for you?" Ellie said, removing her glasses.

"Yes," said Tracy. "I need to get back to Los Angeles and take care of a couple of things. Can you have Jackson bring the car around? I want to catch the afternoon flight."

Ellie's face remained impassive, except for a slight twitch around her eyes. "Anything I can do?"

"Just have the car brought around, please."

Tracy started to leave. Ellie's voice stopped her. "Rob is coming in this afternoon. Can't you wait until then?"

"I'm afraid not."

"He'll be awfully disappointed."

"Can't be helped."

Rising from her chair, Ellie said, "I've got an idea. Why not leave the kids here with us? Go down, take care of business, and come back?"

"I'd rather they were with me. I don't know how long I'll be."

"Of course. Very well then."

Nodding, Tracy hurried back upstairs, almost stumbling as she reached the top. The kids were waiting for her in her room.

"Why do we have to go?" Allison wanted to know. "It's so fun here."

"I have to take care of some business," Tracy said.

"Are we coming back?"

"I don't know."

Allison said, "I wanna live here."

Tracy stroked her daughter's hair. "Wherever we live," she said, "we'll be together. That's the important thing."

As she helped the children get their things together, her mind worked overtime, trying to fit all the pieces together.

What was Rob's role in all this? How much did he know? It was possible he was a complete innocent, being removed from the day-to-day of his operation. But what did that say about the people around him? Was he in danger himself?

Tracy was hoping Mona was mistaken. Maybe it was all a matter of rumors. But some of those puzzle pieces were beginning to fit snugly. That she couldn't deny.

Sandy Joseph murdered. O'Lean Murray framed as the perpetrator. Why? To cover up the fact that Joseph was hit. Hit by whom? Someone from the drug underworld? Or someone from the political world—someone *hired* by that world.

Conspiracy.

The thought was chilling. She'd never been one to go looking for political conspiracies. Most theories of political intrigue were nutty. But not all. Maybe this was one of those. Maybe there was something to this NyDex connection, too. She'd have to think about all this later, back in L. A. Now she had one task—get out.

Finally, the bags were packed. Tracy led the children down the stairs. Ellie was waiting for them. She looked for a moment like one of those holograms that appears to turn and watch you no matter which way you move.

"Is the car—" Tracy stopped when Ellie looked to her right. Tracy turned and saw a man emerging from the living room. He was a powerful-looking presence, sharply dressed, and impeccably groomed. He reminded Tracy of some of the big-time defense lawyers she'd come up against, guys like Jackson Beymer, who wore expensive suits to advertise their success.

"Miss Shepherd, I'm Terrence Hagan. I work for Rob Cavanaugh." He didn't offer to shake her hand. "Rob will be here shortly."

Tracy stiffened. "I'm going to catch a flight to L. A. I'll talk to Rob later."

"It might be better for all concerned if you spoke with him now."

A ripple of fear hit her, fear for her children, mostly. They were in harm's way, and she had put them there. *God allowed it,* was the thought that followed immediately.

Hagan extended a hand toward the living room. "Why don't you and I discuss this in here? I'm sure Ellie would be glad to take the kids into the kitchen for some ice cream, eh?"

"Come along," Ellie said to the children, without waiting for Tracy's approval. The kids hesitated, looking to their mother. She nodded to them, and they followed Ellie to the kitchen. Hagan led Tracy into the living room and offered her a chair. She didn't take it.

"It's not a good idea for you to leave right now," said Hagan. He faced the large bay window looking out at the lake. "We'd like it very much if you stayed."

"I don't choose to stay," Tracy said.

"Well, choice may not be a part of it." Hagan turned and faced her. She noticed a tightness around his eyes and resoluteness to his expression. It reminded her of a picture she'd once seen of a prisoner of war, taken by his captors, showing an indomitable will. That's what Hagan appeared to have. No wonder he was in politics.

"Are you telling me I'm a prisoner here?" Tracy said.

"I'd rather say you were a guest."

"But a guest who is not free to leave?"

"Precisely."

"Are you absolutely nuts?" Her anger was rising. She made no attempt to stop it. "You think you can get away with this idiotic attempt at coercion? What is the matter with you?"

Without so much as a flutter of the eyelids, Hagan said, "I've done many things in my career in politics, Miss Shepherd, and this is not the most difficult decision I've made."

"I could ruin you. I could ruin any career Rob might have. What are you thinking?"

"You know, I once worked for a congressman from one of the southern states." Hagan began to pace a small circle as he spoke. "He was not expected to win in the district, but I had other plans. His opponent was a lawyer, a woman in fact, and when she discovered what she thought was a campaign . . . irregularity, she went to court. You know what happened? She ended up being disbarred." He stopped and faced Tracy again, as if she was to fold up at this point.

She said, "And the point of that little fable is?"

Hagan smiled. "The machine turns, and those who control the machine are the ones who come out on top. Any threat to our position is going to be met with swift and decisive action. I hope this is becoming clear to you."

"The only thing that's clear to me is that I'm dealing with a diseased mind."

The remark got a twitch out of Hagan's face. He pulled his shoulders back slightly. Tracy half expected him to slip off his coat and put up his dukes. But he quickly regained his composure. "The only disease I suffer from," said Hagan, "is being repulsed by losing."

"At any cost?"

Before he could answer, a voice said, "No." Tracy whirled around. Rob Cavanaugh was standing in the foyer.

"Let me have a word with her alone," said Rob. Hagan hesitated a moment, then silently left the room. Rob looked at Tracy and nodded toward the rear doors. "Please?"

Tracy followed Rob outside. Being next to him gave her a mix of feelings. One of them was fear—not so much for what might happen to her, but what she might find out about him.

"I'm sorry you had to meet Terrence like that," Rob said, putting a hand on her shoulder.

Tracy immediately pulled away. "Will you please tell me what is going on?"

"Of course I will." He stepped toward her, his arms reaching out. She raised her hands to stop him.

"Just talk to me," Tracy said. "Why am I being held prisoner here?"

"Maybe I should ask you why you want to leave. I thought we had everything set up. Now suddenly you want to get out. What happened?"

Tracy looked deeply into his face, trying to read his expression. He looked like the sincere suitor, begging for an explanation, but something about his eyes kept her from accepting that. It was like he was watching more than listening. She decided to give it to him between the eyes. "We have reason to believe your campaign is being funded by drug money."

"We?"

"I'm not alone in this. Do you have anything to say?"

"That's a pretty outrageous statement. Maybe I should be shocked."

"But you're not, are you? There's something to this. I want to know what."

Rob smiled, but this time it was more of resignation than anything else. "In politics, and in life, you have to learn when not to ask questions. I'm a political candidate, and there is only one reason for me to be here—to win. I have a whole machinery set up. All I'm interested in is that the machinery runs well. I don't really care about the details."

"I can't believe I'm hearing this."

"Don't patronize me, Tracy. This is the real world."

"No, the world you're talking about is a fantasy. You think you can ignore the law like this?"

"I don't even think about it. I don't have to. I let others handle it for me."

Tracy stared at him. He seemed to shrink in size right before her eyes. "What about your professed beliefs? All your talk about traditional moral values? All a sham?"

"I prefer to think of it as positioning. What do you think politics is all about? Ultimately, it's doing the will of the people, isn't it? If you're elected, you have the chance to do all you promised."

"Who's pulling your strings, Rob? What promises have you made to them?"

"Tracy, like I just said, sometimes you have to know when not to ask questions. Look at all this." He made a large, sweeping arc with his arm. "This can be yours, and the kids', too. We still have something between us, you and I. I can give you a great life."

She shook her head. "How can you possibly believe I'd stay with you?"

"Because I'm used to getting what I want."

The sound of an outboard motor issued through the trees. "Am I free to go, or not?"

"I wish you'd think it over."

"Am I?"

Rob took a step back and opened his arms wide. "Of course. I won't hold you like some prisoner. But I want you to stay."

"I can't."

Rob nodded sadly, but it was a sadness etched in cool thought. For the first time, Tracy felt she was seeing the real Rob Cavanaugh.

"I'll see about the car," he said, stepping back inside. Tracy followed. When he closed the doors behind her, a world disappeared with it.

Hagan was waiting inside. Rob turned to Tracy. "Let me explain things to Terrence. Why don't you go get the kids ready?"

Tracy nodded and started for the kitchen. She caught a last glimpse of Rob and Hagan looking in her direction.

The kids were sitting in front of bowls of ice cream. Ellie said, "Everything all right?"

"I hope so."

"Then you're staying?"

"No. We'll be going."

"I'm sorry to hear that."

*I wonder if you are,* Tracy thought. *What is your role in all this? Or are you as much in the dark as I am?*

A moment later Rob stepped into the kitchen. "The car will be here in a little while. It will take you to the airport, where I'll arrange tickets for you."

At that moment Tracy wished she hadn't found out anything, if indeed anything was there. He hadn't denied the drug allegation, but he hadn't admitted it, either. Maybe it was all just some irregularity that could be cleared up. Maybe she could *help* him clear it up, and everything could be made right.

Her thoughts were a jumble when Ellie announced that the car had arrived. Rob was waiting outside as the kids, suitcases in hand, bounded out, Tracy behind them. "I wish things were different," he said, and she thought he meant it. She also knew there were reasons things couldn't be different.

Tracy nodded slightly, then followed the kids down the path to the black Cadillac with tinted windows. Hagan stood at the open passenger door. He gave Tracy a cool look as she climbed in. Almost immediately the car fired up and pulled away. Tracy's last view of Rob was of him standing, shoulders hunched, in the doorway of his magnificent home.

She turned her attention to the driver. It wasn't Jackson, the jovial chauffeur. This one looked like a hired hand, with his flannel shirt and long, black hair. Tracy thought, from the look of him, that he was a Native American.

Mona had that feeling again, that burden. Tracy needed prayer. She was in trouble. She went to her sofa, her prayer closet in the middle of the room, and dropped to her knees. She began to pray in earnest, her hands clutched tightly together until the knuckles showed white.

The driver was the silent type, not one for idle conversation. Tracy asked if he was heading for the airport. He nodded. But that was it.

"Are you and Rob still gonna get married?" Bryce asked.

"Why are you asking me that?" Tracy said.

"Because we're leaving so all of a sudden."

"Yeah," Allison said, looking up at her mother.

"Can we talk about this when we get back?" Tracy pleaded.

"Don't you love him no more?" Allison persisted.

"Any more," said Tracy.

"Any more," said Allison.

"Let's just put it this way," said Tracy. "I love you two most of all." She smiled then, and thought she noticed the driver with his head turned to listen. For some reason, this made her feel uneasy. Something wasn't right.

She looked out the window and noticed they were on a dirt road. "I don't remember this on the way in," she said to the driver. He did not respond.

"Excuse me," she said, leaning forward. "Where are you taking us?"

Without turning his head, the driver said, "Airport."

"Is this the right way?"

"Yes."

Tracy looked outside again. The thickness of the pines blotted out any sight of the lake or civilization. It seemed like a private road. She decided to sit back and not worry about it. Rob wouldn't have anybody incompetent on his staff. No, competence was not the problem. Ethics was.

The car began to slow down.

"Is there a problem?" Tracy said.

"Maybe," said the driver. He slowed more, then came to a complete stop at the crest of a small hill. He opened the door and got out.

"Why are we stopping, Mommy?" Allison said.

"I don't know." Tracy watched the driver as he walked around the back of the car, hesitated, then appeared at her window. He tapped it, motioning her to get out.

She did.

For the first time she saw him face to face. He was Native American for sure, with haunting, dark eyes. "Come with me," he said.

*Obviously something wrong with the car,* Tracy thought. She glanced back at her children. Bryce was engaged with a puzzle page from a children's travel book. Allison was watching him.

The driver walked several paces away from the car. Tracy took three steps toward him, but when he stopped, she stopped. When he turned, she felt fear.

*He's going to kill me.*

The thought came from the blue, but it made odd, disjointed sense. She backed up a step. The Indian seemed to sense her realization.

"No," Tracy said, taking another step back.

"Don't," said the Indian.

She was at a loss. There was no way she could free her children and flee. Where would she go anyway? And now this horrible thing would happen in front of them. Maybe he would kill them, too.

The Indian stepped toward her, shaking his head.

"No!" Tracy shouted.

And then he was upon her, grabbing her shoulders hard, his hands like steel vices, his teeth bared. She tried to pull loose but couldn't budge. His fingers dug into her skin.

"Stop!" he said. "You're not going to die!"

Tracy ceased struggling. "What?"

He loosened his grip, but not all the way.

"Listen to me," he said. "You will drive the car. Do not go to the airport. Drive to Los Angeles. The man you want is named Kohlbert. Sherman Kohlbert. You will have no trouble finding where he is. He's the key."

"Who are you?"

"Now I'm nobody. And that's the way it will have to be."

"You work for them. You're the hit man."

He said nothing.

"You can help me," she said. "We can bring them down together."

He shook his head. "You can do it alone. I've watched you."

"Please."

Again, he indicated no. "I would be giving up my life."

She couldn't argue with him. As a cooperative witness, there might be some leniency. But murder is murder, and you do hard time for that no matter what.

"At least let me know how I can reach you," she pleaded.

"Unreachable," he said. He turned and walked toward the forest.

"Wait," said Tracy.

He didn't. He began to run. And in two seconds he had disappeared into the trees.

A voice came from the car. "Mommy?"

She went to the open passenger door. Bryce and Allison looked at her. "What's going on?" Bryce said.

"We're going home," said Tracy.

## CHAPTER TWENTY-FOUR

"I'LL WANT YOU to second chair this case," Walt Lindross said. "You know more about it than anyone."

Tracy was sitting across from the district attorney of Los Angeles County in his office on the eighteenth floor. Things had moved swiftly since her return. She and Lindross had gone to the grand jury and secured an indictment against Sherman Kohlbert for the murder of Sandy Joseph. Their star witness before the grand jury had been none other than Detective Stan Willis.

Willis had cracked when interrogated. In monosyllabic tones he detailed how the killing went down, how it had been ordered by Kohlbert through a hit man named Tommy Bear Paw. He detailed the plans of Sherman Kohlbert to push NyDex Systems to the top of the computer world, plans that included buying the influence of a new governor. That couldn't be done directly, but drug money from Sandy Joseph—laundered through dummy corporations with offshore accounts—could do it. Kohlbert owned Joseph, Willis said, but when Joseph looked like he might talk, Kohlbert had him killed.

Putting the hit man at the scene was done through a reluctant witness who went by the street name of Mickey D. The prosecutors didn't even have to call Randall Lefferts, who had been picked up and was now being held without bond. He would surely testify in return for a deal to save his own skin.

Immediately after the indictment, Sherman Kohlbert secured the services of Jackson Beymer, who almost instantaneously held a press conference to denounce this "witch hunt."

So the game was on. Having Beymer on the case would guarantee a full frontal assault on the press, the D. A.'s office, and the system of justice itself. There would be no prisoners.

Lindross, in conjunction with his chief deputy and central trials director, had tapped Hank Conroy to handle the trial. Conroy was considered one of the best trial lawyers in the office, with long experience, and he also had the personality to contend with Jackson Beymer.

Tracy agreed. But she was also glad to be second chair. She wanted to be part of this one.

Nodding, she said, "I'll give it all I have."

"I know you will," said Lindross. "That's why I'm glad you're back. I look forward to having you around here for a long time."

"Me, too."

"By the way, you'll be meeting with an FBI agent named Humphreys on the Cavanaugh matter. They think they know where to find him." Tracy looked down at the light blue carpet.

"You OK?" said Lindross.

"I'll be all right."

"I know it's hard. But to tell you the truth I never liked the guy anyway. Too much Clinton, not enough Truman."

Tracy forced a smile. "What about O'Lean Murray?"

Lindross nodded, his face showing concern. "Right. We'll move to reopen and dismiss. Of course, that's not going to look good, especially to all the victim's friends who were in the courtroom asking for the kid's head."

"How's that going to play? For you, I mean."

"Well, it certainly isn't going to make me look like the king of competence." Lindross laughed. "But it's the right thing to do, and we'll do it. I'll take my chances in the next election."

Tracy's admiration for him grew. *At last,* she thought, *a district attorney putting duty before politics*. That was the kind of boss she wanted to work for.

"Good luck." Lindross stood and extended his hand. As she shook it, Tracy thought once more how she never wanted to sit in the chair behind that desk. All she wanted was to stay in the courtroom trenches and fight for justice.

As she walked down the corridors of the D. A.'s office, Tracy couldn't help but wonder if justice would prevail in this case. Beymer was the best, and if anyone could get Kohlbert off the hook, it was him. Rob and his man Hagan would find the same quality legal help when that all came down. The only answer was to fight. She knew now she was in the fight of her life.

And she was glad she was in it with Hank Conroy. Entering his office after a slight knock, Tracy felt a flow of confidence just by looking at him. He was in his fifties, but his hair was still dark and perfectly combed. Coupled with his selection of only the best suits and dress shirts, Conroy's personal appearance always gave the impression of a man with all aspects of his life in order. He inspired confidence in juries simply because he never fiddled around with papers and notes and books. Everything was in its place in Conroy's courtroom.

Conroy also had that most prized possession of the trial lawyer—a photographic memory. It gave him the ability to recall testimony and transcript pages with almost perfect accuracy. Defense lawyers feared him for that, because they knew they could never snow him. In fact, the only lawyer reputed to have a comparable memory was Jackson Beymer. The Kohlbert trial would be a show just to watch those two in action.

"How you doin'?" Conroy said in his informal way of speaking. He had been raised in one of the tougher sections of Chicago and never lost his street edge. That was another reason juries warmed to him. He seemed like one of them. He never spoke down to the jurors.

"I guess it's you and me," Tracy said.

"Guess so." Conroy leaned back in his chair and folded his hands across his chest. "You ready?"

"Ready."

"Good. 'Cause we're working as a team here. I don't want to be the captain. As far as I'm concerned, we're equals. We'll divide things up right down the line. When I pause and smile for the television cameras, I want you there smiling with me."

"I'm all smiles."

"All right. Let's get to it."

For the next several hours, Hank Conroy and Tracy Shepherd began to lay plans for the trial of their lives.

That night Mona came over for coffee and a video. Tracy had spent a wonderful evening with her children, playing games and laughing and feeling at home again. Then she'd tucked them into bed and read stories to each. It was like having a normal life again.

Almost normal. There was still some unfinished business.

"That's why I asked you over," Tracy said as she handed Mona a cup of coffee.

"I think I know," Mona answered. They were in the quiet of the living room. The night seemed especially peaceful, though very dark.

"When I found out about Rob I almost gave in," said Tracy. "I almost chucked God right out of my life."

"God?"

"Yeah. I couldn't understand why God allowed it. Why weren't there any warning signs to begin with? Why did he let me get sucked in, all the time knowing there was this web underneath it all?"

Mona nodded.

"I didn't have the answer to that," Tracy continued, "or anything that even approached an answer. I still don't, but last night I began to wonder if we're always supposed to know the answer. I wonder if that's the meaning of it. Living without knowing, but trusting anyway."

Smiling, Mona said, "I think you're on to it."

"I may be, but I'm not *in* it. Not yet. Trust is something you can't manufacture out of thin air."

Mona thought for a moment. "You saying you don't trust God?"

"Maybe. That's why I wanted you here. I want you to pray over me. I want it to make a difference."

"I'm not a theologian, but I have a thought about it."

"I thought you might."

Mona laughed. "Basically, my thought is that God can do anything. Profound, huh?"

"I like it so far."

"And the Bible says anyone who calls on the name of the Lord will be saved."

"I don't think my salvation is an issue."

Mona quietly took up her Bible and began leafing the pages. "No, but there's an interesting passage in Matthew . . . here it is. Chapter 1, verse 21: 'She will give birth to a son, and you are to give him the name Jesus, because he will save his people from their sins.' You hear that? *From* their sins. Not just the penalty, but the power. I think that's the full promise."

"To save us from the power of sin?"

"Right."

"Which means save us from ourselves."

"You could say that. So if you call out to God for the very desire to trust in him, I think he gives you that desire."

Tracy was silent for a moment. "Let's go for it."

"Calling on his name?"

"All the way."

Mona smiled. "Since we've got the book open, let's take a look at one more section. Joshua, the last chapter. I love this. They've just conquered the land, right? And now Joshua gathers all the tribes at Shechem . . . and he reminds them of all that God has done for them. Then he says:

*Now fear the LORD and serve him with all faithfulness. Throw away the gods your forefathers worshiped beyond the River and in Egypt, and serve the LORD. But if serving the LORD seems undesirable to you, then choose for yourselves this day whom you will serve, whether the gods your forefathers served beyond the River, or the gods of the Amorites, in whose land you are living. But as for me and my household, we will serve the LORD.*

Mona paused, then said, "So the people chose the Lord. You would have thought it was a no-brainer, right? But Joshua put them through a renewal of their commitment, and that's what we as Christians have to do from time to time. We have to make that decision all over again. Who are we going to serve?"

Tracy nodded. "That's what I feel like. Renewing."

"Then let's renew," Mona said.

And they did. For an hour they prayed together. Tracy felt like layers of scales were peeling off of her, leaving some unadorned essence in their place. The recent past was shed as well, and a new hope for the future took hold. It was good to get back to the basics. She knew she would need them in the days ahead.

## CHAPTER TWENTY-FIVE

ON MONDAY MORNING the principals met in the chambers of Judge Loretta Rymer, Department 109, Superior Court of the County of Los Angeles. Present were Hank Conroy and Tracy Shepherd of the D. A.'s office, and Jackson Beymer along with his clerk, Lisa Robinson, a young, aggressive-looking law-student intern. With her head full of blond curls, she reminded Tracy of Leslie Abramson, the fiery lawyer who defended the Menendez brothers.

Judge Rymer, Hank told Tracy, was "tough but fair. If we keep away from nonsense and stick to the issues, we'll do fine."

"And Jackson Beymer?" Tracy said. "If he tries to pull something?"

"She won't let him get away with anything. At least, I don't think she will."

When Tracy saw Judge Rymer up close in her chambers, she had confidence that the judge would keep Beymer in line. Rymer was in her mid-fifties, with short, steel-colored hair and sharp, sparkling green eyes. After everyone was seated, she asked, "So are we all ready to do this thing?"

"Yes, Your Honor," said Beymer, with a slight smile.

"The People are ready," Conroy said.

"All right," said the judge, "but before we pick a jury let's just get a few things straight. We've got TV in the courtroom, and this is a big media deal, but I'm not going to tolerate any playing for the camera. I want this trial conducted within the four walls of my courtroom, not in the Nielsen ratings. Clear?"

"Clear," Conroy said.

Beymer shrugged, then put his hands out as if to say, "Who, me?"

"All right, then," said the judge. "Twenty minutes and we go."

The lawyers stood and made for the door. Conroy and Lisa Robinson were first out. That gave Jackson Beymer the opportunity to whisper to Tracy. "Well, here's your chance."

"Chance?" said Tracy.

"To watch me in action. You've got a front-row seat." He held the door for her. "Give you a chance to learn a few things."

"Thank you very much," she said, trying hard to keep her voice from dripping with too much sarcasm.

In the hallway, Beymer said, "As I once told you. In the courtroom, I'm God."

Tracy looked him in the eye and did not hesitate. "God does not send people threatening mail."

Beymer's eyelids twitched slightly. He said nothing.

"Oh I know all about it," Tracy said. "The little note, the phone calls. It was that man you were with at Langer's that day, what was his name? Cliff?"

Tracy saw a tightening in Beymer's face, but coolly he said, "I don't know what you're talking about."

"But I know. And you know that I know. Let's just leave it at that."

Tracy walked away. Beymer said nothing else and that, as much as anything, was confirmation for her. Yes, this would be a most interesting trial.

Twenty minutes later, Judge Rymer took her place on the bench. The courtroom was packed with media people, well-appointed onlookers—Tracy took these to be Kohlbert's retinue—and various court watchers, mostly senior citizens who spent their days viewing the real-life soap operas that are open to the public.

Rymer called the case, the lawyers stated their appearances, and then a group of citizens was summoned from the jury room.

The process of selecting a jury. Tracy sat up, all her attention focused on the impending *voir dire*. The term, she knew from law school, was French for "to speak the truth." Her criminal law professor instructed the class that this process is ostensibly the occasion when lawyers can uncover possible bias on the part of potential jurors. But then he told them what *really* goes on is that skilled lawyers try to predispose the jurors to their side of the case with suggestive questions and clever turns of phrase that press close to the ethical limit.

Tracy had her ears attuned as Jackson Beymer got up to question the first group of citizens seated in the jury box.

"Good morning, ladies and gentlemen," he said. His voice was smooth and even. *Like an FM easy-listening disk jockey,* Tracy thought. "I'm going to ask some questions of you now in this process the judge has explained to you, a process called *voir dire*. I assure you, though, it's not as dire as it sounds." Chuckles from the panel, and a charming smile from Beymer.

*He's good,* Tracy thought immediately. *Very, very good.*

"The first thing I need to do is introduce myself. My name is Jackson Beymer, and I'm here to represent a man accused of a crime." He strode over to the defense table and put his hand on the shoulder of Sherman Kohlbert. Tracy noted that Kohlbert was dressed in a conservative blue suit and burgundy tie, virtually the same outfit as Beymer. "This, ladies and gentlemen, is Sherman Kohlbert."

Kohlbert stood up and nodded toward the potential jurors.

*Well rehearsed,* Tracy thought. *Kohlbert looks like a Boy Scout.*

After a pat on the shoulder by Beymer, Kohlbert sat down. Beymer approached the jury box. "The first thing I need to find out is if anyone here knows my client personally. Anyone?"

No one raised a hand.

"Fine. And how about by reputation—his business, his contributions to the community, anything like that?"

*Objection!* Tracy thought. Beymer was testifying about "contributions to the community," painting a sympathetic picture of his client. This was clearly crossing the line. So why didn't Hank object? She looked at him, and he seemed to know what she was thinking. He shook his head slightly, as if to say, "It's not worth it." Sometimes a lawyer had to know when *not* to object.

Tracy turned her attention back to Jackson Beymer. "Now, does anyone know *me?*" Beymer said.

Three hands went up. Beymer looked toward an older man. "How do you know me, sir?"

"Seen you on TV," the man said.

"Doing a trial?"

"Yep."

"What did you think?"

The old man folded his arms. "Pretty slick."

Laughter arose from the panel. Jackson Beymer laughed, too. "Don't know if that's a compliment or not," Beymer said with a chuckle. Tracy watched the faces of the panelists, and what she saw jolted her. They were connecting with Jackson Beymer, almost like he had them in a spell. They had smiles on their faces, like they would if listening to a charming conversationalist at a party.

That's what Jackson Beymer was doing, Tracy suddenly realized. Making this trial like a party . . . *his* party. And there was little that Hank Conroy could do about it. Nothing in the evidence code said a lawyer couldn't charm the jurors.

"Let me ask all of you," Beymer continued, "if I can get an assurance from you that you'll just forget about me and do only one thing—focus on the evidence in this case, because it doesn't affect me, but that man—" Beymer pointed dramatically at Sherman Kohlbert—"a man accused by the government of committing a terrible crime. That's what I need to know, ladies and gentlemen. I'm nothing here. The accused is everything, as the judge will tell you."

*Another good move,* Tracy noted. Getting the jurors to perceive that the judge was on his side.

"If you're willing to assure me of that, will you raise your hands, please?" Beymer said. Every hand went up.

"Thank you," Beymer said. "Thank you. That means more than anything. Now, we need to talk about the burden of proof, the most important aspect of any criminal trial."

Beymer looked directly at a middle-aged woman. Tracy glanced down at her juror questionnaire. Her name was Samantha Desmont. She had described herself as a "wife and mother."

"Now Mrs. Desmont," Beymer said, "the prosecution always has the burden of proving guilt beyond a reasonable doubt. You understand that, don't you?"

The woman nodded and said, "Yes."

"Does that rule bother you?"

She hesitated a moment and said, "Well, it's the law, I guess."

"But you wouldn't find Mr. Kohlbert guilty just because you think he *might* have been involved, would you?"

"No."

"And why not?"

"Because it has to be beyond a reasonable doubt, right?"

"Is that how you understand the law?"

"Yes."

"And can you promise us, Mrs. Desmont, that you will hold the prosecution to its burden of proof—*beyond* a reasonable doubt?"

"Yes."

"And if the prosecution fails to prove its case beyond a reasonable doubt, what will your verdict be?"

"Not—"

Before she could finish, Hank Conroy was on his feet. "Your honor, we'll object at this point. This has become final argument, not *voir dire*."

"I agree," said Judge Rymer. "Move on, Mr. Beymer.

"Thank you, Your Honor," said Beymer with a smile. Tracy nodded and smiled to herself, like a magician who admires the way another magician palms a playing card. Beymer, by *thanking* the judge for an adverse ruling, actually gave the impression of liking what just happened, indicating the judge once again was on his side.

Jury selection lasted most of the day. By the time court recessed at 3:30, it was clear to Tracy what Beymer's pattern was. Back in Hank's office she said, "He's striking followers, isn't he?"

"Very good," said Hank. "You learn fast. Beymer doesn't want people who listen and compromise, you know, like real jurors?"

Tracy laughed.

"He wants opinion makers and strong heads because he wants at least some holdouts for a hung jury. If he doesn't win outright, he wants a mistrial."

"He's also striking the older people," said Tracy.

"Right again. He wants a few Generation Xers on that panel. They'll identify with Kohlbert, who's young and successful in an industry they all understand. They're also more suspicious of the system, a more cynical bunch. That works against us."

"You only exercised three challenges today. Why?"

"My philosophy, Tracy, is to let the jury panel know that we'll pretty much take whatever hand is dealt to us. I got rid of three of the most obvious people who'd work against us. But I want that jury to know we're not like Beymer, trying to get a predisposed jury. I want them to know we have enough confidence in our case that it doesn't matter who hears it."

Tracy nodded.

"No matter what, though," said Conroy, "we've got our work cut out for us. Beymer knows how to play a jury. We've got to watch him every step of the way, and that's going to be your job. Are you ready for that?"

"Hank," Tracy said, "I'm as ready as I'll ever be."

Sitting on the hard chair, with the walls seeming to close in upon him, Stan Willis reached out and rearranged the handguns on his dining room table. He was forming a random pattern, even as his thoughts were doing their own swirl, seemingly without design.

Here, there was an image of his graduation ceremony from the police academy. Right behind it were shadows of the night, a vision of the mean streets, with predators everywhere—from the pimps and dope pushers to the gangbangers and armed robbers.

Now a remembrance of the family he once had—the wife who left and the kids who no longer spoke to him. They were together once, on a trip to Disneyland. The sounds of the amusement park grew louder in his brain, the screams of delighted children . . .

. . . to the screams of the woman who was kneeling beside her dead child, caught in the crossfire of a gang war. Then a *veterano* of the gang with his arms folded over his tattooed chest, nodding like it was just one of those things.

Willis pushed the four handguns around and around, making a swooshing sound as metal scraped against vinyl. The swooshing became the sound of waves on the beach, at night, almost ten years ago. He had driven out to Zuma after a night of drinking with his then-partner and plopped himself in the sand fully clothed. Looking up into the night sky, with the glitter of stars above him, he had never felt so peaceful. It was the last time he remembered ever feeling that way.

Hanging above him was the moon, bright and round, and it became a face: the face of Sherman Kohlbert. It was a face full of the power of the sun, reflecting silver light back at the cop who had just lost the people who were closest to him. It was about a week after his wife had walked out when Kohlbert first contacted him.

The moon face—Kohlbert's face—said everything would be all right, and would he consider eventually moving into private security, with a pay-and-benefits package that was so above anything he could ever hope for that he would feel like the Michael Jordan of law enforcement. The open market was finally paying him what he was worth.

But first there were a few things Kohlbert needed from him in his aspect as a police officer. Little things at first, involving a bending of the rules, not a breaking of the law. That would come later. But it would come.

Then the sound of waves became a crashing sound, louder in his head than anything he would have heard in the real world. He grabbed his head with both hands, covering his ears, but the crashing was inside his skull and no pressure, no covering, could make it stop.

When it became apparent that the crashing noise would not go away, when it was obvious that it would never leave, when the moon face gave way to a blinding white light, Stan Willis reached down with his eyes closed and felt all the guns on the table. Closing his hand around one the way the claw in an arcade game clutches a stuffed toy, he picked it up.

## CHAPTER TWENTY-SIX

ON TUESDAY MORNING Hank Conroy rose to give his opening statement to the jury. He introduced himself and then Tracy, who stood, nodded, and sat back down. He also introduced Mona Takata, sitting in the first row, as the chief investigator on the case.

Then, in simple terms, Conroy outlined the evidence they would present to the jury that would convince them, "beyond a reasonable doubt," that Sherman Kohlbert had contracted the murder of Sandy Joseph.

"It's an old story about greed and the lust for power," Conroy told the jury. "The defendant wasn't happy being a success. No, he had to be the next Bill Gates, show the world that he was better than everyone else. But things are tough in the computer industry. The defendant needed an advantage. He thought he found it in the governorship of the state of California."

Tracy glanced quickly at Sherman Kohlbert. His face was impassive.

"You will hear from a former detective of the Los Angeles Police Department," Conroy continued, "Stan Willis. He was part of the inner circle of this conspiracy; he will tell you exactly how and why Sherman Kohlbert arranged to have Mr. Joseph murdered. And he'll also tell you about his framing of an innocent man for the killing. This is the essence of our case. Everything else will be a matter of details, and all of those details will point to only one thing—the guilt of the defendant, Sherman Kohlbert."

Next it was Jackson Beymer's turn to open his case in front of the jury. It was as Tracy expected—smooth, theatrical, confident, poised, and just about the best opening statement she had ever heard. He explained how this opening was like a "mosaic." During the trial, bits of evidence would be presented—like colored tiles. His opening statement was now going to describe what the picture would look like when all the evidence was in.

And that would not be a pretty picture. He would show a picture of a prosecution case based more upon political motivations than hard facts. "This fantasy that the prosecution has concocted," Beymer said, his voice loaded with contempt, "is all based on circumstantial evidence. So be very clear about what's going on—the prosecution is under tremendous pressure to get a conviction in this case, so they are railroading an innocent man."

Hank Conroy shot to his feet. "Objection, Your Honor! This is argument."

"Sustained," said Judge Rymer. "Mr. Beymer, please restrict yourself to what you believe the evidence will show."

Smiling, Beymer said, "Thank you, Your Honor." He continued his statement as if he and the judge were the very best of friends. Beymer's opening statement lasted twenty minutes. Then it was time for the prosecution to call its first witness.

Mona Takata took the stand and swore to tell the truth, the whole truth, and nothing but the truth. Hank Conroy led her through the initial questions about her occupation and expertise, and then into the details of her investigation. He immediately went into her account of recovering the computer disk from the studio office of Sandy Joseph.

Tracy couldn't help stealing a look at Jackson Beymer. He obviously knew what was coming, the prosecution having disclosed its evidence to him under California's reciprocal discovery rules. What would he do about it? She didn't have long to wait to find out.

"Miss Takata," Conroy said, "what did you do with this disk once it was in your possession?"

"Objection, Your Honor," said Jackson Beymer, rising to his feet.

"On what grounds?" the judge asked.

"May we approach?"

"With the reporter." As the court reporter moved her transcriber to the judge's bench, the lawyers approached for a sidebar, a conference with the judge outside the hearing of the jury. Tracy and Beymer's clerk, Lisa, listened in.

"What's this about?" the Judge said to Beymer.

"Your Honor, I'm going to object to this line of questioning on hearsay grounds."

"Hearsay?"

"Yes. The disk they are talking about contains some ambiguous notations, supposedly made by Sandy Joseph. Leaving aside all the foundational problems, these statements are hearsay."

Hank said, "But the witness is obviously unavailable, Your Honor."

"But what exception to the hearsay rule would this fall under?" Beymer asked. Tracy knew full well what they all knew—the rule against hearsay had certain exceptions, but they were very specific. Beymer, by challenging Conroy to find one, was setting him up for a fall.

"The exceptions," said Judge Rymer, "are for declarations against interest, dying declarations, former testimony and, of course, state of mind. Do the statements fall under any of these?"

"State of mind for sure," said Conroy, looking at Beymer with some satisfaction.

"But the state of mind of Sandy Joseph is irrelevant," said Beymer quickly. "They want to introduce the statements to prove the matter asserted, namely, that my client is guilty. But these statements were made before the murder! How could they possibly be relevant?"

Judge Rymer looked at Hank Conroy. "A fair question."

Conroy hesitated. Beymer looked smug. Tracy reached into the depths of her recent memory and blurted, "Section 1370!"

Her voice was louder than it should have been, within easy earshot of the jury and spectators, some of whom tittered.

"Keep your voice down," Judge Rymer said. Hank Conroy looked at her as if she had just jumped onstage in the middle of a performance of *Death of a Salesman*. But it was Beymer's look that Tracy caught, and it was silent confirmation that she had hit the right note. He looked slightly taken aback.

"Now what was that section?" the Judge said.

"Thirteen-seventy, Your Honor," said Tracy. Judge Rymer reached for a volume of the California Evidence Code and started flipping the pages.

"It's the domestic violence section," said Beymer. "The new one. It doesn't apply."

"Let me look at it," the judge said. She got to the section and started reading. Beymer looked at Tracy now with a slight air of irritation.

"We haven't got any definitive law on this yet," Judge Rymer said, "but on the surface it looks like this may apply."

"I anticipated this, Your Honor," said Beymer. "If you'll carefully read subsection one, it requires that the statement narrate, describe, or explain the infliction or threat of physical injury. There is no such statement here."

"Oh, but there is," said Conroy, taking over once more. "Joseph says on more than one occasion that he fears Sherman Kohlbert."

"And I fear the rulings of our judge, but that doesn't make my statement admissible," said Beymer, eliciting a smile from Judge Rymer. *Not a good sign*, thought Tracy. *He's even charming the judge!*

"All right," said Judge Rymer, turning to Conroy. "Do you have a transcript of the statements you want to present?"

"I do, Your Honor."

"Give them to me. We'll take a short recess, and I'll look at them in chambers. Anything else, Mr. Beymer?"

"Only this, Your Honor. If you should for some reason find that these statements fall within a hearsay exception, I would plead most strenuously that under Evidence Code, section 352, they are much more prejudicial than they are probative. I think the prejudice to my client would be extreme."

"Mr. Conroy?"

"I obviously disagree," said Conroy. "But we'll submit it to you."

The judge informed the jury that she had to take up a legal matter before the trial continued, and dismissed them back into the jury room. A few of them looked annoyed, Tracy noticed. The first witness just got on the stand, and now they had to take a break. Score one for Beymer. Even though the jury couldn't know what was happening, the impression was that the prosecution had made a mistake. Beymer objected, went to the judge, and the judge called a recess.

"Don't worry about it," Hank Conroy told Tracy after the jury left. "There's no way Rymer is going to keep these out."

"I wish I were as confident as you are."

Mona walked over and tugged on Tracy's sleeve. "How'm I doing, counselor?"

"You're the most credible witness I've ever seen," Tracy said with a wink.

"Natch. So what do you think of all this? The judge going to let in the disk?"

"Hank says it's not a problem, but I don't know. There's something about Beymer. He seems to know just what to say."

"So does a ventriloquist's dummy." Mona laughed. Tracy smiled. She went out into the hallway to get a drink of water from the fountain. She felt a few heads turn toward her, then a woman with a pad walked up to her. "Hi, I'm Beth Thomas of the *Times*. Can I ask you a question?"

"You can ask," said Tracy. The judge had not issued a gag order on the case, so technically there was nothing to stop Tracy from talking with a reporter, but there was a policy in the office about the press: Don't give out any information that isn't a matter of public record.

The reporter asked, "Is there some connection between this case and the political ambitions of Walt Lindross?"

"Are you kidding me?" Tracy said.

"That's a denial?"

"Miss Thomas—"

"*Ms.* Thomas."

"Yes, well, this is now off the record."

"Oh, come on."

"Off the record. If I say it's a denial, you'll print that I've denied something that is being manufactured out of whole cloth. But the very fact of printing the denial lends some credence to this speculation. You understand, don't you?"

Thomas hesitated, chewed on her pencil eraser, then said, "Let me ask you this. What about the bad blood between you and Jackson Beymer?"

"What are you talking about?"

"Well, isn't it a fact that you were upset about a case against one of his clients being pled out?"

She was talking about Sollomon. But how did she know so much about it? Tracy could think of only one way. Beymer himself must have been talking to her, giving his spin. Now Tracy was in the position of either speaking up for herself, thus lending more weight to the story the reporter was fishing for, or keeping quiet and letting Beymer's version be authoritative.

"I'm sorry, Ms. Thomas. No comment."

"You make it tough," the reporter said. "But if you change your mind you know where I'll be. Second row."

Tracy nodded. There was something tenacious about this reporter. And she recognized the name. Where had she heard it before? The glimmer of memory said it had something to do with an investigative report about brutality by county sheriffs. Before she could explore the thought further, a voice behind her called her name. She turned and saw Kendra Murray hurrying up to her.

"Miss Shepherd! Praise God!" she said, her arms outstretched. Before Tracy knew it the woman was embracing her. It was a bear hug, warm and all-encompassing.

"How are you, Mrs. Murray?" Tracy said.

"Praise God, I'm wonderful. O'Lean's getting out today."

Warmth spread through her body at the news. "That's wonderful."

"You and me both know God had his hand on us all the time!"

"We sure do."

"And I want to tell you something. God is using you for justice. The Holy Spirit is witness to that."

Tracy smiled. At last she felt comfortable again talking about her faith. "I believe it, too. That's why I'm here."

"Amen and amen. Thank you for everything." Kendra Murray hugged Tracy once more. "I'm going to get my boy now. He's going to go to UCLA, did you know that?"

"I didn't. That's wonderful."

"Do you mind if I call you sometime? Just to tell you how he's doing?"

"Not at all. I'd love it."

With a smile that lit up the hallway, Kendra Murray said, "Bye now!" and walked back to the elevators. Tracy watched her go, giving her a wave as the doors closed. *God really was in all this,* she thought. Everything would be all right.

She checked her watch. It was time to go back in. The judge was going to make her ruling.

As Tracy walked back into the packed courtroom and past the bar to the counsel table, Jackson Beymer slid up next to her. "Are we having fun yet?" he said with a smile.

She said nothing, slipping past him to her chair. His cockiness made her extremely uneasy. Just before she sat down she looked out at the audience and noticed Beth Thomas staring right at her.

*This must be what a germ feels like under a microscope,* Tracy thought.

The bailiff suddenly piped, "Remain seated and come to order. This court is again in session."

Judge Rymer took the bench. "Back on the record in the matter of People against Kohlbert. Let the record reflect the defendant is present with counsel, and all counsel are here. The jury is not present."

She shuffled some papers in front of her. She looked sullen, Tracy thought. As if she was not pleased.

Judge Rymer said, "The court has before it an objection to an electronic document, based on both hearsay and prejudice grounds. I have looked over the transcript of the statements on the electronic recording, provided to me by the People. I found several parts of the document to be irrelevant to this proceeding, and have redacted the document accordingly. What remains is, however, hearsay."

Tracy looked at Hank Conroy. He was looking straight ahead.

"The first question to be resolved is whether these statements fall under any of the exceptions to the hearsay rule. The only possible exception is section 1370 of the Evidence Code, the so-called violence exception. There are five requirements that must be met, one of which is that the statement was made under circumstances that would indicate its trustworthiness. The code section itself tells us what to look for."

*This is taking too long,* Tracy thought suddenly. She looked at the Court TV camera. It was pointing straight at the judge.

"The first factor is whether the statement was made in contemplation of pending or anticipated litigation in which the declarant was interested. I find that it was not. This is a criminal matter, and no offer has been made that a civil action was in the declarant's mind.

"Second, we must ask whether the declarant had a bias or motive for fabricating the statement, and the extent of any bias or motive."

Judge Rymer paused, took a breath. "When I consider the totality of the statements, it is apparent that the declarant was involved in some criminal schemes. These may or may not have involved the defendant in this case—that's another matter. But clearly there existed a motive for the declarant to color his statements in a prejudicial fashion against the defendant. Therefore the electronic document does not qualify as an exception to the hearsay rule."

Once again, the judge paused. Tracy thought, *Maybe she's going to give us a back door.*

"There being no other basis to admit this document," Judge Rymer said, "it is inadmissible."

"Your Honor!" Hank Conroy said, jumping to his feet. "May we be heard?"

Beymer was on his feet like a shot. "He submitted this, Your Honor!"

"We want to be heard!" Conroy insisted.

"No," said the judge forcefully. "You submitted the matter to me. You had your chance for argument. Let's move on."

"But Your Honor," Conroy pleaded.

"No, Mr. Conroy."

Stunned, Hank Conroy said, "Then may we extend this recess to tomorrow?"

Beymer immediately jumped in. "They're unprepared, Your Honor. This is a waste of the jury's time. They should be ready to try their case."

"Thank you for your opinion, Mr. Beymer," the judge said. She glanced at the courtroom clock. "I have a funeral to attend this afternoon. It won't hurt much to end proceedings early today. I recognize my ruling will require some thought on the part of the prosecution. Very well, we'll start up again tomorrow at nine o'clock."

And with that, Judge Rymer left the bench.

Conroy rubbed his eyes. "Just great," he said. "What else can happen?"

"Let's not ask," said Tracy. She looked at Jackson Beymer, who was laughing as he spoke to Sherman Kohlbert.

Tracy took refuge in her office. Needing a break, she pulled out her Bible and began reading the fourth chapter of John. The account of the Samaritan woman fascinated her. Jesus was leading this woman, a social outcast, to the truth about himself—and *herself*—by a clever use of questions. *Jesus,* she surmised, *would have been the greatest lawyer of all time.* Of course, he knew the answers to the questions before he asked them!

The Samaritan woman wanted to avoid the subject of her five husbands and current housemate. She wanted to discuss generalities. Jesus would not let her off the hook. He used his questions to bring her back to the point—that she was speaking to the one who had been promised. Tracy felt a warmth from the distant past. It was the warmth of enveloping faith.

There was a quick knock on her door, and then it opened. Mona stuck her head in. "Tracy!" she said with an odd urgency in her voice.

"What is it? Come in."

Mona entered the office looking dizzy and pale. "Are you all right?" said Tracy.

"No." She slumped heavily into a chair. Her eyes were glassy. "It's Willis," she said.

"What about Willis?"

"He's dead."

Shock paralyzed Tracy.

"He shot himself. Somebody says he did it with a street handgun, obviously something he wasn't authorized to have."

"This is . . . crazy."

"What's this going to do to your case?"

Tracy looked at the ceiling. "It might kill it."

"You mean that?"

"Of course I mean it. He was our main witness, a guy from the inner circle. Without him, we have no one who can testify about any meetings Kohlbert had with any of the people. I don't believe this."

"What about those guys he named? You know, like Rob's right-hand man?"

"You mean Hagan? Without Willis's ID there's nothing to tie them to Kohlbert."

"You know something, Tracy? It's almost like Kohlbert set this up, too. You think?"

Tracy thought. "I'll tell you one thing. It really is like there's some dark force acting on his behalf."

"I heard that. Maybe it's Jackson Beymer."

In spite of everything, Tracy had to laugh. Yes, it was almost like that. Beymer seemed to have some sort of power. Then, suddenly, it didn't seem funny. Who knew what Sherman Kohlbert was like, the way he could pull strings?

Tracy felt like she was shrinking right there in her own office. It was a good thing court was in recess. There was no way she could go back into that courtroom today. And then the question Hank Conroy had asked popped into her mind. It kept popping in and out for the rest of the day.

*What else can happen?*

# CHAPTER TWENTY-SEVEN

THE NEXT MORNING, Tracy arrived early at the CCB. Part of the reason was to avoid the crowd that was beginning to assemble each day for the high-profile case. Also, to try to get some quiet time in her office to gather her thoughts and pray for strength. She was going to need it.

How were they going to make a case without Stan Willis? She had thought a lot about him last night, how tortured he must have been. A career cop, but one who had gone bad. And it all had finally caught up with him. Such things happened, but why did it have to happen now?

She stopped at the newspaper vending machines to pick up a copy of the *Daily Journal*, the Los Angeles legal newspaper, and the *Daily News* and the *Times*. She needed to keep up on what all of them were reporting about the trial.

Newspapers under arm, she rode the elevator to the eighteenth floor and entered the prosecutor's office. A few of the support staff nodded at her as she headed to her office.

She plopped her briefcase and purse on the floor next to her desk, sat down, and spread the newspapers in front of her. All three papers trumpeted yesterday as a series of setbacks for the prosecution. "Ex-Cop Kills Self" was the headline on the front page of the *Daily News*. The subhead read, "Was to be Star Witness in Kohlbert Murder Trial."

The *Daily Journal* was more subdued in its characterizations, in keeping with its reputation as an objective legal journal. But the news was just the same.

By the time Tracy got to the *Times,* she didn't want to read anything else. She only read the headline, "Cop Suicide Throws Trial into Turmoil." That was enough.

Just before she tossed the paper aside, though, she caught sight of a little sidebar story in the lower right-hand corner of the front page. What she read made her hair feel alive with static.

"Prosecutor Puts Faith on Trial" was the headline. The story read:

> Los Angeles County Deputy District Attorney Tracy Shepherd, assisting in the prosecution of Sherman Kohlbert for murder, is taking a rather large view of the proceedings. She sees herself as an instrument of God's retribution.
>
> During a break in the trial proceedings yesterday, Shepherd engaged an unidentified woman in conversation in the courthouse hallway. The woman told Shepherd that the Holy Spirit had told her God was using her to bring justice to the world.
>
> "I believe it," said Shepherd. "That's why I'm here."
>
> Kohlbert's defense attorney, Jackson Beymer, agrees that Shepherd sees herself as a messenger of the Lord. "She's always had that attitude," Beymer said. "I don't know whether to run or bow down when I see her coming."
>
> The trial of Sherman Kohlbert continues today at the Criminal Courts Building.
>
> —Beth Thomas

Tracy felt the first flush of anger rise inside her. It became almost a blinding heat behind her eyes. She crumpled the paper in her hands, with a picture in her mind of Beth Thomas's journalistic neck.

It took her twenty minutes to calm down. By then she'd received a call from Mona, who had read the paper at home. "Remember," she said, "blessed are those who are persecuted for His sake."

Tracy said, "I'm blessed enough. I don't want any more blessings."

"How you doing?"

"I feel like I've been stuck in a cosmic washing machine and I'm on spin cycle."

Mona laughed. "Well, it ain't over 'til it's over, right?"

"We've still got Lefferts. Everything OK there?"

"Yep. He's in protective custody, and we've got two officers watching him like a hawk."

"Why am I not feeling a great deal of comfort right now?"

"You just leave it to me."

Tracy liked the idea of leaving it with *anybody*.

Hank Conroy came to her office about half an hour before court was to commence. She asked him if she had endangered the case in any way. He reassured her that she hadn't. "Maybe it even helped," he joked. If any jurors read the story—in spite of the judge's admonition against it—they were sure to vote for guilt. After all, what juror would want to oppose God?

Then he said something that wasn't so funny. He wasn't feeling well, a little tightness in the chest. "Too much coffee," Tracy warned.

"Yeah, yeah," Conroy said. "But just in case, you be prepared to do some of the trial, OK?"

The trial. Tracy Shepherd head to head with Jackson Beymer. "You just get better," Tracy insisted. "I've had about all the Jackson Beymer I want for one lifetime."

---

The Denny's waitress was disturbed. She was about to get off, after a long graveyard shift, but she still had that one customer in the back corner. It wasn't so much the tip she hoped to earn. That would be measly. It was those eyes, the kind that follow you around, look you up and down, and remember you. He was the kind who would be back, maybe for a little stalking. Her imagination ran wild.

She had a sense about these things, Sally Robbins did. She'd been waitressing for seven years, and you got so you could tell. Especially doing graveyard. All the weird ones came in then—the addicts, wired for sound; the clubbers, who didn't want to go home; the wannabe screenwriters who thought coffee at three A.M. would help generate the next box office smash. And then there were what Sally called "the fringe dwellers," those people with the dark lives who lived somewhere on the edge, and often jumped over it.

This guy was a fringe dweller. He was dark like an Indian, and dangerous like a loser. He had America's Most Wanted written all over his face.

He'd been sipping coffee for three hours straight. The first two hours he did nothing but look out the window, as if waiting for the L. A. dawn to signal it was safe to go home. But then the dawn came, and he got up briefly, telling her not to move anything. *Anything*.

He went to the bathroom, Sally noted, then outside to the newspaper racks. He bought a paper—she wondered which one it was—then glided back to his booth. He read the paper for half an hour, during which time she poured him more coffee and noticed the paper was the *Times*. It looked like he had only read the front section. The other sections were still folded on the seat next to him. Sally wondered if he was looking to see whether the paper mentioned his name. Maybe he was a fugitive of some kind. Maybe he'd committed serial murder all across America and was now on the West Coast, looking for a hole to crawl into.

This was good material. Her boyfriend wanted to write true-crime books, and he always asked her if she'd run across any interesting people on her shift. She'd have a honey of a character for him this time: the Indian murderer, on the lam, who sat quietly drinking coffee at her station, reading the *L. A. Times* and looking out the window, wondering who his next victim would be.

Just as long as it wasn't her. Just as long as he went away before she did, so he wouldn't follow her home.

Sally stayed overtime, doing side work, filling salt shakers, emptying them, then filling them up again. She wiped down the refrigeration locker a half-dozen times. The manager told her to go home. She said she wasn't in any hurry.

Finally, about 8:30, the guy left. Sally peeked out from the back until he was out of sight, then she went to check out his table. He'd left no tip. He did leave the *L. A. Times,* though, all except the front section. Sally scooped it up and plopped it at the coffee station, so others could read it if they wanted to.

She waited about fifteen minutes more, just to give the serial killer plenty of time to put distance between himself and Denny's. Then she drove home and went to bed.

Tracy had to endure several shouted questions from the cluster of reporters outside the courtroom. She put up her hands to indicate "no comment," but this was not heeded. Just before she pushed through the courthouse door she heard a voice shout—she was pretty sure it wasn't a reporter, but after what had happened she was not sure—"Win one for Jesus!" The phrase was dipped in sarcasm.

Once again, court was packed. But there was only one face Tracy wanted to find. He was there, seated in the front row next to Mona Takata.

It was Mickey D, the gang kid who had parked cars on the night of the murder: the one who could testify about the appearance of the killer. Beymer was sure to argue during his case-in-chief that the killer was O'Lean Murray, and he'd have in hand all the evidence the prosecution had used to convict him in the first place. Since there was no connection between Murray and Kohlbert, the case would break down at this point.

But then their next witness, Randall Lefferts, would connect it all up by naming Tommy Bear Paw as the killer, describing him, then detailing the contacts he'd had with him. That should be enough to convict.

Tracy, however, wasn't betting on it. In the few moments she had before court began, she closed her eyes and silently prayed. She prayed for strength, for smarts, for tenacity, and for justice to be done. Later she realized she should have prayed for Hank Conroy. But by the time he joined her, she was in her courtroom mode, and Conroy was feeling ill.

"I don't think I'm going to make it today," he said, almost gasping for breath.

"Hank, you've got to."

"Can't." He was holding his chest with his hand.

"Let's get a continuance and get you to a doctor."

"Judge won't allow more delay. She'll want you to take over."

"We can ask."

Conroy winced. "I hope I'm not having a heart attack."

"You and me both," said Tracy. "You've got to get some help."

It was then that the bailiff ordered everyone to rise, and Judge Rymer stepped up to the bench. She called the case, announced the appearances of counsel for the record, then said immediately, "Are you all right, Mr. Conroy?"

"Good morning, Your Honor," said Hank, ever the gentleman lawyer. "No."

Almost without knowing it, Tracy said, "We'd like a continuance, Your Honor."

Hank shot a glance at her.

"For how long?" said the judge.

"Um, until he sees a doctor," Tracy said.

The judge turned to Jackson Beymer. "Mr. Beymer?"

Rising majestically, Beymer said, "I'm quite sure the People's case is safe in the capable hands of Ms. Shepherd. We all wish Mr. Conroy well, but we have a jury to consider."

"Quite right," said Judge Rymer. "Mr. Conroy, please go get some medical attention. We'll all look forward to your return."

Conroy nodded, turned, and whispered to Tracy, "You can do it." Then he shuffled out of the courtroom, slightly bowed, still holding onto his chest.

"That's unfortunate," Judge Rymer said. "Well, Ms. Shepherd, you get to be the star now."

*Great. Bring on the makeup crew.*

"I'm sure she'll rise to the occasion," Jackson Beymer said with a smile, "or go down in glorious flames."

A few giggles lifted from the gallery. Judge Rymer looked sternly at Beymer, but in a playful way. It was Beymer's courtroom now. Tracy could feel it.

She wished that Jesus would return.

"Let's have the jury," said Judge Rymer.

# CHAPTER TWENTY-EIGHT

FACING THE KID, the clerk said, “Please raise your right hand. Do you solemnly swear that the testimony you are about to give shall be the truth, the whole truth, and nothing but the truth, so help you God?”

“I guess so,” said Mickey D.

If there were an open window, Tracy would have jumped. What was the jury going to think of *this?*

“Yes or no?” Judge Rymer said abruptly.

“Um, yes,” said Mickey D. Then he sat down in the witness chair. The clerk asked him to state and spell his name for the record. He said, “Mickey D.”

“Your given name,” said Judge Rymer.

“That’s the name I was given.”

The judge rubbed her eyes. Mickey D seemed to be hiding a smile. “What name were you born with?” Judge Rymer asked.

“Levoy Allen,” he said. “Wouldn’t you want to change it too?”

Laughter from the gallery. Frozen at her table, Tracy fumbled through the notes Hank Conroy had left her. Hank had made an outline of the questions he was going to ask on direct. Unfortunately, he had an organizational system all his own, based, primarily, on a refusal to use a computer and printer. All the questions were scrawled in longhand on a legal pad, with some kind of number code beside each one. To Tracy, it looked like some Russian message seized during the Cold War.

“Ms. Shepherd,” she heard the judge say. “Your witness?”

Tracy simultaneously stood, grabbed the notepad, and knocked a glass of water onto the carpet. Laughter flew all around her, including from the side of the courtroom where the jury sat. "Excuse me, Your Honor," she said, bending to pick up the glass, and banging her shoulder on the corner of the counsel table.

*Take me home, Lord* . . .

"Um, Mr. Allen," Tracy sputtered. "Where do you live?"

"You want my address? I ain't givin' out my address."

"Just what part of town?"

"South Central."

"And what do you do there?"

"Survive."

By this time Tracy had carried all the notes to the podium near the jury box. She caught sight of a few jurors looking her way. At least they seemed to be looking at her with pity.

"All right, Mr. Allen, were you, in August of this year, approached for a job as a valet at a movie premiere?"

"Objection!" said Beymer. "Leading and suggestive."

"Sustained," said the judge.

Tracy was not feeling good about this. She had not had any time to interview this witness, and if she let him answer in narrative fashion who knew what he'd say? But the judge was right. She'd have to take the chance.

"Were you approached for a job this last August?"

"Yeah."

"What was the job?"

"Parking cars."

"Where?"

"At a party."

"Where was the party?"

"In Hollywood."

"And what was the occasion of the party?"

"A movie."

"Do you recall the name of the movie?"

"Yeah, it was *Red* something."

"*Red Ride 'N the Hood?*"

Beymer said, "Objection."

"Overruled," said the judge.

The favorable ruling gave Tracy a good jolt of energy. She took a breath, stared at the notes in front of her, and went on. She asked specific questions about the night of the premiere, Mickey D's location during the evening, and what opportunities he had to observe people. She even walked him through a diagram that she drew on a white board for the jury. "Always use visual aids," Hank Conroy had counseled her while preparing for trial.

Her questioning of Mickey D took forty minutes. At the end he described the Indian he saw in Sandy Joseph's car. The crucial piece of evidence was in. Then Jackson Beymer rose to cross-examine.

As Tracy gathered up her salad of papers, she noticed Beymer stepping to the podium without a single piece of paper in his hand. By the time she was seated, a slew of yellow and white notes before her, Beymer was casually leaning on one side of the podium, asking his first question.

"Mickey D," he said, "is that what they call you?"

"Yeah," said the witness.

"Who calls you that?"

"Everybody."

"Who is everybody, Mickey D?"

"You know, my home slice."

"Home slice?"

"Friends, man."

"Ah, friends. Your homeboys."

"Yeah."

"And are any of these homeboys members of a gang?"

Tracy knew Beymer would get here, she just didn't realize how fast. She stood up quickly and said, "Objection."

"On what grounds?" asked Judge Rymer.

The only think Tracy could think to say was, "Irrelevant." Fortunately, that was the right thing.

Judge Rymer said, "What does this have to do with his observations on the night of the murder, Mr. Beymer?"

"Almost everything," said Beymer. "I'll connect it up shortly."

The judge paused, then said, "Counsel better approach—sidebar."

Tracy and Beymer, along with his assistant Lisa Robinson, met the judge at the side of the bench. Tracy spoke first. "It is completely irrelevant, and prejudicial, for counsel to go on a fishing trip into this witness's background."

Beymer said, "If I may give my opponent a short lesson on the law, delving into the background of a witness is exactly what cross-examination is for."

"Only if it is relevant," said the judge.

"I will show you that it is, Your Honor. Just allow me a few more questions."

With a sigh, Judge Rymer nodded and said, "Just make it short."

"Thank you, Your Honor," said Beymer with a small bow. Tracy sat down, attuned to everything Beymer was saying.

"I'll repeat the question, Mickey D. Are any of your friends, your homeboys, members of a gang?"

Mickey D's face became sheepish. He shrugged his shoulders and said, "You know, man."

"No, I don't know. Suppose you tell us." Beymer swept his arm toward the jury box.

Masterful, Tracy thought, in spite of herself. By using "us," Beymer was sitting himself right there with the jurors. He was becoming one of them. Tracy's stomach got a queasy feeling. Maybe she would be joining Conroy very soon.

"I don't know, man," Mickey D said.

"You don't know which of your South Central friends are members of a gang?"

Mickey D shrugged his shoulders. Beymer said, "You have to give us a verbal response, Mickey D. Are you telling this jury you don't know who is in a gang, and who isn't, in your 'hood?"

"I don't know."

"You expect the jury to believe you?"

"Objection!" Tracy said. "Argumentative."

"Sustained," said the judge. "Mr. Beymer, tone it down."

"Of course, Your Honor, of course. Mickey D, don't gang members generally have tattoos that identify their gang affiliation? Do you know that much?"

"Sure."

"Do you know which of your friends have tattoos?"

"Yeah."

"So, you do know which of your friends are in gangs, don't you?"

"Maybe."

"Ah, that's a little better than 'I don't know.' We're making progress."

Judge Rymer didn't wait for Tracy to object. "Mr. Beymer, please," she said. But Tracy knew it was too late. The courtroom belonged to Jackson Beymer. She had a terrible witness on the stand, and the jury was going to blame her for it.

"By the way," said Beymer. "You're a member of a gang, aren't you?"

"Who, me?"

"Yes, Mickey D, you, sitting in that witness box swearing to tell the truth. You're a gangbanger now, aren't you?"

"No way, man."

"I see. Do you have a tattoo on your left arm?"

Mickey D's eyes started to dart back and forth. He looked desperately over at Tracy. She looked down at her notes, without seeing any of them.

"Do you understand the question?" Beymer said.

"Yeah."

"Well, would you mind answering it for us?"

"Yeah, I got a tat."

"And is it a tattoo of the number thirty-nine?"

"Yeah."

"Is that for Thirty-ninth Street?"

Mickey D nodded.

"Answer out loud," Judge Rymer said.

"Yeah!" Mickey D shouted.

Beymer said nothing at this point, another master stroke. He just let the image of this witness burn into the minds of the jurors. Finally, Beymer asked, "What happens when a gangbanger rats on somebody from the 'hood, Mickey D?"

The witness, looking defiant now, cleared his throat. "That ain't good."

"Why not?"

"He's liable to get thumped."

"Beat up?"

"That's right."

"Cut maybe?"

"Yeah."

"Or shot?"

"Yeah."

"You ever rat on anybody from the 'hood?"

"No way, man!"

"Why not?"

"I ain't no rat."

"Would you get thumped?"

"Might."

Beymer walked a little way toward the witness and said, "You're not that big, are you, Mickey D?"

Mickey D raised himself up in the witness chair. "I ain't no big dog," he said, "but I can bite."

There was laughter from the courtroom. Tracy saw even Sherman Kohlbert chuckling at the defense table.

"I see," said Beymer. "But there are bigger dogs in the 'hood who wouldn't like it if you ratted, am I right?"

"Maybe."

"A little scary, isn't it?"

"Only if you rat."

"And you'd never do that, would you?"

"Never."

Beymer paused. Instinctively, Tracy knew he now had what he wanted.

"Isn't it true, Mickey D, that one of your homeboys threatened to kill you unless you protected O'Lean Murray?"

"Objection," Tracy said immediately.

"On what grounds?" said Judge Rymer.

Tracy couldn't think of any grounds. She had objected only because she didn't like the way the questions were going. Feebly, she said, "Irrelevant."

"Overruled," said the Judge.

Jackson Beymer said, "Isn't that true, Mickey D? Weren't you dangled by your feet from the roof of a building?"

"Not the roof, man."

"Where, then?"

"Just from my window."

"High above the ground?"

"Put it this way. I didn't want to be dropped."

"And that was a threat so you wouldn't implicate O'Lean Murray?"

"No, man. It was so I'd tell the truth."

"I see. You believe in telling the truth, don't you?"

Mickey D looked at the jury, as if he knew they wouldn't believe anything he said again. "Yeah," he said quietly.

Nodding his head, Beymer looked at the jury, then at the judge, and then said, "No further questions, Your Honor." He walked to his counsel table and sat down.

*So that's what it's like,* Tracy thought, *to be totally destroyed by a master.* She then faced an immediate decision. She could try to rehabilitate her witness with questions of her own, or she could let him go now. The decision was easy. She wanted him off the stand and as far away from the jury as she could get him. Now.

"No redirect, Your Honor," she said.

"Call your next witness," said the judge.

Tracy turned toward the audience and saw Mona in the front row. Mona smiled at her and gave her little "everything is OK" nod—ever the optimist. Then Tracy stood up.

"The People call Randall Lefferts," she said.

Mona walked out of the courtroom to summon Lefferts, who was sitting on a bench in the hallway. Tracy glanced toward the defense table. Beymer was sitting back in his chair, as if he were sunning himself by a Las Vegas hotel pool. He knew things she didn't know, and that was scary.

How, for instance, had he found out about the incident with Mickey D and Rajah? He must have had some investigator to help him. And what was he going to do with Randall Lefferts? She didn't want to speculate, but her stomach felt queasy again.

Lefferts walked into the courtroom looking like a deer caught in the headlights of a Mack truck. His eyes were wide and red-rimmed. This was not a confident-looking witness.

After the oath and spelling his name, Lefferts looked at Tracy. He did not look toward Sherman Kohlbert. This time Tracy was more confident. She had gone over Lefferts's sworn statement to Mona very carefully. She knew the right questions to ask. "Mr. Lefferts, are you acquainted with the defendant, Sherman Kohlbert?"

"Yes," Lefferts said, so softly the court reporter couldn't hear him.

"Pull that microphone toward you a little more and speak up," said the judge.

Lefferts complied, then said, "Yes," again.

Tracy said, "Can you point him out, please?"

Only then did Lefferts look over at Kohlbert. As he pointed he said, "He's sitting right over there."

"Let the record reflect that the witness has identified the defendant," Judge Rymer said. "Continue."

Tracy walked Lefferts through his employment history with Sherman Kohlbert, his basic duties, and so on. Then, when the foundation was laid, she asked, "Mr. Lefferts, did Sherman Kohlbert ever hire a hit man, a man who commits murder for money?"

Lefferts blinked a few times, then very quietly said, "No."

The answer hit Tracy like a baseball bat. She tried not to let the shock show on her face. She asked, "Do you understand the question, Mr. Lefferts?"

"I think so."

"I'll try it again. Are you aware of any time that the defendant, Sherman Kohlbert, hired someone to commit murder?"

"I am not aware of that, no."

A rush of thoughts sped through Tracy's mind. Kohlbert had gotten to him. Somehow, he had let him know he'd better change his story, or maybe this was all a set-up from the beginning. Maybe Lefferts had been planning to do this all along. Who knew? The only thing Tracy had going for her was Lefferts's previously sworn statement. That would be a joke—a prosecutor trying to impeach her own witness. But what choice did she have? The case was running through her fingers like sand.

"Permission to treat this witness as hostile, Your Honor," Tracy said to the judge. The "hostile witness" designation would allow Tracy to ask leading and pointed questions during direct testimony.

"Any objection?" Judge Rymer asked Beymer.

With a Cheshire cat grin, Beymer put out his hands and said, "None, Your Honor."

"Go ahead," said Judge Rymer.

Tracy pulled out a copy of the sworn statement given by Randall Lefferts. She approached the witness and showed it to him.

"Isn't it true, Mr. Lefferts, that you gave a sworn statement to our investigator, Mona Takata?"

"Yeah."

"And is this a copy of your statement?"

"Looks like it."

"And is that your signature on the bottom of the statement?"

"Yeah."

Tracy plopped the copy on the witness rail and walked back to the podium, where she had another copy. "Isn't it true, Mr. Lefferts, that in this statement, on page 2, you said that Sherman Kohlbert had hired a hit man named Tommy Bear Paw to kill Sandy Joseph?"

Lefferts took his time looking at it, then said, "That's what it says."

"You said that under oath, didn't you?"

"I guess."

"Please don't guess, Mr. Lefferts."

"Yeah, I was."

"But now you're changing your testimony?"

"Yeah. Now I'm telling the truth."

Tracy felt a tingling on the back of her neck. Inside, she felt a lostness. Where could she go from here? *Exactly nowhere*. All she could do is bring up other portions of the statement, and Lefferts would deny them. She would be left to argue that Lefferts was a liar, but that he had told the truth when he gave the statement! The jury would never buy that, not in a million years.

"No more questions," Tracy said. She felt like a giant vacuum cleaner had sucked out her insides.

Jackson Beymer stood and strode to the podium. "Mr. Lefferts, let's talk about that statement, shall we?"

"OK."

"Your statement that Mr. Kohlbert hired a hit man wasn't true, was it?"

"No, sir."

"Then why did you say it?"

Lefferts, as if he had been coached by a master, turned and looked at the jury. "I was scared. I was getting threats of prosecution, but they told me they'd take it easy on me if I cooperated with them in nailing Mr. Kohlbert."

"Did they use the word 'nailing'?"

"I think so."

"Who did?"

"Um, that investigator, Ms. Taka . . . whatever."

"Ms. Takata?"

"That's it."

Beymer turned and pointed to Mona, whose face was turning a bright shade of red. "And is that her sitting right there in the front row?"

"Yes," said Randall Lefferts.

Tracy looked at Mona. She knew Mona would never say anything like that. But the big lie was out there now, in strutting glory, like Jackson Beymer himself. How could she possibly shoot it down?

Beymer said, "Why did you wait until now to correct this statement, sir?"

"Because I wanted to do it in open court, so everybody would hear me. I didn't want them to pull any fast ones on me before the trial."

"Just so we're clear, Mr. Lefferts. At no time did Sherman Kohlbert hire a hit man, is that correct?"

"Correct."

"Has Sherman Kohlbert ever done anything that would lead you to suspect he could ever do such a thing?"

"Nothing. He's a businessman, one of the best I've ever known. He's tough, he's decisive, but he respects the law. He plays by the rules."

"Are you aware of any connection between Sherman Kohlbert and Sandy Joseph?"

"There is no connection."

"None whatsoever?"

"Well, I think he saw one of his movies once."

A smattering of laughter from the courtroom. Beymer chose that moment to laugh himself, look at the jury, and say, "No more questions."

Judge Rymer looked at Tracy. "Nothing further," said Tracy.

"Very well," said Judge Rymer to Lefferts, "you're excused." As Lefferts stepped off the witness stand, the judge said, "Ms. Shepherd? Your next witness?"

"May we take our morning recess, Your Honor?"

"No objection," said Jackson Beymer, suddenly a model of congeniality.

"All right," said Judge Rymer. "We'll be back here at 10:30. Let me remind you, ladies and gentlemen of the jury, not to discuss this case amongst yourselves, and do not form any opinion about this case."

*Fat chance,* Tracy thought.

After the jury was out, Mona charged to Tracy. "That liar!" Mona fumed.

"I know, I know," said Tracy.

"What are we going to do?"

"At this point I have no idea."

"He's going to walk, isn't he?" Mona said suddenly.

Tracy couldn't deny it.

## CHAPTER TWENTY-NINE

"WOULD YOU LET ME pray over you?" Mona said to Tracy. They were in Tracy's office with the door closed, with five minutes before court reconvened.

Tracy's thoughts were conflicting, and she realized how fragile her recommitment was. But there was no turning back. She remembered a phrase Mona had used once, one that had resonated with her at one time: *Jesus is Lord of all, or not at all.* This applied to the Criminal Courts Building, too. "Pray away," said Tracy. "And make it a good one."

Mona did. It was an impassioned plea for a miracle.

When the prayer was over, the two friends rode back down to the ninth floor. It seemed like forever. Tracy found herself almost wishing the elevator doors would not open. Or if they did, the crowd on the ninth floor would magically disappear—everything would disappear—and she'd wake up and discover Sherman Kohlbert in jail for murder.

But the doors did open. The crowd was still there, and it was still a struggle to get back into court.

Tracy had only one plan left. She would ask the judge for an early recess and hope she, Hank Conroy, Walt Lindross, and anybody else who was available could come up with something to continue their case.

And if the judge denied her request? She didn't want to think about it.

The judge emerged from her chambers. Tracy looked toward Mona's seat one last time, but Mona wasn't there.

"All right, Ms. Shepherd," Judge Rymer said. "Shall we bring the jury in? You have another witness?"

"Your Honor," said Tracy, "at this time the People would request a recess until tomorrow morning."

"What for?"

Beymer said, "So they can think up how to save their sinking ship."

"You're out of order, Mr. Beymer," said the judge.

"This is a serious objection," said Jackson Beymer, now on his feet. "The People want us all to waste more time, when they obviously haven't got anything. If they cannot proceed now, I ask Your Honor to compel them to rest, and then I will move to dismiss this case."

A heavy silence draped the courtroom. Judge Rymer leaned back in her swivel chair and twirled her glasses in her right hand. Finally, she said, "I'm inclined to agree with Mr. Beymer. Do you have another witness to put on?"

Throat dry, Tracy started to say no, but the word got stuck. Then she heard the courtroom door open. She looked back. Mona was standing at the door vigorously motioning Tracy to come to her. All eyes in the courtroom turned toward the investigator.

"I think Ms. Takata wants to speak to you," the judge said with a grin. The audience laughed.

"May I have just a moment?" Tracy said.

"A moment," said the judge.

Tracy walked to the back of the courtroom, aware that everyone, including the all-seeing eye of the television camera, was looking at her.

"What is it?" Tracy whispered to Mona.

"I've got a witness."

"What?"

"Ask the judge for half an hour."

"To do what?"

"Don't tell her. Don't say anything. Use your charm."

"Mona, I can't just—"

"Do it!"

Tracy didn't know whether she saw desperation or euphoria in Mona's eyes, but things were crazy enough already. What was another crazy request going to matter? Tracy walked the one hundred miles back to her table. "Your Honor, we request just a half-hour recess if the court please."

"Objection!" cried Jackson Beymer.

Judge Rymer paused, this time tapping her glasses on the bench like Poe's raven. Finally, she said, "All right, Ms. Shepherd, one half hour. But by then you must either present your next witness or rest your case. Is that understood?"

Tracy nodded. "Yes, Your Honor."

And with a look that said "I hope you know what you're doing," Judge Rymer left the bench.

During the break, as they continued to sit at the counsel table, Jackson Beymer regaled Sherman Kohlbert with one of his favorite stories. It was about the legendary Los Angeles defense lawyer Earl Rogers, who practiced in the early part of the century.

"One day," Beymer said, "a guy walks into Rogers's office and says, 'How much do you charge to defend somebody for murder?' Rogers looks the guy up and down and says, 'Five thousand dollars.' The guy reaches into his coat and pulls out a bag of gold coins. He counts out five thousand bucks and puts the coins, in a neat stack, on Rogers's desk. Then he starts to leave. 'Hey, where you going?' Rogers says. And the guy says, 'To kill the lousy tramp.'"

Kohlbert rocked his head back and laughed.

"My kind of guy," said Beymer.

Kohlbert nodded. He looked around the courtroom, almost empty now, as if to see if anyone was listening in. Then he said, "So how does it look?"

"It looks great," Beymer said. "Just like I told you."

"You know, one thing you've never asked me."

"What's that?"

"You've never asked me if I'm guilty."

Beymer smiled. It was a question he had answered innumerable times before. "It's not up to me to know guilt or innocence. That's the jury's job. I can look at the evidence; I can look someone in the eye and know how the jury is going to feel about them. I can make the state prove its case, and I can make them squirm."

"You've looked me in the eye," said Kohlbert.

"Yes."

"Can you tell me what you see there?"

Beymer shrugged. "I could."

"Why don't you?"

"You really want me to?"

"Sure."

"All right. I see a man who knows how to get what he wants and how to make his opponents fear him. And you know what? I see myself."

Smiling, Kohlbert nodded. "I thought you did."

The courtroom doors opened, and people began filing back in. It was almost time to start.

"Listen," said Kohlbert. "When this is all over, I want you to join me on my yacht for a little champagne cruise, OK? We'll toast the victory. What do you say?"

"I say . . . I like champagne. You're on."

Beymer turned, looking for Tracy. He wanted to see the look on her face, to try to judge it. He liked being able to read faces. He always knew what the verdict was when he saw the expressions of the jurors as they filed in after deliberations.

Finally, Tracy came in and walked down the aisle, but her expression was odd. It was not defeated, necessarily, but it certainly wasn't confident. It suggested something like a last, desperate measure. She was going to try something. But whatever it was, he, Beymer, would be there to argue against it.

She sat down quietly and began scribbling some notes. Beymer watched her. What was she writing? Maybe it was her last will and testament. Behind his hand, Jackson Beymer smiled.

Judge Rymer returned and called the proceedings to order. She wasted no time: "Ms. Shepherd, do you have a witness?"

Beymer watched Tracy rise to her feet. She looked uneasy, but determined. Tracy Shepherd said, "The People call Tommy Bear Paw."

Whirling, Beymer saw Mona Takata enter the courtroom and, behind her, the man he least expected to see. Immediately, he was on his feet. "I object, Your Honor! This man was not on the witness list handed to us! This is a blatant violation of the discovery rules."

"Your Honor," said Tracy, "this witness was unknown to us until one half hour ago. He came to us."

"This is outrageous, Your Honor!" Beymer shouted.

Judge Rymer said, "Your outrage is duly noted, counsel. But there is no discovery violation if they didn't know about this witness."

"Your Honor, we have no idea what this witness is going to say. We have no way of preparing."

"Ms. Shepherd," said the judge, "do you have an offer of proof?"

"Yes, Your Honor," said Tracy. "Tommy Bear Paw will testify that he was given money by Randall Lefferts to commit the murder of Sandy Joseph. He will further testify to two meetings with the defendant to discuss the details of the hit."

"Mr. Beymer?"

Jackson Beymer, for the first time in the course of the trial, felt a tingling on his skin. "This . . . this is extreme prejudice, Your Honor.

This witness cannot be allowed to testify without a thorough examination of his background."

"It seems to me," said Judge Rymer, "that you can ask him all about his background on cross-examination. Isn't that what cross-examination is for?"

Beymer felt heat rush to his cheeks, and even more when the judge smiled at him. "I object with every fiber of my being, Your Honor," he said.

"Objection noted," said the judge. "Well, this is going to make great fodder for the TV audience, isn't it? I'm not willing to make the jury wait any longer. We'll take a recess until after lunch. At that time I'm going to allow this witness. You'll both have to take your best shot."

"Oh man, did you see the look on his face?" Mona Takata erupted. "It was beautiful! Lord, forgive me for gloating."

"We're not out of this thing yet," Tracy said. They were just outside the D. A.'s office. Inside, in a witness waiting room, sat Tommy Bear Paw.

"I'm telling you, Tracy, this is the miracle!" said Mona.

"We'll see."

"Have faith, girl."

"First, I'm going to have an aspirin." Tracy entered the office through the reception area and made for the water cooler. She took two aspirin for her pounding head, then went to talk to Tommy Bear Paw.

She wanted to know one thing first. When she entered the room, she sat down at the table opposite the Indian. His look was very different from the one she remembered. The last time she saw his face, it was dark and dangerous. Now, it seemed at rest.

"Mr. Bear Paw," Tracy said. "I need to know why you're doing this. Why now? Surely you know you'll be taken into custody immediately after you testify."

"I know."

"And while you may not get the death penalty because you are cooperating, surely you'll remain in prison for the rest of your life."

He nodded.

"And you're still willing to testify?"

"Yes."

"Why?"

"I'm not sure."

Tracy did not speak. She sensed he was looking for another answer. She waited. Finally, he spoke again. "Do you believe that the dead speak to us?"

"I beg your pardon?" said Tracy.

"My grandmother has been speaking to me."

Tracy glanced over at Mona. This was crazy. If he said anything like that on the witness stand, the jury would probably start throwing their pencils. At *her*. Yet there was something in his eyes that told her this wasn't just off the wall. There was something going on in Tommy Bear Paw's mind. Besides, she had nothing to lose at this point. Without something radical like this, the case was as good as lost.

"I've thought of ending my life," Tommy said. "My grandmother has told me there is no honor in that. But there is an honor in you that is not in the people who are against you. There is no reason for me not to tell what I know, and let the chips fall. Then maybe . . ."

"Maybe what?"

"Maybe I'll find something on the inside of a prison that I haven't found on the outside."

Tracy nodded, suddenly understanding without being able to explain. Maybe there was more to Mona's miracle than anyone realized.

For the next twenty minutes, Tracy took notes as Tommy Bear Paw went over his testimony. Mona brought in sandwiches and soft drinks, and before they ate, Mona asked if she could say a blessing over the meal.

For some reason she still couldn't identify, it was not a surprise to Tracy when Tommy Bear Paw said, "Yes."

## CHAPTER THIRTY

TOMMY BEAR PAW was an enigma to Tracy, as he surely was to anyone who knew him—if anyone did. But there was one thing certain about him. He was one of the most effective witnesses she had ever put on the stand.

He told the jury everything, in startling detail. His sharp-edged demeanor, piercing eyes, and unhesitant voice combined with the luridness of his story to create one of those rare occasions—ignoring TV dramatics—where a courtroom was literally in a state of hushed mesmerization.

With Tracy asking an occasional guiding question, he narrated the account of Sherman Kohlbert's murder plan. Over the constant objections of Jackson Beymer, Tommy Bear Paw painted a vivid picture of greed and hubris that was extreme even for the moral landscape of Los Angeles. When his testimony was over, fifty minutes after it began, Jackson Beymer rose to cross-examine.

Tracy could sense the jury and court watchers all leaning forward, not to mention the millions who were glued to their television sets. If there was going to be anything like an OK Corral in the courtroom, this was sure to be it.

"Mr. Bear Paw," Beymer began. "You kill people for money, don't you?"

The courtroom became as still as a desert night.

"Do you understand the question, sir?" Beymer said.

Tommy Bear Paw nodded.

"You'll have to answer audibly," said Judge Rymer. Bear Paw looked at her, then back at Jackson Beymer.

Stoically, Tommy Bear Paw said, "Yes."

"You do understand the question?"

"Yes."

"Then answer it, please. Do you kill people for money?"

"Yes."

"You're a hit man, correct?"

"Yes."

"How many murders have you committed in your illustrious career?"

"I don't know."

"You don't keep count?"

"No."

"Don't keep a diary?"

"No."

"Don't plan on publishing a memoir?"

"No."

"You just sort of wander gloriously through life, picking up an occasional murder job, is that it?"

Tommy Bear Paw shrugged.

"Answer out loud," Beymer said.

"It's a stupid question."

Beymer smiled and cast a glance at the jury. "So you don't have an answer, is that what you're telling this jury?"

"I don't answer stupid questions."

"Oh, well, you just had plenty of answers when Ms. Shepherd was asking the questions, didn't you?"

Bear Paw said nothing.

"Answer the question!" Beymer said, his voice rising suddenly.

"Objection!" said Tracy.

"This is part of cross-examination, Ms. Shepherd," said Judge Rymer.

"I withdraw the question," said Jackson Beymer. "Now, I'll ask you this. Isn't it true, sir, that you approached Sherman Kohlbert and demanded money?"

For a moment, Tommy Bear Paw looked confused. He shook his head.

"Verbally," said the judge.

"No."

Beymer, pacing in front of the jury box, said, "And isn't it true that you threatened to kill him if he didn't pay you?"

"No!" Bear Paw's voice rose for the first time.

Instantly, Tracy knew what was happening. Jackson Beymer was going to ask a series of accusatory questions, none of which had any basis in fact but which, cumulatively, would sound devastating. All Tommy Bear Paw would be able to do is deny, deny, deny, but how would that play to the jury? He had just admitted he was a hit man.

Tracy knew she was powerless to stop it. The judge would allow the questions, leaving it to Tracy to try to rehabilitate her witness. Tracy could object constantly, but she knew juries didn't like that. It would appear she was trying to keep damaging testimony from them, trying to protect her witness. She could do nothing but listen. The masterful Jackson Beymer once again had a witness exactly where he wanted him.

"Isn't it true, Tommy Bear Paw," said Beymer, "that you have a pattern of extorting money from wealthy people?"

Bear Paw appeared to be boiling. "You're a liar."

"Oh really? And you see yourself as a beacon of truth?"

"That's argumentative, Mr. Beymer," said Judge Rymer.

"Thank you, Your Honor. Isn't it true that you have undergone psychological treatment in the V. A. Hospital?"

Looking startled, Tommy Bear Paw hesitated, then mumbled, "Yeah."

"I didn't hear that, Mr. Bear Paw."

"Yes!"

"Ah, and that's because you felt violent and destructive, isn't it?"

"I don't know."

"You don't know why you underwent psychological treatment in the V. A. Hospital?"

Tommy Bear Paw shook his head.

"Out loud, please," said Beymer.

"No."

"Isn't it true, Mr. Bear Paw, that you knew you were a murderer and a coward?"

Tracy started to rise, but held back. She could see some strain on Tommy Bear Paw's face, but he would have to weather this himself. She had warned him about Beymer, advised him that Beymer would try to get under his skin. She hoped now that warning had some effect.

"Isn't that true?" Beymer repeated.

"No."

"You're not a murderer?"

"I said . . ."

"Said what, Mr. Bear Paw?"

"I said I was."

"And a coward?"

"No."

"Isn't it true, Mr. Bear Paw, that in the army, while serving in the Gulf War, you committed murder?"

"No!" Bear Paw's voice jumped out, like a springing lion. Jackson Beymer paused, staring at the witness. Then he slowly walked over to the counsel table and picked up a file folder.

All eyes in the courtroom followed Beymer's moves. Deliberately, Beymer opened the file and read something inside. Then he looked once more at Tommy Bear Paw. "Isn't it true, sir, that a fellow soldier named Dev Traynor died at your side?"

Tommy Bear Paw did not answer. Tracy saw a look of pain flash across his face, then a look of anger. Who was this soldier he was mentioning? What ace did Beymer have up his sleeve? And why didn't she have this information?

Jackson Beymer jumped into the middle of the silence. "And isn't it true that it was you, Mr. Bear Paw, who killed him? Killed him in cold blood?"

Time stood still for a moment. Tracy watched Tommy's face, and almost sensed what would happen next. Tommy Bear Paw would lose it. He would fall back on instinct, on the raw, nonreflective reactions of a man beaten into a corner. He would leap to his feet and jump over the witness rail, his hands reaching out for the neck of Jackson Beymer . . .

It happened. A look of horrific fear flashed across Beymer's face. His soft hands reached up ineffectively to the rough claws that Tommy Bear Paw had entwined around his windpipe. Two deputy sheriffs sprang like cats. One noosed Tommy Bear Paw in a headlock. The other ripped his hands off Beymer's throat. Bear Paw convulsed in their arms, throwing all three of them to the ground. Something like a snarl issued from Tommy Bear Paw. Beymer collapsed backward against his counsel table, holding his neck and gasping. His face was deep red.

One deputy managed to get handcuffs on Tommy Bear Paw. After one final convulsion, Bear Paw ceased his struggling and lay, motionless, on the courtroom floor.

"Take that man back to lockup!" Judge Rymer ordered, her voice trembling. The deputies lifted Bear Paw off the floor and, with his arms clamped to his sides, walked him through the side door.

Judge Rymer took a deep breath and looked at the jury. "Ladies and gentlemen, I'm obviously going to have to confer with the lawyers about this. Please go back to the jury room but do not, I repeat, *do not* discuss with each other what just occurred. Do not discuss this case at all, is that clear?"

The jurors nodded and slowly shuffled out of the box through a rear door. "Are you all right, Mr. Beymer?" Judge Rymer asked immediately.

Wicked red welts popped from Beymer's neck. "I think so."

With unmistakable ire, Judge Rymer turned to Tracy. "Let's all meet in my chambers, shall we?"

The judge was slipping out of her black robe when the lawyers entered. "Do you have an explanation for this, Ms. Shepherd?" she said.

"None, Your Honor."

"I have never had anything like that happen in my courtroom. Never."

"I apologize, of course."

"Accepted. Now, can you give me one good reason why I shouldn't declare a mistrial?"

Tracy could think of none. She shook her head slowly, knowing it was all over.

And then Jackson Beymer said, "We don't want a mistrial, Your Honor."

"Excuse me?" said the judge. Tracy looked at him in disbelief.

Beymer, lightly rubbing his neck, said, "It's simple. We want this case to go to the jury. If there's a mistrial, the prosecution will conduct this circus all over again. After what just happened, I *want* this jury to get the case. I want an acquittal, and I'm going to get it." He looked at Tracy. The arrogance was there, now mixed with a healthy dose of anger.

"Ms. Shepherd?" Judge Rymer said.

Tracy shrugged. "Let's finish it," she said. "But I want it on the record that Sherman Kohlbert waives his right to object to this incident."

"You *what?*" Beymer gasped.

"That's right. You want to proceed with the case. You want an acquittal. But if the verdict comes back guilty, you'll appeal based on witness misconduct, won't you?"

Beymer looked at the judge, as if this was the final insult.

"She's right," Judge Rymer said. "It is within my discretion to declare this trial over, right now, because of legal necessity. This outrageous conduct—and that's what it is, Ms. Shepherd—can be viewed as something that has tainted the entire proceedings. But you, Mr. Beymer, can go forward if you wish. I'll put your client's rights where they should be, and that is at the top. If you want to waive your objection to this incident, I'll let the trial continue. It's up to you."

Now it was Jackson Beymer's time to squirm. Tracy could almost hear the wheels churning in his head. It was like the high-stakes poker games Beymer was reputed to love and thrive in. Was he bluffing? How confident was he in his hand?

"Fine," Beymer said. "I want this jury. I want to see their faces when Ms. Shepherd here gets up to argue. I want to see how many of them actually break out laughing."

With that, he turned and marched out of chambers, his legal assistant at his heels. When the door closed, Judge Rymer and Tracy exchanged looks. The judge shook her head slightly. "This has got to be the craziest case I've ever sat on."

Tracy said, "It's number one for me. And I don't see how it'll be topped." She turned to go. Just before she left, she heard Judge Rymer say, "Keep your wits about you. You'll need them."

Jackson Beymer played the incident to the hilt. He waited until court was called and the jury was seated. He waited until Tommy Bear Paw was again in the witness chair. He waited until all eyes were on him.

And then he stunned everyone in the room by saying, "Your Honor, I have no more questions for this witness." He sat down.

Judge Rymer looked at Tracy. Several considerations shot through her mind. Normally, a lawyer whose witness has been savaged on cross-examination will take another turn during redirect and try to undo the damage. The cost of that, though, is that the opposing lawyer gets another shot on recross.

Tracy wondered what Beymer was doing. Like the poker player he was, maybe he was luring her into a false sense of security. Maybe he wanted her to ask more questions so he could once more goad Tommy Bear Paw, without her having another chance to rehabilitate him. That's when Tracy decided to take a gamble herself. "No redirect, Your Honor."

She looked at Beymer, and he flinched. "Excuse me, Your Honor," he said as he stood.

"What is it, Mr. Beymer?"

"I do have a couple more questions."

"Your cross-examination was concluded."

"Yes, but—"

"Sit down, Mr. Beymer."

He did, heavily. He looked at Tracy, and she knew she had flanked him. She also knew he couldn't stand it.

"Mr. Bear Paw," said Judge Rymer, "you are dismissed." The Indian rose and walked into the custody of the L. A. County Sheriff. He looked at Tracy as he passed the counsel table. He seemed shell-shocked but somehow relieved. He had done what he came to do, and now it was over. Jackson Beymer squirmed noticeably as Bear Paw walked behind him, even though a deputy sheriff was between the two.

"Do you have another witness?" Judge Rymer said.

"No," said Tracy. "The People rest."

Now the ball was in Beymer's court. He would, Tracy knew, make the standard motion to dismiss the case with prejudice—meaning his client could not be tried again. He would argue that the People had not presented enough evidence to make a case. The judge would deny it, as always. Then he would have to decide what sort of a case he would put on, and whether his client would take the stand.

As Tracy was guessing about what Beymer would do next—call for a recess or ask to approach the bench—the defense lawyer rose to his feet. "Your Honor," he announced. "The prosecution has not met its burden of proof. We'll argue the case as it is."

Tracy lost her breath. Jackson Beymer had just made the biggest gamble of all. He was not going to present a single witness! He was clearly banking on the theatricality of the moment, fresh in the jury's collective mind, of the star prosecution witness trying to strangle him. That was his ace in the hole, and he was going to play it.

"Very well," said Judge Rymer. "We'll recess for fifteen minutes, at which time you can begin closing arguments."

"Your Honor," Tracy said quickly, feeling like she was holding the back rail of a bullet train. "I haven't had time to prepare—"

"You have fifteen minutes, Ms. Shepherd," said Judge Rymer, who then dismissed the jury and retired to her chambers.

It was the longest fifteen minutes of Tracy Shepherd's life.

# CHAPTER THIRTY-ONE

HE WATCHED THE TELEVISION in the darkness. With the curtains shut, it was night inside the room, though the day outside was bright.

It didn't matter to him. Day and night had crossed beams some time ago. Unable to sleep, he only rested when his body shut down. Food was no longer a friend. He subsisted on milk and an occasional piece of toast. It had been like this for more than a week.

If anyone had known where he was, they might have told him to get to a doctor. But he knew it wasn't a doctor's help he needed.

The host commentator, one of the Court TV regulars, was interviewing a guest expert, some former prosecutor from New York City.

"So," the host said, "some high-stakes drama in the Kohlbert case."

"I've never seen anything like it," the prosecutor said. "It's just like TV."

The two gentlemen laughed.

"What do you think the closing statements are going to be like?" asked the host.

"I expect Tracy Shepherd to be a little nervous. She looked shell-shocked when the judge gave her only fifteen minutes."

"She's looked a little shell-shocked this entire trial."

"Well, consider what's happened. The lead attorney gets sick, and she's suddenly faced with the task of going up against Jackson Beymer all alone. Her witnesses fold on the stand, and then one of them attacks the defense lawyer."

"Bizarre! But it's done wonders for our ratings."

They laughed again.

"But give Shepherd her due," said the prosecutor. "She has hung in there as well as could be expected. She's shown some toughness in there. I think she'll do all right."

*Oh she'll do all right,* Rob Cavanaugh thought. *She'll do more than all right. She's got someone watching over her.*

He felt his face. A stubble of beard bristled against the soft skin of his hand. He chuckled. When he was on the campaign trail, he'd shaved twice a day. Now, it didn't matter if he looked like the wolfman.

Two days after he abruptly dropped from the governor's race, and one day after a massive press conference where he'd done his best to lie—health reasons, mainly, and the need to reassess the future—Rob Cavanaugh had dropped from sight. Not even Hagan knew where he was. There were days when Rob would open his eyes and have to strain to remember what town he was in and what motel it was.

Nothing was certain, nothing predictable. Except, perhaps, the inevitability of a federal agent or two knocking on the door one day soon. *"We've had a hard time finding you, Mr. Cavanaugh. We have several questions we'd like to ask you. You have the right to call an attorney . . ."*

Back in the days when he was selling used cars in Albuquerque, he'd fantasized about one day just picking out one of the vehicles—he had his eye on a '73 Corvette—and crushing the gas pedal down to Mexico, where he'd live some Kerouac dream about the open road and freedom. The fantasy had returned. He had come full circle, right here to the "prison" of a cheap motel.

He thought of a movie he'd once seen, an old one starring Brian Donlevy. The movie started in a banana republic somewhere during the Depression, and Donlevy was the bartender in some dive. He tells a distraught barfly that he was governor of a state once. Oh yeah. Then in flashback, the movie shows how Donlevy, a bum, teams up with a political boss and actually cons his way into the governorship. But his past catches up with him, and in the end he has to flee the woman he has married and her kids, whom he has come to love.

*That's me,* thought Rob. He actually had been falling in love with Tracy Shepherd. But it wouldn't have made any difference. In the end, just like in the movie, he would have been found out. So maybe a few years in Mexico would set things right, and he'd find a way to come back. Eyes blurry, he looked back at the television set. Court was again in session.

"Ladies and gentlemen," Tracy Shepherd began, "I represent the People of California. And on behalf of the People, I want to thank you for your presence on this jury, and for the attention you've given this case. You will soon be deliberating. The case will be taken away from the lawyers and given to you. That is as it should be."

She took a few steps away from the podium. She was speaking without notes.

"No case should be decided on what the lawyers tell you the evidence is. You are the sole judges of the facts. You are the ones who look into the faces of the witnesses, and at us, and decide what the truth is.

"It is our burden to prove to you that Sherman Kohlbert hired Tommy Bear Paw to kill Sandy Joseph. Tommy Bear Paw took the stand, and you heard him testify. You looked into his eyes. You saw what happened in this courtroom. Whatever I say, or Mr. Beymer says, please remember the look in Tommy Bear Paw's eyes when he told you what happened."

She spent the next half hour going over the judge's instructions on the law. Experience told her that jurors have trouble with legal language; they need to be taken step-by-step through the relevant law. She reminded them that the burden of proof, beyond a reasonable doubt, did not mean beyond all *possible* doubt. "If you just use your common sense, ladies and gentlemen, you will come to the right conclusion."

Then it was time to close. "There is one man you must never forget as you begin your deliberations. That is the victim, Sandy Joseph. He was a man who engaged in some questionable conduct. We all know that. And for that conduct he should have been held accountable—by the law, not by murder. He was murdered in cold blood because Sherman Kohlbert wanted to make sure he would never tell what he knew. Now you, ladies and gentlemen, have the power to do the talking for him. Thank you."

Tracy sat down, drained, but with a deep sense of relief.

Jackson Beymer's closing argument was everything she expected: passionate, theatrical, lucid, and smooth. Beginning with the Constitution of the United States, and the right to a fair trial, Beymer lectured the jury about its duty under the flag, and proceeded from there to discussing the evidence. Naturally, when he recounted Tommy Bear Paw's attack, he played it for all it was worth.

Tracy kept watching the jury. Were they being hypnotized by the master? Was this another vintage Beymer performance, with an inevitable result to follow? Beymer's argument took one hour and fifteen minutes, and then it was Tracy's turn for rebuttal, the final word the prosecution is allowed.

Tracy stood up, not entirely sure what she was going to say. Then somewhere, deep in the recesses of her mind, she heard her father's voice telling a familiar story. She heard herself saying, "Ladies and gentlemen, my dad was in the insurance business, and he used to hear a lot of people say a lot of things to try to get out of responsibility for their actions. I remember him telling me once about the octopus. You know what happens when an octopus is afraid? When it is being threatened? It shoots out a black, inky substance that clouds the water all around it. And in the confusion, it escapes.

"What you have just heard, ladies and gentlemen, is the black ink of the octopus. Eloquent, it was—entertaining, too. But it is meant to do nothing but cloud the waters."

Beymer shot up to his feet. "Objection, Your Honor! This is not argument; this is a personal attack!"

For a moment, Tracy thought she had gone too far. But Judge Rymer said, "This is a characterization of the argument, Mr. Beymer. The jury can sort it out."

With a theatrical sigh, Beymer sat down. He had found a way to get in another word to the jury after all.

Tracy turned back and looked at the faces of the twelve citizens who would decide her case. She was tired and a little confused. Then she stopped at the face of one juror, number eight, a Hispanic man in his fifties. He had eyes that danced a little, and when she looked at him, the thinnest hint of a smile registered on his face.

"Thank you, ladies and gentlemen," Tracy said. She returned to counsel table.

Except for the final verdict, it was all over.

## CHAPTER THIRTY-TWO

BRYCE AND ALLISON were waiting for her at home, both jumping into her arms as she walked through the door.

"You looked good on TV," Bryce said.

"Yeah!" said Allison. "We watched."

Mrs. Olivera smiled. "I hope you don't mind, Mrs. Shepherd. When I got them home from school, they wanted to see you on the television."

"That's fine," said Tracy, hugging her children close.

"Did you win, Mommy?" said Bryce.

"Not yet. We have to wait for the jury to decide."

"How long?"

"No one knows."

Bryce thought a moment, then said. "Can we ask them to hurry?"

Laughing, Tracy said, "I'm afraid not. They get to take as long as they want."

"Aw, what are we gonna do for so long?" Bryce said.

"How about we go out to dinner," said Tracy, "and get a great big dessert?"

"Yes!" Allison said, pumping her little fist just like an American Gladiator.

The phone rang. "Nice goin'," said the voice on the other end.

"Hank!" Tracy said.

"You done good."

"How are you feeling?"

"Hey, I'm gonna live. But I'm gonna be very grumpy for awhile. Bad news for the defense lawyers."

"Do you have a feeling about the case?"

"Trace, if there's one thing I've learned in all the years I've tried cases, it's this: You can never predict what a jury is gonna do. You just have to go in there and do your thing the best way you know how. You did that. You can be proud of yourself."

It was a nice affirmation from a respected member of the office.

"There's only one thing I wish," said Hank.

"What's that?"

"I wish Duke were still around. He would have been proud of you."

Small tears formed in Tracy's eyes. "I wish he were still around, too. There was so much left unsaid."

There was a long pause, then Hank signed off. Tracy had one other call to make.

"Pop?"

"Is that my star?" Hal Shepherd sounded like he was in the room next door.

"So what did you think?"

"I think that TV outfit that goes into court ought to give *you* your own show!"

Tracy smiled. "I wasn't *that* good. There was a lot of stumbling going on."

"You had a whole bunch of us praying for you down here."

"Your prayers were answered, Pop."

"But the jury hasn't come back yet, have they?"

"No, Pop, they haven't. But your prayers were answered just the same."

They spoke for another half hour, and each of the kids got their turn with "Pop Pop." Then, along with Mrs. Olivera, Tracy and the kids went to Johnny Rocket's, a hamburger place decked out in fifties style. Just a cheeseburger, chili fries, and a malt, but it was the best meal Tracy had ever had.

* * *

The waiting game continued the next day. First, in the office, then later in a small Chinese restaurant with Mona Takata. Along with the lunch, Tracy got her first taste of celebrity. A woman from an adjoining table recognized her and asked for her autograph.

"Oh, I just think you're the cutest thing on TV," the matron gushed. "I don't like that Jackson Beymer. Yuck."

Mona had a big laugh after the woman left. "I guess it's Oprah next for you."

"Please," Tracy said. "I have no desire."

"Who do you want to play you in the movie? Sandra Bullock?"

"Go away."

Mona put her hand on Tracy's arm. "How do you really feel, now that it's all over? I mean, the whole thing?"

"You mean everything? From the threats, to Rob Cavanaugh, to a hit man named Tommy Bear Paw?"

"Pretty strange, wasn't it?"

"More than that," said Tracy. "I kept thinking of Job. Not that I've suffered like him, but the fact that he went through some supernatural ordeal, only to come out with more faith in the end. He questioned God about it all, like a good lawyer, and got the whirlwind in reply. But you know something? I don't think he ever looked at whirlwinds the same again. And I don't think I ever will, either."

"And there will be plenty," said Mona, "if you stay in the D. A.'s office."

Tracy nodded. Her cell phone rang, and she picked up. Then she looked at Mona. "We have a verdict."

---

Sherman Kohlbert and his lawyer, Jackson Beymer, stood and faced the jury. Tracy Shepherd did the same. Without thinking about it, she looked at juror number eight again. This time, when he looked at her, he smiled widely.

The clerk took the jury form from the foreman and handed it to Judge Rymer. She looked it over, handed it back to the clerk, who read it aloud. "To the charge of violation of Penal Code section 182, criminal conspiracy, the jury finds the defendant, Sherman Kohlbert, guilty."

Tracy closed her eyes. She was aware of nothing, except one sound that pierced the murmur of the courtroom. That was the sound of Sherman Kohlbert's voice crying, "No way! No way!"

She turned and saw Jackson Beymer trying to console his client. She knew this was not truly over—yet. Beymer would move to disregard the jury's verdict, and the judge would deny it. Then there would be the sentencing, and the eventual appeal. Sherman Kohlbert had the resources to fight, and the lawyer to fight with. But now, for the first time, Tracy felt the events were in the hands of a higher power. Not even Jackson Beymer was good enough for that battle. She was content to leave it there.

Two deputies took Sherman Kohlbert into immediate custody, leading him into the lockup. Just before he disappeared through the door he looked back into the courtroom. Tracy saw his face. On it was a look of profound disbelief. Jackson Beymer walked over to Tracy, looked into her eyes and said, "This thing ain't over, not by a long shot."

"I can wait." She felt no unease, looking Beymer directly in the eyes. He looked like he was about to say something, but then he turned and walked out of the courtroom without another word.

Two of the jurors asked to meet with Tracy. She waited for them in the courtroom. One was juror number twelve, a woman in her early forties who worked for Litton Industries.

"I just wanted to tell you," she said, "I never believed a single thing that came out of that lawyer's mouth."

"Jackson Beymer?" Tracy said.

The juror nodded, then leaned in close and whispered, "You know when that Indian jumped up and put his hands on his neck?"

"Yes."

"I was rooting for the Indian."

Tracy tried not to laugh, but couldn't help it.

"That's how we all felt in there," the juror continued. "He was too smooth. You were not."

"Is that a compliment?"

"We thought you were more human, more trustworthy. Keep up the good work."

"Thank you," Tracy said.

The other juror was the familiar number eight. He introduced himself as Felix Mendoza. "I have a granddaughter," he said, "she's only eight, but sharp as a tack. When she grows up, I wouldn't mind a bit if she turned out just like you."

"That's very nice, Mr. Mendoza."

"Do you think someday you'll run for office, maybe district attorney?"

"I don't think so," Tracy said softly. "I think I belong in the courtroom."

"I do believe that's true," said Mr. Mendoza.

# EPILOGUE

IN THE WEEKS that followed the Kohlbert verdict, Tracy managed to get back to a familiar routine as a trial deputy. Out of the bright lights of a media trial, her life resumed a semblance of order.

And vividness. Time with her kids was all the more precious. Her friendship with Mona had developed into a deep and lasting one; so had her friendship with God. She was reading the Word every morning again and praying. It was sweet fellowship. It was home.

In the papers, she read with fascination about the unfolding federal investigation into the activities of Rob Cavanaugh and the ties of his campaign to drug money. Terrence Hagan had been taken into custody, but he was out on bail. She heard that he was cooperating with the authorities. For the first time, too, she read about Rob Cavanaugh's background. The reporters performed investigative wonders as they detailed his early life as a troubled kid growing up in the Southwest, and the way he remodeled himself into a conservative politician for the nineties. He was missing, believed to be out of the country. Tracy prayed for him regularly, for his redemption.

The other player whose story was being told was Tommy Bear Paw. He was awaiting extradition to New Mexico to be tried for the murder of a state trooper. One Friday, Tracy went down to county jail to visit him. She didn't know why she wanted to see him exactly, except perhaps for a sense of closure. He was the missing piece that had somehow been provided. He had sacrificed his freedom on her behalf. She had to know why.

They looked at each other through Plexiglas and spoke by phone unit. "I just wanted to see how you were getting along," said Tracy.

"Why?" His voice was emotionless.

"I'm not really sure." She quickly added, "Does that sound strange?"

Tommy Bear Paw shook his head. "I've heard stranger."

Tracy paused, then said, "You murdered a man who was very close to me."

"I know. He was your boss."

"He was much more than that."

"I know that, too."

"I should hate you."

"Yes. But you don't, and I know why."

Confused, Tracy said nothing. Then, slowly, as if revealing himself for the first time to her or anyone else, Tommy Bear Paw held up a small Bible.

"A chaplain gave it to me," he said.

"What are you going to do with it?"

"I'm going to read it."

Tracy nodded. "I think you'll like it."

Bear Paw nodded.

"I do want to thank you for coming forward to testify," Tracy said.

Again, Bear Paw merely nodded.

"If your lawyer wants me to write a letter about your cooperation, I will."

"I don't have a lawyer."

"When you get one, in New Mexico."

"I won't get a lawyer. I'll plead guilty."

"But—"

"I did these things. I won't lie."

Tracy imagined the heart attack any defense lawyer would have if he heard a client talk like this!

Tracy looked at the Indian through the glass and said, "I have a feeling your life is somehow just beginning."

Tracy Shepherd drove back to her office, where she sat alone for a long time. The office was as before—windowless and not very pretty, with books and papers and files scattered around. But she loved it. It was a place of contentment. It had not been that way for a long time.

She glanced at her desk—just this side of messy—and took up an envelope that had been there for several days. She wanted to look at the contents again. It was a wonderful thank-you note, written in a simple but loving hand, and a photograph. She held up the photograph and smiled. The picture was of a grinning young man in a T-shirt, standing before an old-style brick building. His eyes sparkled.

The T-shirt, in large blue letters, said UCLA. The young man was O'Lean Murray.